City of Sharks

*

Also by Kelli Stanley

*

MIRANDA CORBIE SERIES
City of Ghosts
City of Secrets
City of Dragons

OTHER TITLES
The Curse-Maker
Nox Dormienda

City of Sharks

✳

Kelli Stanley

Minotaur Books
New York

CITY OF SHARKS. Copyright © 2018 by Kelli Stanley. All rights reserved. Printed in the United States of America. For information, address St. Martin's Press, 175 Fifth Avenue, New York, N.Y. 10010.

www.minotaurbooks.com

The Library of Congress Cataloging-in-Publication Data is available upon request.

ISBN 978-1-250-00675-2 (hardcover)
ISBN 978-1-4668-9310-8 (ebook)

Our books may be purchased in bulk for promotional, educational, or business use. Please contact your local bookseller or the Macmillan Corporate and Premium Sales Department at 1-800-221-7945, extension 5442, or by email at MacmillanSpecialMarkets@macmillan.com.

First Edition: March 2018

10 9 8 7 6 5 4 3 2 1

For all those who watch the watchmen

Acknowledgments

*

Writing a novel may be a long, grinding, and solitary process, but it takes a whole lot of nonsolitary help to see the book through to publication. Top of the list of people to thank is my wonderful editor, Elizabeth Lacks, whose insight, wisdom, and patience helped guide *City of Sharks* to fruition. I'd also like to thank everyone at Minotaur and St. Martin's Press, most particularly Sara Melnyk, Hector DeJean, Kelley Ragland, Andrew Martin, and Sally Richardson. An extra-special thank-you, too, for Sallie Lotz and production editor Elizabeth Curione!

Because writers spend most of their working hours in self-made reveries of one kind or another, we need strong support teams: my literary agent Kimberley Cameron, my foreign rights agent, Whitney Lee, and my film/TV agents, Mary Alice Kier and Anna Cottle, at Cine/Lit. Thank you, super team!

I also have a long list of friends and family to thank for support and encouragement, both personal and professional: Pamela Vaughn, Sam Siew, Andrew Grant, Tasha Alexander, Heather Graham Pozzessere, Dennis Pozzessere, Rebecca Cantrell, Joshua Corin, Shane Gericke, Martyn James Lewis, Ali Karim, Jon and Ruth Jordan, Janet Rudolph, Cara Black, Rhys Bowen, Joe Hartlaub, Margery and Steven Flax, Randal Brandt, Lesa Holstine, Marlyn Beebee, Julie Rivett, Robert Gregory Browne, and so many more friends and colleagues from the writing community that I could fill up a good half of the book with names. Thank you all. A special thank-you to author Julie Kramer, who came up with the title years ago, and to whom I owe a night's worth of drinks or a day's worth of coffee.

Lastly, I'd like to thank you, the reader, for reading and for discovering Miranda Corbie, either with *City of Sharks* or in previous works. Your loyalty, support, and letters of encouragement have raised my spirits on dark days and made pages fly by on brighter ones. If a writer were to be judged by the character and generosity of her readers, I know I'd win the prize. If you'd like to read more Miranda, please let me know, and help spread the word.

No acknowledgments could ever be complete without a tribute to the one person who makes everything possible for me: Tana Hall. It is with the deepest gratitude and most profound love that I thank her for positively everything.

Act One

*

The Idea

"The lunatic, the lover, and the poet
Are of imagination all compact."
—William Shakespeare
A Midsummer Night's Dream, Act V, scene i

One

*

The girl cleared her throat, eyes falling, long fingers intertwining like the cross-hatched roof of a child's game, church and steeple, church and steeple.

Miranda made her voice patient, soft.

"Miss Crowley—even if I can't help you or you don't wish to hire me, anything you tell me is always held in confidence. That's a promise."

"I'll Never Smile Again" drifted up from Tascone's jukebox on the ground floor, Dorsey and Sinatra swallowed by the guttural rumble of a White Front, while the newspaper vendors bawled the afternoon edition and a fog horn bellowed on the Golden Gate, gentle rain from heaven falling on San Francisco, city of mercy for sinners and the sinned against.

Miranda figured Louise Crowley fell into the latter group.

Pink lips opened and shut again, blue eyes clinging to Miranda like a life preserver. Louise took a breath, voice as pretty and delicate as the Dresden china bone structure.

"Miss Corbie, I'm afraid . . . I'm afraid someone is—someone is trying to kill me."

*

Miranda studied the letter again, frowning.

Bond paper, not terribly cheap but not too expensive. Probably available in any moderately sized business office in San Francisco. The typewriter ribbon was fresh, letters evenly struck except for the *t*, which faded on the serif in every instance of "bitch."

There were fifteen in half a page.

She sniffed the paper. Faint whiff of lilac.

"Do you wear perfume, Miss Crowley?"

"Mr. Alexander prefers me not to. He said—he said it distracts him when I take dictation."

Miranda raised an eyebrow. Mr. Niles Alexander, Publisher, held forth in a self-important little office on the sixth-floor corner of the Monadnock. A vain, pretentious man with a Turkish cigar and a lascivious sneer, he sold books and sold out authors, business done with the aggression of a two-cent stockbroker and the manner of an Egyptian prince. She'd cut him short on a few elevator trips after failed attempts to impress and attract.

"What about when you're not taking dictation? Shalimar? Joy? Shocking, perhaps?"

Louise hesitated. "I wear Fleurs de Rocaille sometimes."

A church bell chimed on Mission, long somber note caught by the wind and carried upward until a Municipal Railway braked hard on Montgomery. The secretary turned quickly toward the window, neck twisted in a delicate S curve like a madonna in a Mannerist painting.

The girl wasn't theatrical, the kind of self-made victim who courted and pursued trouble only to roll around in it like a cat in heat. Not particularly hungry for attention, either, and her looks would guarantee her plenty, wanted or not.

Miranda set the letter on the black desk, tapping a finger and frowning again. "Miss Crowley—"

"Please—call me Louise."

"You say you've received five of these over the last two months—about one every two weeks."

The blonde nodded.

"Where are the rest?"

Her eyes stuttered a little. "I—I only kept a few. I burned the first two, thinking they were—they were some sort of prank, you know, perhaps a disgruntled author or someone else who knew I worked at Alexander Publishing. We do get a number of cranks, you know, people who are upset that Mr. Alexander won't publish their novels."

Miranda shook out a Chesterfield from the pack on the desk and flicked the desk lighter. Glanced back to the white bond paper, lines single-spaced and alternating between all caps and lowercase.

Ugly message, ugly letter, typed with heavy, violent strokes.

"I need whatever you kept, with dates of receipt. And a list of your crackpot writers, the ones who think God dictated four hundred pages of Holy Scripture that Mr. Alexander won't publish because he's the Anti-Christ."

A faint smile pulled at the corner of the blonde's mouth. "Do you know anything about the publishing business, Miss Corbie?"

Miranda tipped ash into the Tower of the Sun tray. "Only what I read."

"It's a bit like show business. Agents and authors are constantly trying to get manuscripts to Mr. Alexander. Bigger publishers, New York publishers, might have a whole fleet of editors, but Alexander Publishing is a small house, and Mr. Alexander prefers to do most of the acquisitions himself—though we do keep two editors on staff. Anyway, he's the face of the business and agents and authors target him directly. Most of what is submitted is drivel, frankly, unreadable piles of illiterate junk. Few of the manuscripts—a very small percentage—could even qualify as the lowest form of entertainment."

Miranda leaned back against the overstuffed black leather of her desk chair, eyes focused on the secretary.

"So the list of discontents is long. Thank the 'Do You Want to Be an Author?' ads in the back of the *Saturday Evening Post*. But what about repeat offenders? The ones who won't take no for an answer?"

Louise hesitated. "I'd have to ask Mr. Alexander for permission. We keep records of every legitimate submission, but I've made a few notes for myself on—on troublesome people who come to the office and sometimes demand to see him in person."

Miranda tapped the letter again. "You have anyone in mind for this?"

The crowded writing, black on white, drew the girl's eyes before they closed for a moment.

Louise shook her head. "No."

"You're single, you said. Any fiancé, steady boyfriend?"

Quick, stuttering glance toward the window before she shook her head again. "No one in particular."

"And you say these—these 'accidents' you've described—they've all occurred within the last three weeks?"

The secretary clutched the calfskin gloves in her lap like a rosary.

"The—the shoving incident—"

"Someone tried to push you in front of a White Front—"

"Yes. That was the first. I didn't think anything of it, you know, it does get crowded on Market Street after work and sometimes people stumble, but I'd received those—those letters, so I wrote down what happened once I got home that night. Just in case."

Louise shuddered and opened her shiny, brown leather bag, replacing the gloves and pulling out a pack of Viceroys.

"Mr. Alexander doesn't allow smoking in the office, but my nerves are so jittery I started sneaking one or two on lunch break."

"How fascist of Mr. Alexander."

Louise tittered nervously and lit the cigarette, acrid bite of the cork filter drifting upward with the blue-gray smoke.

Maybe the secretary wasn't quite as demurely naïve as the nervous hands and spit-curled hair and admiration of her swaggering boss would suggest. Fearful, definitely; under attack, probably. But her sangfroid was holding together, the Viceroys a sophisticated smoke, the clothes not I. Magnin, but not the Sears, Roebuck catalog, either.

"Smart of you to write down what happened. How long have you been in San Francisco?"

The blonde tried to smile. "Does it show? About seven months. I'm originally from Olympia, Washington."

"Why did you leave?"

A tight line formed at the corner of the girl's lips. She suddenly looked older.

"You've never been to Olympia. I can tell. Unless you work in the government—it is the state capital, you know—or want to become a logger's wife, there isn't much to do. I saw an ad in the paper for the Dorothy Durham School of Business here in San Francisco, saved the money my father left me—he died when I was fourteen—and I worked my way through the courses in three months."

Ambitious and determined. Louise Crowley was becoming more and more intriguing and less and less just a frightened china doll.

"When did you start work at Alexander Publishing?"

"Immediately after I graduated. I supported myself as a theater usher and—and sometimes a model."

Red suffused her cheeks. The secretary took two quick puffs on the Viceroy, avoiding Miranda's eyes.

The job you don't write home about.

Tascone's juke started up again, Al Stuart intoning "Practice Makes Perfect" with Bob Chester and his orchestra.

Miranda's lips twitched and she said dryly: "Lingerie or the kind on the Gayway?"

The blue eyes flinched. "Miss Corbie—"

"Miranda."

"I put myself through school, yes. But I did it without—without taking off all my clothes. I was—I was a lingerie model, though how you were able to guess—"

"My employment history isn't quite so pure—though I'm sure you've heard about that by now." Miranda tilted her head back, exhaling a steady stream of smoke. "And you're still here, so you're no drooping daisy."

"I assure you, Miss Corbie, I am not shocked easily, nor am I judgmental. What I didn't learn about life before I started working in publishing, I've learned since. I know you were an escort once. What matters is whether or not you can help me now."

The single-set pearl necklace bounced with emotion as Louise inhaled her Viceroy, eyes glued to the window on Market Street, knees pressed tightly together, face blotched with pink.

Tougher than first appraisal, no Pearl White tied to a railroad track, but her jutting chin and straightforward look still couldn't mask the stench of fear. She was drenched in it, sharp tang of sweat and desperation just below the surface, blue eyes hunted, breasts and legs and what was between them the target and the quarry.

Miranda had seen enough women from Olympia or Boise or Topeka walk through the doors at Dianne's, first-timers, second-timers, last-chancers on the Funhouse slide, ride fast enough and quick enough and you'll never know when you hit bottom.

The secretary wasn't there yet but on the way down, maybe, whether an unwilling victim of malice or lust or a woman running from her own shadows, whether someone was trying to kill her or she was stringing Miranda along for reasons unseen.

Miranda ground out her Chesterfield, three strong twists in the glass ashtray.

"I need honest answers. You say you've been with the Alexander Publishing company as executive secretary to Mr. Niles Alexander for approximately four months. After the first two, you started to receive letters."

"Yes."

"Then after the near miss with the White Front, a car almost ran you over in front of your apartment—and that was late at night, about eight days later, correct?"

"Yes. Saturday, September 7th. The first incident was on a Friday, August 30th, and, as I told you, I thought it might be a—a prank or something."

"So the second attempt was when you were off work and had just gone out for the evening?"

"Ye-es." The blonde drew down hard on the remains of the stick before stubbing it out in the glass ashtray.

Miranda frowned.

"Answers, Louise. All of them. No secrets between us, no hiding. Men you know, men you used to know, whoever you were out with that night."

"Miss Corbie, I—"

"Miranda. That's the only way I can help you."

The blonde bit her lip, small white teeth worrying the skin. She didn't look up. "I can bring you the notes I made, Miss Cor—Miranda. I wasn't sure if you'd be able to help me or even believe me, so I brought only the one letter."

Miranda scratched another note in the Big Chief pad on her desk.

"Who were you with?"

Louise was clenching her hands again, voice rising. "I could get fired . . ."

"You could get killed. Name?"

The girl dragged her eyes toward Miranda's.

"Jerry Alexander."

"Niles Alexander's son? Stanford running back?"

"Yes."

More scratches on the Big Chief tablet while the secretary lit another stick, right arm hugging her middle, expanse of heavy black desk between them.

So Louise Crowley had graduated from Olympia with a Ph.D. in San Francisco, by way of Dorothy Durham, Niles Alexander, and Jerry Alexander, star athlete for the Cardinals, her boss's only son and heir. That might explain the fear. The bastard had a reputation, on and off the gridiron. And the father had one, too, in and out of the boardroom, in and out of the bedroom.

Neither of them were known to accept "no" as an alternative, though Jerry was rumored to pay for his flings, favoring Sally Stanford's place over smaller boutiques like Dianne's.

Miranda studied the girl. Blue-gray cigarette smoke formed a cloud around her face, and she was still holding on to herself with her right arm, avoiding Miranda's eyes.

"The last attempt on your life was yesterday, nine days after the car. What made you suspect the chocolates?"

"I'm—I'm not sure. The letters—the car—all of it has made me so nervous, I feel like I should check into a sanitarium. So I asked Roger what he thought, and he suggested cutting them open before I eat them. In fact, he insisted. I'm not prone to reading silly crime stories—"

"You mean the type Alexander publishes?"

"He publishes much more than that, Miss Corbie. Mr. Alexander is a real genius at discovering talent."

"And you showed a real genius for discovering poison in a box of chocolates."

She was almost too quick. "I was lucky Roger was there. There was no return address on the package and I—well, I confess I have read a few detective novels and I thought I'd best examine the candy to see if the chocolates had been tampered with. That's when we found the—the powder. Roger sniffed it and said he thought it was rat poison, and I just—well, I couldn't really believe it, it all seems so absurd."

"In every piece?"

"No—only four out of eight, in the chocolates with crème centers."

"Your favorite kind."

It came out as a whisper. "Yes."

"And you threw out the chocolates and didn't contact the police."

"No. I—I don't want to make a fuss over nothing—"

"Do you know of anyone who has a grudge against you or who has threatened you in the past?"

The blonde shook her head. Miranda sharpened her voice.

"What about Alexander? Are you having an affair? Or are you saving yourself for his son?"

Louise stood up stiffly and reached for the brown leather bag, voice high-pitched.

"I'm—I came to you because you're in the same building and you're a woman and I thought you'd understand these things—"

Miranda tapped the letter. " 'Run you over with a car until you're a bloody pool of guts and brain'? 'Sluts and whores should drink poison and die'? 'You're going to die soon—you've been lucky so far'? Miss Crowley—Louise—the threat in this letter is either personal or playwrighting. If you want me to get to the bottom of it—to find out who wrote it and protect you from any more 'accidents'—I need to know the truth. About your work, about Jerry, about your boss. About boyfriends, about girlfriends. About you."

The secretary slowly sank back into the chair, large blue eyes focused again on the window to Market Street. Her voice was even, remote. The fear had dissipated, replaced with a calm Miranda found disquieting.

"You will take the case then?"

Miranda glanced at the paper calendar on the wall. September 17th. The *Cameronia* sailed from New York today, another opportunity gone, her place on the ocean liner supplanted by a diplomat. One or two more chances before the ship was commissioned by the Royal Navy, one or two more chances to find Catherine Corbie.

One or two chances to save a mother she never really knew.

She turned back to the blonde, composed and sitting still in the hard-backed chair.

"Yes. But on my terms. That means you tell me why you haven't gone to the police and why, instead, a woman on a secretary's salary is willing to pay twenty dollars a day to a private investigator. You'll tell me the nature of your relationships with Jerry Alexander and Niles Alexander—and Roger Roscoe, who so helpfully convinced you to slice open the chocolates. You'll tell me what you're afraid of and what you suspect and whom you suspect."

The girl's face drained to white but her voice remained steady.

"You'll get your answers, Miss Corbie. Tomorrow. Along with the rest of the letters and my handwritten notes on the—the attempts. Tonight Mr. Alexander is throwing a party for a famous author, and he expects me to attend."

Miranda leaned back against her desk chair, a smile at the corner of her lips. Her eyes glinted green.

"But he doesn't expect me. Wangle an extra invite, Louise. I'm feeling literary."

Two

*

Miranda pushed away the buffalo china plate and what remained of the ham and cheese sandwich from Tascone's. She shook out a Chesterfield and lit it with the One-Touch, thinking over her client.

Louise Crowley was back at her desk by now, lunch break over, scrawling out shorthand for Alexander the Great. She'd promised to send down an invitation for tonight's literary salon, calmer than when she walked into the office, hands and legs shaking.

Louise Crowley, small-town blonde from Olympia, Washington. Louise Crowley, young and pretty, a lingerie model, never at Candid Camera or Sally Rand's, just a nipple through satin, an upper thigh pressed against silk. Then Dorothy Durham anoints her, and lo! she finds work with a man known for his taste in nubile young women, taste shared by a prodigal son with a kink for violence and history even more debauched than his father's.

Miranda exhaled a stream of smoke. The girl was terrified, that much was obvious.

But she still threw up a wall Miranda couldn't see through, was still hesitant and hiding behind opaque blue eyes.

Goddamn clients, can't trust 'em to tell the truth. You gotta check their stories, Corbie, and you damn sure gotta get 'em to pay in cash . . .

Charlie Burnett, ex-boss, ex-grifter, always in his cups, a man whose private dick wisdom couldn't save him from himself.

Miranda sighed, reaching for the top of her newspaper stack and picking up the *Call-Bulletin*.

Best to find out now which author she'd be meeting, what dress she'd wear, what pose she'd take, though since Hammett's departure and Jack London's death twenty-odd years earlier, the artistic landscape had shifted toward the well-heeled and the well-manicured, socialists out and capitalists in.

Her finger stopped at Section 4G, above the movie ads for *Foreign Correspondent* and *Meet the People*. William Saroyan's *Something About a Soldier* was opening for three nights at the Little Theater on Washington. "DIFFERENT" SAROYAN COMES TO STAGE IN HOMETOWN blared the headline.

Miranda's frown deepened as she read. Saroyan rejected the Pulitizer Prize for *The Time of Your Life* and was now peddling an "anti-war" satire. The new play featured an anti-fascist army of only boys and old men, with a central theme that all it took to defeat fascism was "a good man living a good life."

Not the same man who dramatized Izzy's, the City's most famous speak, a San Francisco mélange of dockworkers and newshawks, Nob Hill swells and B-girls off Pacific, cioppino of the down and out and those who were never in the ring.

Not the same man who wrote "Have no shame in being kindly and gentle but if the time comes in the time of your life to kill, kill and have no regret . . ."

Not the same man.

The playwright's new method for combating pogroms and purges, countries swallowed and citizens killed, was oh so quaint, so 1936, when the only thing at stake was American honor in the Olympics, not human lives and human culture, good men living good lives ripped and torn and shattered by a Third Reich hell-bent on ruling the world.

Unlike Dos Passos and Hemingway, Saroyan had never been to Spain, didn't know that boys and old men already were the army, first blood, first casualties, along with freedom and liberty and democracy, empty words on a fucking New York stage to Mr. "I Don't Want My Pulitzer Prize." So easy to preach that murder is murder and killing is killing when a bayonet isn't aimed at your thirteen-year-old daughter's throat and your wife's eyes aren't already dead.

Miranda shook her head, stabbing out the Chesterfield.

Saroyan's new pacifist message played perfectly into Charles Lindbergh's speech and radio scripts. And now rumor had it that the new "America First" committee was backing Lindbergh for the presidency, aviator-hero, proponent of eugenics, the man who accepted a medal from Adolf Hitler.

Sieg Heil, Sieg Heil, Sieg Heil . . .

Her eyes fell to a small paragraph below the Saroyan article. Clare Boothe

Luce's *Margin for Error*—an anti-Nazi satire—was opening at the University of California's Little Theater, same night as Saroyan's

Pacifist vs. Interventionist . . . which one would win out on opening night? Boothe Luce's play was a revival, but hell—that just proved she'd been paying attention.

Miranda frowned. The question was whether either Boothe Luce or Saroyan would associate with Niles Alexander. Saroyan was a playwright, not a novelist, and if he decided to trot out a book he probably wouldn't look for a publisher in San Francisco, hometown or not. Boothe Luce never ran short of publishing opportunities and she'd never stoop to Alexander's level.

No, what Miranda was looking for was a name well-known enough but not at the top of the list, someone with minimal press and a good record with society matrons.

On a hunch, she picked up the society pages.

Bingo. Page nine.

ENGLISH NOVELIST TO SPEAK AT JUNIOR LEAGUE AFFAIR

The article announced that Mr. "C. S. Forester, author of *Captain Horatio Hornblower, To the Indies* and other best-selling novels," would lecture at the Junior League's open house at the Fairmont Hotel, October 8th, and that "the noted English novelist is fast becoming a regular commuter between his present home in Berkeley and Hollywood, where Warner Brothers are making a movie version of *Captain Horatio Hornblower* with Laurence Olivier and Vivien Leigh."

Forester was a likely candidate, a writer Alexander would salivate over, and if he was "fast becoming a regular commuter," chances were that he was in town early, in time for the publisher to fête him.

What was it Louise said? "'Throwing a party for a famous author'?" She didn't say "client" . . . maybe the publisher was in full-throttle woo mode, trying to lure Forester away from a larger New York–based company and using the local connection to do it.

Miranda folded the *Call-Bulletin* and picked up the *Chronicle*. The headline stared at her, an ugly nightmare scrawl in black and white: LONDON'S WORST YET . . . NAZI VENGEANCE RAID!

Goddamn it.

She should be on the *Cameronia* right now, steaming to Glasgow, making her way to London and Somerset House to search for any records of Catherine Corbie, not figuring out what to wear for a literary salon.

She opened the desk drawer and pulled out a Big Chief tablet, staring at the hastily scrawled notes, list of leads and ideas, most of them fallow, most of them dead.

Edwina Breckinridge, the old lady and former actress who'd helped her find out what happened to Annie Learner . . . she'd meant to see if Edwina had known Catherine Corbie, alias Maggie O'Meara, during her acting days. A fiver and a bottle of rum would wake up any memory, old lady glad for company.

Then there were her mother's brothers. The Corbie uncles were long gone, Guerrero Street tavern owned by German Lutherans, beer and bratwurst über corned beef and cabbage. No luck there yet, she'd try to track down the sale, if it was ever official, trace her mother's brothers through a land and money trail far colder than the German pilsner.

Miranda rubbed her forehead, closing her eyes. It all took time, time she was spending on cases not her own, on her own. But hell, she was where she'd always wanted to be, no expectations, no strings, at least since Rick introduced her to Charlie Burnett and she started to see a future beyond the red walls of Dianne's.

She looked up at her office, the dust on the Wells Fargo safe, the sun-faded Martell's calendar, the quietness and emptiness, sun motes floating in a stray beam of light.

No wrinkled tie and crooked fedora and bullshit Irish grin sitting across from her.

No Rick.

The bastard had to join the army and miss everything, Freddy Martin opening tonight at the St. Francis, Artie Shaw packing the Rose Room, the autumn warm weather and the chill of the fog, the steaks at John's grill, the last of the Fair.

Treasure Island was closing September 29th.

Hell, the whole world was closing, why shouldn't it?

Her hands were shaking. She reached for the pack of Chesterfields and lit another stick.

No more Rick, no more Magic City, no more "Pageant of the Pacific," but San Francisco carried on and so did the cops, James MacLeod and the State Department helping keep O'Meara and Brady off her back, the gold braid brigade resenting every column she was mentioned in, every crime she helped solve.

Didn't know her place.

Slut. Harlot. Whore.

Who could've been Mrs. Mark Gonzales.

That's Inspector Gonzales, doncha know, married some frail who used to be a good-time girl—for a price . . .

No ring on her finger, no man on her arm, not with the chains it came with, no more Miranda Corbie, no more. Sure, Gonzales was a good cop, one of the two she could trust . . . and there was the way he smelled, the way he moved, the way his body felt and how it made hers feel.

"Just fuck him, honey," Bente had implored more than once. "It's good for you."

Bente Gallagher. Best friend and ex-Bolshevist, still a Trotskyite. A red-haired Viking of a woman for whom the answer to a lost brother in the '34 strike was Russia, whiskey, and athletic young men . . .

Miranda exhaled, watching the smoke sail toward the filing cabinet.

Mark Gonzales wasn't for her. Too rich, too slick, and too goddamn sincere, confusing lust for love and thinking he could mold Miranda Corbie, shamus, ex-escort, and San Francisco bastard, into a country club wife, 1941 model.

He'd be a step backward, a step down the rabbit hole, Alice landing in a Wonderland ruled by the Red Queen, Dianne Laroche. She'd lost herself before, lost and found again, and this time there was no Rick to pull her up.

Miranda flung herself up from the oversized chair, scattering newspapers. She moved to the window, looking down at Lotta's Fountain.

So he wasn't there to help her, to annoy her.

Hell, they'd all be drafted anyway.

The phone rang suddenly, jolting her, and she stared at it for a couple of loud rings before picking up the handset.

"Ducks? Good news."

She exhaled. "Hello, James."

"That's it? No 'Happy to hear from you, James'?"

Miranda sank into her chair and picked up the fountain pen, scratching out "September 17th" under the *Cameronia* heading in the Big Chief notebook. "I'd be happier if I were on my way to Scotland."

The State Department man sounded sheepish. "Ducks, I'm sorry. You know that. But I've got a consolation prize . . . if the *Cameronia* makes it back intact—and the Admiralty holds to its latest pledge not to requisition it until December—I can get you onboard the 26th or 27th of next month. I've booked you a ticket on the *City of San Francisco* for Monday, October 21st through to Chicago, then transfer to the *Twentieth Century Limited*. You should arrive in New York no later than Friday, October 25th."

The pen made circles around and around the word *Cameronia*.

"Miranda? Did you hear me? It's good-bye San Francisco, hello Britain in just a few weeks, and I'll never forgive you if you get your head blown off—"

"Are you sure this time? Absolutely sure?"

His voice was solemn. "As sure as I can be, Ducks. We're running out of time. I want your debt paid in full."

The pen moved on to larger circles. *Scritch, scritch, scritch* . . .

"Miranda . . . are you all right?"

She set down the pen. Outside someone was shouting for a cab, and Tascone's jukebox was crooning "I'll Never Smile Again" . . .

"I'm all right, James. Thanks. Will you be sending me the tickets?"

"Will-call, Ducks. Everything is booked in your name, no trouble antici-pated. Unless you bring it onboard, of course."

"That's fine. Thank you for the advance notice."

The State Department man sounded surprised. "Well, it's a sea change, Miranda, leaving your home and entering a country at war. I know you've been preparing for it since July, but you've got your work cut out for you, apartment and office and all that. And I know you were disappointed about today."

"Disappointment and I are old friends, James. Diplomats come first, I under-stand that. But God help you if you're lying to me now."

His voice strained into the upper registers. "As God is my witness, Miranda, I am ninety-nine percent—well, let's make that ninety percent—sure you'll be on that ship. And the ten percent is only because of U-boats. That is, if you still want to go. You've got it nice, up in Frisco—and deservedly so. You've more than earned your place, and throwing it all away on a whim—"

"My mother is not a whim."

He retreated hastily. "I know, I know, Ducks, I didn't mean it that way. I'm just saying there are other ways to trace her than showing up at the center of a damn bull's-eye, which is what London is right now."

"Let me know if there are any changes, James."

"Miranda, I . . ." The State Department man's words drowned in his throat. He cleared it, voice lower, gruffer. "You can count on it."

She lowered the phone slowly, setting it down in the cradle with a heavy *click*.

Knock on the door, light and hesitant. Red-haired messenger boy from the Monadnock stood awkwardly in the hall, hair gleaming against the white and gray marble backdrop.

"Note for you, Miss Corbie."

"Just a moment."

She retreated to her desk, fetched a quarter from her change purse and pressed it into his hand. The smile lit up his freckles.

"Thanks, Miss Corbie!"

Miranda tore open the beveled-edge envelope. Gold-leafed invitation on a hard-pressed card. "Sky Room—Hotel Empire—8:00 P.M. Mr. C. S. Forester." So she'd guessed right and Forester was the pigeon.

Better wear her finest, since hell, it didn't travel well.

She crushed out the cigarette in the Tower of the Sun ashtray.

Her last case in San Francisco, the city that birthed her and bore her again, Father, Son and Holy Ghost. No more ferryboats, no Pacific, no Dungeness Crab. No American stubbornness and distrust of manners, no pledge of allegiance, no can-do and cut-through, no great gray metal spanning an island and two counties, no red-orange marvel, Wonder of the World, rising from a gateway to paradise.

Fog, sure, but not the kind with green in it, the eucalyptus and Monterey pine and dull throb of fog horns, lighthouse blinking slowly from north of the City. No sourdough bread, no Sam Wo, no No-Legs Norris and Blind Willie singing "Mademoiselle from Armentiers" on a cold night on Grant Avenue, cable cars climbing steep hills straight into the sky.

No city, her city, the city that defined her, that gave her strength to come back once, to come back twice, to return from the dead again and again, the City and Miranda twinned and linked, fissured and broken, but always rising, striving, surviving as one.

Would she still be Miranda Corbie, crossing a foreign ocean on a trek back to Europe, no Johnny this time, no cleft chin and hard-fought muscles, no newsman's drawl and stale cigarettes and late-night poker, no one to watch over her?

She closed her eyes, letting the tears drop down her cheeks, letting them flow.

Three

*

A sign stood on an easel by the elevators, black-inked in an elegant hand: "The Sky Room is closed for a private event."

Miranda glanced around the tastefully lit lobby, Gothic arches, small stained-glass windows and etchings of English cathedrals framed in gold on the wall, dim laughter leaking out from the coffee shop.

The Sky Room was the crown jewel of the Hotel Empire, the former Temple Methodist Episcopal Church and William Taylor Hotel, another eccentric experiment in dry-living and earnest postulation, this one done in by the fact that no visitor to San Francisco wanted to trade in dancing and gin for hot chocolate and the Bible.

Hell, sin was San Francisco's biggest selling point, giving sinners what they were looking for and the rest of the country reason to live by clucking over it. Reverend Sherman's superchurch and sin-free hotel were doomed from the start.

The twenty-fourth-floor lounge opened in '37 as the West Coast's answer to the Rainbow Room and the true salvation of the newly secular Hotel Empire. First of its kind before the barely year-old Top of the Mark made imitation the most sincere form of theft, the Sky Room's famous-first views were still a destination for middle-class Americans and tourists, especially those for whom the sounds of Benny Goodman and the price of better accommodations were just a few dollars out of reach.

Elevator motors clicked and whirred into action, sending a crate down from floor twelve. Miranda smoothed her dress, an off-the-shoulder turquoise silk, low-cut in the back and showcasing her neck and collarbone, diaphanous except for bands of lace and sequins.

No passing for twenty-three, not anymore, but she could still pull off twenty-six, especially with hair newly hennaed and worn down, shining and silky, shoes a silver patent leather, silk of the dress clinging to her breasts and thighs and stomach before falling to the floor in an elegant line.

Footsteps on the polished floor behind her, high-pitched giggles and baritone murmurs.

Miranda turned, ready for whatever the night might bring.

A young man, maybe five-eleven, with broad shoulders and pomaded hair rounded the corner. He stopped in midstride when he saw Miranda, left hand still in the pocket of his double-breasted cashmere coat, right hand holding a brown Borsalino, anemic blond date in pink tulle fading into the wallpaper.

Jerry Alexander, current King of the Cardinal Gridiron. The blonde nudged him in the ribs, and his mouth shut.

Miranda's lips twitched at the corners. "Are you here for the Forester party?"

Jerry Alexander's laugh was as vacuously pleasant as his fair skin and wide-set eyes. "Why—yes." Thrust out a hand. "I'm Jerry Alexander. Niles' son. You are—?"

The handshake was firm and quick, like his running down the field or his reputed taste in escorts.

"Miranda Corbie. I'm a friend of Miss Crowley's."

The manicured eyebrows rose, while his eyes darted over her face and down the length of her gown.

"Louise? Louise invited you?"

"Ye-es." She extended a hand to the forgotten date. "Miranda Corbie."

The blonde accepted two fingertips in a limp embrace, blue eyes burning like dry ice.

"Kaye Harmon."

Not a familiar name, but the new crop of socialites were far from the hardy Brenda Frazier and Cobina Wright, Jr., variety . . .

Jerry's eyes were still struggling to see through Miranda's dress when the main elevator doors drew open and an assortment of businessmen, women in evening gowns, and tourists poured out. She stepped toward a hallway on the right.

"The invitation says to use the freight elevator. I was just headed that way."

He quickened his pace to stay astride. "If you're a regular here, Miss Corbie, I've obviously not been watering at the right holes."

She threw him a sidewise glance.

"I know the Empire well—a friend of mine took out a monthly room here."

"Did she marry or just tire of the place?"

Miranda stopped in front of a nondescript but functional freight elevator guarded by a bored, balding man in a wilted tuxedo.

"He joined the army, Mr. Alexander."

Miranda presented her invitation, strode inside, and pressed the automatic button for the twenty-fourth floor, leaving Jerry still looking for his card and impatiently explaining who he was to the bored man checking names.

With a wobble and a groan, the crate rose slowly, finally opening in the middle of the Sky Room.

Sound struck Miranda with force, bouncing off the six-by-fourteen-foot windows and reverberating around the oblong island bar on the left, all stainless steel and poplar wood with gleaming gold trim.

Every martini was refracted in silver, every stool filled with men in suits or tuxedos, women laughing too brightly in chiffon and silk. Glenn Miller's "In the Mood" played from hidden speakers, blending in with the tipsy laughter, frantic conversation, and—somewhere—a man with anger in his voice and a woman on the verge of tears.

She frowned, pausing by a potted fern, adjusting to the cacophony while her nose wrinkled at the unholy amalgamation of Shalimar, Joy, and Tabu.

In the right corner was a table laden with hors d'oeuvres and a cut-glass punch bowl. Louise stood beside it, speaking to a waiter, dressed in a pastel plum evening gown, conservatively cut.

Miranda watched her for a few seconds, pretty young blonde, congenial and efficient.

Louise Crowley. Hard to believe someone might want her dead.

*

The secretary caught her eye, cut short the waiter's conversation and hurried over with a cocktail glass, threading her way through middle-aged men in tuxedos and potbellies, drawing appreciative glances.

Louise extended the glass to Miranda, smiling guardedly. "Miss Corbie—I'm so glad you could come."

Miranda felt someone behind her. She stiffened at Jerry Alexander's hand on her bare back, rubbing in small circles.

He drawled: "Really, Louise—you constantly amaze me. You should bring your friends more often."

Miranda pivoted sideways from the football player, sliding out from his grasp with a quickness that more resembled a slap in the face. She refocused her smile on his date.

"Louise, I had the pleasure of meeting Miss Harmon outside—along with Mr. Alexander, of course." The girl in pink tulle stared stonily back at Miranda.

The secretary's smile was frozen in place. "Everyone meets Jerry sooner or later. Champagne is in the punch bowl, Jerry. If you'd like something harder, the bar is open."

The running back stood with his legs apart, hands held dumbly at his sides, mouth unsmiling. He grabbed his date's elbow and pushed quickly toward the bar.

"A real Prince Charming, isn't he? And not that you don't look like a Hollywood star, Miss Corbie—you do—but Jerry's like that with so many women that I've lost count. He never stops playing the game."

Miranda sipped the champagne. "We're supposed to be won over or run over. Where's his father?"

Louise tilted her head toward a seating area with the best view. "There."

Niles Alexander, fifty-seven, was holding court, standing in front of the largest window and commanding views of his own. Still relatively fit for a man his age, florid in complexion with an aquiline nose and pugnacious chin, he'd held offices at the Monadnock for seven or eight years. According to Gladdy, her main source for building gossip, he'd undergone plastic surgery.

Whether his transformation was tactile or not, Alexander—originally from Hell's Kitchen and originally named Saul Arnofsky—had remade himself. Russian-Jewish heritage rejected and dismissed, he'd replaced it with a vaguely Continental air, a hint of British reserve, his bank account flush and his politics as strident as a flag-waving mother from Peoria.

The publisher was nodding grandiloquently to two mustachioed gentlemen in starched tuxes, patting the shoulder of a distinguished-looking man next to him. Smart, double-breasted navy suit, glasses, and a long, well-bred English face, too well-bred to flinch . . . C. S. Forester.

Louise followed Miranda's eyes. "That's Mr. Forester. He's ever so polite, but

I don't think he's going to leave Little, Brown for us. Mr. Alexander doesn't have the connections to Mr. Forester's English publisher, at least not yet."

Miranda sipped the champagne again, made a face, and set the glass down inside the potted fern. "So what's this really about? Or is Alexander that delusional?"

"Louise! You look stunning. And who is this ravishing creature in blue?"

The voice was charming, masculine with a droll undertone. Miranda turned toward a tall, thin man of about thirty-six in a crisp new tuxedo. He grinned as his eyes followed the lines of her gown.

Louise smiled. "Hello, Roger. Miss Miranda Corbie—meet Roger Roscoe, one of our authors."

Roscoe placed his hand on his heart. "Such a shade of azure! 'She walks in beauty like the night, of cloudless climes and starry skies . . .'"

Miranda raised an eyebrow. "Are you sure you're an author and not an actor, Mr. Roscoe?"

He took a step closer, smelling of lime and oak. Bent quickly to her ear and whispered, "Are you sure you're a private detective and not Aphrodite?"

Miranda jerked her head upward and met his eyes. Louise interjected smoothly: "Roger writes adventure books and westerns for us, though now he's got a mystery. Don't you, Roger?"

Roscoe stepped away, nodding. "Yes, ma'am. Luckily for me I escaped from my garret and burned my poetry."

"What kind of mystery are you writing, Mr. Roscoe?"

The novelist shrugged. "Whatever kind Niles is buying. I like the Raymond Chandler approach—the man is doing wonderful things for Los Angeles. Surely I could do the same for San Francisco . . . and it helps that we have so many detectives available for research, even in our own Monadnock."

Louise's voice was pointed. "Roger, the champagne's in the punch bowl. Hard liquor is at the bar."

He bowed, eyes darting up impishly at Louise and then Miranda.

"Ladies. Anon."

Roscoe sauntered off toward the punch bowl but made a sudden lurch to the left, tenderly greeting a woman in her mid-forties dressed elegantly in silver lamé.

"Who is that?"

"Sylvia Alexander. Niles' wife."

"Is Roscoe usually so—attentive?"

Louise hesitated, color rising in her cheeks. "Niles is often away on business, and Roger sees that Sylvia has—has an escort when she needs one."

"And Alexander doesn't mind?"

The secretary opened and shut her mouth, cheeks still suffused, then spoke in a low tone without looking up.

"I believe it's called an 'arrangement.' Niles—Niles has a number of . . . well, I'm sure you've heard the gossip. Sylvia has Roger. Roger hasn't written a new book in three years, and squiring Sylvia—according to Bunny Berrigan, our publicity person, it keeps his name in the papers, which helps sell his books— Niles' books."

Miranda arched her eyebrows. "At least it's all in the family. When is Roscoe's new book due?"

"It's overdue. He's very late with it. I—I've got to get back to the table now, Mr. Alexander will wonder—"

"This is the same Roger who was with you when you received the chocolates?"

Louise kept her eyes on the punch table. "Yes. I consider him a friend. Now—"

"Just one more question. When I walked in I thought I heard someone speaking roughly and a woman crying. Have you heard or seen anyone upset?"

"No. Nothing unusual. I'm sorry, but I really must get back . . ."

Miranda nodded. The blonde hurried across the floor.

Miranda opened her white leather handbag and plucked a cigarette from the gold case.

Cole Porter was right. *When writing prose, anything goes . . .*

Miranda stood in a nook by the bar, watching Roger and the publisher's wife.

Something was wrong with Sylvia Alexander.

Something beyond the pink nostrils, the shaking hands, the obvious cocaine addiction.

The woman clutched Roscoe's thin arm as if she were about to be swept out to sea. She was fighting a losing battle, bravely extending a hand or her cheek to approaching guests, sipping something clear in a highball glass but failing at the expected light laughter and brittle conversation, her eyes wide and terrified and searching for a safe harbor.

Roger provided comfort between the necessary niceties, smoothing the transitions and steamrolling over any confusion. Less lover than minder, his behavior suggested the Alexanders' "arrangement" was far less French in style than Viennese by way of Freud.

About fifteen feet away was husband Niles, pontificating his views on literature ("Everyone knows Steinbeck is a Red"), the future of publishing ("De Graaf? An idiot. Cheap 'Pocket Book' editions catering to illiterate rabble who'd rather listen to a ventriloquist on the radio than read a good book—he'll be bankrupt in a year"), and the war ("You're well out of it, Forester. But the navy—your modern-day Hornblowers—will see England through").

Forester stood by uncomfortably, occasionally inching his way toward the bar. The glad-handing and old school tie back-slapping did not go down well with the diffident writer.

Louise hovered behind and to the left of her employer, fetching matches, ashtrays, and drinks for his congregation. And Sylvia Alexander, whenever she glanced the secretary's way, stiffened, her face as tight as a death mask, her thin lips drawn inward, nostrils wide and pink.

Miranda gulped the champagne and handed the glass to one of the circulating waiters, striding across the carpeted expanse of the Sky Room, catching Alexander's eye as she walked toward the group, his audience turning as one, necks craned backwards, conversation faltering.

Louise papered over the pause: "This is Miss Miranda Corbie, Mr. Alexander. She works in the Monadnock."

One or two recognized her name. The rest, including Alexander, just made polite noises while their eyes traveled up and down her dress. Forester threw her a brief smile of gratitude and escaped to the bar.

"A pleasure, Miss Corbie. What is it that you do? Are you interested in publishing?"

Miranda's lips curved up at the corners. "I've recently become very interested, Mr. Alexander."

"But not as interested as she is in a stiff martini. Stand aside, boys—I'll help Miss Corbie to the bar and bring her back home safely."

Young man, brash and dashing, about twenty-four or -five, wide face, mischievous eyes, dapper in a double-breasted green suit. He grabbed her elbow, leading her toward the bar before she could open her mouth to protest.

Seven or eight feet away from the service setup, she shook her arm free.

The curly-haired man grinned at her, laughing softly. "Your photos don't do you justice, Miss Corbie."

She stared at him, recognition slowly crossing her face.

"You either, Mr. Caen. Now, why the hell—"

"Please—call me Herb. And don't worry, I'm not a masher. I'm a newlywed."

"I know. I read your column—when I read the *Chronicle*. Aren't you supposed to be on vacation?"

His grin grew broader. "And where am I gonna go? San Francisco is vacation enough for any man, especially if you're from Sacramento. So . . . what's the City's most notorious female private eye doing here? Do I detect a column item?"

"You know better than to ask."

He scratched his head. "Can't blame a guy for trying. So you're here for business, huh? With Alexander or Forester?"

"What I'm here for, Mr. Caen, is none of your damn business. And I didn't appreciate your interference." She nodded toward the cluster of men around Alexander.

The curly-haired reporter eyed her thoughtfully, biting his lip. "Maybe I jumped the gun. I just figured an entrance like that wasn't exactly low-key, and using your own name meant you weren't undercover, so—"

"So you figured you stumbled on a scoop. Sorry to disappoint. It was a pleasure to meet you."

Miranda turned to leave and he thrust a hand on her arm.

"Wait a minute, Miss Corbie. We have a mutual friend—Rick Sanders. Now that the jerk has joined the army—much to the detriment of my poker game—I hoped you might want to occasionally send a little story my way. 'It's News to Me' isn't exactly an exposé series, but I can squeeze in some controversy here and there, and anything tougher I can pass on to my brothers-in-ink."

Miranda looked surprised. "Rick never mentioned that he knew you."

"He wouldn't, the louse. Wanted you all to himself. But he sent me a line asking me to look out for you, when I could, and, well . . . here I am. So—off the record—what are you doing here?"

The half-Irish bastard . . . always interfering, always worried, and Christ, but she missed him . . .

Miranda's eyes met Caen's, his charm as infectious as the wide-mouth smile.

Goddamn it, what was it about newshawks?

She sighed, linking arms with the curly-haired columnist. "I can ask the same of you. Why this party? Storing up items for when you go back to work, or are you a friend of Alexander's?"

They strolled around the bar, headed in the direction of the coat check, passing Forester behind a Manhattan on one end and clusters of partygoers on the other, most of whom didn't recognize the author whom they were ostensibly there to honor.

The young columnist shook his head.

"Neither, really. I'm acquainted with the Alexanders and I know Forester socially—my sister throws parties for people—Art Shaw's been over once or twice, Saroyan's a friend of mine. Forester thought it might be amusing and has zero intention of changing publishers, either here or in England. Besides, my wife is out of town for the week, and I like this brand of champagne."

No one at the phone bank. Miranda halted the promenade, drawing Caen closer to her in the alcove.

"So why did you whisk me away from Alexander? Sanders was out of line if he said I—"

Caen threw up a hand. "That's between the two of you—whatever 'that' is. Rick's a good friend and he asked me to keep my eyes open. Sister, they were open plenty at the noise you made. Alexander was about to pop a blood vessel, and—I don't know—I just figured it might be better to keep a lower profile. You know, so you could observe and all those things good detectives are supposed to do."

Miranda nodded solemnly, repressing a grin. "You mean shadowing marks and peeping around corners, I assume."

He scratched his head again. "OK, OK, I get your point—right between the shoulder blades. So what exactly are you doing here? And how does hypnotizing Alexander fit into the plan?"

A human freight train hurtled past them, pushing Miranda into the columnist. The tall young woman with imposing red hair braked at the coat check window, turned to Caen, and smiled and waved heartily, while tossing a marten stole at the now-awake brunette behind the counter.

The reporter whispered: "Get ready. That's the storm known as Bunny Berrigan. And I don't mean the bandleader."

"I've heard the name—and not just the bandleader."

"You'll hear more than that when she gets here. She's Alexander's public relations maven."

Bunny was about twenty-eight with a good figure but a slightly bent posture, as if she were trying to apologize for her five-foot-nine height. The gown was custom-made, gold satin with silver sashes. The smile, when she approached, was ferocious.

"Darling Herb—how are you? Where's Bea?"

He grinned. "The missus is visiting her mother—even showgirls have mothers, unfortunately—so I'm indulging in as much free champagne as I can. By the way, Bunny, this is Miranda Corbie."

The redhead extended a firm handshake, no recognition or competition in her eyes. "Nicetameetya." Her voice lowered. "Sylvia? You know where she is?"

"If you mean Sylvia Alexander, as I'm sure you do, she's with Roger Roscoe on the other side of the elevators."

Bunny held her hand to her brow as if scanning the sea for U-boats. "I don't see Sylvia or Roger. Or Jerry. Oh—there's Niles. All right. Take me to her." Demand, not a request.

Caen raised his eyebrows and bowed to Miranda, curly hair gleaming with oil. "Miss Corbie—I'm sure we'll meet again soon."

She smiled. "As long as it's not in your column, Mr. Caen."

He threw her a crooked smile and followed Bunny, who was attempting to drag him along at a faster rate.

Miranda lit a cigarette and stiffened when she felt a hand on her bare shoulder. She pivoted, expecting to slap Jerry Alexander.

Roger Roscoe was looking down at her, deep, anxious lines around his mouth.

"I'm sorry to startle you, Miss Corbie. It's obvious I know who you are. And I wanted you to know . . . something's wrong about Louise."

Four

*

Miranda inhaled the Chesterfield, studying the writer through a puff of blue smoke.

"If you know who I am, Mr. Roscoe, then you know who I'm working for and what I'm working on is confidential information."

He shifted his weight, blue eyes shiny, moisture dotting his upper lip. Cast a glance backward toward the seating area and Sylvia, who sat, quiet and limp, in an overstuffed chair by a window.

"Don't feed me disclaimers, Miss Corbie. Louise must have hired you and I know why—I was there when she received the chocolates. I'm the one who told her to open them up and tried to get her to phone the police."

"Mr. Roscoe—"

"Listen—I can walk you over to Louise right now and she'll verify what I'm telling you. I know why you're here. Don't let's waste time."

No theatrical charm, no poetry. The writer was nervous and twitchy, glancing back again toward where he'd been sitting with Sylvia.

"What exactly do you mean 'something's wrong about Louise'?"

His eyes were grave. "Look, I care about her. She's young, she's naïve—and she's hiding something. I don't know what, but whatever it is—maybe that's what's behind all this. I practically begged her to call the police about those damn chocolates and she refused—tried to laugh it off. But she's scared, all right. Scared plenty."

Miranda tapped ash in a floor tray, frowning. "Any idea why?"

He hesitated. "No—but it's there. I don't think—I don't want to think—that it's Niles, up to old tricks. That's the irony of it all—if anyone at Alexander Publishing is primed for death threats, it's Niles himself."

"By 'old tricks,' I assume you mean seducing small-town secretaries?"

"Yes. Among other things. Niles, I'm sorry to tell you, won't be missed by many people. I'd hate—I'd hate to think he's somehow responsible for this."

She raised her eyebrows. "That's quite an accusation, Mr. Roscoe."

He brushed it away with a gesture. "That's not what I mean. And call me Roger. No, I'm just wondering how and why someone would do this to her, and I can't help but wonder if there's a jealous lover somewhere. She's hiding something or someone, I know it. Perhaps someone stirred up by Niles' flirtation—and reputation."

"In that case, why not target Alexander, too?"

He nodded. "Why not, indeed. Speaking as a writer, I can think of a hundred motives to kill Niles and not a single one to harm Louise."

"He has that many enemies?"

"My dear girl, between the ruined women and the ruined writers . . ." Roscoe sighed. "And I can personally testify to the latter. He convinces young, naïve publishing virgins—and they're all young and naïve if they've never been published, even if they're as old as Grandma Moses or run a brothel—to sign a personal contract. Emphasis on personal. He owns the rights to your future works ad infinitum. So you either churn out pabulum for profit—and a miniscule one at that—or you rail against the gods. And you know how far the latter gets you."

"Then why publish with him?"

The writer withdrew a small silver cigarette case and lit a Lucky Strike, glancing backward again before facing Miranda.

"Thanks to the contract, I have no choice. And that's precisely why I haven't had a book out in three years. B. F. Goodman wants to publish me. He's Houghton Mifflin. I've got a novel I'm really proud of just sitting in a desk drawer. I won't let Niles have it, but I can't get out of the contract."

Miranda examined the end of her Chesterfield. "Unless he dies."

"Precisely. Not that I want that to happen—you may have heard—we still have something of a working relationship and his wife is a dear friend of mine." Roger breathed in the cigarette, eyes shrewd and focused on Miranda's. "But, as I said, I'm far from the only one with a motive. Take Smith, over there."

He nodded toward the bar, where a small, hunch-shouldered man in a wrinkled gray suit jacket was seated at the bar.

"Howard Carter Smith, writes books as colorless as his name, old-news exposés and crackpot conspiracies and criminal life stories ten years out of date. He drinks too much, but that's the gold standard for writers. Smith's trying to make a comeback and you can bet Alexander is riding him hard. Maybe too hard."

Miranda twisted the cigarette out in the standing ashtray, glancing up at Roscoe. "And here I thought all writers did was write."

The author gave her an ironic smile. "We're like actors you know—give the public the image of what they think a successful novelist should be, a writer with a capital 'W,' and sooner or later, so the saying goes, you become what you mimic. Whether or not I feel successful is beside the point. Not all of us can be Hemingway, but we all need to eat."

Miranda inclined her head toward the bar. "Does that rule apply to Forester—or your friend Mr. Smith?"

Roscoe shrugged. "Forester is the quintessential English intellectual. Smith is a misanthropic drunk. Both are variations and roles well played." He glanced backward again. Sylvia was gone.

"I must be getting back. My only motive in talking to you like this was to let you know about Louise. I'm worried for her—and about her."

Miranda nodded. "Thank you, Mr. Roscoe. We may need to speak again."

He bent over her hand, lips dry on her skin. " 'I doubt it not; and all these woes shall serve/For sweet discourses in our time to come.' "

Roger Roscoe, pulp writer with a propensity for Shakespeare.

Miranda stared at his thin, upright back, threading his way through the crowd, the sound of faint, phony laughter and tinkling glass wafting from the bar.

*

The Sky Room was more scenic than advertised, windows to characters and plots more tortured than anything in *Romantic Detective*.

Maybe Caen had a point. Johnny used to call her the Light Brigade, charging where she shouldn't . . .

You're a good soldier, Randy . . . a good soldier . . .

She swallowed another gulp of weak champagne, shoving aside the memory. Navigated the room, focusing on the view.

Herb Caen's ubiquitous grin lit up a dark corner, Bunny Berrigan never relaxing her grip on the columnist. The redhead sat across from Sylvia Alexander and Roger, carrying on a loud and apparently one-sided conversation with the publisher's wife.

Alexander stood nearby, laughing at his own stories of famous-writer gaffes, ignoring his wife and dictating to Louise, watching her, fondling her shoulders, his eyes growing smaller, his skin more red and his mouth more carnal with every passing Scotch and soda.

Jerry Alexander sat slumped in a chair on the opposite end, watching his father, drinking too much and too fast, his date gazing out the big dark window, pink tulle dull and drooping.

Roger Roscoe doted on Sylvia, whose nervous implosion grew with her husband's appetite for liquor. They escaped from Bunny and disappeared together while the party was in full swing, hurrying to the freight elevator, Roger's arm supporting her.

Howard Carter Smith, meanwhile, took his turn in the arena, propelled by Alexander. Short and stocky, about forty-five, thin brown hair plastered to his scalp, the "true-story" writer wore a Sears, Roebuck blue plaid shirt under his wrinkled gray jacket, all mismatched with brown corduroy trousers, cuffs frayed.

Miranda frowned. Not exactly *Esquire*, but his shoes were new two-toned wingtips.

Alexander ignored Smith's glum eye and monotone grunts, praising him to a small circle of hangers-on. Miranda caught a few words like "literary" and "bestseller" and "Alcatraz."

The party burned out in an hour, those at the periphery filtering out to find more and better excitement, others drinking at the bar until they had to be escorted to the exit. Louise was surreptitiously downing a gin and tonic in between shepherding various guests to the elevator instead of the stairs. Miranda cornered her by the now-empty champagne and canapé table, voice low.

"We need to meet. What time tomorrow?"

"I'd almost managed to forget."

"You can't afford to. Chinatown will be safely away from the office. Shall we say noon lunch at Fong Fong?"

The blonde blinked a few times. "Fong Fong? Where is that? What is that?"

"A soda fountain. Eight hundred block of Grant. And don't forget to bring the other letters."

The secretary suppressed a yawn. "I won't. Thanks, Miss—Miranda. See you tomorrow."

Miranda nodded. "Be seeing you, Louise."

A crowd was clustered around the freight elevator, laughing in loud, slurred voices, men and women discussing business and war and politics with the detached amusement of the social register in a country safe from bombs.

She glanced around the pale blond warmth of the Sky Room, Alexander still backlit by the lights of San Francisco, Forester sill nursing a Manhattan, Caen gossiping in a corner with Bunny Berrigan. Jerry Alexander and his date were nowhere to be seen.

∗

Miranda woke early, cursing under her breath at the empty milk bottles in the refrigerator. No oatmeal this morning.

Even twenty-five cents for breakfast was a consideration, especially if she wanted to keep her lease here and at the Monadnock, no more I. Magnin frocks and silly, frilly hats, no more splurging on perfume and moisturizing crèmes.

She was sailing into a war zone, goddamn it. And a penny saved was a penny toward keeping her life intact, the life she'd fought for, the license in her wallet, the apartment on the hill.

The life she wanted to come back to.

She looked around the bright kitchen, yellow light from the living-room window filtering in, wood floors golden, smell of cigarette smoke and coffee.

Hard to believe she was sailing away, sailing across the Atlantic under fire, sailing toward bombs and fires and underground shelters, toward meatless dinners and no milk for four o'clock tea.

Sailing toward a mother she never really knew—maybe—sailing toward the blood and the death she'd left behind in Spain three years ago.

Left behind with Johnny, buried in red Spanish earth.

John Hayes, newshawk with dock-hardened muscles and tousled blond hair, smell of his shirt collar and taste of his skin, the way he threw back his head when he laughed and then grew serious, blue eyes lit with fire over Spain . . .

Miranda took a shuddering breath. Three years ago.

Another lifetime.

And Johnny's friend and her friend, the man who always wanted more than she could give, the friend who'd left New York and led her out of Dianne's, Rick was in the goddamn army now, not Spain, no, but somewhere soon, in Europe or Africa or the Pacific, somewhere where other men would die, bodies blown apart by shrapnel, arms and legs riddled with bullets, streets, walls, roofs the color of blood . . . Rick, who always tried to watch over her . . .

There's a somebody I'm longing to see . . .

Miranda shook herself, holding on to a kitchen chair with both hands. The tightness in her chest passed. She'd eat breakfast at the St. Francis.

✳

Miranda's short heels clicked on the downhill pavement, calves straining to balance, the snug beret and light navy wool skirt tight against her thighs.

What the hell did she actually find out last night? Too much and not enough. Publishing was a business like any other except it wasn't, what with personal contracts and gridiron heroes and misanthropic authors in plaid shirts and new Florsheims.

Louise Crowley was dutiful and pleasant and good at her job, everything a nice girl from Olympia should be. Except someone was trying to kill her, and not even Roger Roscoe's pulp-writer imagination could come up with a reason why.

Miranda frowned. The writer saw fear in the secretary, too, maybe even the same sense of hesitancy, of holding back . . . of hiding something.

Niles Alexander was an exploitative bully, a philandering social climber, and there were no shortage of people who'd like to forget he existed . . . but Alexander hadn't received threatening letters, hadn't been pushed into a streetcar, hadn't been mailed lethal chocolates.

And Sylvia . . .

Sylvia's face was like a death mask last night, small teeth drawn up into a prematurely aged mouth, eyes dark pinpoints of rage.

Miranda looked up at the St. Francis, stern gray visage smiling benevolently, nothing but blue skies and fresh bay air for Union Square.

She frowned again, her stomach rumbling.

The blonde was in trouble, the danger around her palpable. What the hell was Louise Crowley hiding?

✳

Gladys was sitting behind the Monadnock counter, bored and reading *Modern Screen,* brightening when she saw Miranda.

"Miri, sugar, I haven't seen you in days! I've got two packs of Chesterfields and four Lifesaver rolls saved for you with the *Chronicle.*"

Gladys' blond hair was newly arranged in an upswept style that formed a halo of curls around her face. Miranda smiled.

"Thanks, Gladdy. Been working late."

The newsstand girl clucked, eyeing her with concern. "You won't be in any shape to make an ocean voyage, Miri, not like this. I know you're set on finding your mother and all—"

"Gladdy—"

"And I'm not sayin' not to go, even though I'll worry and I'll miss you, and, well, U-boats and bombs and everything else . . . I'm just saying, sugar, that you need to put your best foot forward. We want you back in one piece. That nice Inspector Gonzales isn't going to wait forever, even though he was here first thing this morning, asking about you, and I just think you—"

Miranda held up a hand. "Gonzales was here? What did he want?"

The blonde shrugged. "I'm not sure, Miri, he just bought some cigarettes and Sen-Sen and asked if I'd seen you. I told him you'd been working all hours," she added accusatorily.

"Anything else?"

"Well . . . he seemed worried about something. I think you should call him."

Miranda put a dollar on the counter and turned toward the elevator banks. "I'll do that, Gladdy. Be seein' you—and thanks."

The blonde was distracted from finishing her lecture by a portly man in a gray derby who wanted a can of Sir Walter Raleigh pipe tobacco. Miranda hurried to the elevator.

Gladys was a trusted friend, the woman who'd saved her life when she'd been kidnapped by Martini's thugs. But she laughed at Andy Hardy and wept at one-reelers, resolutely believing in a happy ending and desperately wanting one for Miranda and Mark Gonzales.

Miranda lit a Chesterfield, first smoke of the morning. She'd have to tell her friend the timetable for England had been moved up and set.

But not today.

She stepped in with a middle-aged couple and a young brunette. Hit the button, brow furrowed.

Wondered what the hell Gonzales wanted.

And why she still cared so much.

The crate clanged open at four and the brunette hurried out, hesitating in the corridor, trust fund written all over the Joseph Magnin dress and May Company hat.

"You'll find the Pinkerton offices to the left—big double doors."

The brunette stammered "Thank you very much" before bolting portside. Miranda passed her, grinning, then saw the light under the door in Allen's office.

She strode toward the unmarked door, rapping decisively with her knuckles. A male voice rumbled "Come in."

Allen Jennings, fat, bald, and toughened by more than forty years of life, twenty-five of it spent in gumshoe work. He sat back in his office chair grinning, hands behind his head, an Old Gold clenched between his teeth.

"Well, well, well, if it's not Frisco's most notorious girl shamus. How you doing, Miri? Any news from the G-men?"

Miranda flicked a glance of mock disapproval at him while she crushed the cigarette in a glass ashtray and plucked two lemon drops from the candy dish next to it.

"You're here early. Pulled an all-nighter?"

The Pinkerton chuckled, pale yellow shirt and red suspenders stretched tight against his paunch. "Age, Miri, age. I'm gettin' to be an eight-hour-day man these days, early to bed and early to rise, all that malarkey. The missus likes it that way. What about you? You're not usually here til closer to lunch."

Miranda sank into the chair across from his desk, facing him, and popped the lemon drops in her cheek.

"Too virtuous to sleep."

The laugh was long and hearty before petering out in a coughing fit. He leaned forward, crushing the Old Gold in the ashtray.

"Warn me if you pull a Gracie Allen, OK? Take pity on an old man. And catch me up. Haven't seen you in a week or so . . . you working on something or did your ship finally come in?"

Blue eyes wreathed in wrinkles, shrewd smile.

God, she'd miss Allen.

"Both. Got a call for the *Cameronia* in about a month, if she survives the U-boats. Took my last case and hope I can finish it."

The detective rubbed his nose. "Last case? You're a good op, Miranda. You sure about pulling up stakes? I know you want to find your mother, but looking for someone in wartime is as close to impossible as it gets. Hell, you were in Spain, you know what it's like. Bombs, evacuations, refugees and displaced people everywhere . . ."

"Yeah. I know what it's like."

Her tone was sharper, words quicker than intended. She looked up at Allen.

"I just don't see any other choice. If she's there, I've got to get her out. I'll have a couple of weeks to dig up more information before I go, try to find a lead on where she went. Soon as this case is over."

His gravelly voice was serious as he studied her.

"You'll be missed."

She waved a hand. "Not by the blue boys, not by Martini's old gang, not by the Musketeers . . ."

"Good ops make more enemies than friends. Solitary work for solitary people, and that's us." He held her eyes for a long moment, then looked down at some papers on the desk, clearing his throat. "So . . . what can I do for you?"

She smiled, reading the signal, and stood up. "Nothing much in the way of what I'm working on, at least not yet. It's a local affair—concerns Alexander Publishing, sixth floor."

He raised his thick eyebrows. "Watch out. Cases close to home can come back and bite you—they don't have far to go."

"I'll be careful. You aggravate your wife again?"

She gestured toward his left ankle, brown peeking above the creased, well-worn oxford. Allen scooted his chair back and crossed his legs, ruefully examining his right shoe and thick black sock.

"She was asleep this morning when I left and forgot to lay 'em out last night—up too late playing bridge. All right, Miss Sherlock, get back to your office. I'm here if you need the Pinkerton files."

Hand on the doorknob, she looked over her shoulder and smiled at the stocky man behind the desk, hard muscle softer now, wrinkles around his mouth and eyes, bald head shining under the lamplight.

"Be seeing you, Allen. And thanks."

She shut the door softly behind her and leaned against it, breathing in the stale, musty air of the Monadnock Building's fourth floor.

Just down the hall, the gold lettering on her office door glinted in the low light: MIRANDA CORBIE, PRIVATE INVESTIGATOR.

She closed her eyes for a moment.

Goddamn it, she'd miss her life.

Five

*

L ouise prodded the ginger ice cream with her spoon, doubt creasing her fore-head.

"You sure about this place?"

Miranda looked around. No teenage boys, Chinese and Filipino, crowding the end of the counter. No girls clustered across the room, five in one booth.

We meet . . . and the angels sing . . .

Martha Tilton and the jukebox, Filipino Charlie's gang and Eddie Taka-hashi, the Rice Bowl Party in February . . . eight months and a lifetime ago.

Miranda bit into the burger, swallowing with a swig of ice-cold cherry Coke.

"No one from Alexander Publishing would step foot into a Chinatown soda fountain. Besides—it's a taste of San Francisco."

"If you put it that way . . ."

Louise took a tiny mouthful of the ice cream, laughed, and ate the rest with an appetite. Miranda finished the hamburger and plucked at the French fries, a young man with spectacles and a chocolate-sauce-stained waiter's jacket rush-ing over to replenish her cherry Coke.

"You sure you don't want something else?"

The blonde shook her head. "I splurged at the Carlton this morning—up too late settling with the Sky Room after the party."

"The hotel on Sutter?" Miranda opened her notebook. "That's near where you live at the Glenarm, isn't it?"

"Yes, just down the street."

"And the Glenarm is where the second incident—when the car tried to run you over—occurred?"

Louise shook out a Viceroy from a silver cigarette case and lit it with a tabletop matchbook. "Not in front. About a half block away."

"So on Sutter, half a block from your apartment house doors. You were alone?"

Louise took a sharp inhale. "Yes."

Miranda frowned. "You were out with Jerry Alexander that night. If he didn't park and go up to your apartment with you, why didn't he drop you in front?"

Louise and her small-town provinciality, comfortable in working hard and getting ahead, cash wrapped in plain paper and sent back home to mamma, virtue still intact. Miranda watched it redden her cheeks and neck, the secretary's voice higher-pitched, syllables sharp.

"You've met him. You know what he's like."

"I know he's a probable rapist who gets off scot-free because he's a football star and his father pays for ads in the Cardinal program. What I don't know is why you were with him and what you were doing and how you came to be dropped off half a block from the Glenarm Apartments."

Louise bit her lip, eyes on the Formica counter.

"Jerry was—he was very persistent. Kind, too, believe me, he can be quite charming when he wants something. I'd only been working for about a week or so when he started coming into the office, every day, sometimes more than once. Niles even remarked on it . . . frankly, I was worried about my job and finally just gave in."

Miranda leaned back against the green leather of the booth.

"How far?"

Deeper hue, crimson cheeks. She dropped ashes in the glass tray, second "Fong" at the bottom barely discernible.

"Is this really necessary?"

"Only if you want to know who is trying to kill you."

"It's not Jerry! I mean, you can see he's not—not—insane. Wild, yes, but—"

"That doesn't answer my question. Did you sleep with him?"

Her eyes darted across the drugstore. "I'm starting to regret hiring you, Miss Corbie."

"You know my terms."

Louise looked away, up, down, toward the door, blue eyes starting to well. She twisted out the Viceroy in the ashtray.

"To answer your question, no, I did not sleep with Jerry, and that is why I was walking to my apartment from Larkin. We'd had an argument and I got out of the car."

"Because he wanted to come upstairs with you?"

"Yes."

"Had you encouraged him?"

"I don't think that's any of your busi—"

"Did he become violent before or after the argument?"

The secretary's face contorted. Whatever she'd done with Jerry Alexander and whatever he'd done to her, she didn't think of herself as innocent.

Miranda stubbed out her Chesterfield. "Look, Louise. I don't give a damn what you've done and who you've done it with. What I want is to keep you safe and figure out what the hell is happening to you and why. That means I've got to know who you're involved with—who you've been involved with since you moved here."

The girl sat numbly in the booth. Miranda reached impulsively across the table.

"Louise—somebody tried to kill you. Someone who knows where you work and where you live, who knows you like chocolates with crème centers. We both know what Jerry Alexander is. Tell me what happened."

Louise looked up, tears tracing her cheekbones. Miranda opened her purse and handed her a handkerchief. The secretary blew her nose.

"I can take a blow, Miss Corbie, I know it's hard on a man to not have a good job, I—I understand, women talk too much anyway, we're always looking for a man to save us and then we complain about it. I was—I was attracted to Jerry. But I never intended to go to bed with him. He invited me to his apartment— he lives over on Filbert, by Telegraph Hill—and I said no. Then he wanted to come upstairs. And then he hurt my wrist and—and I need my wrists for my work, for typing, so I jumped out at the next stoplight. At Hyde and Sutter."

"Then what happened?"

The blonde smiled ruefully, gathering composure. She wiped her eyes again with the handkerchief edge.

"Jerry sped by, very angry. He drives a red Lincoln Zephyr convertible. He didn't say anything. I'd walked for most of the block and was crossing on my corner—Larkin—when I heard a loud motor, like a bus or a truck, coming up behind me, and—well, I was just afraid, reacted instinctively. I ran across and leapt for a grocer's step, the shop lights were still on, and then I felt—felt a whoosh, this gust of air, and I think—I think I screamed. The gust knocked me down and I remember looking up and seeing a black car, a four-door I think, ride up on the curb and turn right down Larkin. It all happened so fast, and I was already upset."

"This was about 1:30 in the morning, right?"

Louise sipped the ice water still on the table. "Yes. About that."

Miranda scribbled some notes. "Do you remember the make of the car?"

The secretary shook her head. "No. Only that it was large and loud, so it must have had a big motor. It was definitely a four-door."

"Had you ever seen it before? When you were pushed the Friday before, for example?"

"Not that I recall. It was a common sort of car, except for the sound it made. Not too new, not too old."

Miranda turned a page of the notebook. "Tell me about Alexander Publishing. How many people are in the Monadnock every day?"

"Niles and I are the only people in the office every day, all day. Bunny—"

"Miss Berrigan?"

"Yes, Bunny's her nickname, her real name is Berenice. Anyway, she's in and out throughout the week."

"She's publicity, right?"

Louise nodded, sipped the water again.

"And Emily Kingston and Hank Ward—they're the editors Niles keeps on staff—they're in irregularly, two or three times a week at the most, usually to pick up a submission or pitch one of their own to Niles."

"Any copy editors? Cover artists? Typographers?"

The secretary smiled faintly. "You've been doing your homework, Miss Corbie. Niles mostly uses freelance copy editors and artists, although Emily has been filling in as the main copy editor lately. Our printers supply typographers and layout artists for each project. Copy editors come to the office only to pick up and drop off manuscripts, and artists may meet with Niles once or twice at the most, and again—they're only in the office to drop something off. Most of them never read the book they're working on—Niles just tells them what he wants."

Miranda's voice was dry. "Niles seems to do everything but write the books."

Louise gave a hesitant laugh. "Sometimes the books are practically his by the time he's done editing them."

"OK. Let's talk about the earlier incident with the White Front. That was the week before the car attempt, and you were just off work—six o'clock?"

"Yes. I'd walked down a block to my favorite flower seller I wanted some carnations for my room. Actually, Roger suggested flowers . . . I was feeling rather blue that day, I think."

"Roger Roscoe? He was there?"

"Oh, yes. Roger usually comes in on Fridays for an hour or two. He likes to check up on things, update Niles on his progress."

"I thought he hated Alexander."

The secretary smiled. "Roger is frustrated about his contract. And overly theatrical. Niles can be infuriating, too."

Miranda frowned, tapping the Formica with her pencil. "Roscoe was there when you found the poison in the chocolates and that was Monday."

"Oh, surely you can't suspect Roger! He's a friend, one of the few I've made since I started working here. And he was in the office on Monday because he couldn't come in on Friday last week. Said he had a doctor's appointment. Besides, he lives close to the office and sometimes comes in more than once a week. I'm sure Sylvia has asked him to report on—well, report on Niles."

"And whether or not you're sleeping with him?"

Color rose in her face again. "Which I am not, never have, and never will."

"Has he asked you to?"

"Not in so many words. Look, Miss Corbie—Miranda—I needed a job. I knew Mr. Alexander found me—well, found me attractive. But I never encouraged him. I just try to do my work."

Miranda gazed at the secretary thoughtfully and played a hunch.

"Has he ever suggested—in so many words—that you sleep with a client?"

The secretary's voice was still tired but more sure, color in her face steady.

"Not 'suggest.' Insinuate is the strongest word I could use. He—he has insinuated that I 'make friends' with a book reviewer and one of his authors. I pretended I didn't know what he was talking about."

"Which author? Roscoe?"

She shook her head. "Howard Carter Smith."

Miranda raised her eyebrows. "Why Smith?"

The secretary closed her eyes for a moment. "I don't know," she said wearily. "Smith has no family that I know of, doesn't seem to know anyone socially. Niles is priming him for the *New York Times* list, even mentioned the

Pulitzer. Seems to think the next book is going to be a big, big seller—make him famous."

"What's it all about?"

"You'll have to ask Niles. He handles Smith's drafts by himself—actually locks them in the safe. I never see them, much less read them."

"Isn't that unusual?"

The secretary's eyes drifted toward the large double doors again.

"I suppose it is. The publishing business is pretty cutthroat, Miss Corbie, and there are a lot of competitors out there—even in San Francisco. But honestly, Smith and I barely know one another, whatever Niles intends. He can't possibly be involved in this. He drinks too much and doesn't like people, sure, but not enough to make him target me or anyone else."

Miranda's voice was sharp. "Your impression of Smith or Roger Roscoe's?"

"Mine. And Roger's, certainly. He knows him better than I do."

The blonde sipped the water again, determined denial. No one she knew or worked with was trying to kill her. It was just a stranger, could only be a stranger, someone who knew her address, knew which streetcar she took, knew which chocolates she liked . . .

"Let's get back to the White Front. You bought carnations and were waiting for a car—"

"The #3. I walk two blocks to Sansome and Sutter, that way I don't have to change."

"You take the #3 every day? And everyone knows it?"

"I saw no reason to keep it secret, even if I could. I don't own a car and it's how I get to and from the office every day. We all have our routines."

"Was Roscoe with you?"

"No. Roger left me at—let me think. Oh yes, at Montgomery. I think he was going to get a dinner and a drink at the Palace. That's his routine, too, except on Friday evenings, not Mondays."

Miranda flipped a page. She asked without looking up: "What do you think of Roscoe as an author?"

"He's usually on time, though not as fast as Smith, and right now he's very late with his novel. He's a good writer when he tries. Niles really should let him out of his contract, but he won't, even though he hasn't invested anything in Roger's career. And Niles is like that—as long as someone else wants him, he won't let him go. So I think Roger tries to make the best of things for Sylvia's sake."

"And their relationship is acceptable to Alexander?"

The blonde gave a short laugh. "'Acceptable'? It's utterly convenient for him. Niles doesn't want to think about Sylvia."

Miranda nodded, staring at her notebook with a frown.

"All right. So you were holding pink carnations and waiting for the #3 and right before it pulled up someone shoved you from behind."

"That's right. I started to fall, almost under the car, when an old Chinese woman and a man in a pin-striped suit pulled me back."

"Are you sure it wasn't an accident?"

"I wasn't sure, not at the time. I assumed it must have been an accident. I was embarrassed, to tell the truth. I thought I'd stumbled, had a dizzy spell—it was—well, it was that time of the month—and I sometimes do get dizzy."

"But you still wrote what happened that evening?"

"I couldn't be sure. I could feel a push, a shove between my shoulder blades, and it felt—well, it felt too directed. And that's why I thought maybe one of the crackpots had done it."

"One of the rejected writers?"

"Yes." Louise checked her watch, nervously clearing her throat. "I'm running out of time."

"Just a few more minutes."

Miranda set the pencil down and looked up. "Roscoe figured out why I was at the party last night. He also thinks Alexander makes a much better murder target than you do."

Louise's eyes were wide and puzzled. "How awful! Why would he say such a thing?"

"I was hoping you could tell me. Has Alexander suffered any threats that you know of? Any enemies?"

"Too many. Former authors, current authors, rejected authors, agents, editors, other publishers . . . Niles is not a well-loved figure in the literary world, but honestly, who is? It's a tough business. I mean, shouldn't you be looking for someone, well . . . sick? And the idea anybody would try to kill or hurt me in order to get at Niles—that makes even less sense than one of the mysteries we sent back this morning."

"That's part of your job, isn't it? Screen the manuscripts for Alexander?"

"It wasn't at first, not until Niles felt he could trust me. He really does work hard, you know, and most of the submissions are sent directly to him. Some come through agents, the kind who take a few dollars up front. Every day I stamp 'rejected' on ten or more books. Thousands of people want to write, Miss Corbie. Many of them aren't beyond the fifth grade."

Louise opened her purse and pulled out two envelopes and a sheet of folded paper.

"I've brought what you asked for. The two letters and a list of the people who've threatened us."

Miranda took the rubber-banded bundle and ran her eyes over the list. Five names.

"Both men and women, I see."

"That shouldn't surprise you."

Miranda looked up at the blonde, holding her eyes.

"I need more information. Your daily routine during, before, and after work. Names of people you were friendly with in your former job, in secretarial school. And former boyfriends—men you've dated, men who might be jealous."

The blonde started to slide out from the booth, skin drawn tight over sharp-edged cheeks.

"I must go. I can't be late."

Frozen face, blond hair immaculate, tears wiped and dried. But dry white hands clutched her purse like a life preserver, and fear drowned the blue in her eyes.

"Who is it, Louise? Who are you afraid of? Jerry? Smith? Niles?"

The secretary gripped the edge of the Formica countertop. Words tumbled out.

"I couldn't bear it if this is someone I know. I've worked with Niles for four months—Roger's a friend. Jerry is—Jerry, but not a murderer. Sylvia is too weak to be a threat to anyone but herself. No, Miss Corbie, you should look to the list." She shuddered, tremulous. "There is no one else."

The blonde hurried through the double doors of Fong Fong, the bright Grant Street sunshine momentarily blinding.

Louise Crowley was too scared to stay, too scared to run, too scared to go to the cops.

Determined to find a stranger behind the threats to her life.

Miranda nodded to herself, sipping the last of the melted ice and cherry Coke.

Louise Crowley was protecting someone.

Six

*

Miranda's feet sank in the quicksand of the plush Pinkerton carpet. New brunette at the front desk, hair upswept and piled high in an attempt to mimic the latest *Vogue*, billowy white silk blouse tied with a scarlet bow at the collar.

The girl raised a complexion colored and harmonized by Dorothy Gray, all to the tune of South American Red. One lip sneered.

"Mr. Jennings is not available, Miss. If you care to leave a card . . ."

The tone suggested that any card Miranda might care to leave would be dog-eared and sweat-stained. Miranda smoothed the tight-fitting navy skirt over her hips and raised a hand to adjust the beret, brushing back her auburn hair.

"Ask him to phone Miranda."

"As I said, Miss, if you care to leave a card . . ."

Miranda's lips twitched dangerously. "And as I said, ask him to phone Miranda. I just saw him a couple of hours ago. He doesn't need my card."

The receptionist raised a plucked eyebrow disapprovingly. She was all of twenty-two or twenty-three.

"Miranda . . . ?"

Miranda leaned forward, gloved hands placed flat and square on the top of the desk.

"Corbie. I'm right down the hall. The name's on the door. But then again, maybe that wig on your head is making it difficult to think."

The brunette blanched and then turned red. "Why, I never—"

Miranda pivoted from the doorway. "Exactly, sister."

She strode through the hall and around the corner. Allen would see her later and maybe the Pinkerton files would find something in Louise Crowley's past, something from Olympia, Washington, that followed the blonde to San Francisco.

Something to tell Miranda what—and whom—she was hiding.

*

Miranda turned the page of the Big Chief notebook and frowned at her scribbled notes.

MOTIVE was underlined three times.

Sylvia Alexander? Maybe. The letters read more like a sick fantasy than an actual threat. And yet . . . a shove, a car, a box of chocolates. No fantasy there.

She wrote SYLVIA: JEALOUSY? Stared at the blue ink and followed with ROGER ROSCOE, HOWARD CARTER SMITH, NILES ALEXANDER, JERRY ALEXANDER, EDITOR/EMPLOYEE, WRITER? Miranda quickly added OPPORTUNITY in a separate column, writing the same list underneath, with NILES, JERRY, and ROGER ROSCOE at the top. Question marks for everyone else.

MEANS . . .

Not Jerry, not for the hit-and-run, not unless he hired someone, and that wasn't his style. Women were the goal line, bedded, bruised and personally conquered. Hiring someone else to kill or injure his father's secretary was too passive, too indirect, almost a feminine touch.

Miranda's frown deepened, and she wrote SYLVIA? at the bottom of the list.

Sylvia Alexander seemed capable of fantasy but not reality, not the kind that could command a powerful car and drive it over a sidewalk without hitting a brick wall. Hell, she could barely command her way out of the Sky Room.

Was it a pose, Sylvia's helplessness? Or was she a neurotic snowbird, brittle and breakable, capable only of writing venom but not acting it out?

Miranda tapped the fountain pen against her lips, brow wrinkled in thought.

Sylvia may be fragile but her husband wasn't, not Niles Alexander, a would-be literary tycoon bloated with his own delusions. Add a Shakespeare-quoting novelist who squires and screws said publisher's wife, a scion star running back who graduated from Sally Stanford summa cum laude, an exposé writer who looks like a lumberjack and five little pigs, all of whom wanted to go to market with a book . . .

She picked up the list of rejected writers Louise had given her and studied it.

MILLICENT PRYNE
RANDAL B. BRANDT
ANASTASIA DECKER
IDA WINEGARDEN
GEOFFREY HUTCHINSON, ESQ.

Decker was housed at the Oceanic Hotel, Bente's run-down, low-rent hovel, frequented by strippers, queers, hophead musicians, and a few Communists, though Bente's own politics were ever-evolving, especially after Trotsky's assassination and the Molotov Pact.

Pryne lived in a boardinghouse on Haight, Winegarden in West Portal. Randal B. Brandt lived at the Benson, an alliteratively irresistible choice despite the paddy wagon's nightly visits and the stench of sour laundry. Geoffrey Hutchinson, Esq., gave a law office on Turk.

None of them sounded like a sure candidate for the Napa Valley State Insane Asylum.

Miranda leaned back in the black leather chair and tipped out a Chesterfield from the pack on the desk.

Five names on a sheet given to her by a client she knew was lying.

They all lie to you, Corbie. Sooner or later. Just a matter of what kinda lie. And most important? You gotta figure out why . . .

Charlie Burnett, her old boss, deep in the cups and serious, tricks of the trade. The bastard taught her even after he got himself iced and damned her soul to hell as a private detective, solving his murder, transformation from bait to shamus. Goddamn Charlie Burnett . . .

Miranda stretched and walked to the window, smoke from the Chesterfield curling into an arabesque.

She'd follow her client tonight. Find out what kind of lie she was telling.

And whether it was a lie of omission or a lie of duplicity, Louise Crowley was young, alone, and in trouble. She needed help, needed protection. Needed someone to watch over her . . .

Miranda exhaled, watching a White Front rumble by on the way to the Ferry Building, flower sellers wrapping dahlias. Someone threw in a nickel at Tascone's and punched "In the Mood" again.

Last case in San Francisco, maybe the last case ever, Miranda Corbie, Private Investigator, reinvented and reimagined. Miranda Corbie, the same and not the same, child of Pacific Street in a torn muslin dress, Mills girl dancing the Charleston, English teacher in Salinas and Red Cross nurse in Spain, the woman who finally found herself, found her soul and lost it all, all, buried deep, a death so complete that it became her life, no Johnny, no Johnny, no Johnny. Then Rick and Burnett and James and Sally Rand, and a license in her wallet and she emerged, reborn, the same and not the same, dark and light and shining like the Phoenix . . . like the City, her city, her very own.

And before the sad good-byes, before the fond farewells, before she wrote Rick or called Gonzales or bought Gladys the new hat she'd been eyeing or sublet her apartment to Bente or sent a message to her old man that he'd be on his own, no more vitamin B shots and rye-soaked sprees . . . before she threw back a final shot with Allen at the Rusty Nail, before she dropped a C-note on No-Legs Norris and spun the last wheel at the Club Moderne, Joe Morello crying like a baby, boutonnière wilted and brown . . . before anything else, she made a promise to Louise Crowley, to the piece of folded, worn paper in her wallet.

The same promise she'd made to Eddie Takahashi, to Pandora Blake, to a waitress in Reno and a little girl named Susie Hampton.

Light tap on the frosted glass.

Miranda stiffened at the noise and looked up quickly, watching the office door open wide.

Roger Roscoe stood in the doorway, hat in his hand.

*

"Miss Corbie? Are you otherwise engaged or may I take up a few minutes of your time?"

He held a brown bowler in long, nervous fingers, wore brown corduroy trousers and a dark green sweater under a tweed jacket. She waved him toward one of the hard-backed chairs in front of her desk.

"I've got a few minutes. Have a seat, Mr. Roscoe."

"Thanks." His angular body stretched awkwardly over the wooden chair. His eyes met Miranda's, and he smiled as if sharing a secret.

"I knew you'd want to talk to me about last night. In fact, I was just in the office and Louise wasn't—well, not quite as open as she normally is. Downright reticent, in fact. I attribute this change to advice from you."

"Mr. Roscoe—"

"Please. Call me Roger. I agree, it's far safer to treat everyone as a suspect, though I'm not accustomed to the cold shoulder." He pulled a silver cigarette case out of his breast pocket. "Mind?"

Miranda shook her head. He struck a match and inhaled the Lucky. She nodded at the gold Gump's matchbook.

"In the market for Oriental antiquities? Your royalties must be better than you led me to believe."

He followed her eyes to the matchbook in his hand and laughed.

"Niles is friends with the Gump family—we often have receptions and parties at the store. My royalties are sadly not such that I'm contemplating a Persian carpet or a jade Buddha."

Miranda crushed out her Chesterfield stub in the ashtray. "To address your initial comment, yes, I've advised Louise to be careful."

"To trust no one?"

"If that's what it takes to save her life."

He nodded. "I'm glad. As I told you, I'm worried about Louise and what these attempts or whatever they are portend. The sooner this is cleared up, the better for all of us. Writers are like the lilies of the field, Miss Corbie—or Miranda, if I may. We toil not, nor do we spin, except in our own little minds."

"Louise said you work very hard."

"And so I do. I work more at being a writer than actually writing. But never mind. You said you had a few minutes, let's not waste time on philosophy."

The teeth flashed again, showcasing a dimple in his thin right cheek and chin. Roger Roscoe had charm—and knew how to use it.

"Thanks for being so cooperative." She pulled the Big Chief tablet toward her and opened it to a blank page. "Is Roger Roscoe your real name?"

The novelist gave a short laugh. "I'd like to tell you that my true name is Percival Snodgrass, but alas, my parents—both dead, by the way—were Roscoes and succumbed to the temptation of alliteration. My middle name, believe it or not, is Rodney. My dust jacket copy reads 'From the pen of R. R.'—Niles thinks I'll be more successful as an abbreviation."

Miranda scratched a note and asked, without looking up: "Address?"

"The Ford Apartments, 957 Mission Street. At least until something better comes along."

"Live there long?"

Roscoe sucked at the Lucky Strike and blew a stream of smoke over Miranda's head.

"A year. Nothing's come along yet."

"So it should take you maybe ten or fifteen minutes to walk to the Monadnock every Friday afternoon before dining at the Palace."

The novelist blinked. He reached toward the desk and tapped the cigarette in the ashtray.

"'A hit, a very palpable hit.' You're not a lily, Miranda, though you'll forgive me if I describe you as a rose." He grinned. "I visit Louise and remind Niles of my existence at least once a week. As I explained last night, I'm hoping he'll let me out of my contract, and my strategy—unsuccessful to this point—is one of ubiquity. In short, I'm hoping to irritate him enough to let me go without alienating the already paltry sum I collect. A difficult task, to be sure. I then eat a modest dinner at the Palace to keep my chin up. My jacket photo is in the Library of Congress, after all."

Miranda turned back a few pages. "So why were you at Alexander Publishing the day before yesterday—a Monday—when Louise received the chocolates?"

The lanky author sighed dramatically and uncrossed his legs.

"Have you any idea how difficult it is to stare at a blank page? To give shape and form and mass and direction to the impulses and thoughts and feelings in your head and then craft a narrative out of them? Poets have it easy—they work in outlines these days, no sonnets, no long-form story-poems, except for MacLeish and Benét and a few other holdovers. No, prose is the undiscovered country, the land of wilderness and broken dreams, where you are expected to either be a good writer or a good seller, and God help you if you try to do both."

Miranda smiled.

"I'm not an author, obviously, but I do have a degree in English. I'm not unfamiliar with the pitfalls of publication—nearly everyone who has ever written anything of importance has suffered something, Mr. Roscoe, so you're in good company. I assume your appearance here on Monday was due to—what, officially? Frustration? Boredom?"

"Both. I'm trying to break into a new market—the crime story, as I explained last night. I'm hoping a detective thriller will give me both commercial and literary success, in the way it has for Chandler and Hammett. Cain's an academic, he can live on tenure, but he's not a bad model to follow, either. Anyway, since I live so close to the office I drop in when the mood strikes, and I thought I'd add another day's worth of irritating Niles to my weekly schedule. Plus, I'd missed the Friday before—my annual medical checkup. I'm fine, by the way."

"So Sylvia Alexander is not a factor in when and how often you choose to appear at the office?"

His dark complexion reddened for the first time. He angled forward, cigarette in his hand, blue eyes on hers.

"I love Sylvia. She deserves better than Niles, but she's incapable of leaving him and he knows it. I'd like nothing better than to catch the bastard in a compromising position—thus securing my freedom and potentially Sylvia's in one swoop—but Louise isn't that kind of girl."

Miranda spoke quietly. "Does Sylvia know that?"

The writer's voice was taut. "No. Not exactly."

"How long has she been taking cocaine and heroin?"

He opened his mouth to speak, shut it again. Leaned forward to rub out the Lucky in the Tower of the Sun ashtray.

"You're a better detective than I gave you credit for. She's been using both since I've known her."

"Was she a nerve case before the hop?"

"I don't know. Probably. She—Niles sends her to sanitariums, practically one a year."

"So Alexander basically employs you as his wife's baby-sitter?"

Anger flashed across his thin, dark face. "I'm no baby-sitter. Sylvia is a fully functioning woman, I assure you."

"No assurance necessary. She's functional enough to be jealous of a pretty young girl—maybe even enough to try killing her."

The novelist stood up stiffly, no flash of white teeth, no smile. "I thought you were a sympathetic soul, Miss Corbie. I was wrong."

"I'm sympathetic to my client. Everything and everyone else is open season. Sit down, Mr. Roscoe, this isn't the Mercury Theater and you're not Orson fucking Welles."

The words hit him and he winced, blinking. He sank back in the chair, knees together, breath heavy. A church bell on Mission tolled three.

Miranda said dryly, "So we understand one another. Here's the question: the husband not only OK's the affair, but makes sure you're taken care of for taking care of his wife. Doesn't that make canceling your contract even more awkward?"

Roscoe's cheekbones burnished red.

"The publishing business is full of awkwardness. When a book is rejected or reviewed badly, you take it personally. When your publisher bestows time and money on another writer instead of you, you take it personally. My relationship with Sylvia—and the very slight pecuniary allowance Niles allows me for squiring her places—is merely one small wrinkle in an old hag's face."

He pointed the last words at Miranda. Her lips rose at the corners.

"'A rose by any other name,' Mr. Roscoe. What the hell did you expect when you walked in here?"

"Not this." The smile was strained. "But I'm a brave man, Miss Corbie. Let's finish and get it over with."

Miranda turned a page in the notebook. "Last night you said something about Jerry Alexander, about saving the story for another time and place."

"Jerry has had more escapes than Houdini. Most of them bought and paid for by Niles. He's the primary reason—in my opinion—Sylvia is so . . . so shattered. As it is, his allowance has been cut and the trust fund rewritten and his inheritance depends on him making something of himself and staying out of trouble. That trust fund, incidentally, is Sylvia's money, which answers your question before it's asked."

Miranda nodded, jotting down a note.

"What about Louise? Jerry's pursued her from the beginning."

The novelist shook his head. "Look, Miss Corbie—Jerry sees every woman as something to conquer. He practically grew up in Sally Stanford's place. You know how many rape cases Niles has paid off? Four. And those are the ones that he knows about."

"Is he capable of murder—in your opinion?"

Roscoe frowned, brow wrinkling. "I would think so. Under the right circumstances. I'm not sure how smart he is, but he's certainly violent enough. With Louise, though, he doesn't strike me as the letter-writing type—more like a tire iron or bare-handed strangler."

Miranda raised her eyebrows. "A preview of your new crime novel?"

The writer cracked a cautious grin. "Maybe."

"Two more questions, Mr. Roscoe, at least for now. You were worried last night, and not just about Louise. You suggested she was hiding something, something that could be endangering her or even Alexander. Do you have any idea what?"

Roscoe studied the floor and spoke slowly.

"Louise is crucial to Niles. She is his first reader, his assistant editor, his secretary, his all-around Girl Friday." He looked up, thin face twisted. "I don't know, Miss Corbie. I don't know. What I do know is that something isn't right with her and hasn't been for one or two months. I've even wondered—I'll confess it—if she's not writing the letters herself."

She stared at him.

"And sending herself poisoned chocolates? Why?"

He shook his head slowly. "If I could make a guess, I'd tell you. I don't know. Just a—writer's intuition, let's say. Louise is in trouble, certainly, but I'm not sure it's the trouble we think it is."

Miranda kept her face steady with effort. Roger Roscoe was voicing some of her own goddamn worries. Her eyes flickered over the notes once again.

"Final question: Louise said Alexander is grooming Howard Carter Smith for major success . . . *New York Times,* publicity, awards. You insinuated Niles may be working him too hard. Do you suspect Smith of something?"

Some of the aplomb crept back into Roscoe's demeanor.

"I suspect him of horrid prose. I suspect him of faking facts and muckraking the muckless. Niles has been hinting something about Alcatraz—as if that hasn't been done to death, no pun intended—but you'll have to ask Smith. I warn you in advance . . . he's hardly a gentleman."

"Unlike you."

The smile was lopsided, charm back in place. "Indubitably, dear lady."

Miranda nodded again. "That's all, Mr. Roscoe—at least for now. I'll have more questions later."

"I don't doubt it. I'll be better prepared next time, 'No more be grieved at that which thou hast done: Roses have thorns, and silver fountains mud.'"

He nodded, grinning, and slid through the open door into the hallway, footsteps echoing against the white marble.

Seven

*

Miranda was walking toward the door when the phone rang. A buzz and crackle and then Allen's voice, uncharacteristically dim and barely audible.

"Miri? Got word you called. Can you hear me?"

"Barely. You sound farther away than Murrow and he's getting bombed."

The chuckle came through more clearly. "No bombs here in Livermore, but plenty of land mines. I'm knee-deep in cow dung. Would you believe I'm on a rustling case?"

She grinned. "I always pegged you for a Wild West type. Listen, I need a trace on a name."

A loud motor drowned out his reply. Miranda raised her voice.

"Allen? Allen, can you hear me?"

"Not really. I'll be back to the office tomorrow morning. Can it wait?"

"Sure thing. See you tomorrow. And thanks, Allen."

The phone clicked off while the tractor or thresher was warming up again. She replaced the receiver thoughtfully, picked up her purse, and closed and locked the door behind her.

Glanced at her wristwatch. Three-twenty already, and she'd need to change clothes. Louise would be leaving for her rendezvous with the #3 White Front in a little under three hours.

Miranda stood indecisively in the marble hallway, listening to the hushed women's voices around the corner. Maybe she could push Louise a little further.

When she reached the elevator bank, she punched six.

*

Miranda pushed open the double doors marked ALEXANDER PUBLISHING and looked around.

Alfred A. Knopf had nothing to worry about.

Wainscoting lined the walls, gray paint splotchy, gold-framed scenes from Shakespeare and cheap reproductions of Rembrandt. The waiting area was furnished in thirty-year-old couches, floral patterns dim and faded, with a couple of side tables and lamps on a burgundy-colored carpet. A marble standing ashtray stood in the corner, contents unemptied.

Louise sat behind a newer, more modern desk, blond hair limper than at lunch, stack of envelopes in the outbox to her right. Behind her a thick oak door boasted NILES ALEXANDER: PUBLISHER in gold script. An unmarked door, smaller, plainer, thinner, stood meekly to the right.

The secretary's blue eyes grew wide at Miranda's entrance, then darted toward the publisher's sanctum.

"Yes—yes, I'll make sure he gets the message. No, I believe the print run was already set and he's firm on that, but I—yes, I will double check. Thank you."

She blinked, hung up the phone, and took a deep breath. "Miss Corbie—"

"Why doesn't Alexander install a buzzer? You'd certainly be safer from rejected crackpots."

Louise glanced again toward her boss's office, voice low. "He likes to be accessible."

"Then let him sit where you are. Listen, Louise, I'm heading out of town tonight—another case—but I'll be back in the morning and I'd like to get on Alexander's calendar tomorrow. I also need to borrow an office key."

"A key? Oh no, that's impossible. He'll never allow it."

Miranda held the blonde's eyes. "He'll never know. I'm playing a hunch and need to test the typewriters. Your letters may be an inside job."

Louise paled. "Miss Corbie, I—I told you, I'm sure no one here had anything—"

"I'm not so sure. How many machines are there, by the way?"

"Six. Mine, one in Mr. Alexander's office, one in Miss Berrigan's—her office is through the other door—and another two in the editing office—Miss Kingston and Mr. Ward come in about twice a week, and they share an office but not a typewriter—and one more in our general meeting room, next to Miss Berrigan's."

"Fine. I'll come in either early in the morning or late at night, no one the wiser."

"But I don't have an extra key—"

Miranda's voice was breezy, confident. "That's OK, I'll get yours copied right now before I leave town."

Louise blotched red and white, blue eyes like Wedgwood saucers.

"But—my job—"

"Your life, Louise."

The secretary's breath was audible in the quiet office.

"I— There is an extra key. I'll get it for you." She stood up, walking quickly and quietly through the unmarked door, shutting it behind her.

One Mississippi, Two Mississippi . . .

Miranda grabbed the mail from the outbox, rifling through envelopes as fast as she could.

Uniformly typed, all on office stationery and addressed to various people—one of them Roscoe—probably royalty statements for agents and authors—and an assortment of bills, mostly printing and distribution invoices. In between two invoices was a letter hand-addressed in blue ink to The Greer Home, a sanitarium out on Fulton and 36th.

Miranda frowned, studying the writing, when she heard the doorknob click. She hastily replaced everything.

Louise entered distraught, voice barely under control.

"I—I can't find it, Miss Corbie. It's not there."

"Where do you usually keep it?"

"In the meeting room. We have file cabinets there with extra paper and office equipment, and I always keep the key on a string, hanging from the inside of the top drawer."

Miranda said slowly, "Maybe it fell off. I'm sure you'll find it later when you look again. I can pick it up tomorrow when I come in to talk to Alexander. What time will work?"

The schedule, resumption of order, seemed to calm her a little, though she kept glancing back toward the unmarked door as though the key would walk through it.

"I'm—I'm sorry—I should have told you the truth earlier. I don't—I don't know why I didn't, Miss Corbie. I'm sorry. I should have given it to you, and now—"

"Now you'll have time to find it. It's all right, Louise. I didn't mean to rush you—it's my fault that you panicked. Let's start over, shall we? Will a late morning appointment with Mr. Alexander be possible?"

The secretary breathed in and out for a moment, shoulders moving with her lungs. Then she sank into the squeaky chair and opened a large appointment book.

"10:30 is open for thirty minutes."

"I'll take it."

Louise was writing down "Miranda Corbie" in the empty slot when the buzzer on her desk went off, making both of them jump. The secretary flipped on the intercom, and Alexander's voice burned through like acid.

"Louise—you're late for our dictation."

She looked up apologetically at Miranda, who smiled at her and whispered "See you tomorrow."

Miranda turned from the doorway to wave good-bye to the blonde, but she was already at the publisher's door, steno pad in hand.

*

Tracking someone who didn't know you wasn't difficult.

Don't be afraid to get close, Corbie, and for God's sake, don't run. Look 'em in the eye—hell, you can follow from in front as easy as behind. The rest of it is just waiting and loitering. Bring a pack of smokes and you'll be all right . . .

Charlie Burnett, a lesson with a leer, good advice delivered with bad breath and a pat on the ass.

Tracking someone who knew you—that required more preparation.

Rule One: plant a lie if you can. Louise thought she was out of town.

Rule Two: men can be more invisible than women.

Miranda studied the effect in her bedroom mirror, angling her head back and forth.

Hair pulled back and tucked into a patched and worn fisherman's hat. Levis, baggy and blue, hanging from a cinched belt and rolled up at the cuffs. Shoes, a modified man's boot with soft soles and hard metal toes.

The navy peacoat, double-breasted, hid most of her breast-bulge, and—as she'd learned in Reno—she could always stoop.

Miranda nodded to herself, right fingers sliding over the barrel of the Baby Browning in her pocket.

She was ready for wherever her client might lead her.

✳

6:07.

Louise walked out of the Monadnock in a hurry, cream-colored hat askew, camel hair coat halfway unbuttoned. The blonde, even from a distance, looked harried, chased by Furies Miranda couldn't see.

Miranda shrugged herself off Lotta's Fountain. Brushed past a fat man in a straw hat, slurping water, ignored a middle-aged flower vendor who offered her a mum with a toothy smile, rushed across the end of Geary, the neon lights of DR. FORD—DENTIST and PILES CURED beating down from the flatiron on Kearny and Market, and crossed to the De Young building, ambling along the sidewalk of Market Street toward Montgomery.

The secretary wasn't looking behind her. One of the Italian flower vendors brightened when he saw her, held out a pink carnation, and she smiled, waving the flower away and never stopping.

The Italian knew her—probably the same one Louise bought something from the night someone tried to push her under a streetcar.

Louise was heading for Market and Sutter, walking fast. Miranda hesitated, deciding to hoof it to the car stop ahead of the blonde. By the time she reached the corner of Montgomery and Sutter, she was out of breath, and leaned against an ornate doorframe, half in shadow. Louise hadn't turned the corner onto Sutter yet.

The secretary's hat bobbed into sight, heading straight for the #3 Market Street Railway stop on Sansome. A car was approaching.

Louise was climbing aboard when Miranda scooted in line, keeping her head down, catching odd looks from an old lady in tweed and a heavyset man carrying a tool box.

She slumped her shoulders, face angled down. Handed over seven cents to the bored conductor and peeked up from under the fisherman's cap as she maneuvered to an empty seat in the back of the bus.

Sank into the green cushioned seat and exhaled.

Louise was gazing out the window, taut and tense, oblivious to the other passengers. The blonde jumped when the car started up, smiling distantly at the matron in moth-eaten fur beside her.

Miranda kept her eyes on Louise's back. Taylor, Jones, Leavenworth . . . and Louise still staring out the window.

When the car clanged past Hyde, Miranda hunched forward. If Louise was going home, the no-choice destination for a Wednesday evening with Thursday morning hard behind, she'd step off the car at Larkin, maybe treat herself to a salad at the Hotel Carlton. She'd brush her hair and crème her face and cry in her pillow, and start the whole fucking thing all over again the next day.

Louise didn't get off at Larkin.

The secretary passed the Carlton without a quiver, her own street without a sign of recognition.

Miranda settled back in her seat, legs pressed together, Levis too goddamn itchy.

At Van Ness, a stocky, sweaty man in a linty brown fedora squeezed in next to her, giving her a quizzical up and down. She twisted in the seat, flipped the collar up again.

Franklin . . . Gough . . . where the hell was Louise going?

An elbow suddenly jarred her side, and she gritted her teeth to keep from yelping.

The stocky bastard next to her.

He was grinning, pig-eyes red-rimmed and small. "Sorry—*mister*."

Word was pointed, designed to provoke, just like the elbow in the side. The sonofabitch probably thought she was a nancy boy, wanted to have some fun, maybe follow down an alley and beat up the queer.

Miranda's fingers traced the cold metal of the Baby Browning in her pocket. She grunted, made it as deep as she could.

They were crossing Buchanan. Louise woke up suddenly, gathered her purse closer and looked ahead, poised and ready.

"You hear me? I 'pologized—*mister*. Ain't you gonna thank me?"

Louise was up now, preparing to leave the #3 at Fillmore and Sutter. The bastard next to her sprawled back in the seat, legs spread, self-satisfied smile stretching his fat red cheeks.

"Ain't heard no thank you, and you ain't goin' nowhere til I do."

A woman on the other side of him shook her head slightly. No one else said anything, determinedly content in friendly conversations about the Seals and the Fair and what was playing at the Fox.

The streetcar jerked to a halt and Miranda stood up. The stocky man's legs were stretched out in her path, and Louise was moving quickly toward the rear exit, facing her.

She bent her face down. The bully chuckled.

"Cat got your tongue, sissy? Guess you'll have to keep—"

The metal toe of her boot struck bone under thin wool, aiming for the shin, and the bastard screamed and grabbed his leg while she maneuvered around him and hurried off the #3. She could still hear him yelling when the White Front pulled out into traffic, heading for the next stop.

Miranda caught her breath, eyes darting back and forth for Louise and her cream-colored hat. Found her standing by another stop, the #22 Fillmore line, headed south.

Louise looked from her wristwatch to the quiet, residential street. Miranda drifted to the small knot of people waiting with her, two old ladies, a painter, and a man in a suit.

Five minutes later, the #22 arrived, another White Front, one of the older, smaller wooden cars left over from the Quake. The secretary took an aisle seat in the front, still and composed.

Nearly 6:45. Where the hell was Louise Crowley heading?

Not many people on the car, conversation muted, music wafting from jukes in soda fountains and a few of the bars along Fillmore and Geary. Once past Turk, the secretary made a move, standing up at Golden Gate.

Miranda dismounted with her at McAllister. The neon was turning on, sky red and magenta and orange from the sunset, wide street darkened and quiet, except for cafes and bars and the corner stores.

Louise didn't hesitate. She crossed the street to yet another bus stop, this time the #5 line, transfer clutched in her hand. A blond sailor in crackerjacks loitered under a streetlamp, whistling softly, eyeing the blonde. After a few minutes, two teenage boys in dungarees ran pell-mell down the sidewalk, arriving out of breath from the candy store up the street.

By the time the #5 pulled up seven minutes later, the stop was full.

Miranda's hands were shaking. She needed a goddamn cigarette.

Louise climbed in, settled in the middle. Miranda headed for the back, where the sailor was already sprawled.

Nobody talked except for the boys, who seemed to be arguing over a comic book. The sailor dozed. Louise sat upright, eyes ahead.

They reached the Panhandle and turned down Fulton, passing by the Avenues, one by one, the air colder, heavier, saltier. The sailor stayed aboard, woke up around 43rd, Pacific Ocean pounding sand, screams of gulls and young girls riding the Big Dipper.

By now, it was obvious where they were headed, where Louise was trekking on a cold Wednesday night.

The White Front rolled to a halt, bright neon winking and blinking around them, laughter and music and the out-of-tune calliope, uncanny cackle of Laffing Sal and the smell of fresh blackberry pies and fried chicken.

The driver intoned "End of the line" in a pleasant baritone.

Last stop.

Playland-at-the-Beach.

Eight

*

Playland-at-the-Beach was the City's own ocean-front amusement park, usually full of kids, couples, sailors, screaming high school girls, and carnival grifters in crumpled hats with chippies on their arms, trolling for day jobs or a quick buck to fix an unlucky streak.

Desperate or merry, gay, fey, or on the lam, Playland was the last stop, and not just for the Market Street Railway.

For the last couple of years, Treasure Island and the Gayway almost made it redundant. The Whitney Brothers—purveyors of play and owners of land, moguls of the sea all the way up to and including Sutro's venerable Cliff House—even the Whitney Brothers had jumped ship to run the Fair "amusement zone" when asked by Leland Cutler and George Creel and Mayor Rossi.

To their credit, the brothers let the Gayway concessions run themselves, gave Sally a free hand with the Nude Ranch, and looked the other way when Miranda cracked the Incubator Baby case. And after '39, after the bankers and old money had looked down from the Tower of the Sun, mouths pinched and faces pale, descrying the Whitneys, shaking fingers at the Gayway, and come crawling back when the amusement zone was the only goddamn thing to turn a profit—after that, the Whitneys could do no wrong by San Francisco.

The Fair would be history in eleven days, the City's amusement zones confined once more to Ocean Beach or the International Settlement, Chinatown alleys and the road up Twin Peaks, but tonight Treasure Island still beckoned, Magic City's last, dying splendor, last days to catch a glimpse of French tit in the Folies Bergère or watch Diego Rivera paint or even take another splash in the Diving Bell, Ken Silverman and his new wife Nina still exploring under the Bay.

Miranda leaned against a lamp post and breathed in, salt on her tongue, eyes on Louise and her cream-colored hat.

Playland wasn't playing much tonight. Most of the rides sat still and quiet, grifters and carnies, drunks and hustlers outnumbering marks and tourists two to one.

The blonde turned left down the upper midway, past the Flying Scooter and the Lindy Loop, silent and lonely while the Big Dipper hurtled again down the steep wooden hill, lone scream from a young girl punctuating the heavy air and making her jump. Miranda followed, careful to keep her footsteps quiet, her pace unsteady.

They passed the Tilt-A-Whirl, boys in Berkeley letter sweaters and neatly coiffed coeds waiting for the operator to send them flying; passed the Octopus and the Fun House, Laffing Sal scaring the hell out of a group of little boys on a sneak out; finally turned toward the Chutes Lagoon and the cheaper, more tawdry concessions, the balloon darts and the shooting gallery, shell games and confidence swindles, Madame Lavinsky and your past, present, and future through a cloudy glass ball.

The calliope hiccoughed and the Big Dipper screeched again, smell of black-berry pies hot out of the oven from the Pie Shop mixing with the vanilla ice cream and chocolate-dipped oatmeal cookies from the "It" stand, hot dog vendor trying to outshout the tamale cook.

Miranda's stomach growled.

She hadn't eaten an "It's It" in a long, long time.

Memories flooded over her like the Creamsicle waves, still highlighted orange in the almost-set sun, memories of Chutes-at-the-Beach, the Playland before the Whitneys arrived, of spinning around on the Figure Eight when she was fourteen and nearly throwing up afterward, of sneaking out for longer and longer hours and days, riding the streetcars all the way to the West, the edge, wondering, when she was eight or nine or ten, whether she'd fall off and drown and knowing no one would ever know or care if she did.

Other memories, later memories, less painful, less true, of the Ferris Wheel and the Aeroplane Swing, of the boys from Oakland and Berkeley with their hands on her knees, of the gin flask on her hip. Playtime, gay time, the 1920s spinning around and around, women voting, women smoking, Mills College classes and parked cars with rumble seats, the Black Bottom and white hot jazz, spirits as high as the hemlines.

She remembered trying an "It" when Whitney first sold them, right before the Crash when everybody had a nickel or knew where to get one. After Spain, back in San Francisco, back to the only home she ever really knew, she rode out to Playland once, drifting like the wood on the beach, wandering like the little girl from twenty years earlier.

She bought another "It," but it didn't taste the same.

Louise was threading her way toward the stand now, past a Skee-Ball concession, straight toward the Great Highway, not hesitating, not looking around.

Miranda nodded to herself. The secretary had done this before.

The blonde bent forward against the sharp wind rising from the beach, collar raised, sand starting to blow, and darted into the warm Pie Shop next to the "It" stand.

Miranda's stomach growled again. She hunched over and threw a dime at the hot dog man tucked in a corner next door to the Pie Shop, eye on the door, and ordered a mustard, sauerkraut, and onions as gruffly as she could.

Three minutes later she was devouring it, chewing greedily, face burning from the cold wind, watching the stragglers filter through on the way to Topsy's down the street, smell of fried chicken making the hot dog tasteless.

Footsteps behind her, steady and heavy.

She gulped the rest of the hot dog and tossed the paper boat in a garbage can, slipping back to the "It" concession, the pimply-faced man in the soda jerk hat shivering and dying to close up. Fog was thick and blowing in hard from the sea, wind unrelenting.

A large man with a soft belly—late thirties, wearing some kind of uniform, not police or fire, maybe a security guard—was marching up from the Chutes area. She shrank a little more against the side slat board of the "It" booth, watching him.

His face was set in a grim line, scars on his forehead and cheek. Hair short, arms hanging but not loose, the threat of physicality strutted in front of him, pushing people out of his way before he even got there.

Deliberately, not hurriedly, as if the temperature weren't dropping as fast as the wind was rising, he walked into the Pie Shop.

Miranda lit a cigarette.

Five minutes later, Louise walked out with him.

*

They headed north, passing another Skee-Ball joint, the tamale shop, and Smith's Yum-Yums. Louise struggled to keep up, hand crushing her hat to her head, while the lumbering Scar-Face strode on.

He barked something at the blonde when he reached the corner of Cabrillo, and crossed the street against the stop sign. He glanced behind impatiently when Louise was still in the middle of the road, jerking his head toward the north side of the Merry-Go-Round, and stomped past the entrance of the ride, finally halting in front of another Yum-Yum shop next door.

A couple of teenage boys were playing Skee-Ball and the Big Dipper was doing bigger business, or at least carrying louder screamers. Between the roar of the waves and the clattering, groaning wood and palpable whoosh of the cars and girls in the front seats, the barkers at the shooting gallery and Goofy Village were as silent as Charlie Chaplin.

Louise was shivering, still clutching her hat, and finally joined Scar-Face. She looked up hopefully and hooked her arm through his, leaning against him. He bent over her, face set in harsh, angry lines, yelling something that made the blonde shrink against the slat board wall. A yellow neon sign sputtered above her head, advertising SALT WATER TAFFIES and PUFFED RICE CANDY.

Miranda lingered by the Merry-Go-Round entrance, peacoat collar up, desperately hoping her hat and bobby pins would stay in place. The operator was on the other side of the ride, comparing racing notes with a shooting gallery shill, while a little girl bobbed up and down on a white horse and a young man in a good suit and ingratiating smile held his hand out to a plain young woman with full lips and very thick glasses.

Clat-tat-tat-tat-tat-rattle-rattle-rattle-BOOM . . .

The screamers screamed again.

By now, Scar-Face was gripping Louise's arm roughly. The secretary's face was blank, almost like she didn't know where she was or what she was doing.

No one else was in line for the Merry-Go-Round. Miranda inched closer, still facing the ride, her back to them both, desperate to catch a word.

Scar-Face's voice was rich and booming, a voice used to wielding authority, unused to a demand not being met.

"Whaddya mean 'no'? You work there, don't ya? Jesus Christ, don't you care if I get my goddamn job back? Why the hell ain't you—"

Clat-tat-tat-tat-tat-rattle-rattle-rattle-BOOM . . .

Louise muttered something, drowned by the screams. Miranda risked a quick glance backward. The blonde was visibly upset, eyes red, crying. She tried to disengage her arm, turning to go, and Scar-Face yanked her toward him hard enough to send her sprawling on the cement.

Miranda took a step forward, fist clenched on her Baby Browning, then bit her lip, stomach tight, and turned slowly back to face the Merry-Go-Round. Two round-eyed boys of twelve were waiting in line, staring at her.

She bent her head into the peacoat collar, straining to hear. Scar-Face lowered his voice, not as angry, not as demanding, phrases bobbing above the storm of sound.

". . . Alcatraz, baby, not the fucking Palace . . . Cretzer don't know jack . . . job for life and plenty of kale, you'd like that, baby . . ."

Clat-tat-tat-tat-tat-rattle-rattle-rattle-BOOM . . .

One Mississippi, Two Mississippi, Three Mississippi . . .

She turned toward the white caps on the gray-black ocean, no longer flecked with red through the blowing fog, head twisted just enough to see Louise was standing again, posture bent and crooked, face buried in her hands, left stocking torn.

"Aw, Jesus Christ, quit the bawlin'. It's gonna be me and you again, me and you and the goddamn beach. You like that, don't you baby? You like a good—"

Clat-tat-tat-tat-tat-rattle-rattle-rattle-BOOM . . .

The blonde nodded several times, still not looking at Scar-Face. He finally pried her fingers away, surprisingly careful, and grabbed her by the arms in a clinch, kissing her long and hard. The boys were becoming more interested in the scene than the Merry-Go-Round, but the operator was finally ambling back to take tickets, *Daily Racing Form* marked and tucked under his arm.

Scar-Face put his arm around Louise, and they strolled past Smith's Yum-Yums toward Fulton, the secretary leaning into his uniformed mass.

Miranda watched them go, face momentarily lit by a match. She inhaled deeply on a Chesterfield, watching Louise's crushed, crumpled, no-longer-cream-colored hat wink out in the distance.

*

She splurged on a Yellow Cab, catching one in front of Topsy's Roost. The driver was about thirty, with clean fingernails, and enough San Francisco panache to not stare at her clothes.

She leaned back, head against the brown leather, and closed her eyes.

So Louise Crowley from Olympia—confident, capable, pretty, and smart—Louise Crowley was hiding a brute of a lover, the kind of bastard that thought a hard fuck could always cure a fat lip.

Her fingers twitched, remembering how Scar-Face had thrown the blonde, remembering how Duggan had backhanded her a few months ago, remembering the crooked cop and Kaiser, the sadistic lion tamer on the Gayway.

Miranda's fingertip touched the Baby Browning in her pocket.

No wonder the blonde had been attracted to Jerry Alexander, young, good-looking rich boy whose penchant was the same.

Slap and a kiss, punch and a poke, tear drops in the goddamn beer, boys will be boys and men will be men and hitting women was the only way to show them who was the fucking boss, the man of the house, the wearer of pants, the bearer of prick, all hail, all hail, all hail.

She opened her eyes and lit a Chesterfield.

The women cried and dried their eyes, thinking how goddamn lucky they were. They had a man, after all, a real man with a real temper, not some foppish mannequin or closet queer. Men with hard muscles and short tempers, men who smelled of perfume that their wives couldn't afford, men who would fight off other men and win, men who understood about life and about the darkness under the sheets, the sin that felt so good, mamma, you always told me to close my eyes and let them do it but I wanted to, God, I wanted to, so bless me, Father, because I have sinned, and I've sinned again in liking it so goddamn much . . .

The make-believe Merry-Go-Round of love, around and around she goes, and where she stops, nobody knows, nobody except Louise Crowley from Olympia, content with a pat on the head and a ram between the thighs, torn stockings and bruised arms, the little lady knows her place, gave up on Prince Charming, gave up on herself.

Like Pandora Blake, like Betty Chow, like Phyllis Winters, like nearly every goddamn woman she knew.

Confusing strength with violence, love with sex, need for desire.

Oh my man, I love him so . . .

Never knowing or understanding the difference.

Miranda took a deep drag on the stick, Johnny's face reflecting in the dark glass of the taxicab.

✳

She woke up heavy-eyed the next morning, 6:30, dreams of Spain and blown-off limbs and dropping bombs. Miranda sighed, shifting in her robe, stirring brown sugar into the watery oatmeal.

Scar-Face mentioned something about getting a job back. What was it Louise said at Fong Fong? *I can take a blow, Miss Corbie, I know it's hard on a man to not have a job and be tired of looking . . .*

The phone rang and she dropped the teaspoon against the milk glass bowl.

"I—oh, Miss Corbie—can you—can you come here now?"

Miranda held the receiver closer to her ear. No other sounds.

"Where are you, Louise?"

"I-I'm at work. And—oh, my God . . ."

"What is it? What's wrong?"

"Jesus—I can't believe . . ." Her voice trailed off in shock, breath heavy on the phone.

"Louise—*tell* me—"

Audible catch in the secretary's throat.

"Mr. Alexander—Niles . . . he's . . . he's dead."

Act Two

*

The Plot

"*The poet's eye, in fine frenzy rolling,*
Doth glance from heaven to earth, from earth to heaven."
—William Shakespeare
A Midsummer Night's Dream, Act V, scene i

nine

*

The Monadnock was buzzing when Miranda strode through the doors, Meyer waddling slowly behind, cane barely keeping time on the marble floor.

She peered around a fat man with a cigar to check the magazine and cigarette stand. Gladys didn't see her, the blonde already overwhelmed with curiosity-seekers wanting to know the story about the police cars outside, impatient reporters pressing against the counter.

Miranda's eyes searched until her breath caught, remembering.

No lopsided smile, no crinkly blue eyes, no bullshit half-Irish lilt.

No Rick.

Goddamn it . . .

"I'm sorry to drag you down here this early, Meyer. I've got a feeling Louise might need you."

He brushed off toast crumbs from a pale-yellow shirt, freshly starched.

"If what you told me in the taxicab is true, my dear, I'm sure at least one of you shall."

She squeezed his arm. "Follow me."

Miranda pushed her way to the elevators, waiting impatiently next to an elderly lady in a beaver stole looking for Pinkerton's, and a reporter trying to disguise himself as a less predatory species.

They crowded in, the reporter stepping on Miranda's foot. Meyer spoke in a low voice.

"Miss Crowley must have—"

She gave him a poke with her elbow and made a motion with her eyebrows toward the reporter, who was studying his nails. The attorney nodded.

The elevator emptied on the sixth floor, men and women spreading out in singles and small groups. Miranda grabbed Meyer by the arm and whisked him to the closest corner, HIRAM THORPE, C.P.A. painted on a door in prim black letters.

"As I was about to say, Miss Crowley must have followed your advice and telephoned Inspector Fisher."

Miranda nodded, glancing down both hallways and motioning at Meyer to follow. She moved quickly around the corner toward a rumbling of voices gaining volume with every step. Coats and hats, mostly fedoras with a few derbies, in shades from black and brown to green and blue, blocked their progress at the end of the hall.

Reporters.

Miranda whispered: "Jesus. It's only been a little over an hour since Louise called. Either Alexander must be more important than I thought or it's a slow day in San Francisco. Brace yourself."

Her attorney frowned, cane loudly stabbing the marble in front of him with a series of sharp cracks. A small cluster of the reporters turned at the sound, staring.

"Ain't that the shamus-broad? Miranda Kirby? The one you bastards always run photos on?"

"Corbie, you idiot. She's what's-his-name's girlfriend, the hack from the *News*—"

"Who's the fat old guy with her?"

They started to walk-run toward Miranda and Meyer, shouting questions, sniping at each other, more competition joining the race. Miranda threaded her arm through Meyer's and drew the attorney close.

Goddamn it, they were outnumbered. And no Rick to run interference.

Time to throw on the electricity.

She took a step forward, head up, hips shifting slightly, weight on her left foot. No Elizabeth Arden this morning, no fucking time for allure, just a quick slash of Red Dice lipstick and barely a brush through long hair, navy skirt and simple wool sweater under a long black coat, old pair of black gloves and a navy blue beret perched awkwardly on top.

She struck the pose and waited a few seconds, the reporters gradually quieting, some grinning, fedoras pushed off their foreheads. They formed a perimeter around Miranda and Meyer, one whistling under his breath.

"Jesus, that Sanders was a lucky bastard—"

"Oughta be more good-time girls turnin' private dick—beats Pinkerton all to hell . . ."

"Miss Corbie, what do you know about this case? Were you employed by Mr. Alexander?"

"Hell, I'd like to employ her sometime . . ."

"Lay off her, Simon, can't you see the lady needs some air?"

From behind the second row of reporters another man, young, with curly hair and a peculiarly lopsided smile pushed his way to the front.

Herb Caen.

He studied Miranda, grinning. "I haven't seen anything that enticing since—well, since my honeymoon. Step aside, boys—my middle name is exclusive."

"Now wait just a goddamn minute, glamour boy—"

The columnist held up a hand. "Be good and I promise to feed you all later. Miss Corbie is here to meet me."

"Since when? Does Bea know about this?"

"Sanders joins the army and this jerk gets the girl? What gives?"

"You'd better make with the story, Caen, or you'll be makin' an appointment with your dentist . . ."

"Don't be such poor sports—or ugly wolves."

The columnist extended an arm to Miranda, impish grin adding curl to his hair.

"Happy to be your knight-errant, Miss Corbie. Inspector Fisher is waiting."

The reporters, disgruntled, parted like the Red Sea. Caen walked on his toes, comedic version of Prince Charming, while Meyer protected Miranda from the rear, brandishing his cane and fending off the battery of hurled questions with a flat, well-manicured hand.

She glanced sideways at the columnist. "Thanks. You could've said something earlier."

His eyebrows met his hairline. "And miss that little number you put on? I promised Sanders I'd look out for you, Miranda, but every man has his limits. And sister, do you know how to make an entrance and cause a traffic jam, all at the same time . . ."

Two uniforms were guarding the outer doors of Alexander Publishing, and Caen unhooked his arm.

"You'll find Inspector Fisher inside. He's waiting for you—and your friend, I suppose." The reporter eyed Meyer with curiosity. "And don't make a liar out of me, now—I expect that exclusive when you're done."

He grinned at her, tipping his fedora before backing down the hallway. Miranda looked up at the bulls.

"Miranda Corbie. We're here to see—"

"Yeah, sister. In you go." The older one opened the door for them, holding up a fist and yawning. The office was empty except for Louise sitting on the edge of a chair in the waiting area, biting her nails.

"Oh—Miss Corbie—thank God—"

The secretary flew toward Miranda, face too taut and eyes too wide.

"The reporters came right after the police did, and Inspector Fisher is still in . . ."

She looked toward her former boss's office, weaving slightly. Miranda held out a hand to steady her.

"It's all right, Louise. This is Meyer Bialik, my attorney. He's here to help."

The secretary held up a hand to her throat. "You think—oh, Miss Corbie—"

Meyer bowed, plucking up Louise's other hand and holding it to his lips.

"Please—do not alarm yourself, Miss Crowley. I am here only as a shepherd among wolves." He gave the blonde a benevolent smile.

Her eyes darted back and forth and she nodded, sinking back into a Windsor chair.

Two uniforms emerged from the door leading to the other offices, Bunny Berrigan close behind. The cops slipped inside Alexander's office while Bunny lit a cigarette and stared at Miranda and Meyer.

The redhead was red-eyed but in control. "Who're you?"

"Miranda Corbie, Miss Berrigan. We met the other night at the Sky Room."

"Why are you here?"

Meyer interjected. "Miss Corbie represents Miss Crowley."

"What about you?"

Meyer's voice was smooth. "I represent Miss Corbie."

Niles Alexander's head of marketing frowned, her normally fast-talking, friendly chatter replaced with steel. "What is she, a mouthpiece?"

Miranda said dryly: "I'm a private detective."

Bunny jerked a thumb toward Meyer. "And him?"

"The mouthpiece."

The statuesque redhead smoothed her wrinkled wool skirt down thick thighs. "I knew there'd be one hanging around. Better that than those goddamn reporters. What's the lay?"

"Miss Crowley hired me on a confidential matter, but one that might have a bearing on Alexander's death."

Bunny held Miranda's eyes for a few seconds, drawing down hard on the cigarette before she exhaled.

"I hope you're tougher than you look. The cops're calling it murder."

Louise buried her face in her hands, breath ragged, dry sobs.

"I—I found him, Miss Berrigan—I didn't know what to do—I called Miss Corbie—"

"Yeah, I know, kid, you told me already. Listen, Miss Corbie, I've got a business to run. Those boys in the white coats carted out Niles about ten minutes ago down the back staircase, but Alexander Publishing is in the middle of setting up print runs and fulfilling orders and publishing books—that's why I got here early this morning, figuring I'd beat Niles to the office."

She shook her head, blowing out a billow of smoke.

"I beat him, all right. The poor sap never saw it coming."

"When did you get here, Miss Berrigan?"

"About five minutes after the coppers did. Sylvia Alexander is in there with her son, and she's asked me to see that things are taken care of. You're a private cop, I know, but I'd appreciate it if you can help speed things up a little—maybe talk to that Fisher guy and move it along."

"Inspector Fisher is in the office?"

Bunny dropped some ashes in the overflowing tray. "Takes his damn time. I could publish the Encyclopedia Britannica by the time these bureaucrats make a move."

"I'll do what I can, Miss Berrigan."

Miranda turned to Meyer, low voice.

"Would you stay here with Louise? Try to get her to calm down and tell you exactly what happened. And keep it on the QT."

Meyer nodded. Bunny threw herself in a chair next to Louise with a sigh.

"May as well get off my feet. Try to hurry them, OK? I need to get into Niles' safe."

Miranda opened Alexander's heavy office door, the two uniforms inside starting toward her.

"It's all right, boys. Hello, Miranda."

Inspector David Fisher was grayer than the last time she'd seen him, but still compact and muscular, the small mustache he'd sported a few months ago shaved and replaced with stubble. His mouth betrayed no emotion but his eyes looked glad to see her.

Miranda nodded. "Inspector. Sorry to see you under difficult circumstances."

"Only kind we know. Herb Caen said he'd get you through the front lines outside."

Alexander's office was large by Monadnock standards, with multiple windows facing Third and Stevenson, mahogany desk designed to intimidate. Leather chairs sat in front, cowering in thick red-orange carpet and surrounded by walnut bookshelves, straight rows of Alexander publications broken only by a small alcove with a safe discreetly installed into the wall.

Tucked below it was Sylvia Alexander, shrinking into an overstuffed chair, eyes red and dilated. Jerry sat next to his mother, holding her hands between his. Neither one paid any attention to Miranda.

Fisher motioned toward the mother and son with his head, voice barely audible.

"Miss Crowley said she phoned Sylvia Alexander immediately after she telephoned us. Jerry arrived with his mother about thirty minutes ago, before we could officially notify either one of them. He apparently spent the night at his parents' mansion on Nob Hill."

"He's got his own place—why the old family homestead?"

"We don't know yet, but we'll find out. Seems he has a suite of rooms on a lower floor with a separate entrance, in case he needs it. At least that's what his mother said before she cracked up completely—we made the mistake of letting her see the body get taken out."

Miranda shook her head. "Jerry's not the family reunion type."

"That's an understatement. But you didn't hear it from me."

"What about Bunny Berrigan? What's she doing here so early?"

Fisher suppressed a snort. "The redheaded tornado? She flew in on a broom about five or ten minutes after we got here, said she was planning to get to the office at the crack of dawn because she's got a deadline to manage. She just got out of a preliminary with Grant and Cantrell over there." He gestured toward the two uniforms who'd approached Miranda.

"So what about you? Miss Crowley's your client—that much she told us—but what's your timing on this?"

"Louise called me a little before seven. I forgot to check the clock for the exact time—I was up late last night and groggy. Told her to phone you immediately and I dressed and got here as fast as I could, collecting my attorney along the way."

Fisher gave her a wry smile. "So soon? Thanks, by the way—Miss Crowley said you insisted she ask for me directly. Question is, how much did she tell you?"

"Very little—she was hysterical and from what I got out of her I figured it was a homicide. Louise hired me on a personal matter but the cases may be related."

The inspector raised thick eyebrows. "How? Your client's alive."

"Not for want of someone trying. So what happened to Alexander?"

"We're waiting on a toxicology report from the lab—the deceased had alcohol dribbled down his shirt front—and he was fully dressed, apparently from a night on the town—we're checking that angle, clubs and so forth—but we're pretty sure it wasn't demon drink that killed him. There's also no sign of forced entry on the main office door or this one, so we're looking at anybody who had ready access."

They moved in measured steps toward Alexander's desk. Two gold-framed photos of Sylvia in better times lined the smooth, tawny surface, next to a desk calendar, yesterday's date still displayed, along with a Ronson touch-up lighter and cigarette box and an award from the Rotary Club. All were covered in a fine, dusty powder.

The sticky brown-red pool on the opposite side had stopped spreading across the mahogany some time ago, liquid slowly evaporating, becoming thicker and more viscous, streaks and droplets, spatter and smears, tiny hairs and dust motes trapped like flies in amber, slowly swirling in a Technicolor kaleidoscope whenever the light caught the angle just right.

A matching desk chair leaned back drunkenly, facing the window, as if unable to bear the sight, while Miranda stood and stared at the once-shining wood.

"See that spot where you'd normally put a pen set, if you're the pen set kind?"

Fisher pointed to an empty space between the calendar and the award and she blinked, taking a breath.

"Heavy Bakelite, held two pens on either side of one of those modern-looking female heads—a combination desk set–artistic piece. Somebody, late last night—the ME gave me a three-hour window—smashed his skull with the thing."

To the right of the publisher's opulent desk and chair the thick, bright carpet was crushed, fibers like a forest after an avalanche. Two faint tracks leading from the middle of the room toward the desk itself could barely be made out.

"Was he struck while sitting at the desk?"

Fisher stifled a yawn, shaking his head. "Not enough coffee this morning. It's funny you should ask—"

Running footsteps behind them and a yelp from one of the bulls.

Roger Roscoe was halfway across the room, office door flung wide open. He stopped suddenly, taking it in, thin body jerking, while the uniforms grabbed at his arms.

He looked from Sylvia, still lost to another time and place, and Jerry, who glared back at him, over to Fisher and Miranda. The novelist's blue eyes locked on Miranda's, fearful and faintly accusatory.

The younger cop planted his feet and struggled to hoist Roscoe out of the room.

"Come on, you—"

Fisher held up his hand. "I expect this is Mr. Roscoe. Mrs. Alexander asked for him earlier."

Roger moved toward the desk like a sleepwalker, mouth twisting in a tighter grimace with each step. He stared down at the blood, shiny and glistening under the bright overhead lights.

"Oh, God—poor Niles."

He shuddered, turning his pale face toward the inspector.

"Please—I came to help Sylvia."

"No more dramatic entrances, please, Mr. Roscoe. We'll have questions for you later."

He held out his hands, palms up. "I'll do whatever I can."

Jerry stood up, shooting Roger an ugly look as the older man approached, hand still outstretched. Sylvia rocked back and forth, lips moving but no sound, eyes blind and ears deaf. Roger sank into Jerry's vacated chair and picked up her palm, holding it in his, rubbing it and whispering to her.

Disgust twisted Jerry Alexander's handsome, full mouth. He lit a Lucky Strike and stalked off toward the far-left window.

Miranda spoke softly. "By the way, Inspector—Miss Berrigan asked me to help 'move things along.' She wants to open that safe."

He grunted. "According to Mrs. Alexander—in the few minutes she was able to talk—there's money in there and some kind of precious manuscript, the next *All This and Heaven Too* or something."

The inspector crooked a finger at the tallest of the two uniformed cops in the room.

"Grant, go bring in Miss Berrigan—tell her we'll clear out temporarily as soon as the safe is open and she gets what she needs, but the lab boys will be back and we'll expect her at the Hall this afternoon. And tell her this office'll be off-limits for a day or two."

He whispered to Miranda: "We already dusted for prints—no luck. If this was a robbery, I'll eat my hat."

Bunny Berrigan flew through the door in a red and white blur, landing at Sylvia's feet.

Elegant, dark hair in a bun at the nape of her neck, long thin fingers clenched into a frozen ball, Sylvia Alexander gazed down at her, while Roscoe made inarticulate sounds meant to soothe, the three united in grief, Pietà on the sixth floor of the Monadnock.

Jerry watched them from a few feet away, thrown outside the composition. Anger and jealousy stretched his face as he inhaled the Lucky.

Bunny was pleading, trying to reach the thin woman with dead eyes.

"Sylvia—we've got to open the safe. Only you and Niles have the combination, remember? We've gotta open it up—he told me he kept over ten thousand dollars in there, in case of emergency, and we need it to keep the company running."

Something in her words—or maybe Roger's palpable, throbbing sympathy, ardently applied—finally clicked.

Sylvia stood and took a few haltering steps toward the safe. She reached up a shaking hand to turn the knob first left, then around to the right, twice, then back again, slowly . . . slowly . . . to the left.

No one spoke, the mechanism's *click* the only sound in the room.

Sylvia Alexander flicked the door with her fingers, and it swung open with a sigh, as other sighs were sent to heaven at the sight of several stacked bundles of cash. Bunny stood up and peered into the small, rectangular opening.

Several seconds later, she braced backwards against the bookcase, face blanched white to the roots of her red hair.

"What the hell—Smith—his manuscript . . . Niles said he locked it up just a couple of days ago." She looked around the room like a woman with a lost child.

"It's gone."

Ten

*

Fisher snapped his fingers at the uniforms behind him, yelled something about "prints" and "pronto," then trotted toward Bunny, the redhead still pale, still supported by Alexander's bookshelf.

Sylvia stood apart, face an arctic wasteland. Roger's arm was around her shoulder, the novelist rubbing her arm, mouthing words she couldn't hear.

Jerry Alexander, meanwhile, lit another Camel, staring at Roger and his mother with ever-obvious distaste.

Miranda slid out the door. Questions were coming.

Meyer was all alone in the waiting room, dozing in one of the Windsor chairs.

"Where's Louise?"

Her urgency woke him with a start. "Your Miss Crowley said she had to fetch something for the police from the files." He gestured toward the door leading to the other suite of offices.

"New twist, Meyer. We'll be here a little while longer."

The attorney nodded, yawning. "Your client is rather reticent, my dear. Perhaps you'll have better luck, but she was quite incoherent with me."

The inner office door swung noiselessly, opening into a common area with three more doors facing Miranda. The one immediately in front of her bore a gold nameplate: BERENICE BERRIGAN. The other two were faceless.

All were closed.

No sounds, except for the trampling hooves of running bulls in Alexander's office.

She opened the door on the left. No Louise.

The room was large, with a long rectangular table filling the center, file cabinets, and a few smaller tables—some with cover proofs and piles of manuscripts—lining the walls. A corkboard and a chalkboard hung on the far right, and an older-model typewriter perched on top of a small wooden desk by the lone window.

Powder sprinkled the table surfaces. Miranda looked with dismay at the palm of her glove, and pulled out a crushed linen handkerchief from her purse, using it to turn the knob of the room on the far right.

Dank, dark, and overrun with dog-eared manuscripts, pens, ink, blotters, and two typewriters on two different desks, both scratched and obviously second- or third-hand, the small, windowless hole could only belong to Kingston and Ward, the editors who shared an office at Alexander Publishing.

Not much in the way of personality, other than a *Daily Racing Form* on a leather desk chair with a rip down the middle, and a matchbook from The White House department store near the slightly neater pile of work.

A scratched, unpainted door on the opposite corner of the room was ajar.

Sounds of uneven breathing, a kind of low, panicked hum, shuffles and thumps.

Miranda pushed it open.

Louise was standing in the center of a small supply room, boxes of typing paper, typewriter ribbons, ink bottles, envelopes, and stationery lying in disordered heaps on shelving built into the walls.

Her head pivoted at the sound of the door hinges.

"Oh—Miss Corbie—I was just—just looking for that key, the one I couldn't find last night—I thought it might help the police."

"I thought you said you kept it in the other room—a filing cabinet, if I remember correctly."

The blonde nodded too many times, eyes avoiding Miranda as she squeezed by her and shut the supply room door.

"Yes, that's right, but yesterday was so hectic, and Mr. Ward has borrowed it from time to time, and once he left it in here . . ."

"Louise—forget about the key right now. I need you to talk to me before the police question you any further."

"I—of course, whatever you say."

The blonde led her through the small central area and back into the meeting room, shutting the door and turning to face her.

"I just can't believe it—Mr. Alexander—who would want to do such a horrible, evil thing?"

Miranda studied the secretary. "There's a chance Alexander's murder is connected to the attempts on you."

The blonde's eyes grew big and blue and she put an open hand to her mouth.

Either she hadn't connected the dots or she was a better actress than Olympia, Washington, usually produced.

"That—that's so, Miss Corbie, I hadn't thought of it."

Miranda guided her toward one of the round-backed chairs by the main table.

"Sit down. We haven't much time. Why were you here this morning?"

The secretary's hands gripped the armrests. "We are about to go to press with a large run—a short biography of Winston Churchill, Mr. Alexander's had it on the back burner for some time—and I wanted to get an early start."

The blue eyes flicked back and forth between Miranda and the wall. Miranda nodded.

"What happened?"

"I—I came in like always—"

"Was the door locked?"

"Yes. I used my own key. Then I started to set up the typewriter and I noticed Mr. Alexander's office door wasn't shut."

"That was unusual?"

The blonde nodded. "Niles is very neat and particular and never leaves his door open, whether he's in the office or not. He doesn't like people to know if he's in. Didn't like people to know," she added in an undertone, voice tremulous.

"Then what happened?"

"I—I tapped lightly on the door and called his name. I didn't—didn't hear anything, so I pushed ever so gently and—and the door swung open a little, and I took a few steps toward the desk before I realized—before I actually saw . . ."

The secretary heaved, chest jerking in a spasm. "I knew he was dead. He had to be. I didn't know what to do, I—I guess I called you and then you told me what to do and I called the police and asked for that policeman you told me to ask for and then they came with doctors and the doctors came out of the room and shook their heads, and—and—"

Miranda patted her shoulder, stemming the flood. "I know. What was in the safe in Alexander's office?"

Louise stuttered, breathing faster. "Hi-his safe? Only Niles and Sylvia had the combination—"

"I didn't ask you that, Louise. I'm asking you if you knew what was in it."

The blonde looked up at her, lips parted, breath still audible. "Money. Money for emergencies, Niles said, and his most important manuscripts, books he thought would really leave a mark. S-Smith's new book, I think."

"The one about Alcatraz?"

The eyes grew larger and darker, the secretary's voice higher. "Who told you that?"

"Roscoe. Is it true?"

Louise bit her lip and nodded, red creeping up her neck and cheeks. "It was supposed to be a secret—an exposé."

"Have you read it?"

A slightly longer pause. "No."

The secretary was looking down at the floor. Miranda's tone was dry.

"Too bad. Someone's stolen it."

The blonde looked up as though someone had just shouted "Fire."

"How do you—"

"Sylvia Alexander just opened the safe. Bunny Berrigan checked and found the money but no manuscript."

Louise slowly stood up, eyes blinking. "I should go to her."

A bang signaled the opening of the anteroom door, and Fisher's voice boomed through the cheap wood of the interior offices.

"Miss Crowley? Miss Crowley?"

The two women hurried out of the meeting room, Louise shutting the door behind her, hands automatically brushing off the fingerprint powder on the sides of her skirt. Fisher raised his eyebrows, looking from the secretary to Miranda.

"We're moving down to the Hall for statements, Miss Crowley. We'll need you to come with us."

The blonde looked at Miranda, who nodded.

"Meyer will go with you, Louise. Gather your things."

The secretary moved hurriedly toward the outer office and her desk. Inspector Fisher eyed Miranda, dragging a thumb nail across the shadow on his chin. "You're not accompanying your client?"

She shook her head. "Who else are you dragging down to the barn?"

"Mrs. Alexander and Jerry Alexander. And Howard Carter Smith, if we can find him—seems he's out of town. It was his book that was stolen."

"An exposé about Alcatraz."

The burly cop arched an eyebrow again. "You been holding back on me?"

They stepped into the outer office. Meyer was standing and nodded at Fisher.

"I understand you would like Miss Crowley to make a statement, Inspector. I am representing her."

Fisher made a guttural snort. "Kinda figured that, Mr. Bialik."

Louise stood ready by her desk, quiet and composed, as if she were going to church. Bunny Berrigan and Roger Roscoe were sitting in the waiting area, both silent. Sylvia and Jerry were already gone.

The grizzled uniform on guard stuck his head through the main door.

"Reporters have left, sir."

Fisher nodded. "Then let's go." He started toward the now open doorway, Louise following and Meyer trailing behind. Roscoe rose from his chair.

"I should go with you."

Fisher turned his head back briefly. "No, Mr. Roscoe, I've already told you. We'll be contacting you soon."

The writer grabbed his weathered fedora and clamped it on his head. "I'll at least walk out of the building with you. I feel like I'm suffocating."

The inspector shrugged as the party exited the offices of Alexander Publishing, two cops still flanking the door. The *clicks* of Meyer's cane echoed down the marble halls of the Monadnock.

Miranda took a breath in the silent, still office. She turned to Bunny Berrigan, the redhead slumped in a Windsor chair, staring at the wall.

"You really loved him, didn't you?"

Bunny pivoted her head, eyes locking with Miranda's. They were swimming now, the blue drowning in tears.

Miranda held out a hand to help pull the other woman up.

"Come on. Let's talk."

*

Tascone's wasn't private enough, the dives across the street at the start of Kearny too private, the kind of places where you lined the bar to drink cheap gin and rye, drowning your sorrows while the fat man at the piano banged out "Don't Worry 'Bout Me."

Not the spot for Bunny Berrigan, not today.

"John's Grill, Miss Berrigan. You could use a good steak and eggs platter."

The response was as automatic as Elektro, the Smoking Robot.

"Call me Bunny. Everyone does."

They reached the ground floor, conversation or questions held in check by the need to tread carefully down the Monadnock maintenance stairway. Reporters might still be at the elevators; hell, they could be waiting at the back door leading into Stevenson Alley, too, but the stench of steel garbage cans caked with rot and mildewed mops soaking in cold, black water might convince the newshawks to wait it out in more hospitable climes.

Miranda stepped around a threadbare sock covered in something green and dug in her pocket for a pack of Chesterfields.

"Want one?"

Bunny shrugged, accepting the stick. The women walked around the corner in silence.

"Hope you don't mind going the long way. Figure we're less likely to meet up with a reporter."

Bunny inhaled the Chesterfield, smoke billowing from her nose. "Yeah."

"You need to get to the bank or anything with that money?"

The redhead shook her head. "Sylvia gave me the combination. I took what we needed for one week, in case the printers and vendors demand cash. They do, you know, when there's a hint of instability, and since the company was Niles and Niles was the company . . ." her voice trailed off, and she finished, almost inaudibly, "Can't get much more unstable than that."

They'd almost reached the corner of Fourth when the publicity woman made a strange choking noise. Bunny was staring straight ahead, some color back in her face.

"I don't need breakfast. I'm all right. I've got to find Smith."

Miranda took a breath. "Bunny—the cops are gonna want—"

"I know. That's fine. I'll tell them everything. But first I need to find Smith."

The redhead dropped the butt of the stick, ground it with her black leather pump.

"Thanks for the cig."

Miranda studied her. "You know your relationship makes you a potential suspect, right? They love to put the finger on 'scarlet women'—and your hair color won't help."

Bunny nodded. "Yeah. I suppose so. Though I'd never hurt Niles, and believe it or not, I'd never hurt Sylvia. And I still don't know how you figured it out."

"Experience." Miranda drew down hard on the remains of her Chesterfield, looking up at the other woman shrewdly. "At least you'll know what publicity angles to expect. How long were you his mistress?"

"Three years. We were—we were like an old married couple in a lot of ways, you know?"

"I know you loved him. Makes it harder and easier, all at once."

"Yeah. It was goddamn hard sometimes. Especially because of his reputation, which was mostly just bullshit, though Niles, being a man, did nothing to discourage it. And especially because I care about Sylvia so much. Be a lot easier if I didn't."

Miranda's words were carefully chosen, her tone nonchalant. "At least Sylvia always thought it was the secretaries. Louise must have made things easier."

The redhead opened her mouth and shut it again, before the blue eyes solidified into steel, her mouth a twist of rust-colored wire.

"Good-bye, Miss Corbie."

Bunny turned on her heel and walked back toward the Monadnock. Miranda watched her vanish down Mission Street, frowning in thought.

*

Something's wrong with Louise. . . .

Words of worry from Roger Roscoe, and not only about the secretary.

Were the letters and attempts on Louise a smoke screen, a sleight-of-hand to distract from the real victim, Niles Alexander? Did Louise write the letters herself? Was she guilty of murder?

Miranda tore into the eggs and hamsteak with a knife, mouth a grimace. John's Grill was almost empty, the cooks outside smoking cigarettes, gearing up for the coming lunch crowd from the Flood Building and Powell Street, dishwasher whistling "I'm Nobody's Baby" from the kitchen.

No. She'd seen too many Louises, small-town girls with ambition and fear and crippling self-doubt, tops in the typing pool and beat up in the bedroom. She'd stake her license on the secretary's innocence . . . but not her honesty.

Louise Crowley was lying to her, lying about the book stolen from the office, lying about the key she said she was looking for, lying about the man she met at Playland. What was it he'd said the night before? Something about not getting something from where she worked, something about a "job for life" and Alcatraz . . .

Alcatraz, baby, not the fucking palace . . .

She sat upright. Alcatraz in Smith's stolen book, Alcatraz at Playland.

Too much of a coincidence, and she didn't like coincidences.

Alcatraz was suddenly too popular for a desolate and dreary prison, San Francisco's own fog-bound Devil's Island. Smith writes a book about it, some kind of undercover exposé, Louise's brute of a lover—whose identity and existence she kept carefully hidden—mentions it, Bunny Berrigan abruptly decides finding said author Smith and his book is more important than a Winston Churchill print run deadline.

Alcatraz, Alcatraz Island, damned city, dangerous city, a city of sharks.

And what about Alexander's wife Sylvia, heiress to heroin, and the whereabouts of her rapist running back son? What about Bunny Berrigan and the other editors and Smith and Roscoe himself?

What about the list of malcontents Louise gave her, the would-be writers, the poor bastards that might kill for a slight against their prose, rejection answerable only with homicide?

Miranda pushed the plate away and drained the coffee cup, settling it back on the saucer with a weary clink.

Too many questions.

Maybe Allen would find something on Louise Crowley, some nugget of indiscretion stored in the mammoth Pinkerton files, something Miranda could use to figure out what she knew—and why she was lying about it.

Miranda tossed a dollar on the table, heading out to the bright September sunshine of Ellis Street.

✳

The phone in her office was ringing, and she fumbled for a few seconds trying to unlock the door.

"Miranda Corbie, Private—"

"We have a problem, dear girl."

Meyer, uncharacteristically grim. Miranda sank into her office chair, staring at the sepia Martell's calendar, smiling blond girl, just like Louise Crowley . . .

"Tell me."

Her attorney cleared his throat. "As you know, the inspector was to question Miss Crowley. Before he started—he has been taking statements from

Mrs. Alexander and her son—a report came back from their laboratory. Mr. Alexander's shirt, you remember, was covered in a liquid."

She reached into her pocket and shook out a stick. "Go on."

"The liquid was gin, with a high content of potassium cyanide."

Her throat was dry. "And?"

"The police had already searched the premises but—with this news—the inspector ordered another, more thorough going-over. Just a few minutes ago, he received word that one of his men found a small vial of potassium cyanide in the office."

Miranda leaned forward in the chair, cigarette clenched tight in her fist.

"Where, Meyer, tell me goddamn where—"

His voice was somber.

"Miss Crowley's desk. They're holding her for murder."

Eleven

＊

Meyer was waiting for her, patiently throwing donut crumbs to pigeons on the corner of Washington and Kearny, men in suspenders and stained fedoras warming themselves on the grass of Portsmouth Square, making odds on how much bail the judge would set, watching the coppers and clerks filter through the doors of the Last Chance Saloon down the street.

St. Mary's chimed eleven.

A DeSoto screamed down Washington and made her jump, "Sing, Sing, Sing" blaring through the windows of Chinatown Restaurant, along with the smells of chop suey and ginger-steamed pork.

Miranda lengthened her steps down the hill. Meyer looked up, mouth grim, crumpling the remains of the donut with one hand and casting it to his cooing flock.

She shook out a Chesterfield and lit it with the Ronson Majorette.

"Louise talk?"

Her attorney sighed. "No. She fainted. The Inspector hasn't actually charged her yet, but I expect he will do so momentarily. I am hoping you can help forestall him."

"Maybe. So is she in hysterics or what? Can't they get anything out of her?"

"Miss Crowley has been nearly as catatonic while conscious as she was while unconscious. She does not respond to questions—indeed, she pays no attention to her surroundings at all, which—as you know—can be quite dangerous in a holding cell."

"Can't you get her out on a habeas?"

"I'm trying." Meyer sounded uncharacteristically curt. "Your client—our client—is not cooperating."

She patted him on the shoulder. "It's been a tough morning. Let's go in."

"Did you bring the letters?"

"In my purse. What did you tell Fisher?"

"That you had substantive proof Miss Crowley could not have murdered her employer."

Miranda raised an eyebrow. "Is that all? You oversold me, Meyer."

Her attorney smiled for the first time, wrinkles creasing his fat cheeks as he removed a handkerchief with a flourish and wiped his brow. He replaced it in his pocket, brown eyes steady on Miranda, and tapped his cane for emphasis.

"That, my dear, is impossible."

✳

Click.

The minute hand jerked a notch, electricity humming.

Originally a crisp black-and-white, the clock was now more gray and yellow, stained by the bodies of crushed insects, moths' wings, and fly spittle, dulled by the thick blue smoke of Fatimas and Luckies, swirls drifting upward from the scarred desks and tight lips of cops and captured, lipstick-smeared Kool in the mouth of Pickles' newest girl, vice dick chewing a Camel and giving her the once-over.

Miranda exhaled, blowing smoke over Inspector Fisher's left shoulder. He was slumped forward, muscle on his short, stocky frame softer than a couple of months ago. More gray in his hair, more lines in his skin.

What talent, success, and gutless superiors do to a good cop . . .

She tried again.

"Inspector, look—someone set this up."

He leaned back in his chair until it squeaked, strong fingers running through salt-and-pepper curls.

"Someone not your client?"

"She's not stupid enough to call me, call you, and leave the evidence in her desk—such as it is. Did Alexander die from the cyanide or the blow?"

"We'll know after the autopsy, and I've put a rush on it."

"Who found the vial? And where exactly was it?"

The burly cop looked at her steadily. "I'm supposed to ask the questions, Miss Corbie. You know the drill."

She bent forward suddenly, uneven leg of the wooden chair striking the floor with a thump.

"Make it a whole lot easier if you just gave me the goddamn story so I can help you figure out who murdered Niles Alexander and who framed my client."

"Why do you think your client was framed?"

Miranda waved her cigarette over his desk. "You've seen the letters. You think I'd violate my client's confidentiality and risk more evidence against her if I weren't sure?"

Fisher raised his eyebrows. "What I'm sure of is that you're worried about your client's future as a free woman. Her boss was murdered, she was at the crime scene, poison was found in the drink on his shirt, the same poison found in a small, corked test tube at the very back of her desktop drawer this morning. By none other than Inspector Gonzales, whose reputation—as I believe you know—is unimpeachable."

One Mississippi, Two Mississippi . . .

Fisher didn't usually get under her skin. Gonzales, on the other hand . . .

Tall, tight arm muscles wrapped around her, crushing her close, smell of leather and lime and those goddamn French cigarettes, body aching for abandonment, losing herself, all she was, all she would be, seeking pleasure, enough to forget the pain, die a little, the little death . . .

Miranda leaned over Fisher's desk, stabbing her Chesterfield in the cracked glass ashtray.

Click.

11:32.

She threw the inspector a small smile. Started again.

"Thanks for the information on the cyanide. How I see it is we've got five possibilities. A—the attempts on Louise, her frame-up, and Niles Alexander's murder were engineered by the same person, with the presumed motive the complete annihilation of Alexander Publishing. In this case, everyone connected with the publisher is still in danger, including my client."

Fisher rocked his chair back and forth. "All the more reason to keep her in custody."

Miranda glared up at him, while counting off points on her fingers. "B—the two cases are separate. Someone wants to off Louise, someone else wanted to kill Alexander and did and framed Louise for the crime. Louise is still a target."

"And still safer in lockup."

"C—someone who may or may not know about the attempts on Louise's life decided to frame her for the murder, and that someone may or may not have anything to do with either the murder or the threats to Louise."

Fisher frowned. "Too melodramatic and too goddamn improbable. He'd have to know about the cyanide in the gin. Been reading too many Niles Alexander mysteries, Miranda, or you just stalling for time?"

She calmly unrolled a Pep-O-Mint Lifesaver, offering the roll to the inspector, who waved it away.

"Until you get the autopsy results back, we have no idea whether the cyanide was lethal or pure window dressing—his shirt could have been doused after he was dead. And as for melodrama, what I've learned about the publishing business makes a Cagney picture look like an old ladies' tea party."

Fisher shook his head and opened the top drawer of his desk, lighting an Old Gold. He looked up at her shrewdly.

"Your whole track record reads like something cooked up in Hollywood. Fascists bent on blowing up Treasure Island, Berkeley professors running with Nazis, a dead publisher and a missing book on Alcatraz . . . don't you ever take on cases of lost poodles or philandering husbands?"

She cracked the Lifesaver between her teeth.

"You ever miss a desk job, Inspector, or rounding up girls on the corner of Hyde and Leavenworth?"

He grinned, eyes finally warm. "I always said you were a pip. OK, Miranda—any more theories?"

"Plenty. D—the person who framed Louise is the same person who's been threatening her but did not necessarily kill Alexander, though he or she knew about the murder."

The curly-haired cop exhaled smoke through his nose, forehead wrinkled. "You're starting to lose me. Too *Mary Noble, Backstage Wife*."

Miranda looked up, eyebrows raised, and Fisher stammered, turning red: "My wife listens."

Her lips twitched. "All right. Here's the most far-fetched, melodramatic scenario of all. E—Louise Crowley—the secretary from Olympia, Washington—is a criminal genius who masterminded her own attempted murders, wrote her own letters—which mention drinking poison, by the way—and killed her own boss, by both drugging him with cyanide and crushing his skull with a heavy marble desk set, then forgot to remove the vial of cyanide from her desk while she was alone for ten or more minutes with the victim, waiting for the bulls to ride in and cuff her."

They stared at each other over the pocked wooden surface of the desk, another *click* of the minute hand amid the sobs from the vice desk and the loud boasts of the drunks being ushered down the hall.

Fisher finally smiled again, his lips growing into a grin that erased the age in his eyes.

"I've still gotta hold her."

"Until Meyer gets his habeas."

He jammed a finger on top the letters. "I gotta test these."

"I'm counting on it. You'll probably find they were written on a machine in the office—maybe even Louise's."

His eyebrows reached his hairline. "Holy—I don't get it, Miranda."

Miranda placed her hands on the worn, wooden desk, fingers apart, and pushed herself up. She gazed down at Fisher, eyes somber.

"Louise is being set up. I think she's the killer's Judas goat, leading us down blind alleys until we're too fucking dizzy to see. I think you'll find those letters were typed on a machine she had access to."

The cop pinched his nose. "So what is it you want from me?"

"Information. I want to know the time of death when you get it and what you find in the carpet—any blood, any splatters. I want to know if the ME thinks Alexander was struck while sitting. We both noticed the track marks in the carpet, and we need to find out if the body was struck elsewhere and dragged to the desk—which, incidentally, would not be something my client could do. I want to know about the cyanide as soon as you hear from the lab. And I want to interview Smith as soon as you locate him."

Fisher shook his head. "Jesus, is that all? Berrigan told us Smith's in Monterey, on his way back up here now."

"Good. And if Meyer doesn't get his habeas—"

"You're doubting your mouthpiece?"

"No, I'm doubting the goddamn judge. If he doesn't—"

The inspector grinned, stabbing the Old Gold in the ashtray. "What else do you want, Miranda? Key to the city?"

She bent over the desk, hands pressed flat on the wood, eyes locked onto his.

"I want twenty-four hours to find you Louise Crowley's alibi."

*

Louise sat slumped in an interview room, removed from the tank where they'd thrown her with a battered brunette picked up for moral turpitude and a cynical bottle blonde trying to work the opposite corner on Larkin.

Funny how Sally Stanford and her girls—or even Dianne's, for that matter—never saw the inside of the Hall of fucking Justice.

Fucking justice . . . part of their goddamn job.

Miranda nodded at the uniform, his face red from too many visits to the Last Chance Saloon, blue eyes small but not mean. He nodded back, and she slipped inside.

Convincing Fisher she needed a few minutes with her client to procure said alibi required some dance moves worthy of Ginger Rogers, pretending Louise would cough up what she hadn't for the coppers, the oh, so trusting client who'd tell her everything, enough but not too much, not enough to be held as an accessory or for aiding and abetting.

Couldn't let him know that Louise was holding out and lying to her.

Maybe lying to herself.

Miranda sat down and crossed her legs, pretending that the dingy gray walls and scratched table and hard, uncomfortable chairs were the lobby of the St. Francis. She lit a stick and tossed the rest of her pack of Chesterfields on the table, cellophane making a skidding sound.

Louise sat frozen, arms wrapped around her stomach. Eyes on the floor, wide and unseeing.

Cheeks wet from recent tears.

Miranda cleared her throat. Louise didn't jump.

She was getting nowhere, and the twenty-four hours were ticking.

"Look, Louise. I understand you're in shock and scared, and you can't talk to me or Meyer right now, but we are here to help. We're both working for you."

No response. Miranda tapped some ash on the floor, tried again.

"I've got twenty-four hours to find you an alibi. Meyer is trying to get you out on a habeas. They're holding you but haven't charged you yet . . . though I expect them to. They'd be fools not to."

The clock on the wall—a little fresher than the one above Fisher's desk—struck the minute, an audible *click*.

Goddamn it, 12:03.

Her limited supply of patience was running out.

Miranda blew a stream of smoke toward her left and leaned close to Louise, dipping below the sight line of the guard at the door window, voice lowered to a rasp.

"Look. I know about your boyfriend. I know he's got something to do with Alcatraz and maybe something to do with Smith's missing book. At least, I figure you're afraid he's got something to do with it, maybe that and the murder both, between the office key you can't find and the way you've been acting about it. Hell, maybe you were gonna steal the book for him. I don't give a good goddamn if he's Clark fucking Gable in the sack, Louise, or if you think he's the answer to your small-town prayers, even if he pops you in the jaw and knocks you silly. I think you're a fool if you put up with it, but that's not why you hired me."

The blonde slowly, minutely, began to uncurl her arms, her neck bending upward like a slow-motion swan, turning, turning, toward Miranda, eyes blue and enormous and swimming in tears, surprise and shock and self-hatred etched on her face like acid.

Miranda took a breath and continued, words relentless.

"You hired me to save your life, and whether it's from some nuthouse schemer or jealous wife or Alexander's killer, I plan to do that. Even, Louise, if I've got to save you from yourself."

The secretary was looking at her now, waving back and forth, small movements in the chair, blurry and out of focus. She looked young and lost, unmoored from reason, untethered from the world she understood.

Miranda crushed the stick out in a black knot already burned into the table.

"Don't protect him. Maybe he's not guilty of anything but being a first-class sonofabitch, maybe not. But if you don't talk to me, the cops will get you to talk to them, and then you'll be held as an accessory, if he did kill Alexander, and maybe on an obstruction of justice charge if he didn't. The point is this: I've got twenty-four hours to fix it so they can't keep you in a cell. You've got twenty-four hours to wipe your face and dry your eyes and tell me the goddamn truth."

The blonde kept rocking, eyes looking through her.

Miranda sighed and stood upright, straightening her back.

"All right, Louise. I've said my piece. The rest is up to you. Get word to Meyer when you're able to talk to me. And since I'm looking for your alibi, can you at least muster up a name? One goddamn name?"

The disheveled blonde opened her mouth with an effort, eyes still unglazed, fighting a battle against the panic and fear, the catatonic urge to wrap herself in a ball and start her life over.

Miranda stepped closer, her eyes on the cop at the door and when the bull might break in. She made her voice softer.

"A name, Louise?"

The air came out harsh through compressed lips.

"George." Louise exhaled, and the words came easier the second time. "George Blankenship."

The blonde stared at the wall, fingers clenching and unclenching, breathing in and out, in and out.

Miranda patted her on the shoulder and walked to the door, catching the guard's eye. She nodded.

Twenty-four hours and ticking.

Twelve

*

Miranda crossed Market in a hurry, hand holding down her beret. Hoped like hell the flower sellers would still be there.

Chinese woman selling orchids, Portuguese selling roses, hunched Japanese man selling more roses and miniature trees, Italian lady hawking corsages . . . there.

Packing up for a midday break, almost out of flowers, little man in the stained brown fedora.

She hurried toward him, pushing her way past the Monadnock crowd. "*Vorrei comprare qualche fiore, prego.* Carnations."

Took him a few seconds to straighten up and turn toward her, bushy eyebrows raised in surprise.

"You speak Italian, signorina?"

"*Poco, signore. Che bella lingua and che bella e simpatica gente!*"

His weathered face broke into a wreathe of smiles, thin body energetic, flying everywhere over his half-packed stall to find a carnation for *la carina signorina.*

"*Madò! Lei parla italiano molto bene, signorina. Ma inglese è mia lingua ora, perché sono un americano. Va bene? Cerchiamo di parlare in inglese.*"

She smiled as he handed her a white carnation on a long stem. "*Certo.* We will speak in English. This is a beautiful carnation—it smells heavenly! Have you any pink, by chance?"

"I have only these, signorina. How many you like?"

"I'll take whatever you have left." She continued, voice easy: "My name is

Miranda Corbie. I work in the Monadnock here. A friend of mine recommended you, signore—a young blond lady. She buys pink carnations from you nearly every day."

He paused from wrapping up the flowers and put a hand over his heart. "Signorina Crowley? *Una principessa*! Every day I see her, sometimes so early when I set up my stall, and every night she comes by, always with a smile even when she does not have time for my flowers. Ah, signorina Corbie—tell your friend I thank her. Tell her, *prego,* as I tell you now, you must always make time for flowers."

He bowed, handing her the wrapped bundle of carnations. Miranda palmed him two dollar bills. He glanced down, eyes big, shaking his head gravely.

"Is too much, Miss Corbie. Too much."

"No, signore. You and your flowers brighten Market Street here and make San Francisco more beautiful. It is not too much. What is your name, by the way?"

The Italian looked hesitantly at the money in his hands. "I will owe you carnations, signorina Corbie. My name is Francesco Amore."

"You owe me nothing, signor Amore. But tell me—have you seen Miss Crowley today?"

He nodded quickly. "*Sì*, Miss Corbie. She came this morning early—I set up not too long before. She did not smile like always, no hello for Francesco. *Sta bene, la bionda principessa*?"

"I hope so, Francesco. What time did you see her this morning?"

"*Che ora era? Forse—forse sei e mezza.* Six-thirty."

He searched her face, the lines in his own deepening.

"If she need me, Miss Corbie, *eccomi qua*. I think you worry about your friend. I worry, too."

Miranda patted him on the shoulder, breathing in the gentle aroma of the carnations.

"You've been a great help already, Francesco. *Grazie mille.* I'll be seeing you."

She fought her way into the Monadnock, bundle of carnations held close.

Francesco backed up Louise's story, and that would make it harder for Fisher to charge her—but the Italian was far from a complete alibi. And the bulls, always looking for an easy answer, even if they had to make up the question, would suggest Louise was in the office earlier, doubled back home or some other place to lie low, then walked into the office like a little blond lamb, ready to stage her discovery.

And Louise, according to Francesco, "wasn't herself," a suspicious change in demeanor on the morning someone killed her boss . . .

Gladys squealed when she saw Miranda, running out from behind the counter to wrap her in a hug.

"Oh, sugar, I'm so glad to see you! All this excitement in our own little Monadnock. I had a feeling you were probably up to your neck in it, that poor Mr. Alexander and all."

Miranda handed her the flowers. "Here, Gladdy. I'll just forget to water the damn things."

The blonde blinked large blue eyes, surprised. "You sure? They're awfully nice, and you could probably use a little, I don't know, my mamma used to call it 'sweetness'—you know, things that just brighten up the home, like flowers and pictures and all. Mmm, these smell good, too!"

"No, I'm sure. Take them and enjoy them. You got any cigs for me?"

The blonde walked back around the counter and carefully set the carnations underneath the ledge. "Well, thank you, Miri. And yes, I've got two packs of Chesterfields—just got in a whole new crate."

"I'll take those and four rolls of Lifesavers—Pep-O-Mint and Butter Rum."

Gladys was ringing up the order when she suddenly looked up at Miranda with an exultant smile and the triumphal gleam of anticipated good news.

"I forgot to tell you—that nice Inspector Gonzales of yours—I hope those carnations weren't from him, Miri, because if they were you really should keep them—anyway, he was here earlier and he asked me to give you this note."

She handed over a folded piece of notebook paper. Miranda took it from her friend without looking at it and tossed it into the small paper bag of cigarettes and Lifesavers.

"Thanks, Gladdy. Be seeing you."

The blonde's curls bounced in disbelief. "Aren't you gonna read it?"

"Later. Thanks for saving the Chesterfields."

Gladys' eyes grew large again, her lips turned downward in concern. "All right, Miri. But remember what my mamma told me—you could use a little sweetness in your life."

Sweetness.

Sweet red wine, sweet smell of sweat. Why did he smell so good, no cologne, not even any water to wash in, sweat from lying out on his belly in rich, red soil, made redder with the blood of the men he was writing about, trying to live like them, be like them, capture their quiet courage, their fierce, undying loyalty, their love of country, love that killed their brothers, mothers, children, wives?

Other men had smelled like oakmoss and tobacco, whiskey and spice and leather; other men's sweat had smelled like oil, rancid and flaccid.

But nothing was ever—would ever be—as sweet as his skin, dirty, dusty, un-washed, and dry—the scratch of brown hair against her, the essence of him on her and in her, the smell of the two of them entwined, enshrined, enveloped and one.

There's a somebody I'm longing to see . . .

Miranda closed her eyes and punched the elevator button for the sixth floor.

One uniform was still on duty at the publisher's office, cleaning his nails with a pocketknife, eyes half-lidded and bored. He recognized Miranda with a grunt and she walked past him into the erstwhile castle of Niles Alexander.

Louise's desk was covered in dust. A chair was turned upside down in the waiting room, seemingly for the hell of it.

Alexander's door was closed, but the one to the other suite of rooms was wide open. A high-pitched feminine whine could be heard from the direction of Bunny Berrigan's office.

"But Bunny—I haven't been paid for the last book I turned in, and really—I just don't think I can continue on in this fashion. I'd been planning to speak to . . ." The voice trailed off, slightly confused.

"Niles. I know, Emily, I know. Here—this should help make up for any inconvenience."

Miranda moved closer to the open inner door.

Sound of paper tearing—probably an envelope. The whine metamorphosed into a pleased trill.

"Oh—thank you, Bunny! I hope you know I don't mean to add to your list of troubles, and I'm happy to take on the project—I just—well, you know I must provide for Mother, and I haven't been sure if there would be an Alexander Pub-lishing after today, and—"

Bunny. Curtly.

"There will always be an Alexander Publishing, Emily. I appreciate your understanding. I need the manuscript back one week from today."

"Yes, Bunny. I'll have it done."

Footsteps on carpet, light ones, sound of a desk drawer shutting, chair pulling back. Miranda took a few steps in retreat, quickly sitting in a waiting-room chair.

Moments later, a small woman in her forties—mouse-brown hair, red-rimmed eyes, quick, nervous, and blue—dressed in a long gray dress five years out of date and carrying a large brown-paper-wrapped bundle—wandered out from the anteroom, looking for the exit as if she didn't know where to find it.

She spotted the door and moved toward it, head slightly bent forward. Her eyes lit on Miranda, sitting calmly in the chair, and she yelped, halting in her tracks.

"I—who are you? What do you want?"

The yelp brought fast, heavy footsteps and the person of Bunny Berrigan, out of breath and glaring at Miranda.

"She's a peeper, Emily, works for Louise. Go on home, I'll take care of her."

The mousey woman peered at Miranda through horn-rimmed spectacles. "A—a 'peeper'? You mean there are women who actually work as private detectives?"

"A few. Maybe you didn't hear—we got the vote nineteen years ago."

The woman's face lit up. "Have you met any—any hoodlums? You know, the brunos, the button men, the wrong numbers?"

Miranda rose. "You read too much *Spicy Detective,* sister."

The redhead put a hand on Emily's back, ushering her to the door. "Miss Corbie works in the building. You can interview her later."

"Oh—of course—yes, Bunny. I'll be back in two days with the first corrections." She squeezed out the door and into the corridor, looking up at the cop with a fascinated stare. Bunny pulled it shut behind her.

"One of your editors?"

"Emily Kingston. Niles gave her part of an office and let her call herself an editor—and quietly threw away any books she happened to recommend—too much of an appetite for blood. She's actually a copy editor, one of the better ones."

"Are they all that crazy?"

"For the most part. It's a thankless job, one readers never notice unless they fail at it. What the hell are you doing here, Miss Corbie?"

Miranda looked at her steadily.

"They're holding Louise for the murder. Found poison in her desk."

Bunny fell backward a step. "I'm depending on Louise to help me save this company—save Niles' legacy—you mean the cops actually think she killed him? With poison? But Niles was—the blood—"

"I don't think they think she killed him, with or without poison, but that doesn't matter. They need a warm body to hold accountable, and—unless I can get her an alibi by tomorrow morning—they'll charge her."

Bunny shook her head. "Jesus. Does Louise even have one? An alibi, I mean?"

"Maybe." Miranda dug for the pencil and reporter's notebook buried in her handbag. "Just a few quick answers, Bunny. If you need Louise to help save this mess of a company, help me."

Bunny leaned against the door leading to the editors' offices, eyes on Miranda.

"Let's be clear, Miss Corbie. I don't trust you. I'm fairly sure I don't even like you. But if it means keeping Alexander Publishing afloat for a few more weeks . . . what do you want to know?"

Miranda grinned and held out her hand. "Even my enemies call me Miranda."

Bunny paused before enveloping Miranda's palm in her own firm grip. "How can I help?"

"What's Smith's address? I hear he's driving up from Monterey and I'd like to get to him before the cops do."

"Come into my office and I'll find it for you."

Bunny flung open the door with her name on it and strode quickly to her desk, a modern blond affair. She shoved aside various manuscripts, finally locating a black bound ledger.

"I'm trying to maintain some kind of publication schedule—which is why Emily was in the office. We're also planning a celebration of Niles' life at Gump's—a private party. Would you like an invitation?"

"Very much so. Was Niles friends with the Gump family?"

The redhead nodded while scribbling on a piece of paper, which she handed to Miranda.

"Smith's address in town. What else?"

Miranda glanced down. 1201 California #602. Cathedral Apartments on Nob Hill.

Smith's expensive shoes belied his lumberjack clothes—and so did his address.

"You ever see Louise with a large man, a little rough-looking?"

Bunny raised her eyebrows. "I've seen plenty of men around Louise, but she's always giving them the polite brush-off. Nobody like that, ever."

"OK. You said you called in Emily Kingston. What about the other editor? Has he been in and is he a 'real' editor?"

The publicity woman frowned. "He's as real as they get. Hank Ward. I haven't been able to reach him."

"Let me know when you do?"

"If you can find Louise an alibi and get her back to work."

"It might come down to him. She said he misplaces office keys and one's missing."

"In that case, I'll let you know right away. Anything else?"

"I should try to speak with Sylvia—Jerry, too. Do you know where they are?"

A spasm of pain, immediately controlled, crossed the redhead's face.

"Roger took her to Greer Sanitarium. It's where she usually stays. I wouldn't pursue it, though—Sylvia is worse than I've ever seen her. Her husband murdered—God, even a completely healthy woman would go to pieces."

The publicity woman's eyes drifted to her desk, lines around them thrown in relief. "I'm walking and talking because I have to. Because it's what Niles would want."

Miranda made her voice soft. "And Jerry?"

Bunny blinked a few times. Raised her face to Miranda.

"Jerry, as far as I know, went home like the cops told him to."

Greer Sanitarium. The envelope she'd spotted on Louise's desk the day before was hand-addressed to Greer Sanitarium, apparently the home away from home for highflyers and hopheads who could afford the tuition. Sylvia Alexander would be there for a long time, waiting, maybe in vain, for the grief to become comprehensible and the fog of loss to clear.

"Thanks. Can you give me everyone's address? The Alexanders' Nob Hill residence, Jerry's apartment, Roscoe's place?"

"Just a minute."

Bunny opened up the large black register again, searching with her finger until she found what she wanted, then repeated the process. The third address she wrote from memory, handing Miranda another sheet of stationery.

"Here you go. Is that it?"

"For now."

The publicity woman shook her head. "What if there is no alibi?"

Miranda folded up the paper and put it in her bag.

"Louise has an alibi, Bunny. I just need to find him."

✳

She sank into the chair, pulling the thick Pacific Telephone and Telegraph book closer, green cardstock cover making a slithering noise against the shiny black wood.

Blair, Blanchette, Blanco . . .

Blankenship. Only three in the book.

Only one with an initial G.

G. D. Blankenship resided at the optimistically named Cliff House Apartments, 4740 Balboa . . . close to Playland-at-the-Beach.

Miranda frowned, tapping the book with her finger. Flipped an inch of pages over to the yellow business section.

"The Greer Home, Inc.," 36th and Fulton—a long walk or a short ride to Playland and G. D. Blankenship. She could try Sylvia first and then stake out George.

She reached into the bag of cigarettes and candy and pulled out Gonzales' note.

Miranda stared at it for a few seconds, the "Miranda Corbie" in a strong, sure hand.

Goddamn it.

Found screw-capped test tube of potassium cyanide in the top drawer, right side, of your client's desk. Tube was about half-full, no dust, no prints, 16 × 150 mm. Might want to check scientific or industrial chemical supply companies.

No signature.

Miranda folded the note and placed it in a drawer with the cigarettes and Lifesavers.

Lifesaver.

He'd been that, just a few months ago. And for whatever reason—because he was still in love with her, because he still hoped she'd marry him—Inspector Mark Gonzales was passing on information that could help her client.

Miranda ran a hand down the back of her neck.

Jesus Christ, she needed a shot of bourbon, but no goddamn time. Not enough time to call him up and thank him, not enough time to let him down again, words and anger in her voice belying the heat in her body, the desire in her skin.

Mark Gonzales. And the worst part of it was she couldn't even think of him without that other bastard's face fading in, lopsided grin, bullshit-brown eyes, Irish accent learned from a drunk singing "Mother Machree."

Always there, whether she wanted him or not, always watching. And now he wasn't there but the memory, the presence of him, lingered, always wanting what he couldn't have, Miranda and Johnny, Johnny and Miranda, and in the corner of the room Rick Sanders, the tattered knight in a rented car on a lonely Napa road, the unasked-for assistant in a ridiculous Robin Hood costume, the man who always wanted too much and asked for too little.

Rick and Gonzales, Gonzales and Rick, men who'd tried, men who'd failed . . .

And Johnny Hayes, the one man who'd won.

She walked to the ancient Wells Fargo safe, older than her, older than her mother, older than the goddamn Monadnock. The door opened soundlessly for once, and she was shoving a fin and two Hamiltons in her wallet when someone knocked on the door.

Miranda picked up the Baby Browning from the top level. Watched the shadow behind the frosted glass and said, in a calm voice, "Come in."

Allen poked a shiny bald head around the door. "Don't shoot, lady, I'm unarmed."

She broke out in a grin. "Your timing is awful. I'm just about to leave."

The Pinkerton ambled inside, white shirt stained with mustard.

"Got time for lunch?"

"No. And I'm hungry. Got less than twenty-four hours to find my client an alibi for a murder rap."

Allen plucked an Old Gold out of his shirt pocket. "Jee-sus. Miri, why the hell is it that your clients are usually dead or in jail?"

"I'm lucky that way. This one's got someone trying to kill her, too."

"The same one already on the hook for the homicide?" He struck a match with his thumb but it wouldn't light. "They don't make these things like they used to."

"The desk lighter works, tough guy. And yeah. It's the Niles Alexander killing."

"I go to Livermore and step in cowshit only to find more of the same when I get back here." He studied her, exhaling smoke through his nostrils. "Front-page story again. I don't know how you do it. You need something from me? When you called I was in some shanty of a cow office, helping the feds bust a counterfeiter."

"Thanks, Allen. Anything you can get on a Louise Crowley, about twenty-three, born in Olympia, Washington, and a George D. Blankenship, San Francisco, lives out on Balboa. Especially if there's an Alcatraz connection somewhere."

Thick brown eyebrows shot up his forehead. "Alcatraz? Alcatraz? You gotta be pulling my leg. The most secure federal prison in the whole goddamn country? Alcatraz?"

Miranda grinned, grabbing her coat off the rack in the corner and shoving the Baby Browning in the pocket.

"Nutty, I know. But if you find anything . . ."

He opened the door for her while she brushed against the black and gold letters painted MIRANDA CORBIE—PRIVATE INVESTIGATOR.

"I'll tell you. Jesus, just be careful, OK?"

"I always am. You be careful with the next hot dog." She nodded at his shirt as they walked down the hall.

Allen reached his office door and laughed, one hand on the doorknob, his other waggling a thumb at his shirt front.

"You should have seen the other guy."

*

Mustard and sauerkraut helped fill the bun, and Miranda wolfed down the sandwich, chasing it with a bottle of Coca-Cola.

She checked her watch. Just a little after two.

The wind was starting to blow heavy sand again, straight across the walkway at Ocean Beach. She held on to her beret, flinching at the screams from the Big Dipper, ignoring the popping guns at the shooting gallery and low whistles from the carousel grifter, Laffing Sal's cackle drifting high on the wind, pushing her toward the White Front stop. She paid the seven cents after the conductor told her he'd be leaving in two minutes.

Only about ten blocks up from Playland, the crazy house. And if it was anything like Napa State Hospital—anything at all—she'd need to face it on a full stomach.

Memories of flatly intoned verse from Ecclesiastes, the shrill, inhuman screams behind barred doors, and worse than the tortured patients, Grace, the misnamed behemoth who enjoyed giving pain, and the gynecologist-butcher determined to make America pure again.

Miranda shuddered, shrinking against the back of the seat.

Goddamn it.

✳

Sanitarium. Such a funny word for a nuthouse.

The Cairns Hotel was built right after the Quake, an optimistic attempt to lure tourists to the cold, cold beach and away from the warmer Bay. Then the hotel went belly up and the Greer Home moved in.

She stepped out on the curb, shielding her eyes against the wind, staring at the red brick.

Dim memories surfaced of giving it a wide berth, on the rare days she could find or beg a nickel and hop a train down to the Chutes. Whispers about the mad people who lived there, confined to rooms, chained in beds, carrying knives, kidnapping and killing children if they escaped . . .

Miranda hurried across the street, modest homes and rooming houses and half-century-old workers' shacks dotted here and there, sand filling spaces developers hadn't. Stepped under the large, self-important arch and knocked on the door.

A tall, thin woman with gray hair answered, dressed in a nurse's uniform but not looking nurse-like. She smiled at Miranda, the well-practiced smile of the well-trained seller of snake oil.

"May I help you? Are you here for a preliminary visit, perhaps?"

About as preliminary as it gets, sister. Try never on your fucking life.

She gave the gray-haired woman a charming smile.

"I'm here to see a friend."

The thin woman stepped aside. "Oh, please—come in. We always encourage relatives and friends to visit their families—and of course, they become like our family, too." She gestured toward a desk, large, brown, and confrontational, in the middle of the entrance room—what would have been the lobby of the old hotel.

"You may sign in with Eustacia there—she'll help you."

"Thank you, Mrs. . . ."

"You may call me Matron Peters."

Miranda nodded, and the thin woman smiled graciously, moving off to another area where food smells, boiled potatoes and some kind of meat, were wafting out. Either the kitchen or the dining room. Miranda was glad she'd eaten already, because the smell would've killed her appetite.

She strode to the desk, comforted by the cold metal of the gun in her pocket, and looked up at the dark-haired nurse with the thick, flat eyebrows and flatter eyes sitting behind it.

"Yes? Can I help you?"

A large crash sounded from the area Peters had gone to patrol, followed by a shrill woman's voice scream-crying and what sounded like Peters trying to soothe her.

"There, there, Miss Ann. You don't have to eat the soup if you don't want to. Guard"—her voice became peremptory—"fetch a towel at once."

The woman behind the desk didn't blink, but was getting impatient. "Are you here to see someone, ma'am?"

Miranda opened her mouth to speak and froze. Behind and to the left of the enormous desk and its single-headed Cerberus, a guard was trudging forward from what was evidently the dining room, a scowl stretched across brutish features.

George fucking Blankenship.

Thirteen

*

She recovered before Cerberus could bark.

"Yes, please. I'm here to see Sylvia Alexander. She was admitted just a few hours ago."

The desk guard knotted her thick eyebrows like a rope, not-so-surreptitiously giving Miranda the once-over.

"Mrs. Alexander's a frequent guest. I don't remember seeing you before."

Miranda's smile was unpleasantly pleasant.

"I don't remember you, either. You may tell Mrs. Alexander that Miranda, Bunny's friend, would like to talk to her."

"Miranda—?"

"She knows who I am."

Cerberus shrugged, pressed a buzzer. "You can sit down and wait a few minutes. Someone will take you to her, if she's seeing anyone and the doctor allows it."

Miranda ignored the hint to go away and confine herself to the row of old-fashioned chairs propped against the dark yellow wallpaper. She jerked her head toward the dining-room area and asked casually: "Is that a late lunch or early dinner?"

The receptionist looked up coldly. "Some of our patients have trouble eating at regular hours."

"So all the troublemakers eat together, huh?"

Cerberus sat upright, indignation almost lifting her from the chair.

"Now, see here Miss Miranda or whatever your name is. This is a sanitarium, not a nightclub. Every decision we make—every decision—is for the health and well being of our clients. Do I make myself understood?"

Miranda stepped back, waving her hands in the air. "Perfectly, perfectly. No offense intended. Are you the head nurse, then? I thought maybe Matron Peters—"

Mollified, the woman preened a little. "Matron Peters is head of admissions. I am Matron Kasabian, deputy head of operations. My receptionist is off duty today—emergency trip to the dentist."

"Oh, how terrible. I know how painful that can be. I'm surprised an institution as well run as Greer doesn't have a dentist on-site—"

"We do." Kasabian was curt again. "But employees do not use his services. Now, if you'll just sit down, miss, someone will be with you."

Miranda conceded the ground, and retreated to a chair missing most of the springs in its seat. Fought the urge to light a cigarette.

She craned her neck, peering down the corridor behind the receptionist. It came to an abrupt dead end in front of a faded print of George Washington crossing the Delaware, the dining room apparently connecting through a side entrance.

Sounds of disturbance and the noxious smells had ceased.

Footsteps approached the gatekeeper's desk. Man in the same guard uniform as George.

He was young and heavyset, fat rather than muscular, with dull blue eyes and thin red hair. Freckles dotted his face and hands.

"You buzzed, Matron Kasabian?"

"Yes, Carl. This lady"—she gestured with her head toward Miranda—"wants to visit Mrs. Alexander—Mrs. Sylvia Alexander. She's within the regulation hours, but you'll have to check with Dr. Morrisey."

"He just left, Matron."

Cerberus sighed deeply, a sign of how much trouble Miranda had already caused. "Very well. Talk to Nurse Emerson and get permission from her and the patient. And do it quickly, Carl."

"Yes, ma'am." He waddled off in a hurry, taking a staircase at the rear of the large lobby, heavy treads echoing through the room.

"I forget, Matron—when are the visiting hours over?"

Cerberus looked up and glared at Miranda, then pivoted her head like an owl to check the grandfather clock behind her.

"Three o'clock. You have forty minutes."

"Thanks."

Miranda waited out the next twelve minutes studying the layout of the place. Rooms—or cells—ran upstairs, apparently. The dining room was downstairs and in the front, facing 36th Avenue, probably with the kitchen adjacent. Check-in, complete with Matron Cerberus, in the lobby.

Still the shell of a hotel, albeit one where you paid for electroshocks and needles, alienists analyzing your brain for telltale signs that your stay should be made permanent along with their fees, checks made payable to Greer Sanitarium, Inc., please, and don't forget the incorporated.

Greer and its ilk catered to wealthy clients with dangerous habits, women like Sylvia Alexander, filling emptiness with booze and drugs, filling empty minds with something like purpose. Filling time, filling time, until time or money or life ran out.

And then there were the men and women who used sanitariums like the county dump, dispose of their problems and in due course make a little profit. The sanitariums aided and abetted them, problems locked away for good, forever "taken care of," abandoned along the sands of Ocean Beach like empty bags of salty popcorn and the ticket stubs to the Fun House, relatives laughing with Laffing Sal all the way to the bank, power of attorney in one hand, declaration of incompetency in another.

Ha fucking ha.

Sure, there were some decent places, homes that tried to act a little like one, sanitariums that tried to live up to their name. She'd taken Lucinda Gerber to Dante's a few months back, the best quick recovery joint in San Francisco, even if what you were recovering from was kidnapping and attempted murder . . .

Footsteps again. Carl was finally back.

He nodded at Cerberus. "Nurse Emerson said it was OK, and the lady—Mrs. Alexander—didn't say no."

Kasabian looked up at him, squinting, waited a few seconds. "Very well, Carl. Go ahead and take the lady upstairs."

Miranda felt beetle-brown eyes on her back as she walked toward the staircase with the lumbering guard. Her shoulder blades twitched.

*

They reached the third floor, Carl breathing heavily. Miranda leaned against the rail, voice dripping with hesitant femininity.

"I'm sorry. I'm a little tired of all these steps. Do you mind if we wait for a few minutes before going on?"

She followed up by placing a hand on his forearm. The guard flushed even redder, timing words in between breaths. "Of—of course, miss. We're almost there."

"Sylvia's on this floor, then?"

"Yeah, it's her usual room."

Miranda looked around at the sparsely furnished hallway, burgundy carpet new, a few scattered replicas of Old Masters and landscapes lining the blond paneled walls.

"I'm sure Sylvia is comfortable here."

Carl nodded. "This is the top floor and the best floor. She's got a view."

Miranda laid her hand on his arm again. "You must be very brave to work here. It takes a strong man to help the sick. I find that very admirable."

The guard started to lose his breath again, and not from exercise. He grinned like an idiot.

"Thank you, miss. Some of us have special training. I worked down at Agnews for a time, but found this to be much quieter."

Agnews Insane Asylum, forty miles to the south. Wasn't Napa State, but wasn't the fucking Waldorf, either.

"Greer is lucky to have you, Carl. Do any of the other guards have special training? Is it required? I'm so interested in what you do!"

The guard became expansive. "Well, Bob worked at Napa for a while. Spencer worked at Agnews with me. You don't need that kind of job history, but it helps. Alls you really need is some kind of experience in security. Like George—he never worked in a hospital or nothing, but he used to be a guard at Alcatraz! He tells us stories all the time, about what it's like and all the criminals and things."

Miranda beamed a smile at him. "How fascinating. Does he work with you?"

"George? Only the first part of the day. I start early, get off at five. He does a split shift. One o'clock to five, then one o'clock til five in the morning. I don't know how he gets through it, but he says he makes a little extra money that way, and says it's pretty quiet. What he really wants is to get back to Alcatraz. Now who'd want that? I told him he's crazy—crazy enough to be a patient and have to guard himself!"

Carl finished with a loud guffaw. Miranda smiled, said nothing. The guard choked off, eyes suddenly aware and sober.

"I'd—I'd better get you to Mrs. Alexander, miss. You don't have much time with her."

"Thank you, Carl. I do so appreciate it."

He stomped down the hallway until it ended in a Dutch landscape, fished out a pair of keys, and bent down to unlock the door to room #300. Tipped his hat when he straightened up, spoke hesitantly.

"Here you go, miss. Don't be scared by the lock. That's only in place for Mrs. Alexander 'cause she's on a—on a suicide watch. But Nurse Emerson, she thinks it might help the lady to see somebody. Nurse was up here just a minute ago, checking on her." He looked at his watch. "You got about fifteen minutes. Somebody'll be back to fetch you."

Miranda smiled. "Thanks, Carl. You're a good guy."

His blue eyes shone down at her. "Thanks, miss."

The big man waddled back down the corridor, sneaking one glance behind him and embarrassed to find Miranda still watching. He hurried along, and she waited until his heavy footsteps sounded less like cannon fire.

She turned toward the thick door, bronzed numbered marker new but scratched.

Took a breath, and walked in.

The two windows were thick safety glass, unbarred. Sylvia stood in front of them, searching for the fog, watching it roll in and cover the dunes and cars and buildings and amusements. Her thin body was taut, awaiting interruption or instruction or purpose, rigid and brittle.

She didn't turn around.

Miranda lit a Chesterfield, studying the other woman. Smoke curled from the cigarette in an arabesque, drifting to the window, and still Sylvia did not face her.

"It hurts like hell when they take you off the juice. Make sure you eat something—you're thin as it is. Not that what they serve here is edible, but make 'em bring you something decent. Hell, they can run someone up to Topsy's for fried chicken and biscuits. That would help."

Sylvia's hand jerked a little, but she made no other motion.

"Not that the juice is the foremost of your problems right now. They've got you on suicide watch, so they stand over you when you eat, don't let you near knives and they'll tie you back down on the bed when I'm gone. But maybe you don't mind. Maybe you're a woman who enjoys suffering. Maybe you think you deserve it."

A spasm jerked the other woman's body, her breath visible and hard. She slowly turned to face Miranda, pupils dilated, dark eyes haunted by specters only she could see.

"Do I—do I know you?"

Miranda took a step closer. "Indirectly. I'm a private detective. And I'm trying to figure out who killed your husband."

A drawn-out shudder, and the older woman teetered, losing her balance. Miranda held out a hand to steady her, and guided her toward the small bed positioned against the wall.

"I do know you, though, Mrs. Alexander. I know you're an addict. I know you loved and hated your husband, probably in equal measure. And I know you're not as sick as everyone wants you to believe, not a rubber blanket and electroshock candidate for Agnews or Napa State, at least not yet. If they tell you so, don't believe them."

Sylvia opened her mouth but no sound came out. She tried again.

"You . . . are a friend of Niles'? Yes?"

Miranda searched the woman's dark eyes, looking for the spark she'd seen before, swallowed up now, gone.

Maybe try a different kind of shock.

"No, not a friend to your husband, Mrs. Alexander. But I'd like to think I'm a friend to you, so here's the truth. Your late husband was a cheating sonofabitch. You knew it, you've always known it, and you tried to punish him—first, by holding back money, second by social embarrassment, third, by cheating on him, and finally, last card played, by killing yourself. Except you couldn't do it fast, had to be slow, a slow, poisonous death with plenty of penitential mortification for that bastard Niles. And it didn't really matter who you took down along the way, because you were going down, too, the wife he wouldn't—couldn't—leave, the angel of his business, the bankroll to his career. The one woman he couldn't live without."

Sylvia Alexander stiffened like a greyhound at the track. Then, just as suddenly, the rigidity left her body, and she melted on the mattress, tears flowing down her cheeks without sound or sob.

Miranda pinched out the Chesterfield, carefully putting the stick in her coat pocket, and sat beside the older woman. Straps peeked through the thin blue bedskirt made to prettify the mattress.

"So you got addicted. You're not the first. What started out as a way to punish Niles became your own infinitely worse punishment, your own living hell. And now—now he's dead and you blame yourself and think you have nothing left to live for. I understand that. I know a little of what that feels like. But you're wrong."

Sylvia's eyebrows contorted, fighting the morphine they were giving to wean her, numbing body and mind but never all the pain.

"Wr-wrong? He was my husband . . . I . . . I love Niles. Always."

"I know you do. But if you keep poisoning yourself with heroin—if you keep checking into places like this or even worse, drying out for a few months at a time before you hit the needle again—you'll end up as crazy as they say you are. Listen, Sylvia, you were justified in punishing the bastard, but you should have done it clean and quick and in the open, not with your own body and soul as the blood price. You've got choices, choices on what to do with your life and money that most people can only fantasize about. You want to repent? To atone? To remember your husband? Then do something. Get off the goddamn juice."

The older woman shuddered as though a cold wind was blowing. She wrapped her arms around her thin body, rocking back and forth, words high and monotone, like a catechism.

"Niles never—he didn't mean to hurt me, and he had—had Bunny and so I took Roger, and we were all, all so gay . . . and then Jerry, Jerry hated his father, he wanted to punish him, too . . . it's all my fault . . ."

She choked and coughed as the bed shook, tears tracking high cheekbones, and wiped her mouth with the back of her hand, white skin paper thin.

Miranda sat and watched, voice dry. "The only people your son has punished are innocent girls. And I use that word deliberately, because even if they were selling something, it wasn't what he wanted to buy. But we can talk about that later. Look—I know you didn't kill your husband. I'm working for Louise Crowley—she hired me—and she didn't kill Niles, either. You probably thought Louise was sleeping with your husband, like he'd done with countless secretaries. But Louise isn't the type."

The older woman twisted up her neck to peer at Miranda, flecked spittle and tears still dotting her lips and chin.

"N-no? But—but I thought . . . she was a blonde . . ."

"From Olympia, Washington. She's got lousy taste in men but she kept her professional relationships strictly professional. So please—listen to me, Sylvia. You're a hell of a lot more than just a woman with a husband, dead or alive, cheating or not, or the mother of a son, acting out his parents' sadistic quirks. You're your own person—a human being with position, power, and money—and you can choose to make your life, however long it is, into something more than just a wasted testament to a bad marriage. You can stop trying to kill yourself slowly and maybe, just maybe, learn how to live like a goddamn human being."

Sylvia was slowly working her mouth again.

"Your name is Miranda? What—what should I do?"

"Grieve all you want. But try to get off the juice and get out of here as soon as you do. The real fight will begin when you're back home. And for God's sake, forgive yourself—you're at least as worthy of it as your husband. I'll visit you in a day or two to talk about Louise . . . and some letters she's received."

Sylvia continued to rock, hands wrapped around herself and tears drying, but a look of vague alarm fleeted across the older woman's face.

Miranda rose. Her hand was on the doorknob when a voice, thick and scratchy, croaked from the bed.

"Th-thank—thank you."

Miranda inclined her head without turning around and left the room, pulling the door shut behind her.

Fourteen

*

Miranda leaned against the door. One long fucking day, and just after three o'clock.

She looked up. Footsteps were mounting the stairs.

She plastered a smile on her face, ready to butter Carl. Instead, a scowling face, complete with scars, turned the corner onto the landing, reshaping itself into a grin of appreciation.

Not Carl.

George Blankenship.

He walked quickly and on his toes, surprisingly light for his build. The smile grew with every step.

He came to a halt about three feet from her, looking her up and down. "We-ell . . . Carl told me I wouldn't be sorry, and now I see why. I ain't seen you here before."

Miranda pushed herself off the wall, spoke with a drawl. No need to turn on the lights with George fucking Blankenship, apparently always at attention and never considering "no" an answer.

"That's because I haven't been here before. I'm a friend of Sylvia Alexander's."

He jerked a thumb toward room #300. "The hophead lady? Yeah, she's high class . . . like you, sister. Figures you'd be friends. But you never had a ride so good in one of them fancy cars as old George could give you."

Blankenship licked his lips like a not-so-secret message.

She smiled.

"Is that your name? George?"

"George Blankenship. What's yours, gorgeous?"

"Miranda. Hadn't you better lock Sylvia's door?"

He turned toward the door and extracted a key from his belt. "Now, that's a fact. I almost forgot. Nurse'll be around soon to strap her in again. Why ain't you inside? I walked up here at 3:05 . . . Carl wanted to give you extra time."

"She's resting—poor thing is exhausted. But I appreciate the extra time very much. Please thank Carl for me."

He carefully turned the deadbolt from outside, then straightened up, hands back on his belt. "Why don't you thank me? I'm a lot better to thank than Carl, believe you me."

She started to walk down the corridor. "You are a flirt, aren't you, Mr. Blankenship?"

Alarm crossed his heavy features. "Uh, now, Miss—Miss Miranda—don't mind ol' George, here, just I never seen you before, and you being so nice and so pretty an' all . . ."

Miranda paused midway to the landing, turning deliberately to face him. Laid a hand on his upper arm, and slowly, teasingly, traced his muscles with her fingertips.

"You are a big man, aren't you? Are you big all over, Mr. Blankenship?"

Skin red, he took a step closer to her, breath hot on her face. "Honey, I'm as big as you could handle. Trust me."

She dropped her hand and shook out a cigarette, giving him time to cool down.

"What time are you through this evening?"

Broad grin. "Got a split shift, like always, but my place is real close. I can meet you at five, don't gotta be back to work til one in the morning. Plenty of time, baby, plenty of time."

"You haven't asked me if I'm married."

"Baby, I don't care. And after tonight, neither will you."

Miranda raised a hand to his chest, slowly, and started rubbing it in small circular motions, voice a purr.

"Maybe I won't, at that. I could use a ride in something other than fancy. If you're all you say, I'll have to thank Sylvia for the introduction . . ."

"I'm all I say, baby, and more besides. You won't be sorry. Meet me at the Cliff House Apartments—4740 Balboa. Like I say, I'm off at five, but give me a few to get over there. I'm gonna fly."

He laughed, holding out a groping claw toward Miranda, which she deftly sidestepped.

"Patience, George."

He nodded, sober again, and they walked down the rest of the corridor and the staircase to the lobby, past Cerberus, who pretended to study a chart. George escorted her to the door.

"Thanks for visiting, miss." He chased it with an eye crawl down her body.

"Thank you. Greer's a wonderful place—so glad Sylvia is here." She lowered her voice, let her eyes drift downward and back up to catch his. Languidly pushed out a mouthful of smoke.

Whispered: "In case you're wondering, sport—I'm worth it, too."

She left him slightly bent over with his hands holding up his belt and walked quickly down Fulton toward Playland-at-the-Beach.

Her legs were shaking. She needed a goddamn bath.

*

Long walk to Playland, fresh air and exercise a bracer after Greer. The fog was still blowing overhead, puffs of gray charging up Fulton, scent of wet eucalyptus from the park almost overwhelming.

It was a good smell, a clean smell, and got the taste of boiled meat and disinfectant out of her mouth. Too bad she couldn't scrub the memory of George Blankenship, at least not yet, not until she'd secured the alibi.

She ran her palms down the sides of her skirt, frowning, staring at the Pie Shop.

Sutro Baths would take too long, only an hour and a half before she met Blankenship at his apartment house.

And the rented bathing suits were too goddamn itchy.

She sighed, walked in, and ordered a slice of blueberry pie and a cup of coffee.

The bath would have to wait.

*

The Cliff House Apartments catered to carnies, crooks, and quickies, a small three-storied affair built in the twenties, when "sea air" was supposed to be healthy and gin was the tonic of choice.

No names on the mailboxes outside. "Man." was scrawled on a handwritten sign on the single visible door, letters crooked and uneven. The lobby carpet was faded and threadbare, one lightbulb was burnt out, and a half-dead palm tree completed the décor.

She raised the back of her glove and checked her watch: 5:20.

A dark shape was moving toward her, down La Playa and the rear of Playland. She shook out a Chesterfield, lit it, and watched George run.

He arrived slightly out of breath and tried to pull her into a clinch on the steps. She sidestepped again.

"Wait a minute, big boy, wait a minute. I'm not some cheap two-bit B-girl you picked up at a fleabag. Wait til we're inside."

Blankenship smiled, all teeth, eyes on fire. "You got that right. OK, let's go."

He opened the main door with a key. *Manhattan at Midnight* was playing behind the building manager's door, organ music and Energine Cleaning Fluid, make that grease spot disappear completely . . .

George was ahead of her, impatient. "C'mon. I'm the second floor."

Miranda closed her fist around the comforting shape of her Baby Browning, still in her pocket.

"What's your apartment number?"

George was on the landing now, and laughed out loud. "What difference does it make? You'll see it in a second."

"I might not even notice the room, George."

He laughed again. "That's so, doll. I'm number 211—your lucky number."

When she reached the landing, he was opening his apartment door. The smell of stale cigars and cheap rye and beer filtered through the small, dingy corridor.

George's throat muscles were working in and out, and his eyes were tight.

"Hurry up, baby. I can't stand any more waitin'."

Miranda knotted her stomach, palms slippery with sweat under the gloves, clutching the Browning in her coat pocket.

He held the door open with his thick body, making her squeeze past him to get inside.

The studio apartment was strewn with newspaper and dirty dishes, drapes faded and torn. No decorations and only a few pieces of furniture, a pair of mended brown pants and stained white shirt flung over the saggy-bottomed chair.

George grabbed her hard by the arm, trying to drag her toward the Murphy bed jutting into the living space, open and unmade, yellowed sheets and gray wool blankets balled and rumpled.

"No de-luxe here, baby, as dirty as you like it—c'mon, now, take it off before I rip it off—"

Miranda slapped his hand off her breast as hard as she could. George's face darkened, and he lunged forward.

His eyes grew huge at the gleaming gun in her black gloved hand.

"What the—what the hell—this a game, baby? Cops and robbers?"

Miranda backed up until she was away from the bed and closer to the door, gun trained on Blankenship's gut.

"No game, George. And no ride. I'm here for Louise. Your girlfriend. Remember her?"

His mouth fell open, face red, and his eyes darted around the room, confused, as if the blonde might crawl out from under the bed at any moment.

"Louise—you mean Louise Crowley? What the fuck is this?"

"Your girlfriend, asshole. Louise Crowley. She's in the can and the bulls are about to charge her with murder. That's why you're going to walk into the Hall of Justice and tell the nice men in blue that you and Louise were in here fucking last night—all night, if that's the case. You're her goddamn alibi."

Quick, heavy step toward Miranda and she raised the gun again. The guard's face was purple, contorted, eyes like slits, but the Browning made him keep a perimeter. He prowled it like a tiger in the zoo, searching for an opening.

Miranda kept the barrel trained on him, hand steady.

"I'm disappointed in you, George. You really should learn a little more self-control. See, I'm holding a .25 ACP Browning semi-automatic. It's small, but it's enough to blow a hole in your stomach or anywhere else. And I'm a good shot. Size isn't everything."

His scars stood out stark and shiny white against a flush-red face. He finally came to a standstill in front of a countertop burner, covered with a frying pan thick with grease.

"All right. So Louise is in the jug. So what? And who the fuck are you, other than some bitch with a phony setup?"

"I'm the bitch with the gun, George. And I wouldn't mind using it."

He scuttled sidewise, moving closer. "You? You ain't fired nothing, lady, nothing 'cept blanks."

"I've killed a man with this pistol. I've shot a couple in the knees." She extended the gun, lowering the aim to his crotch. "You, I've got something else in mind for."

Blankenship licked his lips, eyes on the Browning, eyes on Miranda. He sank slowly on the bed.

Miranda gripped the pistol tighter. Now he was more dangerous.

"All right, lady, all right, all right. What do you want? And what d'ya got goin' on with Louise? She ain't got no family."

He said the last word with peculiar emphasis, like a test of some kind. Miranda frowned. What the hell was he getting at?

"She's got me. She hired me. And you're going downtown to testify she was with you last night."

The large man stared at her, sly smile starting to spread, posture more relaxed. He leaned back, propped against the wall, hands behind his head.

"Lady peeper, huh, some kinda do-gooder? Probably hate men, doncha? All right, say I go with you downtown. What's in it for me?"

"You don't lose your dick. The rest depends on whether or not you're the one who killed Louise's boss last night."

George sprang up from the bed like it was electrocuted and Miranda gestured with the gun again.

"Hold on, hold on, I ain't popped nobody, no how, nowhere. And I ain't taking the fall for Louise. Sure, she was with me til I got ready to go back on shift at one—sound asleep, right there." He gestured toward the flattened pillow behind him. "Then she walks down to the streetcar line with me, says she's goin' back to her place. She was still waiting when I was walkin' up to Greer."

Miranda cocked her head, studying him. Something stank, and not just the dishes.

She spoke slowly. "OK, George. That's what you say. So if you didn't murder Niles Alexander, why did you steal Smith's book—the one on Alcatraz?"

The burly guard flinched and retreated until his legs were pressed against the bed.

"Louise tell you? What the fuck do you know, lady? She rat it out? Spill it, goddamn you—"

"Did you steal it or not?"

"You can't prove I ever been near that place—"

"You stole it and then hit Alexander over the head and killed him, didn't you, George?"

"If she told you so, she's a lying bitch trying to save her own neck. I told you, I ain't never—"

"You left Louise and after work took a cab downtown, and you walked in with the key Louise made for you—"

"I don't have no key! I wasn't there!"

"And then you opened the safe—she gave you the combination—and when Alexander came in, you killed him, George, didn't you? Didn't you?"

He swallowed a couple of times, throat muscles bunched like fists. Raised his face to glare at Miranda, eyes granite. His voice was quiet.

"I ain't been nowhere near there, peeper. Never took the goddamn book. You can't prove I did. I was at Greer the whole goddamn night. If Louise told you anything else it was a lie, goddamn ungrateful whore, after everything I did—"

He caught himself, choked off.

Miranda's voice was easy. "Everything you did for her? And here I thought it was Louise who was doing you a favor. After all, you ordered her to steal the book."

Breath in, breath out, raspy and ragged, a wheeze just under the surface while he thought it all over. He flicked his eyes up at Miranda, razor-thin smile stretching scarred skin. Sweat trickled down her shoulder blades and she repressed a shudder.

"Somebody needs to pop you, lady, and that's a fact. I'd do it for free. But seeing as how my gun's in the dresser drawer and yours is loaded . . . yeah. I told her to steal the goddamn book. But she didn't, 'cause I ain't got it. An' according to you, she's in the can, so unless she hid it somewheres, it's where it's supposed to be or somebody else took it, if what you're sayin' is true. Me, I been workin' all goddamn day, an' Louise ain't phoned, so I can't tell you no more. But you . . . what else you know about it, peeper? What else?"

Sweat beaded on the large man's forehead and he wiped his face with his arm.

Wished she knew what the hell it was he was afraid she knew . . .

"Why do you want Smith's book? What's in it for you? I know you worked as a guard at Alcatraz—"

He jumped quickly. Too quickly.

"What's in it for me is my fucking job back. They got a bunch of crooks runnin' things out there, people don't know jack. And this Smith guy, he's supposed to be writing about it, see? So's I figure, if I get the book and bring it to my old boss Link and Warden Johnston, they could hush it all up and I'd get my job back. I don't wanna work with no crazy people, not anymore. 'Specially now.

OK? I didn't steal nothing. I can't even get downtown, not with the split shift—so I asked Louise to do it. See?"

Not pleading, selling. George spoke with contempt, conviction, certainty . . . but he was telling only part of the truth.

Miranda's arm ached and the rancid smell of decaying food and soiled sheets was making her stomach hurt.

Time to fold the tent.

"Here's the dope, George. You and Louise are each other's alibi—to a point, but the point may be far enough. You go downtown, you make a statement saying she was with you, and we'll forget about the book for now."

The smile stretched wider before fading, replaced by doubt, and again he probed, eyes flat and canny and on Miranda.

"What if Louise talks? About me asking her to steal it, I mean, and me asking her to make a key before that, like you said an' all?"

Was that what this was about? Louise? Something Louise might have told her—but didn't?

"Louise hasn't said anything up til now. God knows why. But I'm not Louise, George, and if you don't cooperate I'll make sure your miserable ass is nailed to every broken law I can find until a judge locks you up and you're scrubbing toilets in San Quentin."

His eyes widened at the threat as they stared at one another, Blankenship's breath heavy.

"OK, lady peeper. You can put the gun away. I'll go downtown with you."

Miranda lowered her sore arm, barrel still aimed in the guard's direction.

"You got a phone in this joint?"

He jerked his thumb toward Playland. "Can't afford no phone. There's one out by the Fun House."

"Then we'll walk to the cab stand down by the carousel."

He balked a little. "Who's paying for the hack? I ain't."

"Relax, George, I am. Let's go." Miranda waved the Baby Browning again and motioned him toward the door. "My pistol will be in my pocket and aimed at your back with the safety off, so don't give me an itchy finger."

"Your name really Miranda?"

"Yes. I'm a private investigator."

"Figured you was a lady copper."

Miranda pulled the door shut as he stepped heavily across the landing, not bothering to look behind him.

A church bell rang high on the wind, barely audible between the thunder of the ocean and the shrieks and laughter from Playland.

Six o'clock.

A long ride to the Hall of Justice with George Blankenship and a promised alibi delivered.

And maybe, at the end, some goddamn answers from her client . . .

Fifteen

*

Miranda leaned against the cold stone of the Hall of Justice, watching the neon wink on Washington, watching Chinatown open its gates.

The bail bondsmen across the square were still open, yellow light stabbing the littered sidewalks and cars screaming down Washington, somebody playing a scratchy record of "Scrub Me Mama with a Boogie Beat" from an open third-floor window.

Cigarette smoke drifted and swirled above her, refracted by the lights into a nicotine halo. She nodded to a couple of uniforms hauling in a drunk and disorderly, high-pitched whine of the drunk a soprano accompaniment to the scuffling sound his feet made on the marble floors.

The neon grew brighter, green and red, Coit Tower stark and pale against the black and blue sky. She could almost hear the jazz band from Julius' Castle on Telegraph, smell the steak, rare and dark and seared on the outside, hear the conversation, about Rossi and City taxes, the Yankees and Artie Shaw, about the Fair and the Gayway, about the War and when we'd get in it, about love and the draft and what was on sale at the Emporium . . .

She drank in the sound, the cool moisture of the Bay wind, the unblemished stars.

She'd be gone soon.

Gone to Britain, sailing on the *Cameronia*, sailing across the Atlantic on a gut feeling, trying to find a woman she could barely remember and one she never really knew, a postcard from Westminster Abbey her only guide in a country Hitler was trying to obliterate.

Air raids and the Underground, bombs and fire and the dead in the street, just like Spain . . .

Just like Spain.

Uprooting herself from the only parent she ever had, the only one that stood by her through skinned knees and shoplifted apples and her first period and pregnancy scares, the only one that hushed her, that drowned out the roar of cannons with clanging trains and cable cars, the bellows of horns and ferryboats on the Bay; the only one who played music she could hear, the only one whose beauty she could see, an orange bridge and soaring white tower, all-night diners and fresh-made coffee and neon lights and grand hotels and the scuttle of mah-jongg tiles, only real comfort at three o'clock in the morning when she woke up, sweating, and she couldn't stop remembering and she couldn't get back to sleep.

The only thing she ever loved that never left her.

Miranda breathed in the night on Portsmouth Square. It tasted like sesame balls and chop suey, boiled rice and sweet-and-sour pork.

A car honked, horn loud and shrill through the clear evening.

She turned on her heel and walked back inside the Hall of Justice.

Meyer was still inside interrogation room #1 with Louise and Inspector Fisher and a tall detective from homicide she didn't know. Gonzales and another homicide cop, junior grade with a blond William Powell mustache, were grilling the boyfriend in interrogation room #2.

Fisher's orders.

He'd greeted the arrival of George Blankenship with no surprise. She told him she'd bring in an alibi, and Fisher—the able cop, the good cop—had prepared for one.

She peered through the small barred window on room #1. Meyer was wiping his brow with a handkerchief, jowls quivering at every attack on his client. Her client.

Poor Meyer. What the hell had she dragged him into? Louise had lied—lied to her, lied to him.

The only questions were how much and why.

The secretary sat stoically on a hard wooden chair, smoothing her wrinkled skirt, holding herself together. She nodded once or twice at Fisher, who was leaning forward across the table, his small, muscular frame tense and urgent.

Almost reluctantly, Miranda walked down the hall to the next room, hesitating at the door before peering through the small window.

Blankenship sitting at the table, scarred face grinning, skin sprinkled with sweat.

And standing tall and straight in front of him, tailored jacket and manicured nails and smelling like French cigarettes . . . Gonzales.

She couldn't not look, memory still raw, the feeling of his skin, the scent of his cologne.

Mark Gonzales, Prince fucking Charming, the man who had it all, well-bred, well-placed, politically ambitious, a Dies Committee point man in Mexico, smart enough to take advantage of his disadvantage, the Mexican in an Irish mob, with the athletic grace of a tango dancer and the face of a goddamn matinee idol.

The man who'd asked her to marry him, despite her dubious past and somewhat doubtful future, despite the fact that he never really knew her and if he did could never approve.

Despite, despite, despite . . .

And now he was playing nice cop—a good fit—offering George a pack of Lucky Strikes while the blond cop, fresh out of uniform, scowled threats from the corner. George looked confident, even smart—and certainly not about to break. Gonzales' eyes flickered upward and caught Miranda's. She turned away, walking quickly down the hall.

The phone booth by the entrance was unoccupied, no sobbing wives, no angry fathers, no lost children.

No lonely, aging whores.

Miranda dug a nickel out of her purse and hit the switchhook. "Operator? YUkon 0802, please."

The woman on the other end chirped "Certainly, ma'am," and after a few moments of static, connected her.

"Telephone Answering Service Company. Number, please."

"EXbrook 3333. Miranda Corbie. Read only a message from Allen Jennings or Pinkerton, please."

"Certainly, miss. Let me see. Mrs. Parker, Pacific Telephone and Telegraph, a Miss Gallagher . . . here we are. Message from Allen. Are you ready, miss?"

Miranda gripped the pencil, Chesterfield pinched between two fingers, phone in her left hand.

"Yes—go ahead."

"Olympia connection, Cretzer and Kyle. Sister married to Kyle. Both now on Rock. Guard fired for insubordination. Call me."

Miranda stared at the names written on the crumpled paper, the Schwabacher-Frey notebook creased and stained with lipstick.

"Hello? Hello? Miss Corbie, are you there?"

She exhaled, not realizing she'd been holding her breath.

"Yeah. Thank you."

She hung up the phone, shoving the reporter's notebook back into her purse. Someone tapped her on the shoulder and she spun around, hand instinctively reaching into her pocket.

David Fisher smiled at her, stubble dotting his chin, eyes careworn. "Miranda . . . let's talk."

*

Tick. *Tock*.

The clock hand jerked, fly splatter dotted brown on the yellow-filmed face, chromium trim dulled and reflective of nothing.

Time always at a standstill in the marbled Hall of Justice, the perennial parade of has-beens and never-weres, the woulda, coulda, shoulda winos and the brassy, bitter broads who rented bar stools by the hour.

The tired cops, the crooked cops, the cops who'd seen too much, and the rookies who'd seen too little, and behind stout office doors, the kind with gold seals, the fat, middle-aged men with thinning hair and tight, gold braid uniforms barking orders to hurry the hell up and get someone behind bars, preferably a Commie or a Mexican or one of the labor union boys . . .

The Hall of fucking Justice.

And here she was again.

Miranda shifted her weight in the chair and exhaled a stream of smoke.

Fisher ran thick fingers through salt-and-pepper curls, looking older with every question.

"You sure you don't have anything else to add? Nothing about the missing manuscript or whether or not your client knew the safe combination? You know as well as I do how prominent Alexander was—"

"Not like the murder of a nobody, is it? A nude model at a Gayway peep show or a Japanese numbers runner in Chinatown—"

His hand landed on the desk hard enough to make the paperwork jump.

"Goddamn it, Miranda, you're talking to me, here, not O'Meara! I've stuck my neck out for you before now so don't hand me a sermon. I don't need it."

The cop shoved his chair backwards and shook out an Old Gold. She noticed the tremor in his fingers.

"Now you've got me swearing."

Miranda gave him half a smile by way of apology, twisting out her stub in the cracked glass ashtray.

"It's good for you. Let's out tension."

Fisher struck a match and took his time lighting the cigarette.

"I'll tell you what's not good for me: this case. So how about helping me out?"

David Fisher, good cop, decent cop, the only Jew in homicide and one of the few in the department. A man who understood her, who liked her, and who didn't want anything else from her.

A goddamn rara avis.

And she still had to stall him.

"You're holding all the cards, not me. I delivered what I promised—an alibi. We both know the killer's not Louise or Blankenship, as much as I'd like to see him behind bars and not in front of them. No motive, no means, no opportunity."

Tick. *Tock.*

Fisher sighed, hopscotching his chair in little moves back to the edge of his desk. He picked up the report, made his voice nonchalant.

"Speaking of Blankenship, I'm sure you didn't miss the Alcatraz connection. The press sure as hell hasn't."

She raised her eyebrows. "Alcatraz connection?"

"Come off it, Miranda. The missing manuscript's about Alcatraz—Blankenship worked there as a guard. The evening edition of the *News* is full of hysterical speculation about the book and some kind of Alcatraz hit squad silencing Alexander. Something's obviously up. I was hoping you'd tell me what."

Shit.

There was more to the Alcatraz connection than he could have guessed, and all of it was incriminating for Louise Crowley.

Miranda held up a gloved hand to her mouth. Gave him her best wide-eyed look.

"If I could, I would. And if I happen to learn anything I can divulge, you'll be the first to know. Now, how long are you keeping Louise in the cooler?"

Fisher breathed out smoke through his nostrils. Glanced up at the clock.

"Screw it. Been a long day. I miss my wife." He tapped the report. "This whole thing smells. The more we know, the less we know. We're letting your client go tonight. A few more hours and you can call off your bulldog attorney."

"Not charging her?"

"Not with your mouthpiece threatening to wake up Judge Langdon." He yanked a thumb toward the hallway. "Word from on high. We want a solid conviction, no backdoor deals, no surprises. The papers are all over Alexander's murder, especially with this Alcatraz twist, and your buddy Herb Caen's leading the pack—three dots can say a hell of a lot. We'll drive Miss Crowley home after midnight, keep everything on the QT and make sure the vultures from the press room find something else to peck at. She'll have to stay in town, of course, and we'll pick her up and throw away the key, alibi be damned, if she tries to run."

Tick. *Tock*.

Fisher tapped some ash in the glass. "Blankenship's testimony is what's saved her. Not that we won't be trying to figure a way around it."

"You won't break the alibi, not if Alexander was murdered before 1:30. Can't the ME give you a more exact time? You promised me information, remember."

"Yeah, yeah. Gentleman's—excuse me—gentleman and lady's agreement." He gave her a tired grin. "Okay, so between 11:30 P.M. and 1:30 A.M. is the closest the ME can come. Your Miss Crowley didn't have time to get to the Monadnock if she was with her boyfriend til almost one, at least not on a streetcar. Takes too long and they run on the half hour—the 1:25 was the soonest she could've caught. We checked all the Municipal owls, checked taxi records, too, even asked around at Topsy's to see if she caged a ride. No luck, at least so far. And the doorman at her apartment building remembers waking up when she walked in, about 2:15, and that jibes with the timing and with what Blankenship says."

"What about the cyanide?"

Fisher's face crumpled in disgust.

"What about it? It's not what killed Alexander, I can tell you that. Nothing in his gut but Scotch and soda and steak and potatoes. The gin-and-cyanide cocktail he was wearing was a plant—as you suggested. The lab boys say the body was dragged to the desk—another point in your client's favor, unless she's a lot stronger than she looks or had help from her boyfriend—and the Greer people state unequivocally he was there the whole second shift."

He bent forward and crushed out the Old Gold stub. "We'll be working on his alibi, too. Anyway, looks like Alexander was hit once, close to the safe, then dragged to the desk while he was unconscious and hit some more until he was obviously dead. We're cross-checking the few prints we picked up, once we find the janitor and everyone else who had access to the office."

"So the cyanide was poured on him at the time of the murder?"

"Poured or splashed—the lab boys noted the drops were scattered. We're back to square one." Fisher raised his fist to his mouth, unsuccessfully trying to stifle a yawn.

Tick. *Tock.*

"Not exactly. We know someone tried to frame Louise and we know someone's attempted to kill her."

He waved his hand. "And we know Alexander was murdered but we don't know who did it. And we know some wrong number, either the killer or someone else who decided to visit Alexander Publishing in the middle of the night, muddied the waters and maybe tried to make it look like your client was the guilty party. Someone who doesn't know a whole hell of a lot about murder investigations but reads an awful lot of fiction. No, from where I sit, we aren't moving forward—we're moving backward."

Miranda frowned. Fisher was beaten down, worn raw after one too many fourteen-hour shifts, but he was far from stupid and his pessimism would pass with a good night's rest. He'd soon find out about Louise Crowley's sister—the flesh-and-blood connection to Alcatraz and the Cretzer-Kyle gang Allen phoned about. If he also discovered Blankenship and Louise had planned to steal Smith's book, the motive and the connection would be enough for the cops to charge her, fuck the alibi, figuring Louise and her boyfriend were in it together and had murdered Alexander during the earlier part of the two-hour window. Fisher was under pressure and he'd take the chance, trusting God and his men to turn up the magic carpet Louise rode from Ocean Beach to the Monadnock last night.

But she needed Fisher's help—and she couldn't afford to act like she was hiding something.

"You're exhausted. Go home, for God's sake. And don't forget the letters to Louise—have your men go over them, maybe they'll find something I didn't."

The clock ticked again and Fisher shook his head. "Yeah. I know. I just wish to hell we had a clearer motive."

"For the murder?"

"For any of it. For Alexander or the threats to your client. The murder reads like it was a premeditated crime of passion, and how the hell's that for a puzzle? I mean, look: Mrs. Alexander has all the dough in the family, besides the fact she's fragile as hell and not exactly all there. Jerry's strong enough to clobber someone on the head and move the body around, and he's a punk with friends in high places—but he doesn't stand to gain. His mother inherits everything, and his trust is still contingent on behavior, including keeping his nose clean. That much I know. The rest—*bupkis*." He shook his head again, giving in to the yawn. "Maybe there'll be better ideas in the morning. I gotta get home. Gonzales can finish up tonight."

Miranda nodded. "Gotta get back to the office myself. Mind letting me know when you release Louise? I'd like to be with her when you take her home."

"I'll pass your request along to Inspector Gonzales."

Fisher stood up, sweat stains under his white shirt, blue tie askew and splattered with crusted ketchup.

Miranda held out her hand. "I'll keep you informed."

He held hers briefly and gave her a crooked, tired smile.

"Be sure that you do."

She pushed through the wooden gate and out of the corral of desks and cops and drunks, past the plump woman with the two black eyes, past the college kid with glasses and blood on his trousers.

Meyer was leaning against the wall near Louise's examination room, wiping his brow with a lace-edged handkerchief, crisp shirt wilted, skin sallow and sagging.

"They're releasing Louise after midnight, Meyer. Go on home—Fisher is. Gonzales will finish up, and I've asked them to notify me when they let her go. Get some sleep—please." She squeezed his arm. "I'm sorry for dragging you into this."

He blotted his forehead again. "Nonsense, my dear. This sort of thing helps keep me sharp—I'm not in my dotage yet. And I'm afraid that new homicide man will antagonize young George into saying something unwise, and I want to make sure of him. They'll release Mr. Blankenship soon—before Miss Crowley. I'll stay on hand until she's ready. Will you be at the office?"

He wouldn't back down, even exhausted and damp and mussed and looking twenty years older than usual. Miranda made him promise to call her when they were through with Louise, apologized again for the late hour, for the difficult client, for keeping him up. Meyer protested weakly, leaning on his cane while folding the handkerchief and proceeding unsteadily down the hallway toward the second interrogation room.

She sighed and watched him go, walking quickly past the night desk. Collins was on duty, round head shaved, blond stubble on his chin, one of the bulls who'd never think of her as anything but a whore, a contagion, a cancer on the face of decency, an affront to the City and the country, God Bless America, of thee I sing.

Collins and his ilk. Not members of the German American Bund or the Musketeers or the KKK, they squatted behind police desks and bank counters, in doctors' offices and classrooms, gave sermons from church pulpits and in letters to the editor, Dear *Life* Magazine . . .

Hitler's not so bad . . . got the right idea about Jews . . .

The British brought this on themselves. We've no business joining a European war . . .

FDR's a red and a socialist, like that Harry Bridges . . . What we need here are a few Mussolinis and Hitlers to set things straight!

They'd had enough of the unwashed, the needy, those too-foreign masses longing to breathe free, enough of them here already, bringing their filth and depravity and heretical gods to an unsullied America, to a pristine golden gate, where cops like Collins protected the good citizens, the real Americans, the Aryans of San Francisco.

Miranda adjusted her beret, feeling his eyes burn down her skirt.

"What's wrong, Collins? Pickles run out of under-age girls for you to feel up?"

The blond cop flushed purple, veins dancing at his temples.

"Get outta here. I don't talk to whores."

"You don't pay them, either." Miranda turned to face him, eyes green. "I've been meaning to have a word with Pickles. Your supply's gonna dry up."

The cop leaned across the desk. "You mean like your Irish whore of a mother, Corbie? Runs in the family, don't it?"

The intake of breath was involuntary. She stepped forward, fists clenched, while Collins froze, confusion on his face, police club in his hand.

One Mississippi, Two Mississippi . . .

Miranda caught her breath again and with effort made her voice even.

"I'm not fourteen, Collins. And if I see you at the Settlement again, getting paid off with a girl behind the Monaco, you'll lose more than your fucking bully stick."

A loud screech made the blond cop jump. He shoved the club back on his belt and tried to look officious. Two uniforms were hauling in a B-girl with lipstick smeared across her cheek and another woman dressed in a man's suit, both protesting loudly.

Miranda exited through the large double doors, hitting the air on Portsmouth Square, greeted by a whistle from a lounger under the streetlight across the street.

Her hands were shaking. No time to deal with Collins, not tonight. She was in a goddamn jam, and the only thing she had, the only thing she was, the only map that counted was in her wallet, no Gideon Bible, no fucking *How to Win Friends and Influence People,* just a crumpled, stained copy of a California license.

Miranda Corbie, Private Investigator.

Her client, the blond secretary with pretty skin and even teeth, the capable girl Friday and incapable judge of men, the girl from a small town in Washington State, was a liar and a would-be thief.

And according to Allen and the copious Pinkerton files—according to the cryptic message he'd left her—her client, Louise Crowley, was also the sister-in-law of one of the country's most infamous criminals.

Arnold Kyle.

Miranda hailed a cab cruising down Kearny, a watery-eyed man in a blue cap and a yellow taxi. Gave him the address of the Monadnock.

She'd need to call James, figure out the angle, get an appointment. Interview the warden, cage what info she could.

She leaned back in the cab and closed her eyes.

Arnold Kyle, bank robber and murderer. With his partner "Dutch" Cretzer, he'd recently been transferred from McNeil Island in Washington State . . .

Transferred to Alcatraz.

Act Three

*

The Draft

"And as imagination bodies forth
The forms of things unknown, the poet's pen
Turns them to shapes and gives to airy nothing
A local habitation and a name."
—William Shakespeare
A Midsummer Night's Dream, Act V, scene i

Sixteen

*

I t's not the pale moon that excites me . . .
Dinah Shore warbled upward on an unexpectedly warm breeze, September night in San Francisco.

The Tascone's juke was blaring full volume, velvet notes sliding under the open window of Miranda's fourth-floor office, somehow drowning out the still-rumbling Market Street Railway trains competing with the Municipals, roaring their way to the Ferry Building as though they would drive into the Bay, louder than the shrill whistles from the pool hall across the street, the late-night ramblers and factory workers trudging home, streetlights warm and yellow against the midnight sky.

Oh, no . . . it's just the nearness of you . . .

Miranda shoved the cold Tascone burger to one side of the large black desk and rubbed her eyes.

Still Thursday, September 19th, 1940. Tomorrow still six minutes away.

Her client found a dead body this morning, one belonging to her boss. Was subsequently arrested but not charged, only because Miranda discovered one of two big lies her client kept hidden, this one in the person of George Blankenship, disgraced former prison guard at Alcatraz, now a boorish, brutish raconteur at the Greer Home.

The other lie was a sister, one with an even worse track record in judging men. Said sister was married to Arnold Kyle, partner of Joseph "Dutch" Cretzer, both men bank robbers and murderers, both formerly of McNeil Island, Tacoma, Washington, both now spending the fall season at Alcatraz.

The Pinkerton report—waiting under her door for her and now spread out on the desk—spelled out an old tale and familiar one, of the Crash and small-town girls and absentee fathers and just enough to eat to not look too hungry. The mother tried selling home-canned jams and hand-sewn dresses and eventually took in a lodger.

That lodger was Arnold Kyle, a young man with wide, nervous eyes and no chin, amiable and not bad-looking, but the kind of bo with a one-way ticket to the federal pen, stemming mainly from a relationship with Joseph "Dutch" Cretzer . . . his brother-in-law.

Cretzer was the more dangerous of the two, a thick-bodied, square-headed bird, known for a volatile temper and liking for violence. The two were partners in crime, off and on, for more than fifteen years, talents in place and groomed by Prohibition before the Depression made bank-robbing a career choice.

So Louise's sister Thelma falls in love with the doe-eyed "Shorty" McKay, as Kyle calls himself, and they get married and have a kid, Thelma staying home with Junior while Shorty and Dutch embark on a new, exciting life of travel and hit up West Coast banks for five years. Eventually Cretzer makes the big time—number four on the most-wanted list. And, like all bedtime stories, this one ends, too, with a Minnesota drunk-driving charge for Kyle and a Chicago arrest for Cretzer in '39.

They were both sentenced to McNeil Island, where they lived unhappily but not ever after, until the restless Cretzer engineers an escape of the "You'll never take me, coppers" variety. Caught again, they make another break for it during the trial, and in the process injure a bull, U.S. Marshal Artis J. Chitty. Chitty suffers from a bad ticker and dies from the strain.

Cretzer and Kyle are transferred to Alcatraz.

On August 29, 1940, just three weeks ago, Shorty and George were indicted for the murder of Marshal Chitty. Both faced life or the gas chamber.

An addendum: Kyle's wife—Louise's sister—was currently residing in Oakland, California.

Miranda pushed the report from Allen to the side. Banged open the desk drawer and took out the worn Big Chief tablet. Opened it to the last page of notes.

Outside, the jukebox was quiet, street noises subsided. Far away, like a lost seagull, church bell tolling.

Dong . . . dong . . . dong . . .

Midnight. A brand fucking new day.

She sighed, fishing around her desk drawer for a fountain pen with a cartridge, eyes heavy and dry.

Picked up the pen. Scrawled MISSING KEY.

Louise had her own main office key and access to Alexander's—all she had to do was use it. She could waltz in, twirl the combo, which she could've learned from Alexander or discovered on her own, and steal the manuscript for George. So why the hell would she steal an extra key? Or did she? Was the nervousness— the hesitancy—because of all the other lies? Or was the missing key in the hands of the murderer?

Underneath the entry she wrote: INTERVIEW EDITOR HANK WARD. ASK LOUISE.

New column. JERRY.

Miranda yawned, shaking out a Chesterfield. Why was Jerry at home the night his father was murdered? Exactly how often did he spend time with pater and mater? And, most importantly, where was he between 11:30 and 1:30 last night?

She wrote CHECK ALIBI under his name.

New column. SYLVIA.

Sylvia. Sylvia was a fucking problem. Not completely crazy, but sane enough to hide. Not strong enough to drag a body but weak enough to write letters threatening Louise . . . and maybe plant cyanide in the secretary's desk.

But whoever planted the cyanide would only know about the spill on Alexander's shirt if he or she killed the man or was an accessory. Why bother otherwise? And if she wrote the letters but didn't plant the poison, then who the hell did?

Miranda shook her head, inhaling the Chesterfield. Wrote ??? next to Sylvia, and CALL SCIENTIFIC SUPPLY HOUSES RE: CYANIDE below.

She raised heavy eyes to the clock on the wall. Damn it, where the hell was Gonzales with Louise?

Then there was Bunny. Miranda noted her name and under it wrote TOOK OVER BUSINESS. That much was true, sure, but she'd bet the money in her safe that Bunny was clean and clear, a woman genuinely in grief, maybe not for Prince Charming, but for a man she truly loved.

Bunny was guilty, like Louise, of poor taste in men, guilty of cheating on a friend with her boss—though Sylvia didn't seem to blame her—but goddamn it, Bunny didn't murder Niles Alexander and wasn't the type of woman to send threatening letters or poisoned chocolates to Louise, even if she did have a motive—which from all appearances she didn't.

If she wanted to get rid of Louise, she would have told Alexander to fire her, not kill her.

Miranda set down the fountain pen. Crushed the cigarette stub in the ashtray, rubbed her forehead.

Louise, Louise, Louise. It always came back to Louise.

Who was threatening her, and why? Was it the same person who murdered Alexander and presumably stole the missing manuscript?

A sigh turned into another yawn and she picked up the pen again.

THE MANUSCRIPT.

The manuscript was the one common denominator, the only motive that made even a half-assed kind of sense.

Maybe Smith's book was an exposé of prison malfeasance, some kind of highly explosive and litigious page-turner that would blow the lid off Alcatraz. George hinted as much: if he could get the book and deliver it to his former bosses, he'd get his old job back, his confessed motive to a planned but not executed theft.

Hell, maybe the manuscript explained everything . . . maybe how Ted Cole and Ralph Roe escaped in '37, maybe how Cretzer and Kyle skipped McNeil Island. Maybe . . . maybe it was about how to escape Alcatraz and contained enough dirt to bury the warden.

Was a gang—some associates of Cretzer and Kyle—after Louise, figuring they could put pressure on her to destroy the book? Did they murder Alexander in order to stop publication? Was whatever Smith discovered a threat to the bulls or the hoods? Or both?

And where the fuck was Smith?

The phone rang suddenly, the insistent bells piercing the stillness of the room and making Miranda jump. She picked up the receiver, heart still in her ears.

"Miranda? Inspector Gonzales is driving Louise home."

Meyer's voice was cracked with exhaustion. He was too old to go through this kind of punishment.

"I'm sorry, Meyer. Can I come down there to see Louise? I asked Fisher—"

"No, my dear. Louise doesn't want to talk. She's all talked out, I'm afraid. As am I. Inspector Fisher passed your request to Inspector Gonzales, who very kindly permitted me to phone. He said to tell you that any delay could bring reporters, and that he's sorry to keep you waiting. I know you had planned to escort Miss Crowley to her apartment but the good inspector feels it's safer if he drives her there alone. He said you'd understand."

Miranda clenched the phone in her left hand, eyes swollen and dry from not enough sleep.

Her voice was terse. "Tell him I get it. Go home, Meyer. I'll visit Louise in the morning."

Her attorney yawned. "Excuse me, my dear. Yes. We shall compare notes then. Good night."

"Good night, Meyer. And thank you." She hung up the phone.

Miranda wanted to cry, but no tears would come.

Soft, skittering feet down alleys damp with fog and lukewarm dishwater, white rice stuck between cobblestones. Giggles, grunts, and the unmistakable sounds of a trick being turned, light enough under the moon and the torn paper lantern, lurid shadows splayed against brick tenements, sleeping families crowded seven to a room.

Off the alley and back on Grant Street, music swelled, from Forbidden City and the Twin Dragon, from the sixth-floor windows of the Chinese Sky Room and a scratchy Victrola in the basement of the Li Po bar. A trombone solo melded with the aroma of freshly baked fortune cookies, and a rat stood up on his hind legs on Sacramento, long whiskers still twitching.

Not yet 2:00 A.M. Still early for Chinatown.

Miranda listened to the echo of her shoes on stone, stomach full from a plateful of shrimp fried rice at Sam Wo's. Fog blew in clusters down Grant, giant gray puffs belched from the Pacific assembly line, moist wads of cotton kissing stucco dragons and pagoda roofs, yellow neon snapping and paper lanterns hanging limp, streaks and drops forming puddles on red-painted doors.

She walked, holding the small bag of sesame balls pressed into her hands by the waitress, sent off into the night armed with bean paste and rice flour fried in sesame oil.

Chinatown.

Her sanctuary, her safe place, despite the predatory pimps and tongs selling hop, despite the loud-mouthed tourists and the watered-down drinks, despite the all-night nightclubs and questionable chop suey.

And on Sacramento Street, a dead Japanese boy . . .

Miranda looked up the hill at Grant and Sacramento, rat long gone and shimmied up a water pipe. She managed to find some justice for Eddie Taka-hashi back in February but the war raged on in Chinatown streets, Japanese businesses boycotted, Nanking a wound that time would never heal.

Not in a culture where memory lasted a thousand thousand years, where tradition and honor was continuity and life.

She stared at the wet pavement and darkly shuttered shop, almost hearing the firecrackers and music from the Rice Bowl Party. She shivered from a cold wind blowing down Sacramento and walked on.

Chinatown.

Nothing like it anywhere, not in New York, not in London, not in China. "Chinatown, My Chinatown" the song ran, but it didn't mention that it was a Pan-Asian city, didn't describe the dirty cops and cops on a mission, the stern lady missionaries and kindly whores, the well-used laundry hanging from attic windows, the toothless smile of an old lady selling ginseng, the creak of warped wooden floors and the smell of oolong tea.

Chinatown.

Always there, her ghetto-parent. Squalid and stable, poor in everything but its heart.

And now she was saying good-bye . . .

Someone whistled from Old St. Mary's, and Miranda quickly craned her head, surprised to see No-Legs Norris sitting on his plywood board under a splash of streetlight. She walked across the street, smiling.

"Hello, Ned. It's been a while."

"Too long. Heard on the grapevine that you're leaving. Goin' overseas."

Miranda raised her eyebrows. "Where'd you hear that?"

"Got around a few weeks ago, since that last big case you took on, that Nazi spy shindig. Heard it pretty soon after that. Blind Willie told me."

Miranda rubbed her neck. "I don't know how Willie found out, but . . . yeah, it's true. I'm heading for England, soon as I finish this case."

The thin man's face crinkled like brown wrapping paper.

"I liked the Limeys when I was over. Talk awful funny, but damn good to have with you when your back's up against barbed wire and the foxhole needs bailin' out. When you comin' back home, Miranda?"

"Soon as I can, Ned."

"Show them Nazis a thing or two, won't ya?"

"Gonna try. Say, listen—can you keep an eye and ear out for me? Tell Willie to listen up, too."

"'Course. Whaddya need? More spies?"

"Not this time. You hear about Niles Alexander?"

Ned's brow furrowed while he absentmindedly scratched under his thigh. "The book fella? One in all the papers?"

"Yeah. If you hear anything about his son Jerry or wife Sylvia—or anything at all about the Cretzer-Kyle gang—"

"Them bos on the Rock? The bank robbers?"

"Yeah. You hear anything about their gang in San Francisco, any news, you let me know, usual way. OK? It'd be a big help."

No-Legs yawned, showing one less molar than Miranda remembered. "Sure, Miranda. Be happy to. Make sure you let us know when you leave, me and Blind Willie'll come and see you off."

Kaleidoscope of San Francisco.

No-Legs Norris propelling himself through Chinatown streets, rawhide gloves nearly worn out again, Blind Willie and his pencils, voice high and squeaky like a teakettle whistle. Treasure Island and Sally Rand's lisp, always trying to protect the girls, the Gayway folks and Shorty the midget, Gillespie the beat cop and Phil watching her pour tea at Dianne's, eyes desperate and longing and old.

Gonzales and French cigarettes and his long, lean body, Fisher's face damp with worry and faith. Bente's red hair and bellowing laugh and picket signs and Gladdy's blond, bouncing curls, a "Good morning, sugar!" from the Monadnock stand. Meyer arguing for her, always there, pressed linen shirts and white spats, cane punctuating every point . . .

Neon winking at Joe's Club Moderne and Raphael's appreciative nod over the new City of Paris dress, Joe's protective hand on her shoulder, a *"Bella dea d'amore!"* and proud, fatherly smile. Allen and a shot of whiskey at the Rusty Nail, bald head shining, tough exterior melting like a wax candle. Brown leather booth at John's Grill with Rick, a lopsided Irish grin and battered brown fedora, easy laugh and careworn eyes . . .

She bent her face to hide, digging in her purse, lifted it up again with a plastered-on smile. Dropped two tens on Ned's platform.

"For you and Willie. More later."

He scooped it up. "Thanks, Miranda. Well, gotta be gettin' home to the missus. Don't forget to let me know. Be seein' you."

"Be seein' you, Ned."

She climbed the grade next to the old brick church, turning on Bush toward the apartment on Mason.

She was tired from the long day, the murder discovered, the client arrested, the alibi located. But she wouldn't have too many more chances to stroll through Chinatown to the pale cream and green Drake-Hopkins, not too many more chances for sesame balls and No-Legs Norris and the clang of a lonesome cable car climbing up Powell Street.

Miranda's steps echoed, sounds of Chinatown receding, the occasional Pontiac or Ford whooshing by. Fog wrapped around her like a blanket and the streetlights shone like stars.

She walked and she listened and the tears finally came.

Seventeen

*

Light was already streaming through the bedroom window when the telephone woke Miranda. She reached for it groggily, half-remembering the alarm clock she'd turned off an hour earlier.

Maybe it was Louise, maybe it was Meyer, she should've gotten the hell out of bed at seven . . .

"Hullo? Miranda?"

She blinked a few times and sat upright, an unexpected tightening in her stomach.

"Rick?"

Rick Sanders, friend from New York, friend of Johnny's, oldest friend she had, the newshawk who'd followed her, pestered her, haunted her office, the man who found her in the Napa woods and saved her life and watched over her like a goddamn mother hen, the man who'd introduced her to Burnett, helped get her out of Dianne's.

The man who was in love with her.

"Yes, ma'am. I've completed basic and am looking at a few days' leave before my next assignment. You're speaking to Sergeant Sanders now."

The bullshit half-Irish brogue was gone, replaced by a new confidence, almost a swagger. Miranda reached for a pack of Chesterfields on her nightstand and shook one out, mind still groggy.

"Where are you?"

"You know where I am—right next door."

She lit the stick, remembering. There'd been a postcard from San Diego, explaining he'd changed his mind about the navy—something about forgetting he'd get seasick—and that he was enlisting in the army instead. Then another card from the Presidio saying he was entering basic training. Maybe two or three more after that, the kind with sad-faced comic soldiers peeling potatoes, always scrawled with an update on his progress and a "Hope you're OK" and signed off with a "Be seeing you, Rick" . . .

Rick was stationed at the Presidio. A world and less than five miles away.

"Congratulations. Whatever happened to that school you wrote about—officer's school, or something? Did you get in?"

"Officer's Candidate School. I heard about it last year through a *News* story but the government moves like molasses in January. General Bradley won't have the program up and running until next year, but when they do I can apply. My degree will make me eligible and in the meantime I'm an NCO."

"I didn't know you have a degree."

"B.A. in history from City. That's how I met John. Two Lower East Side boys at the poor man's Harvard . . ."

City College of New York, class of '28, Johnny Hayes, B.A. in political science, track team, newspaper, tight, hard muscles from working the docks late at night, from one too many fights in Irish Alley, confidence like the sun and smile just as blinding, *you're a good soldier, Randy, a good soldier* . . .

"Miranda? You still there?"

"Yeah. I'm here, Rick. So what are you doing for your leave? Any plans?"

Drums started to beat on the other end of the phone and then a trumpet blast, sounds of a marching band. His voice, when he finally spoke, sober.

"Sort of depends on you. See, I'm—I'm probably getting transferred to Washington. Seems the HQ brass wants to tap into my newspaper experience. I've told my CO I signed up to fight when the fighting comes, but in the meantime it looks like I'll be leaving San Francisco a little early. I'd like to see you before I go. Say good-bye."

Miranda stared at the blue flowers on the bedroom wallpaper, cigarette burning unnoticed.

San Francisco without Rick.

The memories without him were old ones, when she wore short flapper dresses and danced the Black Bottom, and as a child before that, when she escaped from Hatchett and fled to Spider Kelly's, the ladies with big bustles and deep décolletage offering her bites of mutton and sips of Irish whiskey.

An older City but always hers, and it was still there, the San Francisco she came back to after Spain, the San Francisco she remembered, the San Francisco where Rick Sanders was waiting for her, new and gleaming with two bridges and a man-made island in the Bay, the City that Knew How, the City she'd never forgotten.

And Rick was a part of it.

When she was in London, huddled in an underground shelter listening to wailing babies and the click of knitting needles and someone playing the harmonica, she'd picture him here still, battered brown Champ fedora pushed high off his forehead, wrinkled suit covered in ashes and yesterday's lunch, hunched over a Royal typewriter, pounding one key at a time, looking up with that goddamn look on his face whenever he saw her, cheekbones strong and blue eyes warm . . .

"That's—that's big news, Rick. And of course I want to see you. I've been meaning to write—"

"You'd make a lousy foreign correspondent—"

"Yeah, I know, I know. Listen, I'm—I'm leaving, too. Finally got a ship berth in just a few weeks. The *Cameronia*. Provided the Nazis don't sink her first, of course, but—"

"The *Cameronia*? You mean you're actually going? You're heading to England in the middle of the Blitzkrieg?"

Miranda looked down at the cigarette clenched between her fingers, red rim eating slowly through white.

"I've got to find my mother, if she's there—I owe her the attempt, anyway—and I was trained as a nurse—"

"For about two weeks from a woman who was flying higher than a kite most of the time. This isn't like Spain, Miranda, it's a new kind of war and it's even worse. Are you sure you want to do this? Absolutely sure?"

One Mississippi, Two Mississippi, Three Mississippi . . .

She crushed out the Chesterfield in the small glass ashtray.

"It's not something I want to do. It's something I have to do."

Silence again. More band music from the Presidio. Rick's voice, slow, quiet, firm.

"That I understand . . . more than you know. Well, then—you have my blessing. When do you leave?"

"Just a few weeks. October 21st."

"Jesus, you don't have much time—"

"Yeah, I know. Planning to close up shop after I finish up the case I'm on."

"Any time to see me?"

"I'll make time."

She could hear the smile on his face. "How about tonight?"

"If you don't mind maybe getting dragged along. I don't know where I'll end up."

"Sounds like old times. And after KP and drills, even the Nazi consulate would be a cakewalk. Pick you up at home or the office?"

"Better make it the office. And I may not be able to dress for the occasion."

"I'm flattered you're treating it as an occasion. You in anything at all, Miranda, is OK with me."

His tone was appreciative, warm, fond . . . but with no hidden longing, no lovesick desperation, just an old friend seeing another old friend for old time's sake. Auld Lang fucking Syne, not the Rick Sanders who'd scolded her and worried over her and stared at her when he thought she wasn't looking, the Rick she'd pushed away, hard and fast, for over two years, the friend who always wanted more.

The friend she hurt.

Whatever else the army had done, it looked like it had cured Rick Sanders, no more lovesick longing, no more possessive, protective worry.

So why the hell were her hands shaking?

"All right, let's say seven o'clock. Your buddy Herb Caen has been a big help on this case, by the way."

Rick laughed, a rolling, hearty sound with a just a memory of Irish in it. She missed that goddamn laugh.

"I figured he would be. Herb's a good egg, and he's got an eye for the ladies—appreciates a well-turned leg. But he's married, so he's safe."

"That's usually when they're the most dangerous. But you're right, he's a gentleman. Thanks, Rick."

Sudden conversation in the background, muffled. Rick's voice, more urgent.

"Miranda? I've got to go. I'll see you at seven."

"Yeah. See you tonight."

Miranda slowly replaced the phone on the cradle, gazing again at the blue forget-me-nots dancing on yellow wallpaper.

*

She dressed in a hurry, digging through her purse until she found Louise's number in her notebook.

Seven rings before an answer.

"Hullo?" Louise's voice was slurry, still asleep.

"It's Miranda. We need to talk."

Talk about her client, about her client's boyfriend, her client's family connections to convicted felons, her client's lies . . .

Louise yawned audibly, teeth clicking together. "Oh—Miss Corbie—yes, I'm—I'm sorry about—"

"Lying to me? If you want my help, Louise, you need to come clean with all of it—about George, about Smith's book, about your sister and her husband and what role you think they're playing in all this. I want the whole story—every word, every possible connection. Or I walk and leave you to the mercy of the San Francisco Police Department. Am I clear?"

Silence. Even breaths, in and out.

"Yes. And you're right, of course, Miss Corbie. I'm—I'm dead tired from last night, and I'm afraid I won't be able to get to work until later in the day. I can meet you at the Monadnock in the afternoon."

Sounds of Louise moving the phone, voice muffled. "And it looks—it looks from my window as though there might be reporters outside. Oh, God . . . am I in the papers?"

"You were last night—I slept in myself and haven't seen the morning editions yet. If the newshawks put a target on your back, that'll complicate things. We can meet at your apartment or I can help get you to work if you'd like."

"I don't know what I want except for things to be normal and simple again and without all these people hounding me . . ."

"Prison is a lot worse than a pack of reporters." Miranda's voice was dry. "And I don't think you've seen the near side of 'normal' for a long time."

Silence again. More shuffling. Louise, when she finally spoke, sounded somber.

"You're right, I—I shouldn't be complaining. Yesterday was so horrible . . . like a bad dream . . . it was all I could do to hold on. Poor Mr. Bialik—without him and without you I'd be in a cell right now, facing prison, maybe even the gas chamber. All right, Miss Corbie. Give me a few hours and I'll meet you at the Monadnock . . . let's make it three o'clock to be safe, as I really should talk to Bunny first. If I feel too outnumbered I'll give you a call, but I've been brave enough with some things and I need to be brave enough with this."

"Good. I'll find out what the papers know and what they don't know and we'll figure out the next steps . . . after we have a long talk about everything else.

Meantime, just stick it out. You run into trouble, call me at the office, and if I'm not there, leave a message with the service."

"If you see Bunny this morning, will you tell her—tell her I won't let her down?"

"Sure thing, Louise. Go on back to bed. Don't worry about Bunny or the hacks outside. I'll see you later this afternoon."

The voice was trailing off now, reassured and sleepy. "Yes, I'm not—not feeling too well. Could use another few hours of sleep. Thanks, Miss Corbie . . . see you later."

Click.

Miranda studied the phone in her hand, stomach rumbling.

Time for breakfast . . . and the fucking morning papers.

*

Miranda swallowed a bite of hotcakes and sausage, barely tasting it. Next to a photo of Wendell Wilkie was LONDON RAID: NAZIS ATTACK FOR THIRTEENTH NIGHT IN A ROW.

Goddamn it.

She turned the page quickly, blocking out the Blitz, Wilkie's campaign appearance in San Francisco and the *Chronicle's* ecstatic welcome to the Wall Street Republican who would restore Greatness to America. Page two, page three . . .

Medium headline: SECRETARY TIED TO CRETZER AND KYLE GANG; HELD AND RELEASED FOR ALEXANDER MURDER.

Could be worse. If not for Wilkie, Louise would've made the front page.

Chances are her client was a page-one headline in the *News* and page two in the *Call-Bulletin,* given the former was hot for any murder, especially with a whiff of the salacious, and the latter was supporting FDR and couldn't give a rat's ass about Wilkie.

Miranda's eyes narrowed and flickered over the article. How the hell did it leak this fast? She hadn't said a word about Kyle and Cretzer to Fisher, carefully protected her client and the motive, and now Thelma Kyle's name was featured in the first paragraph and the whole sordid little tale was opening mouths at kitchen tables across San Francisco . . . and in the Hall of Justice.

Shit. Fisher.

Miranda pushed away the half-eaten plate, hailed the waitress, and lit a Chesterfield. She'd call the inspector, explain it was privileged information, complain about how she didn't see this coming and didn't know who the hell could have leaked it.

Except . . . yes. One person.

George Blankenship.

She quickly scanned the article again. No mention of George, just "the accused was with her male friend on the night in question."

Miranda nodded, jaw set and grim. George Blankenship sold the story to keep his name out of the papers. Greer Sanitarium, with all its airs and graces and pretense toward modern, well-bred, and expensive mental health, would not appreciate any link to suspected murderers or criminals doing time on the Rock. The bastard was saving his job at the expense of Louise Crowley.

She took a puff on the cigarette, blowing a stream of blue smoke toward the Powell Street window.

She'd see how long he'd keep it when she was through with him.

No reporters at the Monadnock, at least not on the ground floor. No Gladys, either, so she couldn't get the skinny on the early part of the morning. Maybe the blonde was on break.

Miranda frowned, thinking about how much she'd miss Gladys, and frowned again when she saw the front page of the *News* ("MURDER VICTIM'S SECRETARY LINKED TO BANK ROBBERS"). The *Call-Bulletin* featured a smaller article on page two, slightly less incendiary ("ALEXANDER MURDER CONNECTED TO CRETZER/KYLE GANG?").

She strode into the elevator, scanning the articles. The Pinkerton offices were busy as usual, but no light under Allen's door. Her own office smelled like smoke and Lifesavers, so she tossed the newspapers on the desk and pulled up the window. Picked up the phone, took a breath, and dialed Fisher's number from memory.

Strange voice, not Fisher or Gonzales.

"Is Inspector Fisher available?"

"No, he's not. Who is this?"

"Miranda Corbie. May I leave him a message, please?"

The gravelly voice rumbled while it looked for a pen. "You the private eye broad on the Alexander case? Your client's all over the goddamn paper this morning. We got the Oakland Police Department angry as hell because they're working overtime tryin' to keep the sister under wraps."

"I didn't give them the story."

"Whatever you say, sister. What's the message?"

"Blankenship leaked. Call when can."

A pause, while the bull on the other end worked out the words, his breath heavy on the phone.

"I'll put it on his desk." He clicked off before she could thank him.

Miranda drummed her fingers on the black wood, picked up the phone again.

"Greer Sanitarium, please. Yes, the one on Fulton."

Connection, ring. "Greer Sanitarium, Incorporated."

Sounded like the gorgon she'd met before.

"George Blankenship, please."

The voice dripped ice. "I don't know where you found that name, ma'am. We don't give out information about employees or guests."

Miranda leaned forward in her chair, eyes glittering. "Listen, sister. I know he works there, so save the spiel. You tell him to call EXbrook 3333 if you want to keep your fucking clip joint out of the evening paper."

Miranda slammed the phone down in the receiver, breathing hard.

Next stop, Bunny Berrigan.

*

Two reporters were lounging against the door to Alexander Publishing. God-damn it. Two or three ink-slingers were harder to shake than a whole pack. She started to duck behind the hallway wall when she heard a familiar voice.

"Why don't you fellows find someplace else to stake out? Louise Crowley isn't here and Bunny Berrigan doesn't want to talk."

Warm, jocular, and flippantly confident. Herb Caen.

Miranda smiled and strode down the hall.

"At least not to us," one of the reporters groused. "They always got three dots for you, Caen."

The columnist preened, stretching a bow tie and a smirk in front of the publisher's door. "Can I help it if I—well, look who it is, boys! Miranda Corbie, the private eye most private eyes would like to give the eye to . . . you here to see Bunny, Miranda?"

The two other reporters, one in blue rumpled pinstripes, the other in gray, trotted toward her, pencils poised, questions in high gear.

"Who're you working for exactly, Miss Corbie? I heard it was Louise Crowley, the accused—is it true her sister's married to Kyle? Is their gang behind the murder?"

"Why wasn't she charged? Was Alexander two-timin' with his secretary? Was it a fit of jealous passion?"

Miranda held up a gloved hand against the onslaught while Caen made clucking noises and took her by the arm.

"Now boys, you know she can't answer questions, just like she knows you can't not ask 'em. So why don't we accept the futility of it all and you two run along home to mamma?"

The younger reporter with sharp features and the blue pin-striped suit clenched his fist and took a step toward Caen, while the older one restrained him, voice resigned.

"C'mon, Ed. We can find someone else to shake down." He led the younger one down the hall, the latter still craning his neck backward and glaring at the columnist.

Caen studied Miranda, his leprechaun smile growing bolder. "I was just on my way to your office. Got a message from Rick this morning telling me I'm off duty for a couple of days as of tonight."

"Off duty? You mean . . . oh, I see. You're my Lochinvar until the real one shows up, is that it?"

The curly-headed journalist made a face. "I wouldn't put it exactly like that. He's just trying to protect you, Miranda. With all this rumble, you need as many Lochinvars as you can get."

"'So faithful in love, so dauntless in war.'" Her lips curled up at one corner. "Thanks just the same. Though I do appreciate the help on fending off the wolves."

Caen executed a short bow and tipped his fedora. "M'lady."

"Rick say anything else?"

"Something about shipping out to D.C. in a few days." The columnist shook his head and sighed. "Thing is, war'll come soon enough for all of us, so why he felt the urge to join up now I don't understand. The boy's a good reporter"— Miranda suppressed a smile at the diminutive, since Caen was a good ten years younger than Rick—"but he's an idealist, determined to tilt at windmills." Caen cocked his eyebrow at her. "You two really were made for one another, weren't you?"

Made for each other.

Like bacon and eggs, like Lum and Abner, like Lunt and Fontaine.

Like the stone chimneys and blue-gray London smoke, the sidewalk cafes and gargoyles on Notre Dame, like the El and the Stork and Katz' Deli, Lower East Side.

Like the sad songs on the *alboka* and the olive oil and Tempranillo, like the streets of Madrid and the red, red earth, red like the blood on ancient stone and old women's faces, like the blood in the riverbeds, pooling where water once flowed.

Red like the blood the hospital couldn't find, no blood, no ether, no morphine.

No Johnny . . .

"Miranda?" The columnist was staring at her.

She blinked, eyes fixed on the gold letters proclaiming ALEXANDER PUBLISHING.

"I've gotta talk to Bunny. She in?"

"Sure, she was figuring you'd show up when Louise didn't—especially after she saw the papers."

"Thanks. Be seein' you, Herb."

"S'long, Miranda. I'll resume my duties when Sanders is back on KP." Caen bowed again, grin wide and mischievous.

Miranda nodded.

She needed answers and she needed them fast, wanted time for her good-byes and her farewells, time to pack up her life and start again.

Louise, George, and Smith were the links, links to Alcatraz.

And Bunny Berrigan was the link to Smith.

Miranda took a breath and opened the door.

Eighteen

*

Thick dust still covered Louise's desk, heavy boots leaving powdery imprints on the burgundy carpet. Voices, raised in argument, filtered from one of the side offices, and Bunny Berrigan was nowhere to be seen.

One of the voices was shrill and sounded familiar . . . probably Emily Kingston, the eccentric copywriter and would-be editor, the seeming spinster with an appetite for crime. A lower voice mixed in, baritone, not bass, loud but not ferocious.

Footsteps.

Miranda scooted backward toward the waiting area.

The door flew open, banging into the wall bumper. Bunny strode out, hair askew and eyes wild.

"Just meet the goddamn deadlines, people! Is that too much to ask?"

The redhead, hand on the door to Alexander's office, glimpsed Miranda and paused.

"So. Corbie. Herb Caen said you'd be up here this morning and I told him I figured as much. Looks like Louise is related to some bad gees. Doesn't make her one. I haven't fired her, so I expect her in. That clear? We've got books to publish."

"Louise said to tell you that she won't let you down. She'll be in later, soon as she gets a little sleep and shakes off the reporters."

Bunny shrugged her shoulders and sighed, gesturing with her head toward the main office.

"In here."

Blood still caked purple on the expensive carpet, red-orange now red-purple in lurid patches close by the mahogany desk. Bunny walked toward the opposite end of the room near the windows and lit a Lucky Strike with unsteady fingers.

"Cops don't want us to work in here yet, but screw it. It's the only place to talk where we won't be bothered. So what the hell's all this about Kyle and Cretzer and Louise and Alcatraz?"

"I don't know. Louise lied to me like everyone else."

"Poor kid. Must be scared stiff, her sister married to a bird like that. You think these hoods ordered Niles' murder? And tried to kill Louise?"

Miranda frowned, shaking her head.

"Kyle and Cretzer are locked up, facing a murder charge. I don't know if they have confederates down here or what they'd stand to gain by killing Alexander or Louise or stealing Smith's book. And why not take the money? Why leave it in the safe? Doesn't make any goddamn sense. Louise promised to come clean when I talk to her today and I've got a whole lot of questions. Said she'll see you first, though—she's still worried about the publishing schedule."

"Well, get her in here. She's got a job, and God knows I can use the help. I just don't want any redhots around here, gumming up the works. She safe enough, you think? I mean, what if they've been trying to off her all this time because she knows too much? What if—"

Miranda held up a hand. "Back up, Bunny. Whether or not this is all related to Cretzer and Kyle, whoever was in that safe the night before last got what they wanted: the Alcatraz manuscript. The person we need to hear from—maybe the only person, other than Louise, who can give us an idea about what is going on—is Smith. Has there been any word from him? I mean, Jesus Christ, I know writers like their garrets, but his book was just stolen and his publisher was murdered and he's the logical one to be in the most danger."

Bunny made a face.

"Writers. Every cuckoo thing you've ever heard . . . they're all nuts. I called Smith in Monterey yesterday. Told him Niles was dead, his book had been stolen, and he'd better get up here because the police want to question him. He said he'd drive up right away. Then he doesn't show, and your friend the inspector leaves me a few messages last night: 'Why isn't he here yet? Is he trying to skip?'"

Miranda murmured: "The bulls aren't known for their patience."

"Well, it's not like I have control over what Smith does or doesn't do. But when the cops landed on Louise I figured we had a little more time before they put out some kind of bulletin on Howard, so last night I called his agent, Charlie Segal, and gave him the score. Charlie didn't know anything about why Smith wasn't here yet—I mean, we're talking about a five or six-hour drive, tops—and he had a fit over the missing Alcatraz book. He hasn't read it, but Howard's been feeding him bits and pieces, and he's been looking forward to his ten percent."

"Niles was spending a lot of money and time positioning Smith, wasn't he?"

"He was. The whole marketing budget went to Smith, by Niles' orders. He was positioning him as the next Dashiell Hammett and John L. Spivak combined. I had a full-scale plan for attacking the *New York Times,* getting his books out to civic clubs, in *The Saturday Evening Post, Time, Life, Coronet,* probably serial rights or an essay in the *Atlantic,* you name it. I even got a couple of Hollywood studio heads interested in a picture version of the Alcatraz book—and that was just through reputation and rumor alone, with no idea of what Smith's really got."

"So this would've been a bestseller."

Bunny shrugged. "It should have been, I can tell you that. You know what makes bestsellers? Not the author or the book or how good it is—that's what everyone wants to believe, but that's the last thing from the truth. What makes a book big and an author rich and famous is marketing and publicity and timing—all of which is controlled by the publisher. People like what they're told to like, and they want to think that what they like has merit. Niles knew that, and he was investing a lot in Smith, as a muckraker and novelist and personality. Luck plays a role, sure, but if you're smart you can fix the game."

"So why isn't Smith here?"

"Because he's a pompous little rich boy who likes to masquerade as a man of the people and drinks too fucking much, if you'll pardon my language."

"You mean he's on a bender in Monterey?"

The tall woman ground her stick out in a floor tray, lines forming on either side of her mouth.

"Looks like it. I called him again this morning. He stays at a boardinghouse when he's down there fishing—goes a few times a year, usually in between books or major drafts. According to the old lady who runs it, Smith hasn't left town yet but hasn't been in all night, either. Probably out drinking with Steinbeck—and nuts to them both. I'm sending Howard a telegram this morning: he either gets here pronto or not only will the Monterey police be paying him a visit and holding him for our own boys in blue but I won't publish his goddamn books. That'll be enough to get him to face the music."

"I hope so." Miranda looked up at Bunny. "You gonna send that right away?"

"I was on my way out when I saw you."

"All right, keep me posted. I'll let Fisher know about Smith and run interference for you."

Bunny's lips cracked into a tired smile. "Thanks. The Gump's memorial for Niles is day after tomorrow. You're invited—eight o'clock at the store, 250 Post. I hope Sylvia can manage it—Roger is seeing her today. He's supposed to let me know." Her lip trembled slightly. "Richard Gump, the press, the mayor, even Forester is coming. Niles would've loved it."

"I'll be in touch. Expect Louise later this afternoon."

"Thanks, Miranda."

Hand on the doorknob, she turned back to face Bunny. "By the way—did the deep voice you were yelling at belong to your other editor—Hank something or other?"

"Hank Ward. He's the only editor, really, other than—than Niles. Freelancers sometimes approach us, agents too, of course."

"Mind if I talk to him?"

"Be my guest. Emily's probably gone by now—she hates working in the same office. But make it quick—he's on a deadline."

"Thanks. Good luck with Smith."

"Good luck to Smith, you mean. If he doesn't get down here today, Katie, bar the door."

The two women walked out of Alexander's office together, Bunny peering around the main suite door before striding quickly down the hall.

The connecting door to the other rooms was still open. Miranda raised a gloved fist to knock on the office door shared by Hank Ward and Emily Kingston.

Audible clicks and the clatter of typewriter keys, slow but steady rate. She knocked again and the typing stopped. A deep voice grunted: "Come in."

She stepped inside, shutting the door behind her and leaning against it.

The small office was more cluttered since yesterday. Three or four large manuscripts covered in red pencil marks lay in disarray on Emily Kingston's desk, along with a half-empty cup of tea in English china.

No Emily.

Sitting at the old, tired desk nearest her with a five- or six-year-old typewriter and a marked-up copy of today's *Daily Racing Form* was a soft, burly man about forty-three, black and gray stubble on his cleft chin, eyes nearly black. His generous mouth was shaping into a grin.

"Well . . . hello. Come on in, sister. Don't be shy."

Miranda noticed the sticky brown residue at the bottom of a small shot glass to his right, the multiple *Racing Forms* and the threadbare jacket barely clinging to the back of his chair.

"My name is Miranda Corbie. I'm a private investigator. I'm here to ask you a few questions, Mr. Ward."

The smile vanished. Ward coughed while he lit a Camel, hands trembling intermittently, and he swore under his breath when the Bimbo's 365 matches took three strikes to light. Then he sat back in the squeaky chair and looked her over, chin out and eyes anxious at the corners.

"So you're a private dick. They're not makin' 'em the way they used to, that's for damn sure. Probably get by on the divorce cases, huh? Lady Eve and the apple in the garden, tempting married men to stray. Well, I'm not married, so what do you want with me?"

"What I want, Mr. Ward, is to know what you were doing the night Mr. Alexander was killed, and whether or not you are in possession of the second office key that Louise Crowley kept hanging in the meeting room filing cabinet. She sometimes found it in the supply room after you used it." She gestured with her head to the closet-like room in the rear of the office.

Ward raised thick, unkempt eyebrows, insolently blowing a stream of smoke toward Miranda's face.

"Look, lady, I know my boss was murdered and I'm broken up about it. But the cops haven't seen fit to call me in, so why the hell should I talk to you?"

Miranda pried herself from the door in one long, sinuous move, sauntering up to the edge of his desk, lips stretched in a dangerous smile. She bent close to him, face only inches away from his, eyes flickering over his map-veined nose and the day-old stubble on his chin.

"You talk to me, Mr. Ward, for a few reasons. Number one, because I asked you to. Number two, because if you don't, the cops I'm working with will want to know why. Number three, because those same cops will be down here to question you soon enough, and I'm your best chance at not winding up in a jail cell. And number four, you talk because you're a cowardly hack who bluffs and bullies his way out of as much responsibility as possible, burying any dreams of being a real writer under a haze of bullshit, whiskey, women, and ponies that couldn't finish the fucking fair circuit."

She straightened up, looking down at the editor with a mixture of pity and contempt.

"So can the goddamn Hemingway act and answer the questions."

Ward's nose and cheeks flashed bright purple against red. He shut his mouth with a snap, ran his hands over unruly, white-specked hair, ground out the cigarette in his ashtray.

Didn't meet Miranda's eyes.

He rummaged in some papers on his desk. Mumbled, "Night of the 18th, right? Night before last? I was at a—at a club."

"Bookie or whorehouse?"

"B-bookie."

"Got anybody who can verify?"

His head snapped up to glare at her and his voice rose in anger.

"It's a goddamn bookie joint, you think anybody'll admit to bein' there? Jesus Christ, I didn't kill Niles, he's the only guy who gave me a break—"

"Look, Ward. I'm not saying you killed anybody. But this case is wide open, and anybody who's got a record of gambling—and possible connections to any criminal activity—well, the bulls'll be looking at it. Closely. This is murder and the gas chamber we're talking about. What about the key—the extra key to the office? It was missing yesterday."

Hank Ward rubbed his chin with a shaking hand. "Christ, I need a drink. Here." He reached into his trouser pocket and pulled out a key. "I had it, forgot to put it back. I'm always forgetting things—ask Louise—that's why she had the key made, tryin' to help me. She's a good kid."

"So you had it the night of the murder."

His voice exploded again, eyes small and red, face taut and fleshy in all the wrong places. The baritone climbed to the tenor range.

"That doesn't make me the goddamn killer!"

Miranda studied him, the sweat on his forehead, the dirt under his chipped nails.

She picked up the key.

"Here's the score. Bunny's in a bind and she still thinks you're a decent editor. I'm not here to cut you down or report you to the cops. But do yourself a favor and line up somebody at the bookie's that might vouch for you. If you picked up a girl, find her again. Get yourself an alibi . . . just in case."

She turned to go.

"Hey, Corbie . . ."

Miranda pivoted from the doorway. "Yeah?"

The voice was small and low, meanness scared out of it.

"Thanks."

She nodded, eyes glinting over the editor's ragged face and rumpled clothes, watching him slump in his desk with his head in his hands.

She slipped out the office door.

Nineteen

*

The answering service offered no news from Fisher or Blankenship, but the bored operator recited an unexpected message from Rick. He was at loose ends, an appointment fell through, so he'd be early and meet her at the office around 3:30.

Goddamn it. She wanted to see him—how much she wanted to see him she didn't think about, the surprise anticipation knotting her stomach—but three-thirty wouldn't work. By then she'd be in a long discussion with Louise Crowley.

Miranda tore out a piece of paper from the Big Chief tablet, and hastily scrawled a note. She could tape it to the door, ask him to meet her at the Moderne that night.

She explained what she could, hoped he'd wait for her. The old Rick, pre-army Rick, blue eyes disappointed, lines at the corners of his mouth, crestfallen and glum, would still understand, knew better than anyone what a case was like, what her job—her life—meant to her.

The cigarette tasted bitter on her tongue and in her chest, and she coughed, rubbing it out in the Tower of the Sun ashtray.

Crumpled the note and threw it in the wastepaper basket.

Everything tasted bitter, what with this fucking case making no fucking sense, and saying good-bye to Rick, to Bente, to Gladys, a forever farewell to the Fair and the Gayway, to Pacifica and White Star Tuna, the Singer Midgets and Sally's girls, the gravel-voiced barkers and the kids on the roller coaster. No more sad-faced clowns, no more Threlkeld scones and Maxwell House, no more coffee, no more San Francisco.

It would be another foggy city, gray with the smoke of bombs and fires, ringed by a circle of water, ocean moat for an island castle. Like Alcatraz, an island, but an island of hope, the only bit left, a little crevice of civilization to build upon, to fight for, to preserve. It would be cold nights and wool mittens and hard, driving rain, speeches from Churchill and the wail of all-night sirens and the prayer for an all-clear, Vera Lynn and the King and Queen and the fire brigades, East Enders making do with even less. It would be long nights in the Underground, watching the tunnels tremble, strong tea when she could get it, eating piccalilli and sausage, leeks and cabbage and whatever fish were left in the goddamn English Channel.

Miranda closed her eyes.

If only this fucking case made sense . . .

Why steal a book about Alcatraz? There'd been other exposés of sorts, most notably *Hellcatraz*, the tell-all by Roy Gardner, the "Smiling Bandit" who killed himself back in January at the Hotel Governor.

She remembered reading about it, about how he posted a suicide note on his hotel room door, warning people not to come in and try to save him because there was poison gas inside. The criminal who cared about innocent lives . . .

Released from stir in '38, he took a job on the Gayway the following year, promoting his book, and she met him once, a tough, garrulous, nervous man, stitched together by an irresistible urge to gamble, running through every cent he made and every cent he stole, until finally, alone, he paid his last debt.

Like Cretzer and Kyle, he'd served at McNeil and escaped before coming to the Rock. Unlike Cretzer and Kyle, he worked by himself.

By all accounts, *Hellcatraz* was a popular enough story, reinforcing the shudders and dread that shrouded San Francisco's Devil's Island like the City's famous fog, but Gardner wasn't killed for writing it or his publisher for publishing it.

So why would Cretzer and Kyle gang members—or anybody else associated with the prison—want Smith's book squelched? And why would George think stealing it would get him his job back?

Miranda flipped open the Chief tablet. Wrote GEORGE = BLACKMAILER?

Short of talking to Smith, George Blankenship was still the best bet for answers.

The black phone on the desk rang, and she jumped.

"Miranda Corbie, private—"

"You could have told me about the Alcatraz connection."

Fisher. Tired, disappointed, mad.

Goddamn it.

She took a breath. "No, I couldn't. Not without violating my client's confidentiality."

"Well, that's shot to hell, so how about telling me what it is you know before I lose all the patience I've got left and hold you on an obstruction charge? Attempted murder, successful murder, burglary, gangsters, Alcatraz . . . what in the hell is going on?"

"Wish I knew. I figure Blankenship leaked the story as a deal to keep his name out of the papers and hold on to his job. What the reporters didn't publish is that George wanted Louise to steal Smith's book for him, for reasons I don't know about yet. He swore up and down that neither of them touched it— and you know the state of his alibi. I left a message at Greer and will brace him for more answers but so far no reply. I'd put a watch on him—if he panics at all, he might try to skip."

Frustration cracked Fisher's voice. "Don't have the manpower right now. Blankenship's not much use to us unless we can break his alibi. What else?"

"I spoke with Bunny Berrigan. She said she's sending a wire to Smith, who's apparently still in Monterey and on a bender with Steinbeck. She expects him here tonight."

"If he's not here in three hours, I'm phoning the Monterey cops to hold him. If I could find a *mishegas* motive for him stealing his own book, I'd arrest the sonofabitch. What about your client? She explain any of this?"

"She's supposed to meet me here at three. She didn't get much sleep last night and there was a pack of press wolves camped on her doorstep this morning. Louise lied to me, Inspector—I'm just as frustrated as you are."

Miranda waited, listening to the clacking of typewriters and a siren somewhere on Kearny, the ambient sounds of sullen B-girls and dime-store boosters.

"I want her back for questioning. I prefer the easy way, so why don't you accompany her when you're done."

It meant another long night at the Hall of Justice, but David Fisher was giving her a break, letting her question Louise before he did.

She let out a breath.

"Thanks. I'll bring her in. Expect us around five."

"All right. I'll get the sister here at the same time. She's at the Oakland station right now, for her own protection—too many damn reporters. We get 'em together, maybe we'll get some answers. Especially when Smith arrives. Anything else?"

"I can let you know what I find out from Blankenship."

"Good. Or I'll bring him in, too. Hell, maybe Warden Johnston will release Kyle for the family reunion."

Fisher's breath was shallow, his frustration as palpable as the sweat on her palms. Somebody was leaning on him . . . somebody big.

"Look . . . Inspector. I'll do whatever I can to help. We've been in tough spots before. I can't see how Alcatraz fits into any of this yet, but I'll work on it—I'll work on the angle. In the meantime, can you do me a favor and send me the report on Alexander—toxicology, what was in his desk, his pockets, all that?"

Fisher's voice was still deadened, partially obscured by sirens in the background.

"Yeah. I'll send over what we've got. Remember—bring in Louise Crowley by five tonight. Or I'm arresting her for obstruction and you'll be next. That clear?"

"She'll be there, Inspector. Both of us will."

Miranda hung up the phone. Then she shook out another Chesterfield and lit it with the Ronson One-Touch.

Her hands were still shaking.

*

Lunch was a tasteless affair, tuna salad sandwich and dried-out French fries at Breen's Cafe around the corner on Third. The only thing she could taste was the coffee: black, bitter, and strong, the main draw, along with location, for the crowd of rumpled, saggy-eyed newshounds who filled the tables, men and an occasional woman filtering down from the *Examiner* building on the corner.

Miranda prodded a piece of cold tomato with a fork tine. She needed a break, needed a way in to Alcatraz, needed to figure out why Smith's book mattered so much, why George thought it was worth stealing, why Niles Alexander had been murdered and Louise Crowley threatened.

And she needed to do it in a hurry.

She eyed the remnants of a *San Francisco Examiner,* Hearst's so-called Monarch of the Dailies, thrown open on the green counter stool next to her, left behind by one of his Hearst Building denizens.

She pushed away the platter and swallowed the last, biting dregs of the coffee.

Louise would be through with Bunny by three, Rick would be knocking on her office door by three-thirty. She'd grill Louise, brace George, wait for Smith. But meanwhile . . .

She glanced up at the grease-spattered clock above the Petty Girl calendar. 12:19.

Time to get acquainted with Alcatraz.

*

Alcatraz Island. Alcatraz Prison.

The Rock.

Windswept, bleak, cold, with an arctic chill that knifed through the Golden Gate and straight into the heart of anyone unfortunate enough to be living there. Hell, visitors couldn't wait to leave, no matter how much they loved their husbands or fathers or brothers, no matter how much they enjoyed the warden's company, the screams of gulls and the bite of salt-sea wind.

Inhospitable, like a weird, far-off planet. Like the ends of the earth, like Dante's frozen hell, an eternal, unmoving, rigid inferno from which no one ever escaped.

Only the birds, the gulls and pelicans the island was named after, flew high and above it, landing on the plants and the few trees, fishing in the churning waters off the sharp rocks and stony beach.

Sure, in the spring some flowers bloomed, and the families of the prison personnel tried to make it a home. They had their Social Hall, the Officer's Club, complete with a pool table, dance floor, and bowling alley. Children grew up in the shadow of the prison, quiet, sheltered, unable to play cops and robbers or wander too far, singing carols at Christmas within earshot of the men behind bars.

There was a small store for essentials, though the women did their shopping on the mainland, making one of the twelve daily scheduled trips to the Van Ness Pier, arriving to freedom at seven thirty in the morning, returning to the island in the afternoon or evening, voluntary prisoners of their husbands' jobs.

But flowers and trips weren't enough.

Alcatraz Island had always been forsaken, a rocky pustule on blue Bay water, first a fortress, then a prison, housing Confederate sympathizers by 1861. Its lighthouse—the first one built on the West Coast—cut through the darkness, warning ships not to come closer, protecting the Bay and the commerce that created a City. After becoming part of a federal penitentiary, it excised hope from the breasts of men, white, black, brown, imprisoned behind cement.

And always, just out of reach, like the varied, beautiful fruits of Tantalus' tree and his pool of fresh, still water, was San Francisco. Lights gleaming, neon winking, strains of music carried high on the wind, never heard behind fortress walls, never carried to the dungeon or Cell Block D.

By '39, Treasure Island made Alcatraz even more of a hell, the soft, colored lights and the big bands, the girls on the Gayway, the music and laughter, a World's Fair, a world of freedom, just two miles away. Another island, almost as close as the City, life in Technicolor, not the dull death of gray, the cold stone, the monotony of minute-by-minute routine, the worry of fending off a stronger, more sadistically bent inmate, the constant threat of physical harm and psychological humiliation.

And then there was the silence.

The silence of the men, silence mandated by the warden, the discipline of a life in a five-by-nine-foot concrete cell, the stoic loneliness that drove some to ever more violence and ever less sanity.

Talking was strictly regulated—both for the prisoners and the men that guarded them. At least the no-talking rule for prisoners was suspended after the first couple of years, deemed too impractical if not too cruel or unusual.

But since 1934, when the new maximum security prison opened, no warden, no prison guard, no employee had ever divulged what actually happened on Alcatraz. About policy or procedure, about what went on, about statistics or the lives of men on either side of the bars.

Maximum security applied to everything on the island.

Not even rumors were allowed to escape.

Despite the edict, despite the moratorium on the press, despite the censored letters and harshly controlled visits ("No discussion of anything about your time in the prison, no discussion of your food, your exercise, your work, your fellow prisoners, and especially no discussion of guards or the warden"), despite it all, the newspapers created stories.

That was their job, after all.

Their narratives relied on the few prisoners who'd made it off or made it out, men like Roy Gardner and his *Hellcatraz*, men who knew they'd be punished for it later but took a chance to be heard, to be listened to.

And what they had to say made Devil's Island look like the county jail.

The "hole," a black, lightless pit where you were fed bread a couple of times a day and, if you were lucky, endured an icy bucket of water, thrown at you once a week to wash off the smell of caked excrement. Henri Young, part of an escape attempt just last year, was reportedly still inside.

The Spanish Dungeon below Cell Block A was where recalcitrant prisoners were chained, medieval-style, in secrecy and retaliation, prison guards with bruised fists taking shifts with men otherwise too hard to crack. The wardens chose the victims, prerogative of rule.

Prisoners weren't usually housed in A, which was used for storage, but sometimes the screams from the Spanish Dungeon sliced their way through the drab cement walls.

Cell Block D was where the chronic hard cases wound up, in a slightly larger cell, isolated, segregated, some cut off even from light. Too much dungeon led to too many medical bills, too many unanswered questions by the newspapers. So men already cracked but not broken, not yet, were confined twenty-four hours a day, every day, alone, unheard, forgotten. Alone even in the exercise yard, where for an hour they learned to walk again.

The average cell, the ones on Cell Blocks B and C, held a cold-water sink, a cot, and a toilet.

Rewards for good behavior.

There'd been countless hunger strikes, prisoners trying to win some margin of life for themselves, find a reason to resist or die in the attempt. Since 1934, four escape attempts, last year's the latest, when Doc Barker was shot down and William Martin, Rufus McCain, and Henri Young surrendered to continued existence and punishment in the hole.

Only Theodore Cole and Ralph Roe offered hope to any would-be escape artists. They patiently filed through iron bars in the prison shop, work detail, each shaving a step closer to freedom and the tantalizing dream that lay just out of reach.

On December 16th, 1937, they escaped in a fog thick enough to blind the watchtower bulls, jumping in the icy water and strong currents, taking their chances on the leopard sharks and the unforgiving Bay.

Warden Johnston was "certain" they drowned.

Hoover wasn't.

Cole and Roe were still listed as the top two men on his most-wanted list. Just last month, a cabdriver claimed to see them in Oklahoma. And so the dream held for the other prisoners, news from the outside forbidden but somehow leaking under the sweating cement and through the iron bars, for the men on C and B and especially D, the men who'd forgotten what it meant to be men, the ones chained in an underground parlor straight out of the Spanish Inquisition or the ones thrown in the hole for a knife fight.

It was self-defense, Mr. Warden, sir, he tried to kill me . . .

Alcatraz justice—prison justice—always so impartial.

Miranda shut the giant bound book of *Examiner* newspapers, the morgue empty except for Rusty, the old beat man from before the Quake and Fire, gently snoring on a stool, his green felt fedora pulled halfway down his face.

Al Capone, Machine Gun Kelly, Barker . . . some of these men were murderers, gangsters, the kind she'd dealt with on the Eddie Takahashi case, the kind she'd met while looking for the man who killed Pandora Blake.

Martini would have made a home on the Rock if she hadn't blown his brains out back in February. And Mickey Cohen, the man she owed a favor to . . . maybe one day he'd be here, too.

It was difficult to feel sympathy. To feel anything.

My object all sublime, I shall achieve in time—to let the punishment fit the crime . . .

Problem is, some of them didn't fit the mold. Bank robbers like Roy Gardner, who actually went out of his way not to hurt anybody. Men who'd started life on the rough side and saw it worsen, Depression sinking them below the law. Cretzer and Kyle weren't public enemies because they left a swath of corpses behind them, but because they robbed banks . . . a far worse crime to the government.

Hell, the West Virginia farm boy with twelve brothers and sisters and no food on the fucking table didn't stop to think about right and wrong or how Wall Street had shuttered the savings and loan and the only factory in town . . . he only thought about how to survive.

And still . . . he could wind up in Alcatraz.

No wonder they tried, dreamed, fantasized about getting out, the only life spark left, the only motivation for anything. Escape was motivation enough, not just escape from the island, pipe dream of the bold, but escape from the endless, biblical punishment.

Escape from pain, escape from threat, escape from fear.

And reading between the lines—between the splattered ink on Hearst's yellow pages and the stories told and exaggerated by prisoners, both current and ex-, the system could be gamed.

Escape of the less notorious kind—and hell, maybe even actual exeunts, an *exitus ex isola*—could be arranged.

Guards could be bought.

Maybe even wardens.

Warden Johnston, dubbed "Old Pussyfoot" or "Old Saltwater" by the prisoners, was, like the wardens in Leavenworth and Atlanta, a political appointee. His associate warden, Edward Miller, had been brought on in '37, and, according to vague insinuations in various articles, was the real sadist. He'd begun his career as a correctional officer and his tactics soon earned him a promotion.

Johnston was the political face of the island. Miller's was the one the men saw in their nightmares.

Miranda stood up and stretched her legs. She stood in the *Examiner* morgue, looking down at the table still covered in papers, and shivered.

The threads were there, waiting for a Howard Carter Smith or someone else brave enough or smart enough to tie them together.

Collusion. Bribery. Scandal.

Plenty of motivation for theft . . . or murder.

Twenty

*

The phone was ringing. Miranda fumbled the key, swore under her breath, and finally pushed the door open, racing to the desk before the bells stopped shaking.

Her bag fell on the smooth black surface with a thud, gloved fingers grasping at the phone.

"Miranda Cor—"

The breath on the other side was noisy, uneven.

"Don't fuckin' call me here—ever. You lose my job for me, you pay for it, I promise you."

Nervous, cowardly braggadocio, delivered in a movie-tough monotone that would make George Raft proud.

Miranda lowered herself into the desk chair, lips stretched taut in a grim smile.

"Gee, George, and here I thought we were friends. Unfortunately, I don't have a way of contacting you in a hurry other than phoning that overpriced clip joint you work for—which, by the way, I'm sure will still retain your services, since you've probably threatened to reveal their list of clients to the papers if they don't."

If Blankenship was planning to blackmail his ex-bosses, he was probably milking his present ones, too . . .

"You—you goddamn bitch—"

Supposition confirmed.

"Save it. You're not out of the water with the murder, not yet—"

"What the hell you talking about? The coppers can't crack my alibi—"

"They'll still try. And trying will bring results and motive, and motive will bring interviews with your employers, past and present. Nobody likes a squealing little pig, George, or worse yet, one who threatens to squeal—not the bulls on Alcatraz, not the San Francisco cops. Besides, I thought you wanted out of Greer. Is the job really worth it?"

One Mississippi, Two Mississippi. His breath was raspier, more panicked.

"Now—wait a minute—I ain't—I ain't no squealer. And I don't wanna see Louise no more, you hear me? I jus' wanna be left alone. Maybe get a new start somewheres else . . . yeah, that's the ticket. Go down south, maybe, they got plenty of these joints in LA . . ."

"No traveling just yet. They're watching you. You run now, they'll put the finger on you, forget the alibi. No, your only chance to shake it—shake them— is me. You work with me, tell me what you know about Smith's book, about why you wanted it and what leverage it gave you—then, and only then, will you be in the clear."

He sputtered some more, but it sounded empty and hollow.

"You? You ain't nothin' but a freak, some lady peeper who thinks she's a tough guy. I don't need you or nobody. I'll take my chances with the fuckin' coppers—"

Miranda hunched over the desk, hand clenching the phone tight, unlit stick between two fingers.

"Listen, asshole, and listen up fast. I know you ratted out Louise and probably got slid a few sawbucks from the newshounds. I know you threatened Greer with whatever information you've scrounged up, just like you were gonna do to the high-ups at Alcatraz. I don't really give a fuck about your penchant for blackmail, but the cops will. That nice little conversation you had about Louise and her family put me, my client, and my license in jeopardy, and that means I'm on your goddamn tail, George, and I promise you—you don't want me there. So you either work with me or against me, and if you wanna stay out of fucking stir—you work with me."

A high-pitched whine rose in volume and wheezed through the receiver. George Blankenship was done.

"Whaddya want? I told you everything before—"

"No, you didn't. You kept quiet about the book because I let it drop and you thought there was an off-chance Louise did manage to steal it and you'd be able

to use it eventually. That didn't happen. Louise doesn't have it—the killer does. So I want the whole skinny, George—all the dope. What she told you about the book, how you were gonna use the information, what was in it for you."

"Don't the goddamn writer know what's in the goddamn book? Why do I gotta—"

"Because you don't wanna wind up living with the men you bullied on Alacatraz and because I fucking said so. Meet me after work. Eight o'clock, my office, Monadnock Building, fourth floor. And George . . . don't be late."

Miranda dropped the handset into the cradle.

She wiped her hands on her skirt and lit a cigarette, but the bad taste lingered.

*

She was rereading notes in the Big Chief when the redhead kid from downstairs knocked timidly on the door, bearing Fisher's promised report on Alexander. Miranda gave him two bits and patted him on the shoulder, pushing the door closed and tearing open the brown paper.

Nothing too outré in Alexander's pockets.

Loose change—what the rich call seventy-eight bucks in folding money—a Greer Sanitarium card, a gold-plated cigarette case, monogrammed, with brown-tipped cigarettes—probably French—inside, a small pocketknife, used for cutting cigars.

Miranda frowned. The business card from a doctor in the Flood building rang a bell. Where the hell had she seen that name, Dr. Arthur H. White?

The Flood housed a lot of doctors, some quacks, some frauds, mostly doing low-end business, not the kind that Alexander would normally visit. Was White an alienist, maybe the one who was treating Sylvia?

She pulled the giant Pacific Telephone and Telegraph book toward her, rifling through the pages until she found the P's. MDs, Ear, Nose and Throat, Eye, Feminine Hygiene . . . and there it was, plastered under Genito-Urinary and Chronic Disease, large square ad for Arthur H. White, 875 Market Street, Suite 1005, phone SUtter 1170.

Miranda looked up, remembering where she'd seen him, where she'd heard about him.

Arthur H. White specialized in syphilis.

He'd been Dianne's quack of choice, if the escorts on payroll, men or women,

ever came down with symptoms. Dianne would speak in funereal tones, her petticoats rustling, the velvet on the walls weeping in contrition, the dogs in the English hunting scenes howling mournfully at the moon.

"French gout," she'd whisper, curls nodding, as she sipped the red wine. "French gout. Best to see Dr. White, my dear, and you'll be back to good health in no time. I hope you've saved like I told you to . . . he isn't cheap."

Syphilis wasn't the clap, uncomfortable and painful but rarely fatal. Hell, some of the girls didn't realize they had gonorrhea until Dianne made them take the twice yearly physical. Syphilis would destroy your mind and eventually your body, and even if you caught it in time to save your life, you could come out a cripple and a monster, pustules covering your misshapen body, features twisted into a nightmare form.

Six months or more of painful shots, but at least it was successfully treated, thanks to Dr. Erlich and his magic bullet. Whether Dr. White knew what the hell he was doing or whether he was selling horse piss and arsenic as a cure-all, Miranda had no idea. Men or women, they never returned to Dianne after they saw Dr. White, and no one spoke of the sufferers ever after.

Unlike Lot's wife, Dianne Laroche never looked back.

Miranda wrinkled her brow, trying to remember the names of the two women and the single man, the whispers that floated in the acrid, stale air of 44 Grant Street, Dianne's insistence on rubbers, the creased, soiled card with ARTHUR H. WHITE in embossed black letters.

Dr. Arthur H. White.

Was Niles Alexander syphilitic?

She shook her head. Didn't make sense, not anymore, not with a steady mistress like Bunny and a former fleet of secretaries. The middle-aged Alexander yearned more for fame and wealth and respectability than the fantasy titillation of forbidden sex.

Not like his wastrel son . . .

Miranda eyes opened wide and she scrawled "JERRY—SYPHILLIS? DR. WHITE? TREATMENTS AT HOME??" on the Big Chief pad.

Maybe—maybe Jerry stayed at his parents when he had the treatments from White. Maybe they wanted to make sure he was keeping at them, not brushing off the disease like some kind of cold.

God knows he had plenty of chances to acquire it, to spread it around. Shit, maybe that's why he was targeting Louise of late, maybe he knew his days of late-night parties at Sally Stanford were over, no more roughing up girls he

picked up at the Wharf. Maybe he was looking for new and unused, or at least unabused.

She turned to the last page of the report. Alexander kept a couple of old jujus in his desk and a silver-plated flask, about a quarter filled with gin. The flask came out clean, no poison, but in his overcoat pocket was a small, cracked bottle of Booth's gin.

There were traces of cyanide in the bottle and glass shards in the carpet.

Miranda nodded, staring through the arabesques of smoke from the forgotten cigarette perched on the ashtray.

Someone planned to poison him. Someone who brought in a bottle of gin—odds are the publisher's favorite—and was surprised before he could transfer the poisoned gin into Niles' monogrammed desk flask.

The killer must've planted the poison in Louise's desk before entering Alexander's office, then was caught, maybe in the process of stealing the manuscript—Alexander returned sooner than anticipated—and tried to bluff his way out. Hit Niles, threw the gin at him.

A struggle.

An improvisation.

Something large and weighty, waiting on the desk.

Then he—or she—dragged Alexander's body to the chair, picked up the bottle of drugged gin from the floor—where it had cracked, soaking the rug fibers—and put it in the publisher's pocket.

Maybe.

She picked up the stick, deep inhale.

She couldn't see, not quite yet.

But the shapes were getting clearer.

*

A sharp rap on the door made her start. She pulled open the front desk drawer and placed her hand over the .32.

Raised her voice. "Come in."

Roger Roscoe pushed open the door, dark features twisted in deep lines.

"Miss Corbie. May I come in? I'd like to speak with you."

No actor's gift of charm today, no writer's wit or flattery. He looked worn, his skin pasty, suit rumpled and askew.

Goddamn it—he'd found out about her visit to Greer.

"No more 'Miranda,' Roger? No more friendly chats?"

"No, I—well, what the hell—why should I prevaricate? I came in here to tell you to leave Sylvia Alexander alone. I mean it."

He sat down suddenly in one of the wooden chairs.

Roger's face was haggard, dissipated, as though he'd been staying up too late and drinking too much. He'd attempted to hide the effects—there were traces of what looked like makeup under his eyes, vanity preserved—but his white shirt, navy tie, and gray jacket were wrinkled and dotted with bits of lint. His presence, his palpable charm, the way he spoke, the way he formed words . . . all of it was off.

Maybe the strain of Alexander's murder, of Sylvia's sudden collapse.

Maybe something else.

Snowbird, maybe? Was that how he bonded with Sylvia?

"I'm sorry you feel that way. But here's a suggestion: You don't interfere with my job and I won't tell you to stop using adverbs. Deal?"

"Your 'job,' Miss Corbie, was, as I understand it, to investigate who the horrible person was who tried to harm Louise. What with Niles' murder—may whoever killed him rot in hell—and Louise's current, er, situation—it seems to me that you no longer have a job at all."

Her voice was silky. "How nice of you to worry about my employment. But you needn't bother. Until I find out who was trying to murder Louise—whether or not the attempts had anything to do with Alexander—she's still my client."

"Even if she's in jail?"

He snapped the words out like a small dog with a vicious bite.

"I see you've read the papers. Words, words, words, Mr. Roscoe. Here's the skinny: Louise is my client. Period. Seeing Sylvia was part of what I have to do to protect my client—and discover the truth."

He was gripping the brim of his derby hard enough to warp it. "But I assure you—it wasn't Sylvia. She had nothing to do with—with any of this. She is a woman wronged, a woman hurt, and I ask you—no, I beg you—please let her be, let her find some peace!"

Urgency and drama, the throb and lilt worthy of a Barrymore. Reminded her of dear old pater, reciting Shakespeare and clutching a bottle of rye, *how sharper than a serpent's tooth* . . .

Miranda leaned back in her chair, eyes on the author.

"Whatever else she may be, Mrs. Alexander is a woman with information—information that could help find her husband's murderer. Maybe even whoever tried to kill Louise, if they're not one and the same."

"She knows nothing, Miss Corbie—Miranda—listen, I—Sylvia isn't well, surely you see that—saw that. She's staying an extra week at Greer now, and I believe it's because of that stunt you pulled. I just came from there—stayed with her for a few hours until she calmed down again. I'm behind on my novel— terribly behind—but Sylvia comes first. 'To be wise, and love, exceeds men's might,' as the Bard says, and I'm afraid I've exceeded mine. I'm at the end of my rope."

Miranda frowned. "Mrs. Alexander seemed better when I left, not worse—"

"You don't know the depths of her illness. I understand Louise is your client but Sylvia needs your help, too, she's a fragile, fragile woman, a frail thing and I—I love her. Talking to her about Niles will only do her more harm. I implore you again—please—at least wait a few days. It won't harm Louise's chances and it might save Sylvia. Wait until she's out of the sanitarium."

"I may not have that luxury. And if I don't, neither will the bulls."

Roscoe rose from the chair, long fingers still mangling the brim of his hat.

"Please. I'll answer any questions, do whatever I can to help you, and of course I've told the police the same thing. Importuning them will do no good, but if at least you could allow Sylvia the peace she needs . . . she's insisted on attending Niles' memorial and then she's going straight back to Greer. And I promise you—as soon as she's out and back home, you can have all your answers, anytime you wish."

Miranda studied the tall, thin man, the lines around his eyes and the creases in his suit.

"All right, Mr. Roscoe. Maybe I'll get a break before then. I don't have much more time to give this as it is."

He sank back in the hard wooden seat, tension relaxed, body less brittle. Gave her a weak smile.

"Nor I. My own mystery is in a wretched state. I left my protagonist in a compromising position and now I can't figure out how to get out of it."

She raised her eyebrows. "Does that happen often?"

"More often than you'd think. Characters tend to take on lives of their own."

Another rap on the door—not as sharp, but heavy and loud—made Roger jump. He looked backward toward the shadow in the hallway, obscured by the mottled glass, then turned to Miranda.

"I should go. You have a client. I was serious about what I said—I'll help you in any way I can. Please call on me."

Miranda nodded. "Thanks. I'll do that."

Roger crammed the hat on his head and tipped it hurriedly. Opened her office door and nodded at Rick, who looked surprised.

"Just leaving, old man. She's all yours."

Roger squeezed by him, and Rick tentatively stepped into the office.

Miranda was already out from behind the desk.

His brown hair was short and he looked taller in the uniform, more confident.

More muscular.

Less like Rick.

She met the blue eyes. He smiled, crinkly corners. She took a step toward him, he took one toward her, a sudden dance.

To her surprise, she found herself kissing him.

His body was leaner, stronger, but his hands were still gentle, his posture straight.

It took her a second to realize that he wasn't kissing her back.

She stepped backward, turned her face away. They spoke at the same time.

"Sorry, I guess it's the uniform—"

"Miranda, I'm—God, I've missed you—"

She felt herself flushing and slowly, reluctantly, raised her eyes to his. Goddamn it, why was this so hard? And what the hell had she done—she wasn't Bette fucking Davis, saying good-bye to a man she loved, no Hollywood scene, just a friend, a good friend, maybe her best friend, a man she cared about and yes, loved, like the friend he'd always been.

And still was.

She took him in again, smiled with pride. Then the smile faded.

"Rick—is it 3:30? My watch stopped and I haven't been paying attention to the goddamn church bells . . ."

He glanced at his wristwatch. "3:42. The taxi took a wrong turn."

"Jesus."

Miranda ran back to her desk.

"Bunny? Miranda. Did Louise—she didn't? No word? No, I assumed . . . yeah. Right away. I'll call you."

She looked up at Rick. "I've gotta go. My client may be in trouble."

He was already on his way to the door. "I'll help, whatever you need."

Miranda grabbed her purse and the cigarette case holding the Baby Browning from her desk.

"A fast taxi yesterday."

She shut the door and locked it behind her, running to the elevator.

Goddamn it.

Where the hell was Louise?

*

Miranda threw a dollar at the grizzled driver, barely glancing up at the Glenarm Apartments, 1140 Sutter.

Four stories, and if she remembered correctly, Louise was on the third floor.

Rick held her elbow while they ran up the few steps to the buzzers and boxes.

Adkins, Waller, O'Shaughnessy . . .

#304—Crowley.

Her gloved finger hit the button with force, held it down for three seconds, an anemic whine droning through the main door.

No answer.

Miranda clenched her jaw, face white. "Goddamn it . . ."

She hit it again, holding down the motor until it started to sputter and a heavyset woman covered in flour threw open a second-story window.

"Lady—take a hint—your party ain't in—"

Click.

Door unlocked. Someone else, tired of the noise, buzzed them in.

Miranda and Rick squeezed through the door into a respectably dilapidated foyer.

No elevator.

She turned to Rick. "Let's go."

They raced up the three flights, feet pounding against the worn brown carpet, Rick outpacing Miranda.

"Knock if you get there first—I don't know what we'll find."

She was three steps behind him when he banged hard on #304, a corner room on the narrow third-floor landing.

No answer. One of the doors behind them opened with an audible crack.

Miranda grabbed Rick by the arm. "Can you break it down?"

"I can try."

He lowered his right shoulder and threw himself at the door. It creaked, some splintering, but held. An old lady in faded gingham crawled out from behind #308, stood in the hallway with her hands folded.

Rick tried again. This time the wood shuddered.

Miranda turned to the old woman. "Call the Super and then call the police—hurry!"

"You ain't the police then? You ain't got no right—"

Third attempt, and this time the hinges gave, one of the panels splintering off.

A sickly sweet odor, like rotten garlic, wafted into the hallway, and the old lady immediately shut her mouth, eyes wide, and scurried back inside.

Miranda held her hands to her face, motioned at Rick. He swallowed a deep gulp of air and ran into the apartment, Miranda close behind.

Louise.

On the Murphy bed, next to a closed window, still in a nightgown, white and cold.

From the small kitchen to the left of the bed, a soft hiss and no flame.

Gas.

Act Four

✳

The Rewrite

"Take pains. Be perfect."
—William Shakespeare
A Midsummer Night's Dream, Act I, scene ii

Twenty-One

*

Rick made a face like a blowfish, exhaled, and picked up the secretary in his arms, while Miranda held her gloved hand over her mouth and ran to the small kitchen area, trying to shut off the gas valve connected to the small, two-burner cooktop. The pilot light was off, the knob on the burner turned slightly on.

Rick grunted at her, jerking his head toward the open door, Louise prone against his chest. Miranda nodded, twisting the burner knob to the off position and struggled again with the gas valve, her hands slipping against the black painted handle. No movement, and the gas was still softly hissing.

She gave up, turning toward the small window sash, and clawed at the wood, grimy and caked with oil splatters and dust, desperate to take a breath, lungs tight and full in her chest. Not strong enough, goddamn it, you're a good soldier, Randy, a good soldier . . .

One last look, a stumble through the one-room apartment, searching for anything out of the ordinary.

There.

On Louise's small occasional table that doubled as a nightstand.

A note scrawled in black pencil, heavy lines.

She picked it up by the corner, lungs almost bursting, and finally rushed out to the landing rail, bending over it and gasping for air.

A balding man in a sleeveless T-shirt, mouth and nose wrapped in a bath towel and holding a wrench, was running up the steps. At the end of the hall, on the floor, with the old lady and a redheaded boy standing over her, was Louise.

Still out of breath, Miranda rushed past the bald man as he plowed toward the apartment. Rick was crouched beside the secretary. He slapped her face lightly, then slapped her again.

"Is she dead?"

"Not yet."

"Land's sakes. She was such a nice girl. But them landlords ain't fixin' things like they was before they sold the building last year. I ain't surprised, no sir, not surprised at all."

The old lady shook her head, turned toward the freckled kid beside her. "Alfie, you go on and tell people to open their windows and air this floor out. Can't have no soup on til we get this gas cleared out. Mr. Foster's done shut it off already."

She nodded toward Louise's apartment. The man in the T-shirt—now damp with sweat and oil—was wiping his forehead with his arm, and walking toward them in an uneven line.

"Aw, Grams, do I gotta?"

She gave the boy a prod with her foot. "I said so, di'nt I?"

Miranda knelt by Louise and dug for her compact. She held it up to the secretary's mouth. A light fog formed very slowly.

"At least she's alive."

Miranda didn't look up at Rick.

"No thanks to me. I should've met her here this morning, escorted her to work."

He lowered a strong hand and pulled her off the ground by the elbow. "Quit beating yourself up, Miranda. I'm sure you did everything you could."

The superintendent—Foster—was staring down at Louise, incredulity twisting his features into a clown mask, as he looked from the blonde to Rick and Miranda.

"I got it off. The pipe was jammed—with this."

His calloused palm held a three-inch bolt.

Miranda gazed at the piece of metal, now twisted and bent, flat against the rough, greasy hands of the maintenance man. She jammed her hand in her coat pocket and pulled out the note she'd found, handwritten and scrawled on a piece of typing paper. Rick read it over her shoulder.

It was my fault Mr. Alexander was killed. I couldn't live with the shame anymore. May God help my sister.

Sirens wailed outside, and heavy feet ran up the stairs.

*

The ambulance took Louise to Children's Hospital on Miranda's insistence, a quick drive to 3700 California. Miranda paid a taxi driver to stay close behind. He was a young man, previously bored, now wide-eyed at the thought of a crime occurring at the Glenarm Apartments, and eager to be in on the game.

Their destination was a graceful brick building that looked more like a university or a convent than a hospital, Romanesque arches forming shadowed cloisters set back from the street. Rick helped her out of the cab.

She stared up at the colonnades stretching out on either side of the entrance.

"You need me to stick around, lady? Maybe take you somewheres else?"

She shook her head, handed him a dollar tip, and the cabbie pulled away from the curb in slow motion, reluctant to go back to canvassing for drunks outside Bimbo's and The Pink Rat. Rick took her by the elbow.

"Look, Miranda—don't blame yourself. Hell, I don't know the particulars and I don't have to. I do know you—and I know you've done everything possible, and probably some things that aren't, in order to protect this girl. So quit beating yourself up, OK?"

She looked up into his eyes, the blue anxious and supportive with a new kind of strength.

Miranda dropped the lit Chesterfield stub on the pavement and crushed it until the tobacco splintered, then started walking toward the entrance.

*

An hour later, she and Rick were still pacing the waiting room, waiting for the cops to arrive with Thelma, waiting for Louise to wake up.

Miranda responded to his questions but offered little else. No sense involving him more than he was already, he was about to cross the goddamn country for the goddamn army, after all, no more rat-tat-tat typewriters and late-night deadlines, no more lunches at John's Grill, no more hot dogs at Kezar, no more Rick.

No more San Francisco, either, her home, her life. She was heading to war, a fucking Bundle for Britain, hoping to save her mother when she couldn't save her client.

Rick and Miranda, Rick and Miranda. Rick and Miranda and Johnny, three blind mice, see how they run . . .

Rick stood by like a good soldier, stood straight and tall, stoic and calm. Supportive, protective. Even patient. She wondered what the hell the army had done to Rick Sanders, the newshawk with the broken-brim Champ fedora and a wisecrack for every occasion. The man with the crinkly blue eyes and the mustard-stained shirts.

The man who loved her . . . or used to.

Then Gonzales walked in the waiting room.

His smile was bright, white, and gleaming, skin just as tan, body just as lithe. An almost imperceptible jump when he looked from her to Rick, and back again.

Miranda blew a stream of smoke from her mouth, and strode forward to greet him.

"Fisher can't make it?"

"No, he will have his hands full questioning Mr. Smith—"

"Smith's finally here? When can I see him? You doing anything to protect him?"

His eyes darted to Rick and back again, strangely hesitant in his tailored suit and country club tie, the cut impeccable, hair perfectly oiled and strong chin with just a hint of stubble.

"You will have to ask Lieutenant Fisher. He was finishing the initial interview with Mr. Smith when I left and Mrs. Kyle was next. Someone will drive her here when he is through. She's very worried about her sister."

"And I'm worried about Miranda."

Rick moved to stand next to her, ramrod straight, posture making him the police inspector's equal in height. Gonzales' brown eyes glanced at him again, this time flashing annoyance, his voice still smooth.

"Ah, Mr. Sanders—"

"Sergeant Sanders now."

"Yes, of course. Miranda—Miss Corbie—mentioned that you had joined the army. Congratulations."

Rick inclined his head. "Thank you, Inspector. Just a few days' furlough before I head to Washington, D.C."

Gonzales raised an eyebrow. "You're leaving San Francisco, then?"

Miranda dropped the cigarette in the floor tray and said: "We don't have time for the goddamn social hour. Can you get this to Fisher and the lab as soon as possible?"

She held up the suicide note from Louise's apartment by one corner, hands still gloved.

Gonzales pulled out his white display handkerchief and plucked it from her, lifting it so that the fluorescent light shone through.

"This is the evidence you telephoned us about? You know, you should have left it in place—"

Rick's tone was light. "Kind of hard to mind the p's and q's when you're trying to save a woman's life and not blow up an apartment building."

Another flash from Gonzales as he lowered the paper, brown eyes trained on Rick.

"Yes, of course. I'm sure no real harm was done." He turned back to Miranda. "You were wearing gloves?"

"Still am. Don't bother looking up the watermark. The paper is from Louise's own desk at work. I recognized the mark and the texture. It's what they use at Alexander Publishing for correspondence purposes, just torn off a regular sheet."

The tall cop studied it. "Is this Louise Crowley's handwriting?"

She shook her head. "No. I don't even know if we're supposed to think so."

"I'm not sure I understand what you mean."

He smelled of leather and French cigarettes, with a hint of oakmoss, standing there, looking at her, eyes holding hers a fraction too long.

She quickly turned to Rick. "Can I bum a stick?"

"Of course, Miri."

First time he'd used his old nickname for her. No "Randy," not now, not this new Rick, the military, disciplined Rick with the shined shoes and the short hair and the new confidence. He'd lost the messy hat and the late-night bags under his eyes along with the half-Irish bullshit brogue and the looks of desperate longing, the stares, the half smiles that he'd worn since New York when she was Johnny's girl, Johnny's girl, never Rick's . . .

Gonzales waited while Rick lit the Lucky. The end of the stick glowed red and Miranda pointed it for emphasis.

"Look, Inspector. This was no suicide. Somebody tried to kill Louise Crowley—somebody apparently tied in with her sister and maybe the Cretzer-Kyle gang. At least that's what it looks like. And if they find out they failed, they'll try again, and go after Smith, too—can't you put a uniform on her door, get them both some protection?"

His long fingers absentmindedly stroked the thin mustache. "There has been no report of any strangers entering the apartment building—"

"Which proves nothing. She's my client, for God's sake—and she came to me because she was afraid someone was trying to kill her, and now they've almost succeeded. Jesus Christ, Gonzales, I just spoke with her this morning! She was tired, maybe even dejected—but she sure as hell wasn't going to kill herself."

The inspector read the note again, frowning, holding it by one corner.

"She was under suspicion, Miranda—we brought her in yesterday, after all, and then her name was in the paper. People under such circumstances often show a marked change in behavior, and that could explain the handwriting . . ."

Miranda shook her head. "That note isn't from Louise—it's written on her paper, she's probably got reams of it at home, plus I'm sure whoever did this to her is the same party responsible for Alexander's murder and the other attempts on her life—all of which center on Alexander Publishing—so no surprises there. But they didn't try too hard or have the time to make it look like her hand or even a woman's. And it was left in plain sight, almost like a warning. Besides, if Louise were the suicidal type, why come to me in the first place? Why tell me she was going in to work this afternoon? And she wouldn't have jammed that damn valve."

Gonzales smiled at her. "Unless she didn't want to risk changing her mind. As for suicide, if Miss Crowley was involved in Alexander's murder—we found the cyanide in her desk, remember, even though her alibi has thus far held—she may have been overwhelmed by guilt."

Rick, uncharacteristically quiet, finally gave an unmilitary-like snort.

"Pigs may fly someday, too, Gonzales. That doesn't mean we'll live to see it."

Miranda looked up at the tall cop, eyes challenging his. "I'm not sure of much, but I'll stake my license on the fact that Louise Crowley did not try to kill herself. Who the hell is going to blow out a pilot light to commit suicide? Sure, the burner was turned on a little, but still—too long a wait. No, this is a setup, Gonzales, and the killer is trying to cover his tracks. He didn't know one of the windows was cracked open, figured an eight- or nine-hour sleep would kill Louise off. The only question is where Kyle, Cretzer, and fucking Alcatraz come in."

Silence. Rick was still flushed a light pink, eyes flicking between Miranda and Gonzales. The inspector was staring at the Formica floor. He raised his face to Miranda, muscles taut against his cheekbones, eyes sober. He nodded.

"I believe you. Others may not. We are waiting to see if her prints were found on the valve."

"They won't find any prints other than the maintenance man's."

"Perhaps. That would lend credence to your theory."

Another silence. An ambulance wailed outside and Miranda started, eyes jumping toward the double doors they'd wheeled Louise through over an hour earlier.

Gonzales cleared his throat. "Miranda, I know you wish to stay here and wait for Miss Crowley to regain consciousness—"

"I figure Fisher sent you here, Gonzales, and I figure why. I'll go downtown. All I ask is that you put a man with a gun on Louise's door. She'll wake up—she's got to wake up—and when she does, she'll know something, anything, that will help us catch this sonofabitch. I've got some ideas I can run by Fisher, but right now it's imperative that you keep Louise safe and the goddamn reporters out."

"Hey! We're not so bad."

She turned to Rick, half a smile. "Some of you, anyway."

Gonzales nodded and stepped toward the door. "I will call a guard for Miss Crowley, then drive you to the station." His eyes barely flickered over the man in uniform. "You too, Mr. Sanders, if you wish."

Rick smiled, teeth showing. "Sergeant Sanders. Thanks, Inspector."

Miranda twisted the Lucky in the floor ashtray, knocking more ash to the floor.

"You still coming, Rick?"

He stood next to her, took her by the elbow.

"Hell, yes."

For a second she saw the old Rick, the old look, before it was subsumed in tight-jawed discipline and military posture, dissolved like the sun on a foggy day or the last, magic light on Treasure Island.

She studied him. Her tone was light.

"Sorry about our dinner date."

"It's not over til it's over. And we've got time."

He smiled at her, secure, confident, content.

Miranda shivered as though a cold wind blew through the room, and Gonzales poked his head through the door, summoning them to the exit.

Twenty-Two

*

Five years dropped from Meyer's face when she walked through the doors of the Hall of Justice, Rick beside her. The attorney shook his hand vigorously, wrinkles stretched in a wide smile.

"Congratulations, my boy, congratulations. Delighted to see you again."

"You as well, Mr. Bialik. I've got a couple of days' furlough before my transfer—thought I'd spend what time I could with Miranda."

The portly attorney wrinkled his brow. "Transfer? But you're not leaving us, I hope?"

Miranda interrupted, eyes scanning the crowded hallway, thick with uniformed cops and the usual assortment of shoplifters, B-girls, and juju dealers.

"He's headed for D.C., Meyer. Strictly here for auld lang syne. Where the hell is Fisher? Gonzales said he'd meet us."

Meyer looked from one to the other, smile faded, and cleared his throat.

"Still questioning Mrs. Thelma Kyle, I'm afraid. We can wait in here." He stepped toward an unmarked door across the hall. "I'm sure the good inspector will find us as soon as he is ready."

Miniscule window on the door meant interrogation room, small and sparsely furnished, five cheap chairs and a wooden table, scarred and pitted with black cigarette burns from too many late-night questions and not many satisfactory answers.

A chunky, thin-haired man sprawled in the corner chair, legs spread out in dungarees and new Florsheim loafers, shirt like a mechanic, no tie. His head was tilted back against the wall, mouth open in a rumbling snore.

Smith.

Miranda silently motioned for Rick and Meyer to sit across the room from the author and lowered herself into the wobbly wooden chair closest to him. Then, very deliberately, she clapped her hands.

Smith's eyes popped open and he jerked back, head banging against the wall.

"So good of you to drive up here, Mr. Smith. Not like anything has happened to interrupt your fishing trip—just the theft of your book, the murder of your publisher, and the near-murder of your publisher's secretary."

The stocky writer yanked himself into an upright posture, hands smoothing his shirt and pants, eyes blinking. Rubbed his nose and looked sharply at Rick, Meyer, and back to Miranda.

His voice was thick, like a mouthful of marbles.

"You that dame private eye, right? Corben or Karp or something?"

"Corbie. Miranda Corbie. Louise Crowley hired me."

He grunted. "Niles pointed you out at the Sky Room party." He cleared his throat, stretching his thick eyebrows in a grimace, and finally looked awake. "Something happen to Louise, too?"

"Didn't they tell you?"

Smith snorted. "They didn't tell me anything. Asked me five questions for five minutes, then stuck me in a damn room. I've been waiting to talk to some inspector or lieutenant or whatever they call themselves, drove straight here from Monterey this morning. What's happened?"

Rick said: "Someone tried to kill Louise Crowley, that's what's happened." He walked over to Miranda and stood beside her.

Smith peered up at him. "Who the hell are you? And what's the army got to do with anything?"

"He's the man who saved Louise's life. And a friend of mine." Miranda glanced up at Rick. "Look, Smith, this is complicated, but everything—the theft of your manuscript, Niles' murder, the attempts on Louise's life—the reason she hired me in the first place—all of it points back to your Alcatraz book. The bulls are eager to talk to you and so am I. What the hell's in it?"

His brown eyes were shrewd, voice suddenly clear. He pointed at Meyer, who was smiling benevolently, eyes half-closed, hands folded in his lap.

"That your lawyer?"

Miranda looked back at Meyer in surprise. "Yes, but that has nothing to do with—"

Smith shook his head, thin hair plastered to his skull. "Uh-uh. I'm not talking to anyone, much less a peeper, until I see my own attorney. Sonofabitch is in court all day down in Palo Alto, and my worthless agent—they're all worthless—is on holiday at a goddamn dude ranch in Arizona, but as soon as the attorney gets here the coppers can go hang. If someone murdered Niles to steal my book, then it's worth something. And before I discuss what was in it, I want some protection—financial protection. Protection for my investment."

Miranda stared at him. Rick made a disgusted noise, and sat down in another chair. Meyer cleared his throat.

"Mind you, Mr. Smith, I'm not an intellectual property specialist, but unless you have another copy of the manuscript—or can find the one that was stolen—there is no investment to protect."

Smith looked at him stonily.

"The investment is here." He tapped his forehead. "Whether or not the cops find the final draft. I can always rewrite it. I've got a memory like fucking Nestor."

Rick spoke sharply. "I don't know who Nestor is, but I hope he remembered his manners better than you do, Smith."

Smith shrugged and patted his shirt for cigarettes, finally locating a half-empty pack of Pall Malls.

"Miss Peeper here strikes me as a woman who understands English."

Miranda's mouth curved into a tight-lipped smile.

"Oh, I understand English, Smith—even the ugly patois you make of it. For the record, I don't think academic pretension mixes very well with common-man slang, so I suggest sticking to one or the other. Nestor may have been the oldest Greek leader in the *Iliad,* but he was also a conceited hack."

Smith raised his eyebrows while he lit a stick. "Well, what do you know? A female shamus who knows Homer. Wonders never cease."

Miranda bent forward, eyes trained on his face. "You think so? Here's another one for you: a blue-blood pseudo-intellectual who slums with hoi polloi writing something about Alcatraz worth killing over. If you've got half the memory you brag about, Smith, then you won't have any trouble recalling what you wrote when the cops question you about it. And if you don't answer, then whether your lawyer gets out of court or not, whether your agent gets a saguaro cactus stuck up his ass, whether you can reconstruct your precious magnum opus and make a dime off it, you'll be held on an obstruction charge. Inspector Fisher may not wear Florsheim shoes and descend from the fucking *Mayflower,* but he's the man you'll see and right now he's out of patience. In fact, Smith, you should enjoy meeting him—he's a real man of the people."

His eyes bounced between Meyer, Rick, and Miranda, mouth tight-lipped and small. His fingers—thick with well-shaped, manicured nails—played with a matchbook from the Lodge Tavern.

"I'm not sure what sort of game you're playing, Corbie. And whatever you may think you know about me, know this: my books are mine, a part of me, and they represent a great deal of work, for which I demand and deserve compensation. That said, I will, of course, cooperate with the police."

Inspector Fisher's voice growled from the back of the room.

"I'm glad to hear it, Smith. I'll look forward to your cooperation in just a few minutes. Miss Corbie?"

He glanced at Miranda and motioned with his head for her to follow. Meyer and Rick stood up. The burly cop arched his eyebrows. "What is this, an entourage? I'm only borrowing her for a couple of minutes."

He turned his back and walked out the door. Meyer started to follow, and Miranda shook her head.

"Don't worry. If Fisher says a couple of minutes, it's nothing serious." She threw Rick an apologetic look. He shrugged.

"I'll see you when you're out, Miranda. I'll just keep Meyer and Smith here company."

The squat, thin-haired author looked up, eyes narrowed. Miranda stared down at him.

"Thanks. And Smith . . . I'll be in touch."

She gave the author another long look before following Meyer out the door.

"You get under Smith's skin or something, Miranda?"

"Let's just say I was wearing him down for you. He's got the bright idea that the stolen book is a valuable property—valuable enough to kill for—so he doesn't want to tell what was in it. Oh, and he won't say hello without his mouthpiece."

Fisher shoved the door to the squad room with extra force. "Five minutes alone in a cell with Big Louie and that bastard will be pissing his pants."

A woman sat in front of Fisher's desk. Slumped over, narrow shoulders hunched in a V as she stared at her lap. Dishwater blonde, hair hennaed into a reddish tint, in a dress that was expensive about three years ago, now worn-out and faded, hanging loose in all the wrong places.

Eyes wide and deep and blue, haunted by regrets.

Whether for actions or inactions, Miranda couldn't tell.

"Miss Corbie, this is Mrs. Kyle, Miss Crowley's sister. Mrs. Kyle, this is Miranda Corbie. She saved your sister's life today."

The cop's voice, as muscular as his body, was uncharacteristically quiet. There was kindness in it and sympathy, lining a deep well of exhaustion.

The woman looked ten or more years older than Louise, skin dry and pasty, as if the sun were a luxury she could no longer afford. Miranda remembered the newspaper article from this morning: Louise's sister was only twenty-seven.

The last few years hadn't been kind to Thelma Kyle.

Thelma raised her face—bone structure still delicate, cheek bones too sharp.

"I—I must get out to my sister—be with her when she wakes up—but I wanted to meet you, Miss Corbie. I know what you've done for Louise."

Miranda sat in the chair next to her, impulsively laying a hand on the other woman's arm.

"I'm sorry, Mrs. Kyle. I should've seen this coming."

The other woman's voice was quiet. "I don't think anyone could have done that."

"Mrs. Kyle, Louise didn't try to kill herself. Someone tried to kill her."

Fisher shifted in his chair. "Now, wait a minute, Miran— er, Miss Corbie. I brought you in here because Mrs. Kyle wanted to meet you before she left. You and I can go over any specifics after I deal with Smith."

"Inspector, Louise didn't write that note and you know it. They must've shown it to you, Mrs. Kyle—was it her handwriting?"

The dishwater blonde was hesitant.

"N-no, not anything like how she normally wrote . . ."

"But the other one was." Fisher's voice was tired. "We found another one."

Miranda gripped the edge of his desk, gloved fingers pressing hard against the wood.

"Where? Why didn't Gonzales tell me? What did it say? Let me see it—"

Fisher held up a hand. "Hang on, Miranda. Mrs. Kyle, we've got the car standing by if you'd like to get to the hospital . . ."

The woman's voice was low but firm. "I think—I think I'd like to hear what Miss Corbie has to say, Inspector. If you don't mind."

The cop looked from one to the other, tiny beads of sweat dotting his forehead. Thelma Kyle stared at her lap, rubbing her hands back and forth.

One Mississippi, Two Mississippi . . .

The inspector sighed, glowering at Miranda, and picked up the phone. She took out her cigarette case while he barked orders, lighting a stick and offering one to Thelma, who shook her head. Fisher let the phone drop with a clang and lit an Old Gold from the pack on his desk.

"All right, the evidence is on the way down. Now explain yourself."

"You didn't find any prints on the gas valve, did you?"

"No."

"Louise wasn't wearing gloves when we found her. You think it's plausible that she decides to kill herself, writes one note that looks like her writing, according to you, and another one that doesn't, puts on gloves so no prints show up on the valve or the notes—I know you haven't had time to test the first one, but no prints on this new one you discovered, right?"

The inspector made a grimace and nodded his head.

"Fixes it so the valve can't be turned off without a wrench and the nearest window won't open—neglecting to shut the one that's warped and open a crack—and then takes off her gloves and puts them away with her things while she blows out the pilot light, ever so lightly turns the burner knob on, and lies on the bed in nightclothes waiting to die? That sound reasonable to you, Inspector?"

Fisher stared at his cigarette. "Frankly, no. But two notes—"

"Exactly. TWO notes." Miranda leaned forward in the chair. "This is a setup—it's been a setup from the beginning."

Thelma Kyle wiped her eyes with a yellowed handkerchief. "Miss Corbie— my husband—I'm divorcing him, you know, it will be final soon, Louise was helping me through it—he had nothing to do with any of this. Louise told me— she told me about those letters she got, and she tried to laugh about it, and I've—I've been terribly worried about her, and I just couldn't believe she tried to—to—"

"I promise you she didn't, Mrs. Kyle. Look, Louise came to me because someone was threatening her and had tried to kill her. Then her boss was murdered and Smith's manuscript was stolen and the police suspected her, and even suspected—don't deny it, Inspector—that she was faking the murder attempts, trying to cover her own tracks."

Thelma interjected with urgency, raising her voice. "Louise would never hurt anyone—ever! She even stopped—stopped writing me when Shorty—I mean, my—my husband—before he got sent up, anyway, and didn't write again til he was in prison. How could they even think—"

"It's their job to think of every possibility, Mrs. Kyle. And just so you know, Inspector Fisher's one of the good ones."

"Thanks, Miranda." His tone was wry. "Go on."

"So then she has an alibi for when Alexander is killed—"

Fisher interrupted. "Who you found—"

"And you can't break it. Meanwhile, word gets out in the papers about Mrs. Kyle and Cretzer and her husband."

"And?"

"And Louise is found, nearly dead, with a note she didn't write but one that implied she was involved in or knew something about Alexander's killing and— even more importantly—that it had something to do with you and your husband's gang. 'God help my sister'? That doesn't sound like the same Louise Crowley that was trying to help her sister get a divorce, does it? Or the same Louise Crowley that hired me to protect her."

The blond women with the haggard faced raised her eyes to Miranda's. "That's—that's true. It's what I've been telling Inspector Fisher. Louise was the strong one—she was helping me, making things better for herself. She never liked Shorty—my husband, I mean—never liked any of it, but she wasn't a rat, never, never. Oh God—what if—what if she doesn't wake up?"

Thelma Kyle held her face in her hands, body wrenched, hunched over in grief. A cop in a sloppy uniform, shirttail hanging out, approached the inspector and handed him a manila folder. Wordlessly, Fisher handed it to Miranda.

"The note's inside. We found it in a desk drawer."

Miranda studied the message. Same office stock paper as the one she'd found on the night table. Handwriting much more like Louise, even if the wording wasn't.

If I can't have the man I'd love, I'd rather not live at all. I'm sorry for all the harm I've caused

Miranda looked up. "Ends rather abruptly, don't you think?"

The tired cop shrugged. "Maybe it was a rehearsal piece."

"In more ways than one. Notice the motive is completely different? Sounds like it was written before Alexander was killed, not after."

Thelma was reading over her shoulder and shook her head, still trembling. "That's not Louise's writing. It's an imitation."

The inspector scratched the heavy stubble on his chin, misery etched in every wrinkle. "You sure, Mrs. Kyle?"

"I know my sister's handwriting, Inspector Fisher. That's how we've been communicating since—since I never saw her while Shorty was on the lam. This looks a little like hers, but the e's aren't right. Neither are the i's. Louise dots them differently than that."

Fisher's thick fingers drummed the desktop as he looked at both of the women, frowning.

"So what's your theory, Miranda? That Louise is an innocent victim? Hell, everyone's innocent on this goddamn case—beg your pardon, Mrs. Kyle—no one's guilty. That's the problem."

She glanced up at the clock on the wall then back down to Fisher.

"Someone is framing Louise as a fall guy. I think this second note proves it. Someone was setting her up with those letters, the attempts on her life— someone who wanted to make them look like a self-made alibi, easily destroyed by cyanide in her desk and a suicidal confession. Someone who had access to her and who may be connected with the Rock."

Fisher slammed his hand down on the desk. "Christ, Miranda, you expect me to believe—"

"That Louise is innocent? You're goddamn right I do, because she is. Who- ever killed Niles was after Smith's manuscript—Alexander's murder was probably planned for a later date but he surprised the thief. Just look at the sequence: she gets threatening letters, probably written on a typewriter in Alex- ander's office. You test those yet?"

He shook his head. "No time. We've been working on the alibi with Blan- kenship."

"Test them. I'm sure you'll find they were typed there. Then she says she was almost hit by a car and receives chocolates with poison in them—probably pow- dered cyanide, since that's what was in Alexander's gin and what was found in her desk. Then Alexander's murdered, she's suspected, and the next day suppos- edly tries to kill herself but was actually—reading between the lines of the note I found—bumped off by bad company, since the handwriting is obviously not hers. The result's the same, either way, whether you believe the suicide or she's knocked off by a button man. If she's dead, she can take the blame for everything."

Fisher stared at her, his wide thumb grazing the shadow of beard on his chin.

"Maybe—just maybe—you've got something. But I don't like it. I don't like two notes and I don't like the cyanide. Hell, I don't like the whole goddamn—excuse me, Mrs. Kyle—case. Reads like something in *Dime Detective*."

"I agree with you. But we've got another problem and it's urgent. When Louise wakes up she'll be able to identify who knocked on her door. There was no struggle, no sign of strangers, according to Inspector Gonzales, and she was in her nightclothes—which means whoever she let in was someone she knew or at least wasn't afraid of. So she's still in danger . . . and so is everyone connected with Smith's book, from Smith to Mrs. Kyle."

"But—but my husband and Joe don't have any gang, Miss Corbie, that's what I've been trying to tell the inspector! Sure, Shorty talked to that man Smith, he wrote me about it from McNeil, but all he told him was what was already in the papers, that's what he said, and they don't have a gang—it was just them two, always just them two!"

Miranda nodded. "I don't disbelieve you, Mrs. Kyle. But whoever's behind this is somehow connected to Alcatraz or your husband. You're in danger. So is your sister. So is Smith. I asked Gonzales to put a watchdog on Louise's room, but that's not enough. I think—if Mrs. Kyle agrees—we should let on to the newspapers that the murder attempt on her sister was successful."

Fisher's mouth opened and shut with a snap. "Miranda, you know what the hell you're asking? With every goddamn hack—excuse me, Mrs. Kyle—on this story and the DA and the chief down my throat, you want the whole police department to tell the public Louise Crowley is dead?"

"Yes. Because some uniformed bull will fall asleep on duty and forget he's supposed to watch her, or someone will send flowers or another box of chocolates. Two notes and a change in motive? Too much goddamn evidence. That means improvisation—a departure from the plan. And that makes this bastard even more dangerous, whether or not he's part of some kind of Alcatraz conspiracy. Which may or may not exist. Maybe Smith can tell us."

She leaned forward, twisting out the cigarette stub in the overflowing ashtray. Mrs. Kyle stood up shakily, hand on the back of Miranda's chair.

"Mr.—I mean Inspector Fisher, please—I'd like to see my sister now. I'll—I'll agree to a-a body guard, if that's what you and Miss Corbie think best. And I will agree to—to tell the newspapers that Louise . . . that Louise didn't live. I just hope—I pray—that it doesn't—doesn't become true." She fell into the handkerchief again, sobbing in heaves. Miranda rose and put a hand out to steady the younger woman.

"Your son is where, Mrs. Kyle?"

"My—my mother, in Washington. I sent him away as soon—as soon as I could."

"Did Louise ever write you about George Blankenship? About their relationship? He's not—she went to the mat for him, and frankly, I can't figure out why. He's a bad gee—a bully and a coward."

Thelma looked up, cheeks wet. "We—I guess we're attracted to the wrong kind of men, Miss Corbie. Louise never wrote me about this George—but if he helped her in some way, she'd be loyal. She stopped writing when—when Shorty—she didn't want to have to rat, so she cut her own sister off. That's Louise."

Fisher stabbed out the Old Gold and rose from the desk.

"I'll have someone drive you over to Children's, Mrs. Kyle, if you don't mind waiting a few minutes."

The blonde stood up, nodding, and wavered through the partition gate and out the door.

Miranda spoke in an undertone.

"I'll pay for Louise—if she does make it—to be put in a sanitarium—Dante's, they're discreet. Give me a week, Inspector Fisher. One week to finish this before I get ready to leave San Francisco."

The cop ran thick fingers through his gray and black hair. Sweat made circles around his armpits and ash and mustard stained his tie.

"I'll try to push it through about Miss Crowley, but no guarantees. What about your boyfriend? Can he help?"

Her forehead wrinkled. "You mean Rick? He could make some calls—and Herb Caen will help, too."

He muttered, as if to himself: "Jesus. Keep a lid on an attempted murder, lie to the goddamn press, find a killer, shut down goddamn Alcatraz . . ."

He looked up sharply at Miranda. A light was still flickering in his eyes behind the layers of dirt and sweat and exhaustion.

"Anything else, Miss Corbie? Can the San Francisco Police Department do anything else for you?"

She cracked a grin. "Yeah. Don't bring George Blankenship in until after I've talked to him. I'm heading out there now. I've convinced him you're after his pathetic ass and I'm his only hope."

Fisher fell back into his chair and started to chuckle, shaking his head, the sound growing louder in the crowded room until a middle-aged bookie three desks down interrupted his confession to watch the inspector laugh. Fisher wiped his eyes with his shirtsleeve.

"A pip. A goddamn pip, that's what you are, Miranda Corbie. San Francisco sure in hell won't be the same without you."

Twenty-Three

*

She passed Smith on the way back to the waiting room. He stared stonily ahead, not looking at her, tense and stiff. He was escorted by a uniform, not Gonzales or one of the other homicide cops, and he shook his arm when the bull tried to lead him down the hall.

Quite the temper had Mr. Smith . . .

Meyer was still sitting in the dully-lit waiting room, nodding to sleep, shiny black cane supporting him in a semi-upright position. Rick rose when she walked in.

"Any news?"

"Yeah. I've got to make a call and take a taxi down to Playland right away."

The tall man in the uniform grinned. Almost looked like the old Rick, the one she drove away . . .

"You got a sudden hankering to ride the Big Dipper?"

She smiled, shaking her head. "No, got someone nearby I need to brace. Louise's boyfriend—her alibi for Alexander's murder. He was going to meet me in the office at eight, but I can't wait that long. Not now."

He glanced at the watch on his wrist. "That should put us at Whitney's in time for our dinner. Come to think of it, I'm hungry for a tamale and an 'It's It.' Been a while."

"You don't mind?"

He grinned again, pushing up his cap like it was a Champ fedora.

"Hell no, Miranda. I told you I'm in for as long as you and my schedule allow. Besides, I—well, I need to talk to you and Playland's as good a place as any."

She looked up quickly. Meyer cleared his throat.

"My dear, are you finished, one hopes, with Inspector Fisher? At least for to-night?"

"Yes. At least I think so. Go on home, Meyer . . . it's going to be a long evening. I'll let you know how—how Louise pulls through."

He stood up, wobbly on his feet, and shuffled closer. Patted her on the arm.

"Miss Crowley is a strong young woman, my dear. She'll survive." He yawned, covering his mouth with a fist. "I'm sorry—haven't caught up on my rest. Phone me tomorrow, please, Miranda."

"I will, Meyer. And thanks."

They watched him tap his way down the marble hallway and lean against the double doors, pushing them open.

"I'm gonna need you to do me one last favor as a newshawk, Rick—or a former one."

"No such thing as an ex-reporter, Miri, you know that. What's up?"

She glanced at the clock on the wall. "I'll tell you in the taxi if we can find one without big ears or a big mouth. We'll need your pal Caen on this, too. Can you find a driver while I make this phone call?"

Rick nodded. "Sure thing."

She watched him stride through the doors, Bay blowing in, sand and sea and a ship overseas, when you comin' back, Miranda, when you comin' home?

She shook herself, and shut the wooden door of the phone booth with a slam.

George had a playmate.

Matthew the janitor, about forty-five, thick of body and brain, with small, shifty eyes and nerves like a hophead. Noises from the upstairs dining and kitchen area filtered down to the dim basement room he'd led them to, along with smells of fatty roast beef and creamed potatoes.

Rick looked at the peeling walls and mildewed mops with distaste.

"Why's he meeting you here, Miranda? I thought you said he's off work at five and it's after six now."

She threw a glance at Matthew and sat gingerly on a three-legged stool splashed with gray paint.

"I guess George wanted backup and the woman at the desk would recognize me if we came in the front door, so his lackey here took us through the back entrance, sight unseen."

She wrinkled her nose at the tin bucket of dirty mop water, took in the magazine pinups and crude drawings from jo-jo books pasted on the walls. "His apartment's a shit hole, too."

The janitor giggled, teeth yellow and throat red, nostrils pink and scaly. "You got a nasty mouth, lady. You might upset me with that mouth."

Rick walked deliberately toward him. Matthew backed up against some steel shelves holding boxes and cleaners until a box of White King soap flakes tottered and fell off the rack.

"W-what? I ain't said nothing. It ain't my fault he ain't here yet. It ain't my fault."

"I'm sure you're as innocent as a lamb." Rick's voice was dry. "But why don't you just shut the hell up."

Heavy footsteps from the staircase around the corner. Matthew's eyes got bigger, grin of triumph and anticipation.

"That'll be George. George'll tell you. George knows everything, he knows I ain't done nothing wrong, doncha George?"

Blankenship stood before them scowling, large hairy hands holding his belt, brutish features taking in Rick with surprise and disappointment.

Miranda rose from the stool, lips curved upward in a satirical smile.

"What's wrong, George? Did I forget to mention I was bringing company? Silly me. No, I brought two friends this time. The Browning's in my pocket."

Matthew let out a whistling sound between his teeth.

"You ain't said nothin' 'bout guns, George—I don't like guns!" His head pivoted back and forth as he backed closer to George. The larger man snarled at him.

"Shut the fuck up, Matthew. This is business. She ain't gonna shoot you."

Miranda casually withdrew her hand from her coat pocket. Rick stood beside her, tensed and waiting.

"That's right, George. Business. So if you were thinking of getting the jump on me with your gunsel over there, thinking now that Louise is dead your troubles are over and you don't have to play along . . . well, you're not much known for your thinking, are you?"

"I told 'em, George, told 'em you knew everything an' I didn't do nothing." Matthew licked his lips, gaze flickering over the guard. "I di'n' do nothing, George, now did I?" he repeated softly.

Blankenship ignored him, flush of anger slowly draining out of his face, practicality sinking in. He nodded, thumb on his teeth, looking at Miranda and Rick.

"You keep the cops off my back?"

"I said I'll try. They'll bring you in for some standard questions about Louise and they'll want an alibi."

"But the papers say she tried to off herself, don't got to have no alibi for a fucking suicide—"

"You'll need an alibi, George, and the papers don't get everything. They don't even know Louise is dead. You'll be all right as long as you can explain where you were this morning between about 9:00 A.M. and 1:00 P.M."

"I was sleepin' til eleven, then I ate at the Koffee Klub an' went back to work early. Jawed with Matthew here."

The janitor giggled again. "You sure did, di'nt you, George? I can jaw real good, jus' ask him. He ain't murdered nobody, whatever that dame says. Her mouth ain't clean."

Rick's mouth tightened with distaste. "Let's get on with this. And get rid of him."

Matthew was backing up against Blankenship again. "I ain't done nothin'! Don't let him talk to me like that, George—I ain't done nothin' wrong!"

"Go upstairs and finish work and don't say nothing to nobody." Blankenship barked out the order, eyes not leaving Rick's face. "I'll talk to you later, Matthew."

The janitor slipped back to pick up the mop and bucket then slid past George again, heading slowly up the stairs, pink nostrils flaring, eyes glued to the larger man.

Miranda waited until they heard the footsteps stop and the upper door click shut.

"Spill it, George. Why'd you want Louise to steal the book?"

He looked from her to Rick again, hesitant, face growing redder, until the words came out in a flood.

"'Cause I wanted my fucking job back is why! Ain't got no cause to fire me, no more'n they had on Al or Petey or anybody else. I figured stealin' this book would get me back in with Link and Miller."

"Miller the associate warden?"

"Yeah. But Link—he's head of the prison guards an' Miller jus' does what he tells 'em when it comes to hirin' and firin'. Them bastards got you by the curlies—even when they fire you, you can't tell nobody nothin'."

Miranda stared at him thoughtfully. "Why were you fired?"

"For nothin'. Don't matter. What matters is I want my goddamn job back."

Panic filled George Blankenship, panic and embarrassment and even a little shame, unusual combination in a bully and abuser. She papered over his discomfiture, asking smoothly: "Just start at the beginning, George, with the book. How did Louise know about it? Did she read it?"

"She heard Smith an' Alexander talkin' 'bout Shorty Kyle—her own brother-in-law—an' she panicked. She knew Smith was writin' about the Rock but didn't know it was about Shorty and Cretzer, too. So she wrote—maybe called, I don't remember   her sister and finds out it's true . . . Smith talked to 'em when they was up in McNeil, before they got transferred."

"Was she worried that she'd lose her job if Alexander found out? About her brother-in-law, I mean?"

"That's so." He removed a pack of Camels from his jacket pocket and lit one with a Koffee Kup matchbook. "That's why she snuck a look. Di'n't even tell me nothin' then—told me after she'd got a peek."

"How'd she do it? The book was locked up."

He nodded, growing more comfortable. "Yeah, when it was finished. But a few weeks ago he was goin' through changin' the words or whatever and she got a hold of some new parts—you'd'a had to ask her how she did it, too late now—and told me about it—finally."

"What did she tell you, George?"

He grinned, the Camel clamped between his teeth. "Easy Street, peeper. Easy Street. Louise said that Smith talked to Kyle and Cretzer all right—before and after they escaped from McNeil. That's what them changes was about. An' after they was caught and knew they'd be comin' here—when they shot that bull up in Washington—they gave Smith an earful. They told him that every pen's got a system 'tween guards and inmates and even wardens, too, a lot of times, an' no place was escape-proof, not even Alcatraz. That's how they got offa McNeil in the first place. Then Smith wrote it right there in black an' white for the whole goddamn world to see. Guards in cahoots wit' prisoners, takin' bribes and kickbacks, same as the fucking brass."

Miranda glanced at Rick. His eyes were wide and eager, two-inch headline and a byline burning behind them.

"And you know—from experience—how accurate that report might be . . . don't you, George?"

This time he grew bigger, more expansive, end of the stick glowing bright red. "You bet I do. An' they—Link and Miller—they know it. I ain't gettin' jack from keepin' my mouth shut, am I? That Smith was writin' 'bout how the ginks on the outside contact their buddies, how it works, how the wheel's greased. An' he was gettin' money—good money—for it, while I was cleanin' bed pans for rich widows snortin' too much dust." He shook his head with disgust. "Ain't no point in keepin' quiet, not anymore. Not without gettin' somethin' for it. So's I told Louise to steal the book."

"And she didn't want to?"

"Hell, no. She may a' been good for a roll in the hay and she's dead now, an' I'm sorry an' all—but Louise weren't no genius. So there she was, rubbin' her hands and worryin' over maybe losin' her job, and I told her—I told her if she takes the book I'll give it to Link. He'd know what to do wit' it—burn it, probably, but make sure Miller knew 'bout it. Make sure we get somethin' outta it. An' if she just lifted the goddamn thing she wouldn't have to worry no more about her sister or losin' her job or anything . . . an' I'd get my old job back, with a nice, fat bonus. Shit, I coulda counted on retirin' with a goddamn gold watch."

He snorted, tossing the cigarette stub on the cement floor.

"But she didn't steal it. And instead, you're still here at Greer . . . and Louise is dead."

The guard looked up at her quickly. "I ain't touched Louise, like I told you on the phone, and nobody's pinnin' that on me. She killed herself, pure an' simple. Never was real stable. Hell, I met her when she was lookin' for work, helped her out of a jam even then. Now what about you, peeper? You gotta keep your side of the bargain—keep those bulls off my back."

Miranda made a motion toward the stairs with her head, signaling Rick. "I'll try to buy you time, George. Time to find yourself a waitress who saw you at the Koffee Kup."

"Me? Why do I gotta find somebody? You do it—you said you'd—"

She stopped at the foot of the stairs and turned around to face the guard.

"I said I'd help keep the bulls at bay. Not find you an alibi." Her eyes bored into him, voice silky. "Why did they fire you from Alcatraz, George? What was the cause?"

He reddened again, stepped backward. "None a' your fucking business, bitch."

Rick started down the steps. Miranda thrust out her arm to block him, eyes still on George's face.

"I'll protect you from the cops, George. But someone's killed Alexander and Louise. Somebody who's got something to do with Alcatraz. So maybe it's not just the cops you need to worry about."

The guard's eyes widened, black pupils darting between Miranda and Rick.

Miranda climbed the stairs and didn't look back.

*

Smell of cotton candy and shrill screams from the Big Dipper, music from a calliope, different from the Gayway's, not quite as melodic, not quite as entrancing. Sound of sand and surf and seagulls, cars honking in the parking lot, and Laffing Sal's cackle drifting from the Fun House, high on the wind, growing stronger as they walked down Fulton.

HaaHAHAhaahaaHAHAhaahaa . . .

Rick peppered her with questions: What else did she know about the Alcatraz connection? Was it a gang, like Tony Lima's boys or with connections to Cretzer and Kyle? What was she doing to protect herself and was she telling Fisher?

Miranda's stomach growled. She cut a left corner and they walked through the Standard Oil station on 48th, treading carefully around an oil patch, watching the line of kids at Laff in the Dark and couples lined up at the Ferris Wheel.

HaaHAHAhaahaaHAHAhaahaa . . .

"Fisher will get it out of Smith, Rick. I'm working with him, not for him. Christ, I'm hungry . . ."

He rubbed his nose. "Me too. I'll lay off grilling you til we get something to eat, but I still want to know what you're planning . . . if you can tell me."

Menacing, mechanical laughter, the shrill cries of coeds and gulls and frightened children, and a car speeding by on the Great Highway, Sing and Swing with Sammy Kaye blending and bending with Playland . . .

Let there be you . . . let there be me . . .

Miranda paused for a moment, smiling, and raised her hand to his cheek, tracing it softly with a gloved finger.

"I'll tell you what I know. I'll even tell you what I think. But first, let's get a goddamn hot dog."

Rick grinned down at her, took her arm, and led her back down Fulton along the concrete and wire fence protecting Playland, drawing closer to the screams, smells, and the sound of crashing waves.

✳

They stuffed themselves on tamales and hot dogs, man with a handlebar mustache and a stained white apron giving them funny looks when they came back for pretzels and peanuts.

They strolled by the Octopus and the Lindy Loop and took a spin on the Tilt-A-Whirl, where Rick almost lost his hat. They played Skee-Ball and rode the Big Dipper, the wild wind and sudden drop making their cheeks puff out, the shrieking wood and screaming children more frightening than Miranda wanted to admit, too much like Spain.

Too much like Spain.

They toured the Fun House while Rick ate an "It's It," and studied the new mechanical hostess, Laffing Sal, Whitney's newest edition to Playland, she of the cackle that belonged in Greer or maybe even Napa State. Sal leered like a drunken sailor but was far less terrifying in person—it was her laugh that sent shivers through the backs of children, reminding adults of parochial school nuns and Elsa Lanchester in *The Bride of Frankenstein*.

The protector of Playland and by extension, San Francisco, Sal kept the specter of war at bay and frightened away the ghosts of 1906 . . . surely the City, like Rome with its Colosseum or London with its Tower, couldn't fall as long as Laffing Sal kept laughing . . .

Miranda, grinning, fed her another nickel.

Rick pulled her out of the Fun House and led her to the games, where he threw baseballs at bottles and won a kewpie doll for her, and finally, out of breath and out of change, horizon line gray and pink against a wine-dark sea, they entered the Pie Shop for coffee and coconut cream.

HaaHAHAhaahaaHAHAhaahaa . . .

They talked and Miranda told him about Alexander and Louise and Bunny and Smith, told him about James and London and the *Cameronia*. Told him, a little, about her fears and her dream of finding her mother . . . the mother he'd helped her discover.

HaaHAHAhaahaaHAHAhaahaa . . .

He looked at her soberly throughout, interjecting reporter-type questions on what she thought was going on with Alcatraz and Smith's book, questioning her about Louise and what the blonde really knew, about whether pretending Louise was dead would really work.

Then, when the pies were done and the coffee was half-empty from a third refill, Rick began, his voice blending against Sal's piercing laugh and the ambient noise of Playland and the soft music they were playing inside the white and black shop.

Looking for yesterday . . . most any day I spent with you . . .

He held her eyes, brown against blue, and there was understanding in them and warmth, and not a little pain.

"Miranda—I told you I wanted to—to talk—"

She stubbed out a cigarette end from a new pack of Chesterfields. "I thought that's what we've been doing. Talking. And having a little—well, fun, I guess." She leaned across the table and covered his hand with hers. "It's meant a lot to me, Rick." She paused, cleared her throat, the words coming out with no control, no protection.

"You mean a lot to me."

A couple of months ago the words would have made him turn red and stutter and then puff himself up. A couple of months ago he would have tried to kiss her, saying something earnest about her and John and New York and Spain.

A couple of months ago she wouldn't have said them.

Now he looked away from her nervously, patting her hand with his free one until she pulled hers out from under. She looked him over, the leaner face, the erect posture, the tougher, more guarded emotions.

Miranda shook out another cigarette and he lit it with a lighter. His hands were shaking.

Hers were, too.

You're a good soldier, Randy, a good soldier, so charge ahead, into the Valley of Death, ours is not to wonder why, ours is but to do or die—

"Rick—what exactly did you want to talk to me about?"

He swallowed. She noticed it dispassionately, emotions shut off, shut them off, goddamn it, the closet's locked, the old man's drunk, Hatchett won't let you out for hours . . .

"I—I, well, I've said everything before and I don't want to rehash it, Miranda. But the army, I . . . I learned a few things about myself. I love you. I always will, I think you know that. But I'm not like John, never was. Never should've tried to be. I can't lead you into danger. I can help you as a friend, and as a friend I'm always here when you need me, I hope you know that. I respect you as a—a person, Miranda, not just as a woman. I admire you—you're like Amelia Earhart and Eleanor Roosevelt and Texas Guinan all wrapped up in Rita Hayworth, and I don't want you to—I'd never ask you, never again, I told myself—never ask you to change."

She drained the coffee cup and shoved it to the side of the table. Flicked her eyes up, met his.

"And?"

He swallowed again. "I—I just wanted you to know how I feel, Miranda. You're my friend—probably my best friend—but I realized—I realized I wanted something . . . something more. Something you can't give me. I told you I have furlough and I've got two days to spend with you. That's because—that's because I'm heading up to Santa Rosa for the rest of my week. I—there's a girl, Annabelle, and—well, I'm meeting her parents."

The Big Dipper roared, the windows of the Pie Shop rattling, as a middle-aged couple with two kids walked inside and ordered a strawberry rhubarb packaged up.

HaaHAHAhaahaaHAHAhaahaa . . .

Deep inhale on the Chesterfield. Thank God for cigarettes. James said they'd kill her, but not today.

Not today.

He looked up at her nervously. "So—I just wanted to, to tell you, Miranda—I meant what I said, I'm here for anything you need until day after tomorrow—"

She murmured: " 'You gave me hyacinths first a year ago. They called me the hyacinth girl.' "

He wrinkled his brow. "What? Hyacinths? Miranda, are you—"

She raised her face, rubbed out the cigarette, grabbed her handbag.

"Nothing, Rick. Nothing at all. I'm very happy for you and Annabelle. Is she a blonde?"

He looked startled. "Why, yes, she is—"

"I'm sure she's very pretty and Santa Rosa's a nice little town. Nice people live there. I'm truly happy for you and truly grateful for everything you've done."

"Well, I'm not through yet, I've got to call all the boys and Herb and make sure they stay on the same page about Louise and I've got all day tomorrow to get out to Alcatraz with you—"

She shook her head. "No, I think you'd better not, Rick. I think—if it's all the same to you—I'd very much appreciate it if you could just make those calls for me."

"But Alcatraz—"

She interrupted him smoothly, standing up. "Alcatraz is a federal peniten-tiary, remember, and I don't want you to get in trouble. There could be some sort of army regulation—"

"I don't think there's—"

"It's all right, Rick. I'll be all right. Let's just call it a night right here . . . I've got to get out to Smith's place, anyway, and try to set up the Alcatraz trip."

Rick slowly stood up and looked at her, mouth like a sad clown.

"Then I probably won't see you again before you leave for London."

She nodded. "Forward your post address when you get it. Bente'll make sure I receive important mail."

He took a step forward. "Miranda, I—"

She put up her hand to stop him. "I'm happy for you. You deserve everything life can give you—a wife, kids, nice house, a good career. I want you—I want you to be happy, Rick."

He looked down at her, the blue in his eyes sharp and clear like a cold win-ter's day. Miranda took a deep breath and reached upward, gently kissing his cheek.

"Be seein' you, Sanders."

She pushed open the door against the cold wind, feeling his eyes on her back, never looking behind.

HaaHAHAhaahaaHAHAhaahaa . . .

Miranda bent her head against the wind and walked toward the Great High-way and a taxi stand.

> *Yet when we came back, late, from the Hyacinth garden,*
> *Your arms full, and your hair wet, I could not*
> *Speak, and my eyes failed, I was neither*
> *Living nor dead, and I knew nothing.*

Twenty-Four

*

Living or dead. Which was she?

Hail the cab. Yellow Cab. Wanna Yellow Cab, lady? Just dial TUXedo 1234.

1-2-3-4, A-B-C-D, no more lopsided grins, no more bullshit brogues.

No more Rick.

Miranda leaned back against the worn brown leather of the taxi, a '35 Ford. The cabbie was talking, animatedly, trying to make eye contact in the rearview mirror. She saw herself respond like a machine, like something out of *Things to Come* or that old German horror picture where all the workers live underground, hoping for a savior.

Saviors were hard to come by in 1940.

Better to stay underground, where the worms are, where the bones lie, where the flesh decays.

Underground.

Miranda tried to light a cigarette but that just reminded her of Playland, Playland and the man she drove away, like all the men since Johnny, the ones who deserved it and the ones who didn't. The ones she despised and the ones she cared for.

And finally, the one she could've loved . . .

All of them guilty of not being Johnny Hayes, all of them guilty of wanting her, one way or another, usually her body, always her beauty, fading now, growing older.

Miranda exhaled against the window, distorted reflection of white face and auburn hair wavering like water, yellow streetlights bright and garish, until she was swallowed up again by darkness and the black-green of Golden Gate Park.

Her looks would leave her like everything else, just like that medieval morality play she read at Mills'. Everyman's left with nothing but faith, slung on a dung heap like Job, stinking in his own excrement, thank you so much, Yaweh, thank you so fucking much.

Faith's a little hard to come by when you keep trying to believe, trying to escape, and the closet, the bottle, and the belt keep coming back, day after day, caught in a trap not of your own devising, trap of pain, waking up to it, going to sleep with it, pain your lullabye, not Irish ones, no, just the bottle, the closet, and the belt, and the knowledge you weren't good enough. Not good enough to be wanted.

Not good enough to be loved.

Pain coming back, over and over . . .

Not like the men she drove away.

Phil, the old cop trying to find his lost youth, paunch quivering with excitement, policeman's ironed shirt stretched tight while he watched Dianne pour tea . . .

Gonzales, who wanted to marry her against his better principles, a Mr. Darcy nobility she neither wanted nor appreciated, a rich Mexican cop with a bright future and hard muscle that sparked desire in her flesh . . .

Flesh, flesh, the Way of All Flesh, and *your very flesh shall be a great poem,* said Walt Whitman, and so it was.

Keats wrote it, wrote it for her.

La Belle Dame Sans Merci.

O what can ail thee, knight-at-arms, Alone and palely loitering? The sedge has withered from the lake, And no birds sing.

No bird song, no mercy for herself, not since she lost John. No mercy for her friends, the few who cared about her, Bente and Meyer and Gladys and most of all Rick, the man who'd helped make the City her home again, the man who loved her, who saved her life, her knight in mustard-stained armor.

The man she drove away.

The lights were coming faster now, the neon bright with possibility, the snap and crackle of electricity, the promise of hard liquor and soft women, the hope of loneliness assuaged, the sound of a scratchy Victrola and a slamming door.

Faster, now, faster, like the lights of Playland, so Miranda lit a cigarette, watching the cigarette form a wall of gray smoke between her and the flashing lights, taxi motor humming like a juke in the corner bar.

She found me roots of relish sweet, And honey wild, and manna-dew, And sure in language strange she said "I love thee true."

Too late, too late, too late. Too late in 1937, no time to stop the shell, stop the bomb. Too late on the twentieth of September, nineteen hundred forty, too late to build again, too late to discover, too late to receive absolution from her ghosts, the ones who watched over her, the one she'd lived for when she wanted to die.

Our faults may not lie in the stars, O Bard, and maybe we are the remedies which we oft ascribe to Heaven, but then you wrote *Romeo and Juliet,* didn't you, and you knew, you knew, we are all Fortune's fools . . .

A year, a month, a week, a day.

Maybe even a fucking hour, and it might have worked, it could've worked, blindness gone and sight restored.

One less harsh word, one less shove aside.

One less goddamn moment of self-pity and self-absorption, one less.

One more day to tell him she loved him.

To tell herself.

And there she lullèd me asleep, And there I dreamed—Ah! woe betide!—The latest dream I ever dreamt On the cold hill side.

The cab was slowly crawling up California, the cabdriver prattling on about the Seals and a horse at Bay Meadows and London getting bombed and whether or not war was coming. She made the appropriate noises, plucked out a dollar bill from her wallet in readiness.

The City stretched before them from the top of Nob Hill, dark hills, dark water, red, blue, yellow, and green neon glistening, glowing, sparkling, ready for anything and willing, too, not respectable, no, not the marrying kind.

Not the marrying kind . . .

Miranda smiled perfunctorily at the cabdriver, climbed out at 1201 California.

She left the kewpie doll in the backseat.

She straightened her back, wind in her face, and stared up at the Spanish-style apartment house, just across the street from Grace Cathedral.

A tony place, the kind with a sleek-haired young man waiting to greet you, the kind for a writer who had money or knew how to make it.

An apartment for someone who was going places.

She lit another stick with a shaking hand.

Hell, she'd gotten what she wanted, hadn't she? She was a friend, treated like a friend. That's all she'd wanted from men since Johnny, treated like something without a goddamn target between her legs, treated like a human being, not a pair of thighs and a pair of breasts, not a promise of a hot night and a hand job in the backseat.

That's all she'd wanted.

But not, she knew now, too late, too late. Not, she knew now, from Rick.

> *And this is why I sojourn here*
> *Alone and palely loitering,*
> *Though the sedge is withered from the lake,*
> *And no birds sing.*

Miranda blew a stream of smoke into the black night.

Then she climbed the stairs to the front of 1201 California Street and wiped the tears from her cheeks.

*

She hit the buzzer for 602. The typewritten address card read SMITH. A sleek-haired young man, evident proponent of Wildroot Crème Oil, looked up at her curiously from the modern curvilinear desk, blond wood shining.

She smiled.

He hit a button and let her in.

"I'm looking for Mr. Smith—Mr. Howard Carter Smith."

The young man smelled of bay rum and cheap tobacco but he was fresh-faced and ambitious and he leaned forward with his arm on the desk and leered just a little.

"He went out a few minutes ago but I'm available."

Old pain, new pain, and for a moment she thought about it, about blotting out the night. About blotting it all out, losing herself again, drifting, drifting, like the wood washed up on Baker Beach, like the broken china from shipwrecks off Land's End.

Then she remembered the license in her wallet.

Remembered the blond girl in the hospital.

No, goddamn it, no going back . . .

She smiled again. "I won't ask what you're available for. Mind telling me where he was headed?"

The young man sighed with resignation. "No, I guess not. Mr. Smith usually goes down to the Lodge Tavern. Sometimes he doesn't come back until very late and he's in no condition to . . . well, you know."

He followed up the line with a wink. Miranda raised her eyebrows in mock innocence.

"I don't have the faintest idea of what you're talking about. But thanks for the information . . . junior."

His face fell momentarily, then the natural exuberance of youth and a high-quality hair oil picked him back up.

"I'm here all night if you get bored. Got plenty of pep! Lots of vitamin A."

She nodded on her way out the door.

"A word of advice: go easy on the fastballs when you're pitching woo."

He stared after her, mouth open, while Miranda stepped into the cold night September air of California Street, the gray stone of Grace Cathedral lit by passing cars.

Next stop, Lodge Tavern.

*

460 Larkin and the Lodge Tavern was a long, slow slide down the slope of Nob Hill into the working-class lowlands of San Francisco.

About a mile away. About five thousand miles away.

Small, squat, and dark, the bar was full of longshoremen and factory workers, with a sprinkling of Irish cops thrown in for good luck. Italian, Irish, a smattering of Poles, long faces with tough, pockmarked skin and knuckles scraped dry from too much abrasion against shipping crates and other men's chins, they sat around a long ancient bar, still shiny from constant use, pulling pints of Acme beer or the occasional Old Crow whiskey, telling tales about the wharf and the ships and the '34 general strike.

Perfect place for a writer of means to pick up the patois, to burnish his credentials as a man of the people, rather than a man of the bourgeoisie.

Just don't tell 'em where you live.

Smith was seated on a stool in the middle, nursing a gin and tonic.

Hell, he even had the wrong goddamn drink.

The denizens—and a few of their women—looked up when Miranda walked in and kept looking. She felt a shuffling, a drawing together of ranks.

Ironic that she, not Smith, was the fucking outsider.

She walked over, tapped him on the shoulder. He pivoted around slowly, unevenly. He was already out on the roof.

"Yeah? Oh . . . you. The, the, the peeper dame, Corben or Kirby or somethin' . . ."

"Corbie. Miranda Corbie. I need to talk to you, Smith."

At the utterance of "peeper" the louder voices fell silent before beginning again, louder than before, and the man in the dark gray fedora next to Smith hopped off the green stool and gestured toward it, bowing to Miranda.

She gave him a nod and perched on the leather. A bald man in a dirty white apron, age indeterminate, approached her from behind the bar.

"You want something, lady?"

"Yeah. Best bourbon you've got. Make it straight, no ice."

He grunted, ignored the dollar bill she'd casually thrown down.

The men around her didn't.

Miranda looked up at Smith.

"Louise is dead."

The writer shrugged elaborately. "Shorry to hear it. Nothin' t' do with me."

She leaned into him, voice low. "Bullshit. You're up to your eyeballs in it. We need to talk about the Rock. About your sources. About your goddamn book that people have died for."

He opened his eyes slowly and elaborately, the way drunks always do. "I gotta lotta books. Jus' finish'd another one, matter o' fact, so f'rget goddamn Alcatraz. This one's better, no int'rviews necessary . . . gonna win me the goddamn Pu-lit-zer. Besides, I already told everythin' to the coppers. Go talk to them, lady. Get offa my back."

"I haven't been on your back, Smith. Not yet. You'll know when I am."

One of the men on the other side of Smith made a grunting noise. "I'd know, honey. I'd know in a heartbeat."

Miranda frowned. The bar was too full, too crowded, and too public. She picked up the shot glass in front of her and threw the whiskey down her throat, lungs and stomach burning. Grabbed Smith by the arm.

"C'mon. Let's go back to your apartment."

A couple of the other patrons whistled and the man next to Smith elbowed him. "Now's your chance, Howard. God knows you ain't gonna get a better offer."

Smith looked up blearily and planted his feet.

"I'm not goin' anywhere. I'm stayin' here til they throw me out. Go 'way, dick-lady. Go 'way."

Miranda looked from the red, stubborn face of the writer—drunk, but pretending to be even drunker—to the worn, tired faces of the men and women surrounding him. She hopped off the stool, nodded to the bartender.

Faced the man with small eyes and new Florsheim shoes wavering in front of her.

"You can't hide, Smith. Not from the cops, not from me. I'll expect to find you at the Gump's party tomorrow night. If I don't, Fisher will haul your ass to jail and keep it there . . . for your own fucking good."

She tossed a five-dollar bill on the counter.

"Keep an eye on this goose for me, boys . . . and nibble one on me."

She walked out of the Lodge Tavern to an accompanying cheer of whistles and claps.

No late-night dinner at the Moderne, not tonight.

She grabbed a hamburger from the Hotel Oxford cafe, extra onion, extra pickle, extra ice in the Coke.

Ate methodically, machine-like, while Frank Sinatra warbled from the jukebox.

Food gave her something to do.

I'll never smile again . . .

She walked home, six long blocks, avoiding Chinatown, avoiding the Moderne, avoiding anyone she knew.

Tomorrow she'd call Fisher and Meyer and Bente, tomorrow she'd talk to Allen and buy more sticks from Gladys. Tomorrow she'd brace Bunny or chase down Smith, find out about what he'd written. Tomorrow she'd call the hospital and see whether Louise made it through the night.

Tomorrow and tomorrow and tomorrow . . .

She'd rejoin the world tomorrow on a trip to Alcatraz.

Tonight was its own prison.

She limped up the last hill slowly, catching a glimpse of Raphael around the corner, choosing which blonde to let past the red velvet rope. Her legs ached from the exercise but the pain was real, tangible, localized, the kind of pain that she could endure, appreciate, even savor.

Pain as pleasure, pleasure as pain, *semper idem, semper idem. Gladiator in arena consilium capit,* too late, too late, too late.

She pulled open the heavy door to the Drake Hopkins, gust of wind fighting her. No Roy, no Leo, no one at all in the lobby. The stairs squeaked in protest, and she gripped the oak banister, out of breath by the time she reached the fourth floor.

The door swung open. Apartment still smelled like coffee. Miranda walked into the kitchen and turned on the light. Bent over the cold coffee grounds and inhaled, deep, earthy aroma.

Burnett told her once, when he was very drunk and just scored a pair of C's on a surveillance job. He told her to remember the victories, remember the booze, remember the dough. Remember the grunts and moans and the first fifteen minutes in the backseat when she was seventeen, remember the men she kissed and made love to and the ones she slapped.

Remember her mother's face.

Then, he said, with a philosophical mien and his fingers wrapped around a bottle of Four Roses, forget it all.

Because nothing mattered but that goddamn piece of paper in your wallet, the paper that made you free, beholden to no one, that didn't tie you to an assembly line or a desk or a typewriter.

The paper that didn't tie you to anything . . . or anyone.

She found the number in her reporter's notebook and left a message for James, the gravelly voiced woman with a slight Southern accent sounding half-asleep. Two in the morning in Washington and she hoped he'd deliver, making a few phone calls when he woke up, make sure she was on the list for a boat ride to the Rock. She hung up, waited for the line to clear, and called Fisher.

He wasn't in but the desk sergeant wasn't Collins and he recognized her name.

"You that lady gumshoe I heard about, huh?"

She made noncommittal answers and an effort to sweeten her tone. If James fell through, Fisher was her only hope. She didn't want to wait, not with Louise's life and maybe Thelma's and maybe even Smith's in jeopardy.

Alcatraz was next, even if she had to swim with the fucking sharks.

Miranda dropped the handset into the cradle and started to undress, trailing clothes into the bedroom.

The yellow wallpaper with the blue forget-me-knots nodded and beamed at her, all singing, all dancing, Broadway revue of flowers, here's rosemary, that's for remembrance, pray you, love, remember . . .

Rick helping her find a clown and a little girl across four hundred acres of Treasure Island. Rick seeing her for the first time since New York, meeting at Lotta's Fountain. Rick telling her about Burnett, Rick dressing up like Robin Hood, Rick driving up to the Napa Woods and saving her from suicide or a fucking lobotomy . . .

She sank down on the edge of the bed and poured herself a shot of Old Taylor, the whiskey strong and sweet, scorching as it slid down her throat. Took out her wallet and looked at it, the folded-up and worn piece of paper with her name on it.

Remember, Burnett said.

Remember.

Twenty-Five

*

The bull from Alcatraz took his time.

He was checking the list for civilian passengers, the free-to-go kind, no transfers from Leavenworth or McNeil today, no bank robbers or post office bandits, no men who filed too many writs and raised too much hell or who wouldn't take incarceration with the docility the government demanded.

Miranda shivered.

Seven thirty, and the fog was still thick at the pier around Fort Mason, the dim outline of the steam ferry *General Frank M. Coxe* barely discernible.

A group of schoolkids, various ages, descended from the boat, chattering about Tyrone Power and Clark Gable, shopping with their mothers then maybe a picture at the Alcazar, the boys swaggering around the dock, playing cops and robbers, Saturday morning the most exciting time of the week.

A couple of women shooed them off toward a White Front stop, mid-thirties to early forties, working-class matrons with frowsy hair and sales-rack dresses, women who followed their husbands to prison and lived just outside the walls, just outside the violence, women who thought they were lucky to get the free housing and never asked too many questions about what happened inside.

Women who looked at Miranda with suspicion and curiosity, one to another. She could make out the word "visitation" and "moll" out of the mouth of the mousey blonde.

The bull peered up from underneath his cap. "Says here you're meetin' with Warden Miller. Got it wrote down in pencil."

She gave him a smile. *That'll give the blonde something to fucking talk about.*

"That's right. Thanks, Officer. What time does she leave?" Miranda nodded toward the *Coxe,* a sturdy-looking passenger ferry with a shallow draft and plenty of room. Steam belched from the boat's funnel and made more fog.

The bull narrowed his eyes, looked her up and down. "You some kinda news-hen, lady? Figured you was here to see one of the big trouble boys, though that kind usually take the *McDowell,* the regular transport boat. Maybe you got some pull with the army or somethin', but you won't get no news outta the Rock—we don't talk, see? Nobody talks. It's against the rules."

"My name's on the list. My business is my own."

He looked hard at her again, then dropped his eyes and shrugged. "Whatever you say, lady. Jus' tryin' to save you from pukin' your guts out. It's a rough ride this morning, even if it's only a mile. You don't look like no sailor to me. Got ten minutes til launch."

Miranda shook out a Chesterfield from the pack in her pocket.

"Thanks. I might surprise you."

She huddled under the black Persian lamb coat and lit the stick, the damp air and Bay wind blowing out the lighter twice. The women left, still whispering, herding the children and clutching grocery lists. A couple of men in dungarees, probably civilian workers at one of the shops on the island, loitered by the boat, talking to the captain.

Miranda inhaled the cigarette and reread the telegram James sent this morning.

All set 7:45 A.M. Fort Mason, Coxe ferry. Seeing Miller. Ask abt Roy Gardner, Rufus McCain, Henri Young, last hunger strike, mat shop fire. Call after.

She studied the words, drawing down hard on the stick. James came through for her, but not just for her. It was a long shot whether he could get the potentates of Devil's Island to see a private investigator . . . especially a non-Pinkerton, non-male private investigator whose name was in the paper too goddamn much. That he had succeeded—and on such short notice—meant that the State Department or James' own connections wanted her to learn something and report back.

Something the Bureau of Prisons wanted checked up on? Punishment maybe, the cruel and unusual kind. Something to do specifically with Roy Gardner, Henri Young, and Rufus McCain.

She closed her eyes for a moment, huddled against the cold Bay wind, trying to remember what she'd read.

The hunger strike was just a couple of months ago, dutifully leaked to the papers by the civilian workers and maybe even careful bulls who liked a little folding money. Over one hundred inmates, protesting conditions on the Rock, and only about a month after a mysterious fire broke out in the mat factory. Funny that James mentioned them both.

The fire wasn't much, though the papers ate it like candy—a fishing boat heard the alarm and thought it was another escape. Refusing to eat wasn't much of a bargaining tool and the strike petered out, like most strikes on the island, with the ringleaders locked up in whatever hole Johnston deemed appropriate. Initiative and energy required hope, one of the first casualties on Alcatraz.

Besides, the warden had hoses he could shove down your throat.

About six or seven months before the strike, around the turn of the year, Roy Gardner committed suicide at the Hotel Governor. The author of *Hellcatraz* was just too tired, he wrote, to continue on. He apologized, posted his warning sign on the door, and left a tip for the maid before inhaling potassium cyanide.

She looked at the telegram again and frowned. Gardner wrote the most infamous account of the dungeons—what the bulls called "disciplinary segregation." And he wound up dead. Whether he'd been encouraged, no one thought to investigate.

Then there was McCain and Young. They'd taken part in the infamous escape attempt last year—the one that cost Doc Barker his life. No one really knew what happened to the would-be escapees, since the United States Attorney opted out of pressing charges . . . again, for reasons unknown.

There'd been five men involved in all, one a black inmate named William Martin. She remembered Rick talking about it—since Alcatraz was completely segregated—hell, they even had separate barber chairs in the prisoner barber shop—and the press made sure to play up the race angle. Five white men making an escape attempt was one thing. Four white men and a black man was quite another.

She nodded, mouth grim. Whatever they'd done to McCain and Young and the other survivors, she was willing to bet Martin had it a hell of a lot worse.

Miranda took one last inhale on the cigarette and dropped it on the wooden pier, crushing it with her pump.

She'd ask about Martin, too.

*

The waters were choppy, the way Miranda liked them, and she faced the prow, salt-spray biting her cheeks and hair.

The bull who checked her in was inside the warm cabin, shivering underneath his peacoat.

Two civilian workers, mechanics or machinists, sat together talking, shooting an occasional glance through the window to where Miranda stood like a figurehead.

She took a deep breath, tasting salt, eyes blinking, leaning into the wind as they sailed by Treasure Island. Soon there'd be screams from the Roll-O-Plane and numbers ringing up on the Giant Cash Register, the excited shouts of kids and the roar of the Roller Coaster, Sally's girls sharing a cup of black coffee and stories from the night before, Ken Silverman testing the diving bell, his new wife Nina beaming when he speaks of the wonders under the sea.

Only eight days more for the Pageant of the Pacific, the Magic Carpet, the Magic Island, conceived as an airport, born for a Fair, testimony to a peace that would never be in our time.

Back in New York, The World of Tomorrow would last another month before it, too, became yesterday.

Miranda watched the fog wrap around the Tower of the Sun.

The ferry ride was only about fifteen minutes. Better make the most of it.

She sighed, and made her way to the cabin.

Once inside, she sat opposite the men on the long, narrow wooden bench, shiny with wear. The younger one kept staring at her, the older one growing irritated.

"Christ, Zach, ain't you heard me? I tol' you five times already—that presser's gonna blow if we don't order a new valve soon, I don't give a damn what the warden says. Can't run no rubber mat factory without a goddamn presser, can we?"

He was grizzled and gray, younger, probably, than he looked, with ancient grease stains on his dungarees and a carefully mended coat. The younger one was late thirties or early forties, dark brown hair and beefy, with a map-veined nose and protruding gut. Weak blue eyes crawled over her.

"Yeah, yeah, I heard you. So we get a message to Meat Head and fill out a request. Alls we can do is warn 'em, Mitch. We ain't the bosses. They been keepin' a tight fist on supplies since the fire, anyway—you'd think we was the crim'nals, way they act."

He spoke slowly, eyes lingering on Miranda's legs. He looked up and she met his eyes.

The bull was on the other end of the cabin, leaning back against the windows, gently snoring. She gave the workman a long, slow smile.

He sat up straight and leaned forward. "You here on a visit, lady? "Pop Gun" Kelly, maybe?"

The older man nudged him in the ribs. The younger one ignored him.

"George gets a lot of visitors, does he?"

"Yeah. Not all of 'em as good-lookin' as you, though. What's your name, doll?"

Her lips twitched. "Miranda. Say, I overheard you say you work in the mat shop. Ever find out what caused that fire a few months back?"

Zach raised his eyebrows. The older one, Mitch, shook his head and made a low growling noise.

"We ain't supposed to talk about it, angel. But between you, me, and the deep blue sea, I think it was a joe named Hensley. Leastways, that's what Link says."

"Link? Who's that?"

"That's what some of the birds call Linkletter. He's captain of the guards, just got promoted. Used to be lieutenant, but he's Meat Head's main boy—"

"Zach!" High-pitched warning from Mitch. The small dock was coming into view now, huddled beneath the looming desolation that was Alcatraz.

Zach grinned sheepishly. "Sorry, lady. Ain't supposed to talk about the Rock."

Miranda nodded, and scooted forward on the bench, peering through the dirty windows. The lighthouse shone a cold beam on the Bay, waters gray and dark gray, kelp and seaweed floating on top before drowning beneath the current. Wreathed in fog, the island was bigger than it looked from the safety of San Francisco: massive rock, steep climbs, and a long, low steel box of a building, coffin of living men, clinging to the hard, dark gray sandstone and struggling for survival against the wind.

A few plants clung to the sides of the island, some native, some plantings by the warden's house and before him, the army, living emblem of civilization and the dominance of man against nature.

Seagulls swooped and pelicans flew low, cormorants cleaning themselves after a dive.

No other signs of life.

The bull woke up from his morning doze with a loud grunt. Miranda started busying herself with her handbag, said it nonchalantly.

"Is 'Meat Head' what the prisoners call the associate warden?"

Zach glanced over at Mitch and stood up, the ferry slowing down and rocking as it slipped toward the dock, a couple of men emerging from an outbuilding and throwing ropes to secure her. The mechanic leaned over Miranda. He smelled like bacon grease.

"Yeah. But I'm surprised you don't know that, seein' as you're Kelly's girl an' all."

The bull finally stood up and stretched, his lips moving while he counted the passengers on the boat. Satisfied, he stood up and started giving orders.

"All right, you men, get ready. First you, lady, ladies first, even on Alcatraz."

Zach pressed into her, close whisper. "I work in the new industrial building, mat shop, Zach Russell's the name. Make plenty o' kale, too, case you get lonely, sittin' around waitin' for 'Pop Gun'."

Miranda smiled and stepped away, pulling her gloves on tighter. "Oh, I'm not here to see Mr. Kelly. I'm here to see Associate Warden Miller."

She nodded at the ashen-faced mechanic and took the few steps up to the deck, the guard already outside and reaching down for her hand.

The small ferry was rocking against the wooden dock and the two men had thrown a plank over the gap between the boat and the platform. Miranda held her beret down, wind yowling in a disconcerting shriek as it whipped around the island, fog patchy and dense as it clung to the already decaying buildings perched around the mooring.

The bull helped her across, rough hand supporting her as if she were a child. Zach and Mitch headed up the hill to the right, Zach avoiding her eyes. The men on the dock chatted with the boat captain for a few minutes, before the *Coxe* sailed into the salty wind once more, next stop Angel Island.

Miranda watched the boat pull into the choppy water, remembering why she'd made the journey, remembering the catch in her throat this morning before the nurse at Children's came on the line, Louise "still unconscious but expected to survive." Maybe the secretary would remember something and be able to communicate it . . . maybe she wouldn't. One way or another, Miranda wasn't leaving the Rock without some goddamn answers.

She shivered and turned toward the shore, staring at the fog-wavy outline of Coit Tower, the squat gray solidity of pier after pier.

Roy Gardner had it right.

Forget the small, enclosed cell, forget the howling, freezing wind. Forget the physical threats, the predatory advances of other prisoners, the dark, cold dampness of isolation, depredations and deprivations a man could survive. Forget even the atrophy of regimentation, the hopelessness of fighting back, the death of identity and ego lost, a number among three hundred.

It was the quick glimpse, a white reflection of the Ferry Building.

It was the smell of coffee and chocolate, born high on the wind.

It was the lonesome note of a cable car, drowning out a fog horn, sailing down the hill from California and Grant.

To see and smell and hear and yet never touch San Francisco.

The real hell of Alcatraz.

An anxious "Hello there!" fought above the whistling wind and white froth batter of the waves. A fat little man was quickly walking down the steep road, waving his arms.

He arrived, slightly out of breath, and skidded to a stop in front of her.

"You Miranda Corbie?"

She nodded.

He threw out an arm, encompassing the low, hulking main cell block on the island's crest and the more ornate, human, Spanish-style architecture of the warden's house between the prison and the lighthouse. His smile was broad, teeth yellow.

"Welcome to Alcatraz."

Twenty-Six

＊

The little man's name was Henry, an accounting clerk Miller sent to escort her. He ushered her through the hulking main entrance and to the right, still panting and heaving from the steep climb to the main building. They walked past the officers' lounge and captain's desk, where a sullen-looking man eyed her suspiciously, and into a grim, prim waiting room, windowless and too cell-like for her comfort.

A chipped placard on the door in front announced ASSOCIATE WARDEN, EDWARD J. MILLER. To the left, the reassuring sound of a typewriter floated through a half-open door: the office of the warden's secretary, the supposed nerve center of Alcatraz.

"He'll—he'll be with you in a few minutes, Miss Corbie. I gotta be getting back to my ledgers. It's been a real pleasure—I didn't know Hoover even allowed lady agents!"

Henry wiped his brow, beamed at her, and retreated to the wing on the other side of the entrance.

So that was the score. James insinuated in whatever telegram he sent that she was working with the FBI. A private investigator, yes, but one sanctioned by the G-men, the kind that never showed up on *Gang Busters*. She wondered who James was really feeding information to and why.

Miller's door opened suddenly, and a man who looked like a cross between Herbert Hoover and Al Capone stuck out his head.

Short and squat with muscle long gone to fat, he wore a blue suit, carefully pressed. Deep creases fell downward on a round, unpleasant face, and his hair was thick and dressed like Hoover's, oiled and parted in the middle. Mean little eyes measured and weighed her like a butcher, adding up the numbers and arriving at a total by the time they reached her face.

No wonder they called him Meat Head.

She stood up and plastered on a smile.

"Warden Miller? I believe you're expecting me. Miranda Corbie."

He nodded toward his office.

"Of course, Miss Corbie. I arranged for Henry to meet you when I received the wire from Washington this morning. Rather sudden request, and spur-of-the-moment, I must say—it was 5:00 A.M. when we received the call—but we are always pleased to help the Bureau."

Miranda followed him inside, taking in the small, dark office Miller called home.

"Thanks—I hope I haven't been too much trouble for you."

"Not at all, not at all. Alcatraz Penitentiary is run with great precision. We can react instantly to any situation."

Her lips twitched. "You mean like last year's escape attempt?"

Miller hitched high-waisted trousers and sank into the large desk chair. His tone was frosty.

"Miss Corbie, Alcatraz is a new style of prison. It houses the worst of the worst of federal prisoners, men who would kill at the slightest provocation or even for the sheer joy of it. Naturally, this type of hardened criminal presents a challenge—a challenge this prison was built for and one we more than meet. And remember, please, that Barker and the others *attempted* to escape—they didn't succeed. Thanks, of course, to the diligence of our troops and organization here at Alcatraz."

She nodded. No print of FDR on the wall, standard issue for most government bureaucrats, but Warden Johnston stared down at them, unsmiling, and there was a posed photograph of Miller with J. Edgar Hoover next to an oval-framed portrait of a frumpy woman who could only be his wife.

"Ever find out what happened to Cole and Roe?"

"Drowned." Miller snapped it out while rifling through small piles of papers, neatly stacked.

Miranda perched on one of the hard-backed oak chairs lined up in front of him.

"By the way, Warden Miller, I understand there was a fire in the mat shop recently. Did that have anything to do with the hunger strike or the escape attempt last year?"

He raised his head, black eyes shiny and hard.

"Only in the sense that the fire was started by Hensley—a labor agitator and the man behind the hunger strike. He's a dangerous menace and a Red, and we've taken steps to ensure he won't be able to influence the other inmates."

"Does that mean he's in solitary?"

"Isolation, yes. Now, Miss Corbie—"

"Along with Henri Young and Rufus McCain?"

The warden stiffened in his buttoned leather chair.

"I was told you were to ask a few questions about Joseph Cretzer and Arnold Kyle. I fail to understand the connection."

Miranda gave an elaborate shrug. "Cretzer and Kyle are known for escape attempts and Young and McCain nearly succeeded. I was wondering where they are. Along with William Martin, of course."

Color rose in Meat Head's cheeks, setting off the white line down the center of his scalp.

"Are you working for the Bureau of Investigation or the Bureau of Prisons, Miss Corbie? You sound like one of those well-meaning Washington types. They've learned through the years that it's best not to interfere with how Warden Johnston handles things here—in fact, with the new improvements he's convinced the BOP to support, there won't be any more escape attempts."

She raised an eyebrow. "How often does the Bureau of Prisons come by? After every strike or just every escape?"

"Escape *attempt*."

Tense and tight, Miller bent toward her, desk pressed into a doughy gut, posture full of violence. All he needed was a club in his hand.

He'd been a guard, she'd read—a guard like George Blankenship. A guard like so many she'd seen, lining up men on Spanish streets . . .

The associate warden's shoulders slumped and he leaned back in his chair once again, tone softened, body shrunk back to flaccid middle age.

"As I said, the BOP has learned that Alcatraz can't be managed on a blueprint. We don't receive many visits from them or anyone else. In fact, I doubt if you realize how fortunate you are to be here." He tapped the sheet he was holding. "I know Director Hoover, and I must say—I'm surprised that he would allow his agents to work with a private detective, especially a female. You are licensed by the state, I trust?"

Miranda's lips curled at the corners. "Oh, yes, Warden Miller. I'm legitimate. And I do realize how difficult it is to get any information out of Alcatraz. The newshawks like to say it's as difficult to break into as it is to break out of."

"Pack of sensationalists. Just look at what they did with Gardner—made the man out to be some kind of hero! They print lies and coddle maniacs, every one of them."

"I don't think anyone's out to coddle maniacs, with the exception of some former politicians in Europe and certain members of Congress. And we would still like to know where McCain, Young, and Martin are."

Miller looked up, better controlled this time, a typewritten sheet of paper clutched in a flipper-like hand.

Miranda met his eyes, smile glued in place.

"Isolation," he snapped.

"Martin, too?"

He sucked on his upper false teeth for a few seconds. "Alcatraz is a federal prison and of course is segregated, as I'm sure you're aware. He's in colored isolation. And before we proceed any further, Miss Corbie, you'll sign this."

He pushed the paper at her.

"You agree to keep this interview and any information which you may receive confidential."

She picked it up. "If I don't?"

"Your interview is terminated. I doubt that your employers at the Bureau would appreciate that." He flattened a thick hand on the desk. "Come now, Miss Corbie. I allotted fifteen minutes for you. I suggest you not waste any more time."

Miranda's eyes glimmered green.

"Pen?"

He shoved one at her wordlessly. She scratched her signature and pushed the paper and pen back across his desk.

"I'll need a copy of that."

"I've included a blank form in the packet I've prepared for you, which will contain some basic information on Alcatraz and the report Warden Johnston received on Joseph Paul Cretzer, dated the 18th of April. I doubt I can add any information to that but I am available to you"—he checked his wristwatch—"for the next eleven minutes."

Her voice was dry. "So you've said. Mind if I smoke?"

Remnants of Cuban cigars, smoked to the flat, smeary stub, filled his ashtray. Miller jerked out a nod.

Women didn't smoke, not in his world. Didn't vote, either, and never asked questions beyond how many olives he'd like in his fucking martini.

Miranda lit a Chesterfield, taking her time.

"The main reason I'm here today, Warden Miller, is this: a book purporting to be about the inner workings of prisons, including Alcatraz, was stolen from a San Francisco publishing company. The publisher was murdered during the theft and his secretary was killed at home a day later. The author is under police protection."

Miller grimaced. "When you lie with dogs you get fleas. There are too many books of that sort, anyway—preposterous lies, all of them, starting with that reprobate Gardner's. But what's all this got to do with Cretzer and Kyle?"

"The author interviewed them before their transfer here. About corruption and bribery in prisons and how they escaped from McNeil—"

"There is no bribery here and certainly no corruption, Miss Corbie, and I resent any implication of such a thing. As for escape, Alcatraz, as we've demonstrated, is escape-proof. Cretzer and Kyle won't even make an attempt."

Miranda blew a stream of smoke out the left side of her mouth.

"There's more. The secretary was seeing a man who used to be a guard here. He was fired."

The sudden breath was sharp and quick.

"Fired? Who was it? Our men are all clean and sober—good men, every one of them. I pride myself, Miss Corbie, pride myself on our Alcatraz troops. I was a guard myself and attained my present position through hard work and clean living, and that's the lesson I instill in my men. They know they can come to me with any problem, no matter how trivial—"

She held up a hand. "Just a minute, Warden. I'm not finished. When the secretary told him about the book he asked her to steal it. She didn't, but the point is this: he believed if he showed it to you and a guard named Linkletter that he'd get his job back. Now, I—we, I should say—would like to know why this ex-guard would think such a thing."

Meat Head looked around the desk, at the photo of Hoover. Wet his lips with a gray tongue and then raised his head to stare at her with shiny black eyes.

"If a man was fired from Alcatraz, Miss Corbie, he can hardly be trusted as a source of information. I'm surprised—shocked, really—that you and your associates would even bother with such prattle. The man in question is obviously bent on revenge. As for Linkletter, he is Captain Linkletter now. He is above reproach, as his promotion demonstrates. And my own reputation speaks for itself."

She smiled, teeth showing. "Of course. But I'd still like to see Captain Linkletter."

Pudgy fingers crunched the piece of paper in his hand. He caught himself and smoothed it out on the desk.

"Captain Linkletter cannot possibly hold any interest for you or your associates, Miss Corbie. And our time is nearing the end."

She stared critically at the glowing red end of the Chesterfield.

"Someone's taking an interest. More than one someone. And they're all listening to George Blankenship."

No widening of the eyes, no sign of surprise.

He'd been expecting the name.

"Blankenship, Blankenship . . . oh, yes, I recall now. Insubordination. George Blankenship was terminated for insubordination after employment of just a few months. He came in with a good record, as I recall, working in other institutions. No wonder he's spreading lies and insinuations—an angry man, from what I remember. Definitely insubordinate."

She leaned forward, knocking ash over the cigar remnants in his plain black ashtray.

"May I see Captain Linkletter, Warden?"

Miller stared at her, full mouth twisted, fists clenched. Sweat started to bead up on his forehead and the sides of his neck.

He stood up quickly and strode to the door.

"Linkletter—get in here."

Miller mopped his head with a handkerchief. The sullen-looking guard who'd been holding down the captain's desk knocked softly on the open door. The warden waved him in, shutting the door behind him.

Link was a big man, at least six-two, mostly muscle. His uniform was specked with lint, unkempt and dotted with mud. His jaw was sharp, but not sharper than the light blue eyes underneath his flat hat. He gave Miranda a sideways examination, a quick up and down before facing his boss.

"Sir?"

Miller made a motion with his head and Linkletter moved to stand at attention behind him, more private bodyguard than prison bull, a praetorian for 1940 who would look at home next to Rudolph Hess.

"You remember George Blankenship, Linkletter?"

The light blue eyes grew opaque. "Yes, sir. What about him?"

"He's been shooting his fool mouth off and may be involved in a murder. Spreading lies and rumors about Alcatraz, making insinuations that he could get his job back by coming to us with information." Miller held on to the guard's eyes and spoke carefully. "I've explained to Miss Corbie here—she's working with Hoover's men—that he was fired for insubordination."

Linkletter glanced at Miranda and back to his boss. He held his hat in his hands, huge body oddly paralyzed.

"I'm not sure what you want me to say, sir."

Meat Head shifted in his chair, impatient. "Just tell her what you know about Blankenship, Linkletter, when and why he was fired. You handled it."

The flat bull cap went around in a circle. "Yes, sir. I did. But you—I don't want to get in trouble with the G-men, sir—"

Miller's hand hit the desk with a thud, making the papers and the guard jump. "Does she look like a G-man to you? We both know—both of us—that you've done nothing wrong. I gave you an order, Linkletter. Maybe you want to go back to the night shift."

Miranda uncrossed her legs and crushed the Chesterfield stub in the ashtray.

"Maybe I can help you, Captain."

Her eyes flickered up to the sharp-angled jaw, to Linkletter's muscular face.

Now or fucking never.

"George Blankenship seems to think you have something to hide. Something to do with certain prisoners getting certain privileges, something to do with Joseph Cretzer and Arnold Kyle, and something, maybe, to do with the rash of attempted escapes over the last couple of years. He says he's tired of keeping his mouth shut and wants his old job back and was planning to stop a book from being published in order to protect you—and blackmail you." She glanced over at the warden, sitting tensed in the chair, then back to Link, hat clutched and bent between massive fingers.

"My question, Captain, is simple: What does Blankenship have on you and Warden Miller?"

Cannon fire, thunder in the night, shriek of warplanes, and the bomb you never hear, you're a good soldier, Randy, a damn good soldier, and the men in uniform, the police who kept order, they lined up the men from the brigade against the ancient gray stone, blood and bits of flesh hitting the wall, and they fell down, fell down, fell down . . .

Miller's broad face ran colors, splotchy, stretched skin a rash of red and whites. Linkletter shifted position, pale blue eyes narrowed, muscles poised for action, his neck red and bulging against the color of his uniform.

One Mississippi, Two Mississippi . . .

Miller's voice was unexpectedly flat against the silence.

"Blankenship was a bad guard and he couldn't measure up and he got fired, end of story. We got nothing more to tell you except good-bye. I read up on you this morning, 'Miss' Corbie, made a few phone calls." He patted one of the pieces of paper on his desk as if it were a puppy. "I know all about you. You'll never work for Hoover again, you can count on that—and don't count on getting that license of yours renewed, either. I've got friends in high places, too—plenty of 'em."

Miranda took out another Chesterfield and tapped it on the edge of the warden's desk three times before lighting it.

"Cards on the table, Warden Miller? I'll play a hand. You're the second associate warden Johnston's had, and the last couple of years haven't been very good for the prison, have they? Maybe Johnston needs to know what I know— what my employers know. Maybe he'll wake up from his nap in his nice big office and realize he's tired of making apologies to the BOP and San Francisco. Maybe he'll realize you'll make one hell of a good fall guy. Maybe you'd like to go back to busting heads at Leavenworth along with your bruno boy here." She nodded at Linkletter. "If not, start talking. My fifteen minutes aren't up yet."

Miller's mouth compressed into itself, eyes wide with shock.

"He shouldn'ta been fired, not George, knew there'd be trouble, sir, I told you, but I can fix it, I can fix her, too—"

"Linkletter!" Miller regained control. "That's enough." He glanced up at Miranda, wiped his forehead with the limp handkerchief again. Pulled at his ear, rocked a little, back and forth in his throne.

"Blankenship was an insubordinate fool, a moron with a low IQ who should never have been hired. He was guilty of—of behavior that we don't tolerate in our inmates, let alone our troops. Our guards are top men—all top men."

Top men in uniform, like the men in Spain, like the men in Germany, keepers of order, keepers of peace . . .

"Top men? With Linkletter here at the summit? Some of the—let's call them 'top men,' shall we?—that I work for are wondering why Alcatraz gets strike after strike. They're wondering what happened to Rufus McCain and Henri Young and William Martin and why the U.S. Attorney didn't charge them for the escape attempt. They're wondering about the fire in the mat shop and why Rufe Persful chopped off his own fingers and Roy Gardner killed himself. Maybe you can respond to those 'top men,' Warden Miller. And explain why exactly George Blankenship thinks he can blackmail you into giving him his job back."

Miller raised his face, emotions under lock and key, shut up in isolation. He glanced up at Linkletter, who stood tensed, pale eyes fixed on Miranda.

"My message from the Bureau of Prisons said to cooperate with you, Miss Corbie. It also said your purpose in coming to Alcatraz was to find out more about Cretzer and Kyle. To that end, as I mentioned, I've prepared a small packet of information, including the special report given to Warden Johnston by the Bureau of Prisons."

Miller pushed a manila envelope toward her with his fingertips.

"We do not expect nor will we experience any trouble from Mr. Cretzer or Mr. Kyle. Alcatraz has a habit of subduing even the most hardened, recalcitrant criminal type." He bared his teeth at her. "Your fifteen minutes are up, Miss Corbie."

She looked from one to the other.

End of the road.

"I think you're wrong, Warden Miller. I think there will always be strikes and escape attempts on Alcatraz . . . as long as you're running it. Just as I think Rufus McCain and Henri Young are holed up in one of your dungeons on water and bread every three days, shitting in the dark until their minds rot out. And whatever they're going through, William Martin's getting it worse."

She stood, dropping the cigarette in the warden's ashtray and twisting it until the tobacco splintered. Her eyes flickered over the two men, Miller seated and Linkletter standing at attention behind him.

"Blankenship'll talk. Whatever he knows, we'll find out. And whatever Smith dug up on Cretzer and Kyle, we'll find that out, too. And if it ties into two murders in San Francisco, one—or both of you—may reap what you've sown. Maybe *your* fifteen minutes are up, gentlemen."

Miranda scooped up the envelope and moved to the door.

Miller's voice rose behind her.

"We sacrifice our lives to protect people like you, Corbie. Good, honest men living next to degenerates, all night, all day, so you can lead your life, free to go to the pictures or some two-bit roadhouse, free to fornicate or drink or whatever women like you do. We pay for your sins, you and millions like you. We pay for your freedom. You should get down on your hands and knees and thank God and Warden Johnston that we keep these men under control and off the streets. It doesn't matter how, not to the mother with five children to raise or the accountant with a late-night job. It never matters how. All that matters, Corbie, is that we do it."

Miranda turned around in the doorway. She looked at both of them, the bull behind the warden, the pale blue eyes and the others shiny and hard, like the shells on black beetles.

She spoke the words as if to herself.

"Quis custodiet ipsos custodes?"

Then she pulled the door shut with an audible clack.

Miranda stepped toward the left, looking for Henry.

She shivered and her hands were shaking, knives at her back. . . .

Linkletter's light blue eyes, memorizing her.

Act Five

*

Publication

"Whereof what's past is prologue; what to come,
In yours and my discharge."
The Tempest, Act II, scene i

Twenty-Seven

*

The *McDowell* pulled up to the dock, regular Alcatraz transport boat, ready to take workers and wives back to the mainland, back to civilization.

Christ, the small wooden ferry was the most beautiful boat she'd ever seen.

She waved and smiled automatically at Henry, who wiped his brow and began the long climb back up the hill.

Nice little man. Couldn't help where he worked . . . or for whom.

No flirtatious carpenters on the fifteen-minute trip to shore and Miranda stayed seated inside the cabin, studying the packet Meat Head Miller thrust at her.

She'd seen all she ever wanted of the Rock.

The report on Cretzer—and it was mostly about him, with very little on "Shorty" Kyle, other than some information on his wife, the former Thelma Crowley—found no "psychotic" trend, just a "very desperate, cold-blooded individual." The rest of the small gang they worked with, off and on, had been apprehended. No other known criminal associations, no ties to the families, to the bootlegging dynasties, to the big-money men like Capone or her old acquaintance Mickey Cohen. No, Cretzer was just a simple jobbie with a ruthless streak, determined to escape, aided and abetted by the fact he figured it was the only way out alive, solution to the hopeless dead-end of a long, long sentence.

She frowned, shaking her head.

If he couldn't handle McNeil, Alcatraz would kill George Cretzer more surely than the gas chamber. But this time, other men would go with him . . . innocent men, maybe, guards who weren't part of whatever scheme Miller was running, men who just wanted to do their job and live their lives, grateful for a tough haul, quiet in the face of corruption and cruelty, not willing to rat on their fellow bulls.

A blue shape wavered, reflecting in the window, and she quickly turned her head, expecting to see Linkletter standing in front of her.

She took a deep breath. Just one of the laborers from Alcatraz, stretching his legs.

Jesus Christ. More rattled than she expected.

Miranda stared out the bleary window again, Van Ness pier fast approaching.

She was looking for a killer, a clever one. Someone who could improvise, who could react, someone who'd killed Alexander and thought he'd killed Louise. Someone whose motive she still couldn't quite see, picture as foggy as the goddamn window.

The boat lurched slightly as it pulled in, and Miranda carefully slid the papers back into the office envelope Miller gave her.

Maybe she was looking for a man in a uniform.

*

She grabbed a hamburger at Tascone's, ravenous for meat, cherry Coke sweet and carmelly with the crinkle-cut fries. She read over the report again—the story of Cretzer before he came to Alcatraz.

Spent 120 days in isolation, fed a "#435 diet" for the first 10. What the hell was that? Spiders and piss?

> *Inmate is considered an outstanding problem on account of his attitude and determination to escape and he would not be particular about what method he uses . . .*

Meat Head must be sweating bullets over Cretzer, one more attempt, one more round of bad publicity and his head might be on the chopping block. Miller and Link, Link and Miller and throw in Blankenship, the ex-bull and aspiring blackmailer . . .

She frowned and pushed the plate aside. A sailor, drunk already, put a nickel in the jukebox and hit "In the Mood," weaving and leering his way toward Miranda's counter stool.

Miranda checked her watch. Only 10:45. Maybe Allen had some answers on why George Blankenship was fired, maybe the voluminous Pinkerton files and government connections mouthed more than the word "insubordination."

She threw a quarter and a dime on the counter and hopped off the stool, bumping into the sailor.

"Stand aside, swabbie."

He laughed, blond hair flat and sweaty under his hat. He stank of stale beer and cheap perfume and stood his ground, waving like a forget-me-not in an ocean breeze.

"Ain't ya in the mood, lady?"

She grinned, gently shoved him backward, and headed through the door.

The Pinkerton sat back in his chair, spring squeaking, hands behind his head, beaming like a proud father at a piano recital.

"You're a crackerjack shamus, Miranda Corbie. Crackerjack. Who'da thought the little girl down the hall would get herself an interview at Alcatraz?"

Miranda popped two lemon drops in her mouth. Looked up at the bald, stocky detective with a tired frown.

"For all the good it did me—I'm confused as hell. Alexander's murder and the attempts on Louise look like something personal, not a professional bump-off by a couple of trouble boys—especially with said trouble boys locked up on Alcatraz, and most of their associates lodged in hoosegows around the country. Then the manuscript's stolen, George Blankenship crawls out from under a rock—make that *the* Rock—and Louise's sister turns out to be Thelma Kyle. So what is it, Allen? What the hell is it? Am I missing something?"

"Seems to me like you've covered all the bases."

"Not enough, not nearly enough. If I could just figure out how the Alcatraz connection works . . . I mean, there's a connection somewhere, isn't there? There's gotta be. Something's going down with George and Linkletter and Miller—something blackmail worthy. Graft? Grift? Who the hell knows?"

Allen Jennings shook his head, tapping ash from a lit Lucky into a glass tray.

"The record I found was a cable from the LA office—and the part about Blankenship was penciled in. All it said was 'insubordination,' nothing more. As for Cretzer and Kyle, we get regular reports from the Bureau, so tracking your Thelma was easy—got the whole skinny on her. I'll see if I can dig anything up on Linkletter—he looks like your best bet. I can get you the dope on paper as soon as Hedy Lamarr takes a hike." He made a face and a motion with his head toward the receptionist's area at the front of the office, and Miranda laughed.

"Another one who wants her name in lights?"

The Pinkerton grunted. "Or on a marriage certificate. She's been throwing herself at everything in pants that walks by."

"That's why I just knock on your back door. I get tired of the up-and-down with a Lady Esther voice."

"Eh, female jealousy. Nothin' quite as sharp, not even a stiletto. Seriously, though, Miri, I'll get you what we have, but I don't think it's anything you don't already know—unless I can find a line on that Linkletter bull. Sounds like you hit it off with the Thelma Kyle dame . . . maybe try another round?"

"Thelma'll want to see her sister as soon as she wakes up—if Louise is still Louise, I mean. Doctors don't know how her brain's gonna come out of all this." Miranda shook her head, spoke glumly. "I can't help feeling like I'm looking at everything upside down—or inside out."

The detective scratched the gray and black stubble on his chin.

"Some cases'll do that to you. What you need is a break so your head can reshuffle the deck. Why'ncha go out tonight? Hit the town, catch a band, dance a little. If Sanders is still on leave—"

Miranda's voice was sharper than she intended. "He's in Santa Rosa." Her eyes flicked up to meet Allen's. "And I don't have the time."

She gathered her handbag and stood up from the chair.

His voice was soft.

"I'm here if you need a sounding board."

Miranda smiled. "Thanks, Allen. Don't know what I'll do in London without you."

His face crumpled but he grinned, skin tight around his eyes.

"Duck, mostly."

She laughed. "We'll get back to the Rusty Nail before I leave, OK?"

The Pinkerton nodded and rubbed his nose, large pores red and shiny.

"That's a confirmed date."

Miranda smiled once more before slipping out the door and into the hall of the Monadnock.

*

She pulled the Big Chief notepad closer, glancing at the watch on her wrist.

11:52. Hoped she could catch the inspector before lunch.

"Fisher here—that you, Miranda?"

"Yes. Just back from Alcatraz."

One Mississippi, Two Mississippi . . .

"Alcatraz? The prison? How in the hell did you get to Alcatraz?"

"Don't yell into the phone, Inspector—we need to be discreet about it. I was serious when I asked for a week to clear this up and I figured I'd start at the hot spot."

"Hot spot? Christ, it's goddamn Alcatraz! How in the hell—"

"Look, I don't have time to explain even if I could. Point is, something smells. There's a guard named Linkletter—Miller's right-hand man—he's the one Blankenship wanted to peddle Smith's manuscript to—"

"Miller? Associate Warden Miller?"

"Inspector, please—"

"You're in deep, Miranda, too deep for me." The cop at the other end of the phone took a breath. "But go ahead. I know why and I won't ask how. Miller and Linkletter, you say? That's who Blankenship wanted to blackmail?"

"Yeah. Linkletter was promoted—he's captain of the guards now, in addition to serving as Miller's private Gestapo. Only information I could get on Shorty Kyle was a bulletin written by the BOP, outlines the facts on Thelma and an alienist's evaluation of both prisoners. When I asked about Blankenship, they threatened me—Miller not in so many words, but Linkletter wasn't as circumspect. All they'd admit to was firing him for 'insubordination,' but there's something more. Something went down, something they're trying to cover up. I think you should bring in George and hold him on whatever you can."

Rat-tat-tat of typewriters, a screaming child, and a guttural drone of voices were drowned out by a siren. Miranda held the phone away from her ear for a moment.

"Inspector? You there?"

His voice was heavy. "I'm here. But Blankenship isn't. I pulled a man off another detail last night to watch him and he gave him the slip."

Shit.

"Haul in a janitor at Greer by the name of Matthew—he's a playmate of George's. He'll know something. We grilled them yesterday evening."

"You and Sanders?"

Miranda reached for the pack of Chesterfields and shook one out. "Yeah. Blankenship thought he'd get the jump on me. Boy's always thinking—good thing he doesn't do it so well. Brace Matthew and you'll find George, Inspector—and find him quick. What about Smith? He still under wraps?"

"Yeah, we've got him locked down and so far he hasn't shaken the tail. Looks like he's the only one who can really spill the goods . . . presuming he remembers what was in his own damn book."

"He on a bender?"

Fisher snorted. "He's got two speeds—drunk and drunker. Wouldn't give me much without his lawyer—oh yeah, he's got a mouthpiece by the name of Crosby, no relation to Bing except for a love of ponies—a high-stakes gambler and a slick sonofabitch, excuse my French. Anyway, Smith coughed up nothing specific about Alcatraz, just some general hoohaw about how Cretzer and Kyle never had a chance. Insisted he had no idea why Blankenship or anyone else would want to steal the book, other than it was gonna be a bestseller and worth a pretty penny. I spoke to his agent, too—Charlie Segal. He's flying in from Arizona, already on the way—should be here tomorrow morning."

"Mind if I try to get some sense out of him?"

"Out of Smith? Be my guest. He's at home or should be. His pattern's been to sleep til one or two in the afternoon and stay up all night. The boys are complaining about it, but I can't hold him on anything, not with Crosby watching him like a broody hen. And he wouldn't agree to official protection, so this is the best we can do."

"At least the morning papers carried the story about Louise—it's the one way and only way we're ahead of the killer. The hospital said they're expecting her to live, but we don't know the extent of damage to her brain, not until she wakes up. That dovetail with your report?"

Fisher grunted. "Yeah, I got the update last night. I thought you were nuts at first, but you were right, keeping her under wraps is a good plan. Got two of my best men down there and Gonzales is overseeing them personally. Mrs. Kyle asked if she could wait for her sister to wake up so she's down there, too. No word, not so far."

"Any witnesses at the apartment house?"

"Maybe. Neighbor saw a milkman on the stairs yesterday morning—later than a milkman should be, and not the usual Meadow Glen dairy. Here's the trouble: the ME and the hospital docs think Louise's pilot light had to be shut off for longer than just yesterday morning. They calculated the size of the apartment, the rate of the leak, and the fact that one of the windows was cracked open, hemmed and hawed til I was about to pop a blood vessel, and then said they didn't think it was likely she could've inhaled as much as she did if, say, a phony milkman somehow got in her apartment—while she was there—and blew it out."

"Did they give you an estimate?"

"Half-assed. They thought 'the night before' was reasonable, but couldn't be more specific."

"Any signs of a break-in?"

"Not a one. I hope to hell Miss Crowley makes a full recovery—for her sake, and ours."

Miranda blew a stream of smoke at the faded Martell's calendar on the wall, blond girl in pigtails.

"Me, too, Inspector. Me, too. Please keep me posted, especially if you dig up something on Linkletter or if Blankenship turns up."

"I will. You do the same. And for pity's sake, Miranda—for the sake of my blood pressure—stay away from federal penitentiaries, OK?"

She cracked a laugh, and hung up the phone.

No answer at the number James gave her, so she left a message.

Nothing too specific, nothing too obvious. She owed him the information he'd asked for, but he'd need to collect it directly. Maybe Miller was bluffing, maybe he wasn't, but Hoover and his trigger-happy troops weren't gonna gum up the works, not now, not when she was on the point of saying good-bye and maybe even hello. She wasn't sure how much pull James had, how much power, and the *Cameronia* seat had been too hard to come by.

Miranda pulled the phone closer. Two more phone calls before she could brace Smith.

She dialed Meyer's number, starting to worry when the ring count passed five. His lightly accented voice finally answered.

"Meyer?"

"Miranda? How are you, my dear? What—what time is it?"

"About twelve fifteen."

"Twelve fifteen?" He cleared his throat, sounding embarrassed. "I have been rather tired the last few days . . ."

"You needed to sleep, Meyer, for God's sake. You were up all night with Louise—"

"Miss Crowley! How is she?"

"The doctors expect her to live and said she's showing signs of regaining full consciousness. They're hopeful it'll happen today."

"Thank God." The lawyer spoke quietly, reverently. "I thank the Holy Mother for her intercession."

Miranda's voice was sober. "She might wake up with brain damage, Meyer."

"She will be well. I am convinced of it."

"I hope you're right. Listen, I just wanted to let you know about Louise. Get some rest. I'll phone with any developments."

"Thank you, my dear. I have some case work to review, as a matter of fact, so"—long yawn—"Excuse me—it is very fortuitous that you called."

She smiled. God, she'd miss Meyer, her attorney, her former client . . . her friend.

"Be seein' you, Meyer. Sweet dreams."

Miranda lowered the heavy black headset back into the cradle and stared thoughtfully at the phone. She picked it up again, closed her eyes until she remembered the number, and dialed.

Two rings.

"Alexander Publishing, Bunny Berrigian speaking."

"It's Miranda Corbie, Bunny. Louise is gonna make it. We're just waiting for her to regain consciousness, and they think it'll happen today."

The whoof of relief came over the phone's receiver, Bunny's voice scratchy. "Well, thank God for doing something right. Poor kid. Thanks for letting me know. Listen, I've gotta run—"

"I do, too. Any editors in the office today?"

"Just Hank. Why?"

"Might want to visit some in their natural habitat later."

"Then try the nearest bar. Say, I should let you know—Sylvia's out of Greer. She and Roger are getting married."

Miranda sat back against the black leather chair, eyes blinking. "Married? Isn't that a bit—soon? I saw Roger yesterday and he said she'd tried to harm herself . . . didn't sound as though she were ready for the real world, such as it is—not that Greer is anything other than an expensive clip joint, but still . . ."

Bunny sighed. "I know, I know. At least they're not tying the knot until after the memorial. I think they said Monday at City Hall. Listen, I really do have to go—"

"When you say 'they,' I take it you mean Roger, right? You haven't actually spoken to Sylvia?"

"Nope, I saw them both. Swooped in like two lovebirds to tell me the happy news. She seemed more stable than I've seen her in years, so I'm happy for her. She's recuperating at home."

Miranda frowned. One fast about-face from the woman Roger described as suicidal . . .

"Thanks, Bunny. I might drop in later. Keep your fingers crossed for Louise."

"You bet I will." The redhead spoke fervently.

Miranda hung up the phone once more, staring thoughtfully into space.

She shook herself, threw a couple of packs of Chesterfields in her purse and checked for the Baby Browning.

It lay in the cigarette case, loaded and ready, dark brown dull against the shiny gold.

Little gun, insignificant weapon to a man like Martini, until she blew his brains out against a bathroom wall.

Red and white, red and white, and the sick, soft splatter, *pop-bang* reverberating, around and around and around . . .

Miranda closed her eyes. That was seven months ago and Smith was no Martini. Alexander's death, the attempt on Louise—whoever was behind it was no professional, even if there was a connection with the Rock.

She took a breath and walked through the office door, locking it behind her.

Glanced up and read the letters on the glass, black paint starting to chip:

MIRANDA CORBIE—PRIVATE INVESTIGATOR.

No sense in repainting. Before too long, someone else's name, someone else's office.

Someone else's door.

She stared at the words until they blurred, then walked down the empty fourth-floor hall, shoe taps ringing on the gray stone floor.

Twenty-Eight

*

Miranda leaned back, shielding her eyes, and stared up at the Cathedral Apartments, 1201 California Street, just a country club application away from Grace Cathedral.

Nob Hill, still home to nobs and snobs and members of the Pacific-Union Club, yanking strings with the mayor and God, the closest hill to Heaven in San Francisco.

They controlled the market, controlled the banks, and tried like hell to control the unions, though they couldn't control Harry Bridges, so they kept trying to deport the poor bastard, Red Menace always more threatening than simple German businessmen.

She took in the long, golden lines of apartments and expensive hotels, the stately private temples to commerce and capitalism and silver mines, the private chauffeur lounging against a Bentley, smoking a cigarette, the woman in the leopard coat looking at a packed cable car, simply too amused.

Nob fucking Hill.

What passed for old money in a City built by cheats and frauds and the sweat of gold fever, and built again by optimists and dreamers and sharp-eyed newcomers, the kind who recognized an opportunity when it burned down around them.

It was a long slow skid down to the plants and factories on the other side of the city, the cheap apartments on Laguna, the creaking boardinghouses along Telegraph Hill, even to the Monadnock and the De Young Building, where railway companies hawked vacations to Tijuana and private detectives chased sweaty husbands in out-of-town hotels and newshawks pounded out fairy-tale stories about the sugar cane heir and his snowbird girlfriend . . . one mistake, a misspoken word, a sudden raise in rent and an even farther tumble to the Tenderloin and Chinatown, where Blind Willie sold pencils and No Legs Norris pushed himself through slop-filled alleys on a platform made of plywood, where Chinatown beat cops held assignations in dim alleys, and B-girls retired, old, at the age of twenty-one.

Miranda sniffed the cool air, breeze blowing through her hair as she held on to her beret.

No plywood here, not for Howard Carter Smith.

She hit the buzzer, number 602. No sleek-haired young manager behind the desk today.

A man she'd been watching stepped away from the shadows, smoking a cigarette. About forty with a gut, face covered in stubble, hair cut close to his scalp under the stained brown fedora.

He took three steps forward, got a better look at her, and sauntered back to the shadows, resuming his lean against the cold stucco.

She glanced over and he tipped his hat.

Her lips twitched a smile, and she pushed twice more, short staccato bursts designed to wake up a drunk and irritate the neighbors.

She waited thirty seconds then held down the immaculately white button, buzz grinding through the sedate lobby like the wrong fork at dessert.

A door slammed somewhere above, and footsteps thudded down the steps, muffled by a well-bred carpet.

Smith.

He was wrapped in a blue silk bathrobe, monogrammed, thin hair plastered to his head, skin ashen and gray, chin and cheeks unshaven. His thick body jerked and stumbled its way to the door, which he flung open, eyebrows knitted together in a long line of rebuke.

Miranda squeezed in before he could open his mouth.

Her eyes flickered over him, from the lamb's wool slippers to the HCS emblazoned on his chest. His robe was stained and sweaty and he smelled like Scotch and dried puke.

"Invite me upstairs, Smith. We need to talk."

*

He wavered while he stared at her, trying to figure out who she was and why she'd pried him off a couch and into the cold, hard world of responsibility.

"You—you're that, that dick-lady, Corbie—"

"Congratulations—you got my name right." She looked around the lobby, from the dust-free crystal chandelier to the purple orchids on the eighteenth-century marble-and-gold table, poised like a butler by the staircase.

"No elevator? Let's walk."

His forehead wrinkled. "Elevator's 'round the corner. What're you doin' here, lady? I thought—I thought I told you to dust last night . . ."

Miranda started up the stairs, footsteps barely registering against the blue carpet, gold balustrade shining.

"I'm not that easy to blow away, Smith. I suggest we talk upstairs—that is, unless you want your neighbors to know why you're such a popular boy down at the Hall of Justice."

He blinked a few times, waking up, thick body drawing itself together, muscles tightening. He pulled his robe together more securely, frowning, and climbed after Miranda.

His voice was a growl. "Second on the left, sixth floor."

She didn't bother to reply. Smith started to pant after the third-floor landing, and was breathing hard by the time they reached six.

The door to #602 was a thick number, highly polished. Smith coughed, fumbling in his robe pocket. "I forgot my fuckin' key . . ."

"Did you even lock it?" Miranda pushed on the heavy door and it noiselessly opened about a foot.

Smith glared at her, and proceeded inside. She pulled it shut behind her.

The apartment looked like something out of one of those Joan Crawford or Ginger Rogers pictures where the girl makes good or makes bad or somehow climbs all the way from a department store counter to a ritzy penthouse.

The theme was pale wood, lots of gold and white and yellow, modern, angular furniture and a wide view of the Bay, which she could just glimpse in the small opening of the shut drapes. No clutter and surprisingly few books, with one small wooden case lined with Smith's own and a few, select editions of other writers. Opposite doors presumably led into a kitchen and dining-room area on one side and the office, bathroom and bedroom suite on the other.

The living room itself was a standard arrangement of expensive chairs, glass tables, and a large, overstuffed sofa. A thin wool blanket and silk pillow lay crumpled against the blond fabric. Below, specks of vomit still clung to the long, tan fibers of plush carpet, a small puddle, not yet cleaned up.

Smith noticed her looking and mumbled: "Maid's off today."

She shrugged and sank down in an armchair. "Mind if I smoke?"

"I mind you being here, lady. So cut to the chase."

"I'll take that as a 'no.' Why don't you put on some coffee, Smith? I'm gonna be awhile."

The thick-bodied man glared at her, eyes red-rimmed and bloodshot. Then he padded through the swinging door on the right, and Miranda could hear him opening cupboards in the kitchen.

She lit a Chesterfield and exhaled, looking around. An empty bottle of gin and half a bottle of Van der Hum still littered the glass coffee table, along with an overflowing ashtray and about three dirty glasses.

Smith barged back through, looking considerably more awake.

"Emily Post's satisfied, Corbie. Now talk." He threw himself down on the couch, inelegantly sprawled, small brown eyes still blurry and mean.

Miranda blew a cascade of blue smoke. "That's your job."

"Listen, lady, I'm two seconds away from phoning my attorney and throwing you out on your ear—"

"No, you listen, Smith, and listen well. Crosby's not gonna get you out of talking, not today. Two people have been murdered—two people connected to your Alcatraz book."

The writer's face contorted in a recalcitrant snarl.

"And I've got the same thing to say to you I say to the coppers—not my fucking problem. So why don't you—"

"'Not my problem'? Such a man of the people, Smith. Such a muckracker. I'm surprised Steinbeck lets you into Monterey."

"John knows I can buy the drinks. And don't question my politics, Corbie— you've got no goddamn idea."

She bent forward, tapping ash in the overflowing crystal tray. "Oh, I've got an idea. And I'm not the only one. Try J. Edgar Hoover on for size."

The stocky man blinked a few times and sat up straighter, arm off the couch and hands in fists on either side of his body.

"Hoover? The Bureau? What are you talking about?"

"Alcatraz, Smith. The Rock. I paid a visit to Associate Warden Miller and a bull named Linkletter this morning. I put cards on the table and you were the fucking ace. But Miller didn't want to play and threatened to call Hoover. Linkletter's his goon—capable of murder, I'd say—and from their reaction, it looks like you stumbled on some information either about them or related to them, information that your book contained and that George Blankenship was going to use to blackmail them with."

She inhaled the stick while color cascaded over Smith's pasty face. No words, not from the man who arranged them for money. His stubby fingers clutched at the monogrammed robe.

"You mentioned my name? Told them about my book?"

"I just said so. Whatever you've been hiding, whatever you wrote, whatever sordid mess you dug up on Alcatraz, your surprise party is over. Maybe you're too stubborn or stupid to realize you're in danger, maybe even from the same men, and frankly, I don't much care if you pay the price for it. What I do care about is that you're endangering people, innocent people. I don't know how much money you think you stand to gain from rewriting the Alcatraz book, Smith, but you're no Lincoln Steffens or even John Spivak, and the charade's gotta end—now."

She ground out the stick in the crystal tray.

The writer swallowed, face now ashen and red around the eyes. He looked up at Miranda.

"My family—if Hoover finds out about my—Jesus, it could ruin me." He ran a hand across his forehead. "All right, I'll talk. Seems to be the only way to protect myself."

He stood up unsteadily and walked toward the portable bar, pouring a shot of rye into a shot glass. A faint hissing noise wafted under the door to the kitchen.

Smith mumbled, without looking at her, "I'll get the coffee. How do you take it?"

"Black."

He was gone for under a minute but long enough for Miranda to take out her reporter's notebook and jot down "Ask Bente about Smith." He backed through the swing door, hands full with two cups, and handed her a jadeite mug before heading back to the bar, pouring another stiff shot into his coffee.

"Easy, Smith—I need you to stay sober."

"This won't even make a dent. What do you want to know?"

The writer seemed almost pathetic, arms heavy, mouth drawn downward.

She sipped the coffee and set the cup down on the glass table, taking up the notebook.

"Understand this is as off-the-record as I can make it, but Fisher will need some details."

Smith waved a hand. "Doesn't matter. Not now."

"Why would Blankenship want to use the book for blackmail?"

He shifted nervously against the couch. "I can't—can't be sure, because I never mentioned Miller specifically—too much of a legal risk—but the name 'Link' was in the margin notes of the original manuscript before Niles edited it. So were some other names."

"In what context?"

The thick-bodied man gulped the coffee and whiskey before looking away from her, facing the draped window.

"I talked to a couple of men who knew Gardner—"

"Roy Gardner?"

"Yeah. And others who'd made it out. The book wasn't just about Alcatraz, you know, but that's how Niles wanted to slant it—that's why he had me rewrite some of it a few weeks ago, to make it all about Alcatraz."

"Go on."

"What they told me—well, it's about the guards. Not all the bulls, mind you, there are a lot of good men in these prisons. But the BOP didn't used to be so choosy, and from what I've heard they're trying to clean up their act, boot the crooked ones."

Miranda was scribbling words furiously. "You mean they took bribes?"

"Bribes? Oh, hell, yeah. That's expected. Jailbirds get a whole list of the ones to hit up, prison by prison. You pay to access the information, and it's maintained, inmate by inmate, passed along to other men in other prisons when they get transferred. You get better food, privileges, privacy—pay the bulls to look the other way. You can even crack the joint, if you're willing to take the risk— that's how Cretzer and Kyle made the break at McNeil—they got to the right guard at the right time."

"So Blankenship wanted to steal your book because Cretzer and Kyle were transferring to Alcatraz and you were about to blow the lid off the bribery?"

Smith scratched his chin. "You tell me. Cretzer said he knew he could bust out of Alcatraz—he'd been briefed on the bulls to pay off. I asked him if that were so why Kelly and "Creepy" Karpis were still there. He just smirked and said Kelly was there because he wanted to be there, and he was running things from his cell. Cretzer's goofy, a dangerous sonofabitch. I didn't trust what he told me, but Alexander shat in his pants when I told him I got that interview. Blankenship's girlfriend, the one who got killed—didn't she have something to do with Cretzer?"

"No, with Kyle. She was his sister-in-law." Miranda frowned. "Seems like too much of a stretch. Miller and Linkletter are crooked, all right, but they don't seem crooked in that way. They're bullies—they like power more than money. Blankenship is just the type who'd take a payoff, but he's not working on the Rock anymore. Was there something else, something besides graft and bribes and corruption? Something personal on Miller or Linkletter or both?"

Smith was staring into the empty coffee cup, face red and skin stretched tight.

He mumbled "Excuse me" and walked over to the bar, pouring more rye. He came back to the couch, still avoiding her eyes, and drank half the cup in a go. Miranda waited patiently, never taking her eyes off of him.

He finally looked up. "All right—there is something else. And it's how I heard the name 'Link'—I assume that's your 'Linkletter.'"

Miranda leaned forward in the chair. "What, Smith? What did you hear?"

He drained the coffee cup again, veins stark in his nose and cheeks, and set it down on the glass table with a clank. "It's not pretty."

"I was in Spain three years ago. There's not much I haven't seen."

The writer stared at her, surprise and admiration flickering across his features.

"All right. You asked me, and I'm telling you." Smith swallowed. "You know it's—it's hard on men in prison . . ."

"If you're talking about sex, Smith, a lot of them have problems outside of prison, too."

"Well, when a man's there for years and he doesn't have female company . . ."

"Yeah, I know all about that, too. What's it got to do with Linkletter?"

Smith kept his eyes on the carpet stain, small, brown, and unfocused.

"There are men in every prison who—who provide services to the others. In return, they're protected. Most of the time, in most places, who does what to whom happens—happens naturally, if you know what I mean."

Miranda spoke slowly, skin prickling on the back of her neck. "I do."

His head was rigid, eyes still on the dried vomit. He spoke in a low voice.

"Not on Alcatraz."

Miranda bent forward, body tense and tight.

"Smith—what do you mean?"

"There are some guards on the Rock—Link was mentioned as one of them—who select which prisoners are gonna—gonna provide services. Then they break 'em in. And they do it to men in solitary, too, sometimes, especially the colored ones."

Color drained from her face as she stared at the thin-haired man, sitting hunched on the expensive couch in the Hollywood-set apartment, speaking in a near whisper.

Talking about rape on Alcatraz.

*

"Smith—Jesus Christ—"

The writer scratched his nose. "Yeah. I felt pretty bad when I heard about it. Niles and I went around and around—he was the only one who knew about the bribery and the—the other thing. And he wanted to milk it for all it was worth but didn't want to get sued, so I spent fucking forever rewriting the goddamn thing."

She stared at him, the red-veined nose, the thick, hairy fingers, the soiled robe that cost a month's worth of wages to a man at the Del Monte plant.

"Why the hell didn't you report it, Smith? Do something about it?"

"I was doing something about it—I wrote the goddamn book, didn't I?"

Miranda shook her head. "Not enough. Not nearly enough."

Smith rose from the couch in a swift move, as if trying to run away.

"Listen, lady, you don't know me. So yeah, I come from money—born to it. But I was also born with a goddamn conscience and some talent, too, and I'm trying to use it as best I can to help the proletariat."

Proletariat. Prole-fucking-tariat.

"You a Communist, Smith?"

"Yeah, I'm a Communist. That's why I'm—Jesus, if Hoover finds out I'm a member of the Party, my father'll cut me off in a heartbeat."

Miranda stood up slowly, watching the hunched-over writer trapped like a fly against the window pane.

Her voice was wry. "There are worse things than being poor."

By now, he couldn't hear her. His voice rose and fell, alternately whining and pleading and arguing for clemency, while his body seemed to shrink, thick hands clinging to the gold brocade drapes.

"'Smith,' what a laugh. All I wanted was an—an identity, something beyond my father and the family and that dry, dead house, something my brothers and sister couldn't do, couldn't have, some way to get—to get noticed, for God's sake—my talent's not in Wall Street or washing machines, my talent's in words and syllables, in commas and exclamation points—in what we say and how we say it and silences that are louder than all the words we write . . . that's what I wanted, my dream, and—and the Party needs me, appreciates me. Which is more than I can say for my father."

Miranda looked around. "He's got enough appreciation to pay for this."

"Because he couldn't face having a failure as a son. It takes years to become a successful writer, years and luck and a publisher who's willing to back you. I was on the verge—with Niles—and then the manuscript was stolen. At least—at least I've got my novel, and it's good, damn good. Christ, if I can just keep Hoover off my back—maybe I should skip Party meetings for a while . . ."

"That might be a good idea. In the meantime, I'll ask a friend of mine to keep her ear to the ground."

He looked surprised again. "She a member?"

"Yes. And Smith, if I were you, I'd stay sober. Might even help with the writing."

He pulled the robe together and shivered.

"No, you're wrong. All good writing comes from here"—he tapped his stomach—"and sometimes a drink's the only way you can get to it. It's not easy, you know, sitting around, pouring out your guts and your soul on a blank piece of paper, wondering if you're crazy or if the people who read it are—wondering if anyone will read it. Wondering if you'll be attacked or condemned by the Legion of Decency or if you'll be hailed as a visionary hero, if you'll never see true success because you're decades too early and won't be appreciated until you're too fucking dead to care."

Smith shook his head. "I'd better get dressed. If I'm not mistaken, Niles' memorial is tomorrow tonight. I've got things to do and I'd like to show up at least a little sober."

Miranda started toward the door. "I'll see you there, Smith. Like I said, I'll do what I can to protect you. From Hoover, from the press, from the killer. But for God's sake—protect yourself."

"From what? Life? Forget about it, Miss Corbie. But thanks for keeping my many secrets."

Miranda turned and locked eyes with Smith for a moment. Then the door shut firmly, swiftly, quietly in place.

Twenty-nine

✳

Alcatraz.

The Rock.

The hell she hoped to never see again.

Men trapped, criminals yes, maybe they robbed banks like Gardner, the gentleman bandit, maybe stole a car or maybe even killed someone. And they were shut behind steel bars, locked on an island for the safety of society and the American Way and most of them probably deserved it, some even pain and death, a snapped neck, body flailing in the wind or a jolt of electricity shuddering through their legs or a gas canister, seeping in, nowhere to run.

Whatever it took to stamp out the malignancy of their lives, lives that had taken so many others. Innocent lives, lives like Betty or Edward, lives like the Chinese women packed like rats in the hold of a ship, lives like the Jews in Germany, tortured, burned alive, Night of the Broken Glass now one long night across Europe, lives like the last black man lynched from a swamp oak in Tallahassee, Florida.

Miranda shook her head, inhaling the cigarette.

Hell, she'd hoist the rope, pull the trigger, throw the fucking switch.

Personal vengeance, personal justice.

But this wasn't personal. This was torture, humiliation, rape. Not in the name of a victim, not in the name of a survivor's family, not in the name of any humanity.

No, these were men in prison guard uniforms who represented the whole fucking country.

Quis custodies ipsos custodiet? she'd asked. Hell, no one. They all wanted to forget, forget the men locked on an island, no reporters allowed. Forget the Roy Gardners. Forget the William Martins.

Forget rape.

They had it coming, the men in the boardrooms would say. They had it coming. Like the women in bars and apartment houses, offices and schools, cars or warehouses or the woods in back of the fucking barn . . .

Rape and rape victims always forgotten, always to blame, your fault, Susie, your fault, what did you do to provoke him? What did you do wrong?

Weapon of war directed at women, mothers, daughters, sisters, grand-mothers, front-line casualties from Nanking to Poland, unseen detritus of the battlefield, never calculated by the generals, never patched by Red Cross medics, never blessed by chaplains.

Blood and pain and brutal fear, so much worse than death. So many looking for death afterward, better dead than face the shame, the shame that somehow they weren't fast enough, weren't strong enough, weren't good enough, no, not good enough to be protected by whatever god they worshipped, whatever name they'd called to for help.

Their fault, always their fault. What did you do wrong?

Some lived but couldn't bear the stirring of life from the ultimate violation of it. Others, more numb or lonely or determined to survive, carried the memory with them, carried and fed and bore it, nursed and nurtured, child of rape but loved nonetheless.

And when there wasn't a war, no legitimate reason for killing, no sanction for murder, there was still the target on women's backs, still the dimly lit alleys and cheap hotel rooms and backseats of cars, still the country club dances and college fraternity parties and swimming pool parties in Beverly Hills.

Still the suicides, the botched abortions.

Still the ditches where the bodies were found.

Miranda clutched the gold cigarette case in her coat pocket, clutched it tightly, thinking of the small gun inside and the first time she'd used it to kill a man.

Outside the phone booth, noises from Twin Dragons filtered through, someone ordering chop suey, a fat lady from Des Moines speaking too loudly to the Chinese waitress.

She'd call James again. See if the State Department was worthy of its title;

see how far Smith was willing to go. See if they'd stop what was going on at Alcatraz.

In the meantime, there was Louise.

She took a deep breath, and dialed the number for Sally Stanford.

✳

The crowds at the International Settlement weren't as thick as usual—only one navy ship at port—but the House of Pisco was still packed with locals, tourists, cons and grifters, with a smattering of Pickles' girls sipping colored water through long, red straws, looking up with big mascared eyes at butter-and-egg men from Boise.

Not bad for three o'clock in the afternoon.

"In the Mood" played for the hundredth time on the juke while Miranda threaded her way past the brunette at the bar downing a second Pisco Punch, and gave a nod to Pickles, who barely moved her red-sashed mouth in acquiescence.

Pickles didn't name Mike "Spider" Abati as the bastard behind the sudden youth she was pushing. She didn't have to—Sally did, and Sally was too connected to give a damn and didn't like the competition anyway. But the redhead folded when Miranda brought it up, folded and gave her the key to Jerry's room, freshly rented for the afternoon. Pickles felt better about it when Miranda told her Jerry's medical condition.

Pickles didn't like Miranda knowing her business and she liked Sally Stanford knowing it even less, but she was an old hand, and she knew when it was time to fold the tent—or cull a regular.

The stairs climbing above the right side bar were too worn to creak. Miranda clutched the skeleton key in her right hand, palms still sweaty from the showdown with Pickles. She turned to the right. Fourth door down.

The key turned noiselessly and she pushed open the door.

Jerry Alexander lay naked on a worn, rumpled bed, face turned to the window, deeply asleep. A young girl, elfin face, maybe fifteen or sixteen, bones outlined on her back, was sitting upright, stroking the hair on his chest.

She looked up and saw Miranda and screamed.

Miranda slammed the door shut and Jerry woke with a start, voice slurry, eyes bloodshot.

"Wha—wha—Keezie—where are you? Keezie?"

The girl grabbed a sheet thin enough to be tissue paper and jumped out of bed, backing into a corner like a frightened kitten.

Miranda looked at her. "Get some clothes on. You're finished."

Jerry finally realized there was a stranger in the room and scrambled for something to cover up with, finally clutching at a pillow.

The girl said, defiantly: "He paid me to stay the whole day. I want to stay."

Miranda looked at her again and this time the girl threw the sheet back to Jerry and scrambled into a torn pair of underpants and a skirt.

Jerry Alexander was awake now. He sat up against the scratched, dull headboard, clinging to the sheet and the pillow, staring at Miranda, still in shock.

"Keezie—that's your name, isn't it? Find Pickles after you leave here. She's got more money for you. You're gonna have to see a doctor."

The girl had fastened on a small brassiere and cotton sweater and her defiance returned.

"Why? I ain't pregnant. I don't see why I gotta listen to you—who are you, anyway? Who the hell are you, lady?"

"I'm the one who's making sure you don't get syphilis, kid. Get the hell out of here and do as I fucking well say."

Keezie's large blue eyes grew larger and darted toward Jerry, who wouldn't look at her. She took a few breaths, looking back and forth at him and Miranda, and finally ran through the door, banging it behind her.

Miranda nodded her head. "All right, Jerry. Let's talk."

*

The light inside the Pink Rat was bright enough to reveal the stubble lining Jerry's chin, the purple-brown circles under his eyes. He could still move well— athleticism not wholly lost, not yet—but between the syphilis and the treatments and the never-ending merry-go-round of sex and booze, drugs and highlife, he'd reach sixty before thirty.

He clutched the large coffee cup, staring down into the black liquid as though it were a crystal ball.

"How did you find me again? I—I wasn't much awake when you told me the first time."

"I called Sally Stanford. She said I'd find you at Pickles'. I didn't bother to try you at your apartment."

He slurped the coffee. "You know Sally?"

"An old friend. I used to work for a former associate of hers."

Jerry Alexander brushed some sandwich crumbs off his fifty-dollar suit, wrinkled and stained and still smelling like gin.

"Oh yeah—that's right. I'd heard you were—I'd heard about you." His bleary eyes flickered over Miranda. "I remember you from that party my father threw for Smith. Sky Room, wasn't it?"

Miranda blew a stream of smoke over his left shoulder. "Do you remember that Sally threw you out six weeks ago? Do you remember Dr. Arthur H. White, or that if you don't keep your appointments with him you'll die, brain and body rotted out?" She leaned forward, pointing with the stick. "Do you even remember that syphilis is contagious, Jerry? Or are you such a cold, selfish little bastard that you just don't give a shit?"

Red flared over his face and his hands clenched into fists on the table.

"Listen, lady, it's not like I don't pay them—I pay them well, and sometimes I don't even use them the whole day, sometimes I just—just mostly talk and sleep—"

"And fuck, Jerry. And as long as you're fucking them, you're spreading the disease. And the girls you're fucking, whether you pay them or not, don't own a trust fund to pay for their goddamn medical bills."

Watery eyes held on to hers for a few seconds, then wilted, face caving into itself. He mumbled: "Always doing something wrong, always, never 'Good job, Jerry' unless it's on the goddamn football field. My—my body's the only thing I've got, only thing I really own. Running to the goal post, only time my father ever paid attention and my mother . . . shit, she's talked about killing herself so often I almost wish she'd just do it."

His face constricted and he looked up again quickly. "I-I'm sorry. I didn't mean it. Of course I didn't mean it. It's just—I don't like Roscoe."

"How long have they been so close?"

"I dunno. A year, maybe. Look, I didn't mean it. I—I love my mother. But she's been talking about driving off the Golden Gate Bridge and jumping out of planes and inhaling cyanide since I was a kid. Just seems to have gotten worse lately. And now, of course, with my dad—my dad gone . . ."

He turned toward the wall and swallowed hard. Miranda tapped some ash from the Chesterfield into the small aluminum tray while someone dropped a nickel in the small juke in the corner and Bing Crosby started warbling "I'm Too Romantic."

"You know she's marrying Roscoe on Monday."

The coffee cup hit the Formica with a clank. "What? I can't believe—no one's told me—marry? Roscoe's nothing but a lounge lizard, a, a gigolo for God's sake . . . Dad's barely cold and the bastard's already figuring on how to steal everything out from under me . . ."

Tremors built from hands to arms to legs, a rumbling, roiling boil.

"And, and, my mother—goddamn it, how—how dare she? How fucking *dare* she? Serves her right if he knocks her off, Niles—Dad—was just *murdered* for God's sake—"

Miranda's voice was sharp, designed to derail the freight train of rage.

"So was Louise. Your father's secretary—and your former date."

He took a gulp of air and deflated. "Yes, I know, I'm—I'm sorry about that. Louise probably—probably told you about us. I liked her, I really did. You—I think you're too smart to think I had anything to do with either her death or, or, my father's . . . but Sylvia—my mother marrying Roscoe—that's just too much. I can't bear it. Does she think I'm going to take this? Just take it?"

He started to jump up and Miranda reached a hand out to stop him.

"Sit down. We're not done."

"We're done when I say!" he snapped, then slowly sank back down on the leather seat, Miranda's eyes holding his.

"Sit down and listen, goddamn it. I'm no alienist, but you've got a problem. Maybe you didn't get enough love from Mommy and Daddy, maybe too much. Maybe your whole family's been crazy for generations—I don't really give a goddamn."

She crushed the Chesterfield out in the ashtray until the tobacco splintered.

"What I do know is this: You're through taking your anger out on women. Paid or not, whore or not. Maybe beating up whores—or giving them syphilis—gives you some kind of kick, some kind of revenge on your mother. But you won't be finding any open doors in San Francisco, not if I can help it. From Chinatown to the International Settlement, the City's closed, Jerry. Not for sale."

Miranda slid out from the small booth, looking down at him. His powerful shoulders and arms were slumped and lifeless. He already looked old again, anger evaporated, rage his only fuel.

Her voice cut through the stupor. "Or maybe you are just a sick, perverted bastard with an Oedipus complex who killed his father and a would-be girl-friend."

He raised his face to hers, spoke quickly. "I didn't kill my father. I was staying with my parents while I was getting the treatments. That's why I was at home that night."

Miranda's eyes flickered over his rumpled, expensive suit, his still-shaking hands.

"Go home. Sober up. See Dr. White."

She left him huddled in the dark booth, hunched over an empty coffee cup.

*

The phone was ringing when Miranda finally limped back to the office, foot pinched from a piece of loose shoe leather. She slipped out of the navy pump and hopped to the desk, handbag sliding across the sleek black surface.

"Miranda Corbie."

"Miranda?"

She maneuvered to the desk chair and sank into the overstuffed leather.

Gonzales.

"Yeah, it's me. Just walked in. What is it, Gonzales? Louise? Did she wake up? Is she gonna be all right?"

His voice was soft. "Yes, that is the reason I called. Miss Crowley did regain consciousness, and her sister is with her now. She has not been able to speak more than a few words, but she shows no sign of brain damage."

"Thank God." Miranda exhaled a long breath and slumped in the chair. "Thank God. When can I see her?"

"She is too weak to see anyone right now. Even her sister has been given only a few minutes. Telephone the hospital tomorrow, and perhaps she will be strong enough then. Though you must know, Miranda, that her memory is affected. The doctor says she may not be able to tell us what happened for days, weeks . . . possibly longer or not at all."

"That's OK. As long as she's OK." She shook out a Chesterfield from the pack in her bag. "Thanks for letting me know."

His tones were warmer now, almost caressing. "You are most welcome. I would—I would like to see you, Miranda. I'm leaving here at seven. Would you consider meeting me for dinner?"

Miranda lit the stick with the desk lighter. Took three goddamn tries and it didn't help that her hands were trembling.

"I'm planning to eat at the Moderne tonight."

"May I join you at seven-thirty?"

Deep inhale on the stick, then a long, steady stream of smoke toward the window.

"I'm not the best of company these days, but sure, Gonzales, if you want to."

"Very well. I look forward to it."

She dropped the phone in the cradle with a loud clang, and exhaled another stream of smoke.

✳

The State Department was busy but James wasn't in—she left him another cryptic message and told the woman with the machine-like voice on the other end that it was urgent he get back to her.

Miranda frowned, staring at the phone, then pulled open the desk drawer and found the Big Chief tablet.

A publisher had been murdered and his secretary almost, and the crimes—the motive, the means, and the opportunity—still didn't fucking fit.

Maybe all the circumstances pointed to Alcatraz for the motive—Alcatraz and what happened behind locked bars—but there were too many personal touches, too much inside information and access for this to be just about a pair of gangsters or the rival gang that guarded them. How would Linkletter know about Louise's apartment? How would Cretzer know she liked chocolates or that Alexander drank gin?

Miranda studied the notes, shaking her head. There was a connection somewhere—maybe Blankenship, maybe Smith, maybe someone else.

Her finger traced the numbers Bunny gave her, numbers belonging to the desperate and deluded, would-be writers Louise called the "crackpots."

She glanced at the clock, opened the phone booth, and started to dial.

Millicent Pryne. Shy older woman, voice barely above a whisper. Ran a boardinghouse. Wrote reams of romance, mixture of *Wife vs. Secretary* and *White Collar Girl* with *Gone with the Wind* thrown in for good measure. Eager to let Alexander Publishing know she'd turned to spiritualism and her newest novel was being dictated by a relative of Marie Antoinette.

Check.

Randal B. Brandt. Middle-aged accountant with a thirst for blood. Hard-boiled was his game and his hero was tougher than Spade, liked women better than Marlowe and knew law better than Perry Mason . . . his responses were congenial, precise, and detailed. Too detailed, in fact, as his latest book was a whopping 957 pages and he hadn't quite finished it yet. Asked Miranda if she knew any Communists he could interview for the last few chapters. She smiled weakly and hung up.

Check.

Anastasia Decker. Anastasia was sleeping, Miranda was told, as her job at Bimbo's kept her up all night. She was the "girl in the goldfish bowl" and had aspirations of being the next Gypsy Rose Lee . . . Miranda left her number with the bored roommate, just in case.

Check.

Ida Winegarden. No answer, no answering service. Miranda frowned and underlined her name.

Geoffrey Hutchinson, Esq. A so-called mouthpiece with suspiciously bad grammar. He stumbled around, admitted he'd written a book, admitted he'd gotten angry over his treatment by Alexander Publishing. She suggested they'd reconsidered their opinion, asked when he was available. He swallowed the bait and tugged hard at the line, ready to meet her tonight, as he lived only fifteen minutes away. She held him off, said she'd call him in a few days.

Miranda bit her lip, bothered by Hutchinson's proximity to the office. Made a note to telephone the State Bar and see if his credentials were real.

Check.

She stretched in the chair and phoned Bunny Berrigan, telling her Louise regained consciousness with no lasting damage. Asked casually if Emily Kingston was in the office.

"Can you ask Emily to meet me here tomorrow, say three o'clock?"

"I'll ask her. What's it about?"

Miranda's voice was dry. "Tell her I'd value her opinion on the case."

Bunny chuckled. "Don't be surprised if she grills you. She's a bloodthirsty little dame and she's mentioned you a couple of times already—I'm sure she'll say yes. But I don't think Emily's got a connection with Alcatraz."

Miranda yawned, glancing at the clock. 5:17.

"Sorry. Neither do I. But ask her anyway, OK?"

"Will do. You find Smith, by the way? Is he coming to the memorial tomorrow evening?"

"Yeah. I imagine he will, if he can stay sober enough to remember. I'll be there, too."

"Good. It's—it's hard to even think Niles is gone—I—I haven't been able to get enough done—I keep expecting him to walk through the door . . ."

Bunny's rapid-fire voice was now slow and it rose on the last word, syllable cracked and broken.

There's a somebody I'm longing to see . . .

Miranda spoke gently. "I know. I'll see you at the memorial, OK?"

The redhead cleared her throat. "Yeah. Got books to edit. So long."

Miranda had just replaced the phone in the cradle when the bell rang again.

"It's Fisher—that you, Miranda?"

"Yeah. Gonzales phoned me earlier about Louise—"

"Good news—great news—but that's not why I'm calling. Those letters—the ones Miss Crowley showed you—typed on her machine. You were right."

"I wish I'd been wrong."

The cop snorted. "So do I. I don't know which way is up anymore, but I know this: George Blankenship is on his way to LA. We cracked Matthew. I gotta get Blankenship in custody by tomorrow or I'll be back to rousting drunks out of wharf-front bars."

She traced a circle with a pencil, around and around, on the Big Chief tablet cover.

"We need to talk. Someplace not in your office."

"You got something for me?"

"Tomorrow. I need to get my thoughts in order. You're not the only one spinning on a goddamn merry-go-round."

Pause, while typewriters banged out reports in the background and the sounds of a siren and a woman's sobs poured through the receiver.

"Miranda . . . don't hold out on me."

She spoke wearily. "I'm not, Inspector. I was at Alcatraz this morning, remember? I'm tired and hungry and have a dinner waiting at the Club Moderne. I'll meet you at eleven. We can go to Sam Wo's to talk."

"The Chinese place up on Washington?"

"Yeah. Meet me in front at eleven. And don't worry so much."

She grinned at the cascade of words pouring out of the receiver and dropped it in the cradle.

Thirty

*

Another redhead was warbling "Embraceable You" at the microphone. Clark bowed, hairpiece almost hitting the floor, and Jorge flashed a dimple deep enough to swim in.

Potted palms, soft lights, seashells, and grappa. Kansas City tourists and couples from Pasadena, local drunk in a rumpled tuxedo nursing a shot glass of rye, fat old ladies dressed in sequins, eyeing Blue Book matches for unmarried daughters.

A lounge lizard was giving her the eye until Benny the barman tapped on his shoulder and shook his head. She could almost hear Vicenzo calling out numbers for the magic wheel in the gambling room behind the stage.

Joe Merello's Club Moderne.

Home.

Gonzales rose from the table, teeth white against smooth, tan skin.

"Miranda—you look lovely."

"Thanks. You're early. Everything all right with Louise?"

He pushed her chair in and resumed his seat. No tuxedo, thank God, just a well-tailored double-breasted silk suit, navy blue, with a paisley tie and a cream-colored display handkerchief.

A less elegant man would have chosen red.

Gonzales smiled easily under the trimmed mustache. "Everything is well, Miranda."

Her eyes met his while the orchestra and girl-singer limped through the finish. Goddamn it, her palms were sweating. . . .

Jorge appeared at her elbow. "Wonderful to see you, Miss Corbie. The regular tonight?"

"Yes, please, Jorge. Joe here?"

"He's in the back." The waiter winked. "But he'll come out if he knows you're here."

Gonzales cleared his throat. "Steak Florentine with linguini, please, and a cold tomato salad for an appetizer. House wine."

Jorge raised his eyebrows and nodded, shooting a glance at Miranda. She grinned.

"Tell Joe hello for me, Jorge. I'd like to see him."

The Argentinean bowed like a bullfighter and danced away on his toes. Miranda flicked a glance at Gonzales.

He was still staring at the black velvet dress with open admiration. She'd paired it with small emerald earrings and a matching necklace, nothing too ornate, and her hair was upswept in a chignon that kept threatening to tumble down.

She started to take off her gloves. "Thanks for calling me today."

"Of course, Miranda. I was glad I could report good news. And I have a bit more for you."

"What? You found fingerprints? Got an ID? Somebody saw some—"

The cop shook his head. "Nothing like that. But we did find **George** Blankenship. He was in Buellton."

Miranda's forehead wrinkled. "Buellton? Where the hell is Buellton?"

"About two hours north of Santa Barbara. He apparently bought a used car—emptied his checking account—and broke down just outside the town. It is a small place, and a neighboring policeman saw the wire we sent and arrested him. We are waiting for him to be transferred."

The soft whisk of a gaudily flourished dinner napkin reannounced Jorge. He presented Miranda with a bourbon and water, no ice, and used the napkin to uncork a bottle of red wine from Sonoma, pouring it with exquisite delicacy into Gonzales' glass.

Miranda sipped the whiskey, watching the play of shadows on Gonzales' face while he tasted it, the broad shoulders and muscled arms beneath the deceptive silk, and remembered how his skin smelled the night they'd eaten at Julius' Castle.

She stared at him, eyes wide, palms sweating again. She could forget for a while, forget with Gonzales, sate her body, quiet her mind. It had been so long, so long, since she'd last felt anything . . .

"Fuck him, Randy," Bente implored last time she'd seen her. "Just fuck him and forget him. Works for men and it works for us, too."

Bente said to fuck him.

Gladys, her other friend, the starry-eyed blonde behind the cigarette counter, Gladys thought Mark Gonzales was a dreamboat, a Kearny Street Cesar Romero. Gladys wanted her to marry him.

And Rick . . .

Miranda swallowed the whiskey and set the glass down with a clank.

Three blind mice, see how they run, had to be blind if they were her friends, friends never lasted, never stuck around, they got blown up by mortar shells or married blondes in Santa Rosa, what the hell did her fucking friends know?

"Miranda—Miranda? Are you all right?"

"Yeah. Sorry. Thanks for telling me about George. He didn't kill anyone but he might have more information that could lead us to who did. I'm just worried about"—she leaned closer over the bourbon and dropped her voice—"Louise. The fact that she's alive is the only card we hold, and the longer we hold it, the bigger the chance it'll slip."

He nodded. "That is so. Now that she has regained consciousness, Inspector Fisher is pulling the twenty-four-hour detail as of tomorrow morning. He has no choice—we don't have enough manpower."

"Figures." She frowned, studying the glass of amber liquid, then drained it. Wiped her lips with a napkin, Red Dice smearing the white. Looked up and held Gonzales' eyes.

"I'm confused as hell. Been swinging around in circles trying to figure out what's going on." She shook her head. "Maybe I'm just tired, but I feel so goddamn useless."

Gonzales reached a large, warm hand across the table and held hers. His voice was soft.

"I see the waiter coming with our dinners. For the rest of the evening, let us pretend, you and I, that we are just two people spending time together. You will—you will be leaving San Francisco soon, and I will be returning home in not too many days . . . we may not have another chance."

Warm skin, smooth but masculine, with strength in the fingers and softness at the tips . . . skin that felt oh so goddamn good against hers, skin that would feel good around her, on her, in her . . .

She shuddered suddenly, and spoke in a low voice.

" 'Though we cannot make our sun stand still, yet we will make him run . . .' "

"Miranda?"

Jorge and another waiter arrived with two large platters and another bourbon and water. She looked up at Gonzales' puzzled face and smiled gently.

"That would be fine, Mark. Let's pretend."

✳

They talked about the end.

The end of the Fair, the end of the world. Hitler and Mussolini, how long the British could hold out, how long America would pretend it resided on a different planet. No thank you, my appointment book's filled, can't be bothered to save civilization as we know it, keep ourselves to ourselves, stay out of all that Your-O-Pee-An mess, and besides, that Hitler may have the right idea after all, country's not the same as it used to be, put America first, America first, America first . . .

They talked about less toxic things, too, about what was playing at the Fox and the Alhambra, about whether Artie Shaw was better than Benny Goodman, about whether another racehorse could ever equal Seabiscuit.

Music swelled from the stage, "The Way You Look Tonight" and "On the Sunny Side of the Street" and "Let's Fall in Love," and Miranda had three bourbon and waters and threw her head back and laughed, his strong hands clutching her back, black velvet pressed against begging skin, and she laughed and she danced, losing time, losing place, losing pain.

Joe tapped on her shoulder, beaming like a grandfather, red boutonnière fresh in his creamy-white jacket. He kissed her on each cheek, patted Gonzales on the shoulder. *"Bellina mia"* he called her, making her promise to see him again soon.

And Miranda danced, her hair fallen down around her shoulders, her body leaning against his, warm and strong, resistant and receptive, until the orchestra broke, and the clock moved past midnight, and the glass slippers threatened to shatter.

She wiped her mouth, leaning with one hand on the table.

Time to get her wrap. Time to go home.

They walked out together, her arm through his. She leaned against him, shivering, gusts of fog down Sutter Street dampening the black velvet.

Still a line to get inside Joe's, still neon glowing, still taxis ferrying couples to the Top of the Mark.

Still chances to take in a night that would never end.

They walked up the steep grade on Mason, his voice as warm and reassuring as his hand on her arm and back, as the words he was speaking, as the promises he made.

Part of her listened and part of her didn't care. She just liked the cadence, the sound of it, like poetry, the kind that might make you cry after you read it but you couldn't stop because the words were so beautiful.

Roy was on duty and he stuttered something, Adam's apple bobbing, eyebrows raised in surprise.

Not used to seeing Miranda gay and smiling and holding a man's arm.

Not in this apartment, not ever.

They walked the four floors and stopped on the second landing because her shoe slipped. He caught her and they kissed, long, deep, everlasting, his hips pressed into her, his warm hand traveling up her bare back.

They resumed the climb, Miranda leaning against him, until they reached her doorway. He was still saying things, words she couldn't hear, didn't understand. She unlocked the door and they walked in and she shut it and he took her, took her hard, folding her body backward and kissing her, tongue in her throat, hands under the dress and cupping her breast.

She gasped, skin responding, every pore hungry, and she was trembling, every touch both pain and pleasure, and she tried, oh, she tried to shut it out, shut out the voice, shut out reason, shut it out, shut it all out . . .

A sound.

Maybe a car horn outside, maybe the shout that followed it.

A voice.

Maybe in her head, maybe memory, a strong voice, laughing but serious, a voice that had never tried to change her, that had never tried to own her, not really.

A voice that wanted to love her, protect her, watch over her . . .

A face.

She pried herself out of Gonzales' grasp panting, holding her dress up against her camisole. He looked surprised, dazed, eyes blinking. His voice was thick.

"You—where is your bedroom, Miranda, we should—"

"We shouldn't. Not now, not tonight, not ever."

He blinked again. Straightened his dress shirt. Rebuckled his belt.

"Miranda, I—I don't understand—"

A plea.

She glanced down at his trousers. Met his eyes, spoke sorrowfully.

"I'm . . . very, very sorry, Mark. I shouldn't have let this happen. Truth is, I'm—I'm very attracted to you. And I like you. And, well . . . that should be enough, I mean, we're both adults, and this is 1940, not 1840. But my—you know my history. It's been a long time since I've . . . since I've felt this way. And I'm not sure—truly not sure—if I'm ready for it."

He picked up her hand and held it in his. "I can help you, Miranda. Please. You know I—I asked you to marry me. The offer still stands."

She looked into his eyes, brown, hurting, warm and deep.

Filled with desire. Filled with wanting her.

Her voice was soft.

"I appreciate that. But you know I don't love you. And I don't, truly don't, believe you love me. I told you before, Mark—you don't know me. Our bodies like each other, but that's not enough, not anymore. I—I found it once before, a long time ago, before Spain. I found what it was like, when you loved someone, really loved him, and he loved you. And nothing was ever the same, and for a long time I never expected to ever find that again and so I didn't care, didn't feel. But I—I'm not that young anymore. I'm thirty-three years old and I'd like to find out if maybe—maybe it might be possible to find—find it again. I'm sorry. I'm truly, truly sorry."

Gonzales' tan skin paled, and he nodded. He brushed his shirt front, rebuttoned his coat. Picked his hat off the floor.

He tried to smile. "At least you did not strike me on the nose. Remember?"

She smiled. "I remember. And I hope—I hope we can stay friends."

He took a breath. "We will be friends, Miranda. But it may be that we must be friends from a distance." He opened her door, and started to walk through, turning his head back once. His eyes met hers.

"I hope Mr. Sanders realizes how lucky he is."

She stared at him as the door swung shut.

Easy come, easy go . . .

Lee Wiley, warbling the song of life.

Miranda wiped another layer of makeup off, skin pink and white through the darker pancake foundation.

She shouldn't have let herself go, like a free woman, like a woman with no past and no future, a woman marking time, no promises, no expectations.

She'd already lived like that, spent her youth in the backseat of cars and the dark dance floors of speakeasies, dancing the Black Bottom, downing gin from a flask.

Small pleasures, maybe, replacing the childhood spent in dresses too short and thin, trying to recapture the only joy and gaiety she'd seen and born witness to, the women with the big bustles at Spider Kelly's, the honky-tonks and nickelodeons, ragtime piano and Sophie Tucker and the bars up and down Pacific Street.

Then came the Crash and the Depression. All the king's horses and all the king's men shook their heads and scratched their chins and retreated to Long Island estates and Washington enclaves, not looking out the window at the apple seller who used to own the corner market.

Misery again and plenty of it, but this time she could help, maybe, help make it better for herself and others, migrants in Salinas and Santa Clara, and she taught English and mended her clothes and saved her pennies and held her breath like everyone else.

FDR rode up on a white horse in '32 and told everyone we had nothing to fear, and there was the NRA and a whole alphabet soup of hope, the FCIC and FDIC, the SEC and FHA and TVA and WPA and everything else the president could throw at the economy and a people hungry for food and work and clothes.

Hope and fear, fear and hope.

Miranda dabbed more almond oil on a ball of cotton.

She found hope and she found joy and fear followed, followed her to New York. Hope opened her third decade with foolhardy bravery, contagious and intoxicating and liberating. They ignored the fear, shoved it aside, let it hide in a dark corner like a neglected child.

They would liberate Spain together, she and Johnny, and return to New York riding high.

Glorious love, let's fall in love, I can't give you anything but love because love is here to stay, baby, here to stay until it all burned up, red and orange like the sun above Madrid, like cannon fire on a moonless night, like the smell of cordite and sweat on skin, like blood staining a Spanish street and the bandage in her hands . . .

Back to San Francisco, where she'd spent her thirties in one-night hotel rooms, chasing time.

Chasing time.

Then she walked into Burnett's office and eventually into his job, changed it and made it her own, worked for Burlingame hostesses and Nob Hill strippers, worked for insurance companies and bookies and lawyers, looked for lost kids and missing memory books and the married men who kept a wife in every port.

She shook out a few more drops of almond oil and wiped the skin around her eyes.

Another wrinkle at the corner.

Her days of looking twenty-three or even twenty-five were disappearing fast. Clock's ticking, Miranda, clock's ticking, gather ye rosebuds while ye goddamn well may . . .

Gonzales would go home, take a cold shower. She'd felt pleasure in his touch, body responded faster than she could think. She wanted to have sex.

But part of her was still hoping to make love.

She was thirty-three, she told him. Running out of time, like the whole world. Would she ever, could she ever, create? Ever have a child? Should she?

She stared into the mirror, the Dorothy Gray crème still white around her green-brown eyes.

Why are you waiting, Miranda? Who the fuck are you saving yourself for?

But now that it ends, let's be friends . . .

Friends.

Irish-bullshit brogue, battered fedora. Not tall enough, not strong enough, not handsome enough.

Not Johnny enough.

And then he'd come back and he was himself, not trying to be Johnny, not trying to be anyone but Richard Sanders.

She closed her eyes.

Rick. The second man she'd lost.

Thirty-One

✳

Miranda woke abruptly at 4:13. She sat up, glanced at the clock, eyes wide open, sweat trickling down her back.

A noise.

Bad dream? Nightmare about Alcatraz? Jesus Christ, maybe she just heard a goddamn cab horn and thought—

There—another step. Footsteps outside her bedroom, creak of the floorboards.

Fuck.

Someone was in the apartment.

Linkletter? Goddamn Linkletter?

She quickly slid to the edge of the bed, careful not to let it squeak too much. Stood up on bare feet, suppressing a shiver underneath the thin nightgown.

Neon from the Cottage Market up the street on Bush filtered down Mason and through the sides of the window curtains, pale, lurid glow of pink and yellow. A car drove by, gears grinding.

Gotta get to the nightstand, slide the drawer open slowly, slowly . . .

More footsteps, light but steady, then a rustle and the squeak of the kitchen door.

Miranda held her breath.

He was searching for something . . . and saving the bedroom for last.

Her fingers found the Astra in the barely open drawer. She'd brought it home to clean it and tucked it away in the nightstand, too busy. Baby Browning was in her purse, still in the living room.

She eased open the drawer, cradling the Spanish pistol delicately. Always too heavy and hard for her to chamber, but it was Johnny's gun.

Johnny's gun, Johnny's gun . . .

Another squeak from the kitchen door. Footsteps were getting louder.

She lifted the Astra, balancing the weight of it, the comfort of the long barrel and sturdy grip.

Felt like all eight bullets were in there.

She only needed one.

Miranda crouched, moving sideways on the bare wood floor, bottoms of her feet sticky. She positioned herself in front of the closet, behind the swing of the bedroom door.

One Mississippi, Two Mississippi, Three Mississippi . . .

The doorknob was turning. She could see it only dimly, but heard the distinctive churn of metal on metal. She slowly slid the safety lever down, fingers damp and cold against the Astra.

The knob stopped turning. Had he heard the click? Goddamn it . . .

She held her breath, listening for his.

No shadows moved in the shallow pool of gray light that eked under the door. He was making sure she was still asleep.

The door edge cracked and more light carved in. Not enough to see the empty bed . . .

Her palms were sweating. She held up the heavy gun.

The crack grew wider.

Her wrists were hurting and she was shaking like a goddamn leaf, fucking flimsy nightgown, she'd sleep in trousers from now on, what the hell was she doing, anyway, thinking she could fucking sleep?

The door was open about two feet. He shimmied through, carrying a flashlight.

Don't make a noise, Miranda, don't even fucking breathe . . .

The round beam of light shone first on the floor, then to the right, where her vanity was, lingering on the perfume bottles and makeup. She could barely make out a tall form, long coat and hat.

He tossed the beam to the window and slowly stepped forward. The flashlight traced the wallpaper, the rug on the other side of the bed, the edge of the mattress, and finally, inch by inch, to where the bedclothes were thrown back . . .

"Got you, you bastard!"

Miranda raised the gun in both hands. The barrel dipped toward the intruder's gut.

He stepped back, flashlight on the empty, disheveled mattress, then trained it on Miranda's face, blinding her.

You're a good soldier, Randy, a good soldier . . .

Her finger squeezed in reflex and the Spanish pistol fired, recoil throwing her hard against the closet door.

She blinked, eyes watering, desperately trying to see.

She clambered upright, moved away from the closet door, shoulder and neck aching. The Astra was still in her hands, shaking, still pointed toward Linkletter. The dim shape across the room grunted—he was alive, then, and maybe she nicked him. She could make him out now . . . the bastard was stooped over, gripping his leg.

Coat was open, hat was off. The man was tall, dark haired, and stocky.

Not Linkletter.

"Fucking bitch . . . ," he snarled.

The flashlight was still in his hand. Before she could step forward, he flicked up the beam at her eyes again and then threw it at her.

The heavy metal grazed the side of her face. Miranda yelped in pain and stumbled backward against the closet, holding a hand up to her left cheek.

The intruder scrambled through the bedroom door, limping.

She heard the outer door slam shut.

*

It took a while to clean up.

He'd made a mess of things, overturning couch cushions, ransacking her purse. Her Baby Browning was still there and everything else seemed to be, too, but her face hurt too much to be sure of anything except anger and fear and a sense of satisfaction at the blood on the bedroom floor.

Her cheek was swollen—not broken, thank God—and she'd have a black eye.

Guess she could count herself lucky.

She called Roy, and he brought her bandages, ice, and some aspirin while she grilled him. Why had he allowed a stranger past the desk in the middle of the goddamn night?

The thin man swallowed hard, said a fortyish man in a dark suit and hat said he was visiting Mrs. Farber on floor three, knew her name and everything.

Miranda nodded, wincing.

She phoned Bente and the redhead came over, dragging Old Man Nielsen in tow. The quack gave her a shot, over protestation. Fisher would wait til morning, after Roy calmed down her neighbors on the fourth floor and told them a story about an exploding coffeepot.

Bente sat up in the chair while Miranda lay on the couch, morning light sliding down from Nob Hill. Images flickered through her head like a peepshow, Gonzales smiling and a blinding light, Johnny's gun and Rick's face, Linkletter's eyes and a blond girl in the hospital . . .

"But I need to talk to Louise," she murmured. "Need to talk to Louise."

Bente sighed. "It's six o'clock in the morning, Miranda. Sleep for three hours, for God's sake. You'll look like shit when you wake up and you don't want to scare the poor girl."

Miranda repositioned her cheek against the ice-filled bandage and didn't dream or feel anything for the next three and a half hours.

*

She woke up to pain.

Pain in her cheek, under her eye, pain in her back and shoulders, her hands and arms.

Miranda crawled out from under the blanket and headed to the kitchen.

The smell of Hills Brothers coffee eventually woke Bente, who padded in on bare feet, eyes widening.

"Jesus. Maybe you oughta go to the hospital and get an X-ray."

Miranda looked at her over the edge of the cup. "No bones broken. I just look terrible. Need more ice. Gotta try to get the swelling down before the Gump's party tonight."

The redhead yawned, pouring the rest of the coffee into a chipped mug. "Gump's? The store for the hoity-toits? Why the hell you going to Gump's?"

Miranda gave her friend a shorthand version of the last two weeks while the redhead trailed her from the kitchen to the bedroom. She outlined the Alexander murder, skipped over Rick except to say that she saw him, and eliminated the near miss with Gonzales.

She omitted the *Cameronia*, too . . . her appointment with Fisher was at eleven and she still had to talk to Louise. Telling Bente she was leaving the country for a blitzkrieged England would just bring on more pain.

Miranda stared at herself in the vanity mirror, trying to keep from flinching as she ran a finger down the side of her cheek and the purple bruise under her left eye.

"So that's the skinny. A dead publisher with a hophead wife and a syphilitic son, a missing book about Alcatraz, a secretary the world thinks has been murdered with family connections to the Rock and an ex-guard ex-boyfriend with an inclination for blackmail. Plus the Cretzer-Kyle gang, whoever's left, and Alcatraz itself, including an associate warden and a captain who should be locked in their own goddamn holes. It's a goddamn mess."

"Like everything else you get involved with. So what about this creep last night? Where does he fit in?"

Miranda carefully slid a navy blue cotton dress over her head. "I don't know. I thought he was the guard from the Rock, Linkletter. But I got a glimpse of him and I've never seen him before—and I don't even think he was the killer. I mean, he didn't pull a gun, he was searching the apartment, he didn't move like a hood. He acted more like a . . . like a cop," she finished slowly. "Like a professional . . . like a fucking G-man."

She turned quickly to her friend, grimacing at the twinge in her shoulder.

"Bente, you still go to Party meetings, right?"

The redhead shrugged. "Yeah. Not as much as I used to. After the Molotov—"

"I know, I know. Listen: do you know Howard Carter Smith? He's a writer, a drunk and a spoiled little rich boy playing anarchist—sound familiar? It's his book about Alcatraz that's missing—"

"Wait a minute—is he pudgy, balding, about so-big, looks like he hasn't been laid in ten years? Wears new shoes? That him?"

"Yes—to a tee. You know him?"

"I've seen him at meetings. Always nervous, sweaty. A real paranoic, I'd say. Always talking about Marx and the proles and his own latest book in the same breath, if you know what I mean."

"I do. Would you say he's sincere? Forget the whole Blue Book background for a minute. You think he means what he says, that his politics are real?"

Bente hesitated. "Jesus, it's hard to say . . . especially now. They've really clamped down on members since the Pact—and a lot of people left the Party because of it. I don't go to meetings much, not anymore, whole thing just kicked my guts out. Not the same kind of give and take it was back in '34, you know? Just haven't gotten around to making it official, really . . . so yeah, if I think about it, I guess he seems sincere enough. Not a spy or anything, if that's what you're worried about. Just a—a schmuck, more than anything else. A rich, dopey, desperate schmuck, craving a connection and attention. Smith the schmuck."

Miranda nodded, stepping into a pair of worn and comfortable navy blue pumps. "Thanks. One more thing: You know an Anastasia Decker? She lives at the Oceanic."

Bente raised her eyebrows. "Stacia? Hell yeah, I know her. She's from Cleveland, strips at Bimbo's. Girl in the Fishbowl. Wants to be the next Gypsy Rose Lee or Pearl S. Buck, whatever comes first. Why, she involved in this mess?"

"Maybe. She's one of the rejected authors Louise said might want revenge."

Bente snorted. "Stacia? Revenge? No offense, but your client's loony or reading too many *Spicy Detectives*. Stacia wants money, fame, and respectability, in that order. She might be a lousy writer but she's a good kid at heart. Her act's classy. Sends dough back to dear old mother in Cleveland and doesn't blow the wad on juice or dust or the ponies. No, she's sensible, Miranda, even if she's got ambitions."

Miranda nodded, studying herself in the bedroom mirror. "Thought as much. Thanks, Bente. Thanks for everything. C'mon, I'll buy you breakfast before I meet Fisher."

Bente brushed lint and bread crumbs off her brown sweater and straightened her wool skirt, running fingers through wild red hair. The seam in her stockings was still crooked.

She yawned. "Eggs, bacon, and a good cuppa Joe. Your coffee stinks."

*

Fisher stared at the bowl of barely touched chow mein.

"The food here is good. You should eat."

Murmuring laughter punctuated by soft titters and whispers filtered down the narrow staircase. A bell rang, and a small, fine-boned waitress of indeterminate age wiped her hands on a green-stained apron, grabbing two dishes from the dumbwaiter and hurrying past them with an order of fried rice.

Fisher shook his head. "I was hungry when I walked in . . . but not anymore. No offense to the restaurant. I'm just—I don't know, Miranda. Sometimes I wonder why the hell I'm a cop."

"Because you give a damn. Even if there's nothing you can do. Like I've said before: you're one of the good ones, Inspector."

"I'm good? Because I eat my gut out when a sonofabitch like Linkletter comes up clean? Because I'm worried about whatever *farshtinkener* bastard did that to you? Because I'm tired of looking the other way every goddamn day and shutting my eyes when I see what I'm not supposed to see and shutting my mouth when I hear 'em whispering about the 'kike' in homicide?" The stocky man ran thick fingers through his black and white hair. "I'd sleep better if I wasn't so 'good.'"

"I didn't expect you to find dirt on Linkletter. Too many friends in high places. Got a friend of my own looking in, well . . . other files."

"Pinkerton?"

Miranda sipped the jasmine tea. "I'll let you know if something turns up. In the meantime, Blankenship is on his way north, right? Not that I think he's the murderer, but if we can get him to testify about Linkletter—"

"It's proof for the BOP. You sure Linkletter wasn't behind that?" Fisher gestured toward her face.

"Yes, I'm sure. I never saw the man before last night. And I don't think Linkletter is Alexander's killer, either. He should be locked up in his own dungeon for a few dozen years, and I'd love to help put him there—but he's not the one we're after."

"Then I'm charging Blankenship. Yeah, I know—and I don't care. There's pressure on me, Miranda, and not just from my own conscience. As soon as the sheriff arrives with Blankenship, I'm locking him up."

Someone on Washington started playing "Red River Valley" on a Chinese violin, while the smell of roasted pork and duck fat drifted in from the downstairs kitchen. Miranda stared at her swirling tea leaves.

"I'm close, Inspector—close. Once I talk to Louise, maybe the pieces will finally start to fit."

"Let me know when they do."

She drained the teacup and stood up, gesturing to the chow mein and egg rolls, mostly untouched.

"You really should eat your lunch. If I weren't full from breakfast I'd join you. Try some of the mustard on the egg rolls."

"S'OK. Whatever I can't eat I'll take home—I'm off early today. Worked late last night . . . and you know you should've called me," he added accusingly.

Miranda gave him a lopsided grin. "Next time someone breaks in and I shoot him, I will. Meantime, go home and get some rest."

Fisher picked up an egg roll and dipped it in the saucer of hot mustard.

"You're right, stuff's not bad. But rest? Not tonight. I promised my kids I'd take them to the Fair before it closes. Another ride on the Roll-O-Plane."

She raised her eyebrows. "I didn't know you had kids. How old?"

"Thirteen and ten. They teach me what's important."

"What's that?"

His eyes met hers. "*L'chaim*, Miranda. *L'chaim*."

✳

Louise was asleep. Her eyes darted back and forth under thin, delicate skin, blue and white.

Miranda looked up at Thelma, nodded toward the waiting room. They passed the beefy uniform sitting on a chair by the door. He glanced up and grunted, picking his teeth.

Miranda led Thelma to a corner and lowered her voice to a hoarse whisper.

"Anybody here but the doctors this morning?"

The blonde shook her head, shoulders slumped. "I ain't seen nobody. Been watching Louise." She yawned, and Miranda noticed some of her teeth were missing. "The copper out there came in about nine-thirty this morning. I stayed all night 'cause they told me there wouldn't be no twenty-four-hour protection, and I'm worried sick." Her eyes met Miranda's. "Sombody tried to kill my baby sister, Miss Corbie . . . I want the sonofabitch dead."

"I know. That's the only way you'll feel safe. We'll catch the bastard, but in the meantime Louise'll be able to go home soon, and we've still gotta keep her under wraps. She can't go back to her apartment—"

"I want her with me. She belongs with me."

"That's fine, but you need rest. Until we get some answers and throw more smoke at the newshounds, they'll track you back to Berkeley and you'll both be in danger. So get some sleep while the flatfoot's on duty and come back tonight—he'll be here til around nine, from what the inspector told me. They cut the protection to twelve hours."

Thelma brushed stray hair from her forehead and yawned again.

"Maybe you're right. Gotta keep my strength up. I got enough cash for a few more trips."

Miranda dug in her purse and shoved a ten-dollar bill at her. "Take it. You can rent a room downtown for a night or two—however long the doctors make us wait."

The blonde looked at the bill in Miranda's hand. "I don't know what you think of me, Miss Corbie, but my family's never been beggers."

"I know, Thelma. But you can't be seen riding the train to Berkeley. Best just stash yourself somewhere—call me and let me know where, here's my card—and then come back tonight."

The blonde nodded, and finally took the bill by the corner, folding and tucking it into a worn leather purse. "You—you get in trouble with your man, Miss Corbie?"

"A stranger broke into my apartment last night. I shot him in the leg and he threw a flashlight at me."

Thelma's blue eyes grew huge. "You think it was the same one? Same one that tried to kill Louise?"

"No. But I do think the visit was related. Look, Thelma—I know the cops grilled you pretty hard. Is there anything—anything at all, even if it doesn't seem important—that you can tell me about Alcatraz and Louise? Particularly about George Blankenship or a guard named Linkletter?"

The blonde spoke slowly. "Well, she called to ask about whether I had enough money for Shorty and whether he was OK. That was right after we got word he was getting transferred. She was scared—told me she'd read some of a book at the office and didn't know how bad things were, and said maybe she'd find a way to get some extra money and be able to help. I asked her what she meant—McNeil weren't so bad, Shorty said, but Cretzer was hell-bent on breaking out, he always is, the loony bastard—excuse my French, Miss Corbie—anyway, I'm divorcin' Shorty and I told Louise it was finally over, and she seemed to calm down. Never did tell me what she was so worried about though. And she never mentioned that Blankenship fella but told me a man she was seein' helped her get a job and Louise always sticks by anyone who does her a good turn . . . does—does that help?"

"I think so. Look, did the doctor say we can wake Louise? I need to ask her a few questions if we can."

"They wake her up about every three hours. It's just a little before that now—let's try, Miss Corbie. Maybe she'll remember more. She knew who she was and she knew me last time, but didn't remember her boss or the murder or nothing."

The two women entered the room again, cop watching them with disinterest. Louise was in a different position, head turned, and her mouth was moving. Miranda glanced at her sister, then gently placed her hand on Louise's shoulder.

The woman—thinner, almost skeletal with her china-white skin and blond hair tight against a small frame—stirred, moving her head to the left. Thelma bent down over her sister and whispered.

"Louise—Louise, it's me, Thelma. Wake up, Louise. Wake up. Time to wake up . . ."

Louise didn't breathe for a moment then suddenly gasped for air and opened her eyes, blinking rapidly. Miranda stepped back.

Thelma said: "That's how she's been waking up. Doctor said she'll get better." She bent close to her sister again. "Louise—it's me, Thelma. Your sister Thelma. How are you feeling?"

It took a few more seconds for Louise to fixate on the anxious face hovering above her. She swallowed. Her voice was hoarse. "Can I—can I have some water?"

Miranda reached for the glass on a tray table next to the bed and handed it to Thelma. Louise took it gratefully, draining the cup. She licked her lips and looked around, eyes landing on Miranda. She blinked, brow furrowing.

"I know you. You—you—you work in my building. You're—you're famous, aren't you?"

Miranda smiled. "Infamous, maybe. My name's Miranda Corbie, Louise. I'm a private investigator. And your friend."

Recognition flitted briefly across the blonde's face. "Corbie—Miranda. I know you. I like you. I think I—I hired you. And I . . . I didn't tell you the truth, did I?"

Miranda and Thelma looked at each other and Miranda leaned closer. "About what, Louise?"

"About—about—about George and me. And, and . . . what was his name? Handsome and rich . . . shoulders like Clark Gable, but too rough, and he hit me, just like George . . ."

"Jerry? Jerry Alexander?"

The blonde inhaled sharply. "Yes—about Jerry. Was gonna tell you—but then . . . I got so sleepy . . . so sleepy. Couldn't stay awake—not even for the milkman . . ."

Miranda's voice was sharp. "Milkman? You remember a milkman, Louise?"

Her voice was weaker. "I'm hungry. Can I have some chicken soup? Mama always makes good chicken soup . . ."

"Louise—please try to tell me. It's important. What milkman?"

"I dunno." The blonde was starting to sound like a tired child. "I want some soup. Milkman brought me a free bottle but it wasn't cold. Made me sign something for it . . . left it outside the door, I think, I don't remember. Didn't drink the milk. Was gonna tell you about George. Then I . . . fell asleep."

She looked from Thelma to Miranda, eyes wide. "Can I have my soup?"

*

Miranda closed her eyes, trying to picture Louise's door before Rick broke it down.

There wasn't a bottle of milk in front of it, full or otherwise.

A nosy neighbor did remember a milkman on Louise's floor that morning . . . someone from a company who didn't normally service the area.

Miranda watched the traffic from the taxicab window, speeding toward the Monandnock in fits and starts, driver with a five o'clock shadow three hours too early, hairy hand slamming on the horn when someone pulled in front of him.

A phony milkman was too much finesse for Linkletter or Miller.

Too much goddamn finesse.

And that's what was wrong with the case: too much of everything. Too many clues, all leading to too many places and too many people. Too many motives, too many different styles, a fucking crazy quilt of murder.

She lit a Chesterfield while the driver rolled down his window and yelled at a middle-aged woman in a yellow sedan.

OK, start at the beginning. Someone tried to kill Louise—or at least make Louise think so. Why?

So the secretary could be the fall guy. Louise was in a frame—set up to take the rap for Alexander's death.

Planted cyanide, letters typed on her machine. Jealous wife, pretty girl, too-obvious murder attempts, like something out of one of those genteel books where someone dies of strychnine poisoning right before a tennis party, murder as an inconvenience.

Miranda took a deep drag on the stick.

Fuck that.

Louise was the patsy, that's why there were two notes found in her room. She was supposed to kill herself out of guilt for the Alexander murder . . . but then the Alexander murder didn't go to plan.

Miranda closed her eyes again, remembering the murder scene, the detritus of a struggle, the spilled gin on the publisher's shirt. Niles Alexander surprised his killer and his killer struck back, panicked.

He improvised.

And that led to the second note. After Blankenship leaked the Rock connection, after Louise's personal history became a newspaper headline and beauty parlor gossip. The motive for her presumed death refined itself, became opaque: could be suicide, shame for her criminal ties or role in Alexander's murder, could be murder most foul, committed by the same criminals.

The real murderer wanted to cross all the t's and dot all the i's and make sure all ends were covered.

Didn't sound like Linkletter, whose technique would be more obvious. Didn't sound like Miller, who had the brains but not the creativity. But Linkletter and Miller had the only real motives for stealing that goddamn book . . .

Miranda threw a dollar at the cabbie and hopped out at the corner of Third and Market.

Fucking crazy quilt.

Thirty-Two

*

Miranda punched the fourth-floor button, striding out with two customers for Pinkerton and one for the Mexican Railway.

No reporters, thank God.

She turned the key in the lock and picked up the manila envelope marked "Miranda" that had been slid under the door.

Allen—the Linkletter file. She was about to open it when the phone started to ring.

"Miranda Corbie, private invest—"

"Miranda? James here."

She sank down slowly in the black leather chair. "What's wrong? You calling to tell me I'm bumped again? No trip?"

"Why do you think something's wrong?"

"Don't bullshit me, James. I've been trying to reach you for a couple of days, now—news for you and the BOP—and you finally phone me and sound like an undertaker with a head cold. Just tell me—give it to me straight."

The State Department man sighed. "Your trip is still on, Miranda. But— you're not going to like this—you've got to lay off Alcatraz. Let it go."

Miranda groped for her handbag and shook out another Chesterfield.

"Let me guess. Miller got to Hoover; Hoover got to your boss; you're getting to me. Does that about cover it?"

Electric crackles and a distant roar.

"James? You there?"

MacLeod's voice was heavy. "I'm here. Just . . . let it go."

She leaned forward, edge of the desk pressing into her stomach.

"You know what I found out, James? You the least bit curious?"

"Miranda, I told you—"

"Rape. Rape of prisoners by prison guards. That's what's happening, James, behind concrete walls on a godforsaken little island in the middle of San Francisco Bay. The black prisoners are disproportionately victimized, of course. They're segregated already, so that makes it easier. I don't know how the payoffs work, not yet, but Smith probably does and I can get more information out of him. That's what was in his book—the Alcatraz book—and that's why George Blankenship was gonna use it to blackmail Linkletter and Miller—"

"Stop! Just . . . just stop, Miranda. If—if I can do something, I will. Believe me. But right now, Hoover's got everyone whipped up about the Reds—and he's got you labeled as one. Yes, Miller complained, said you were an agitator and wanted to abolish the prison system. He said a whole lot of crap. Right now, kid, you're radioactive, and anything you say will be disbelieved because you say it."

She blew a stream of smoke before replying, watched it sail past the Martell Liquor's calendar on the wall and fall apart by the Wells Fargo safe.

"What if I told you someone broke into my apartment last night? Someone who nearly broke the side of my face with a flashlight—someone who was careful, clean, and smart and looked like a professional?"

MacLeod spoke slowly. "I'd—I'd believe you, Miranda. But I always believe you, Ducks. You know that."

"Do I, James?" Her voice was soft. "Last time I looked, I wasn't living in Spain under Franco, or Germany under Hitler. Last time I looked, Bureau agents didn't break into innocent citizen's apartments."

"Listen, Ducks, you're going to be sailing soon anyway, just let this go . . ."

"And tell what to my client? Sorry, I can't catch who tried to murder you because the United States of America operates their own Gestapo? Because Hoover's got a hammer and sickle up his ass and a hard-on for Hitler?"

"Jesus . . ." the State Department man swallowed hard. "Listen—I'll try to do something on my end. Type up whatever you got on the Rock and send it to the address I gave you last time. That's still good. But please, Miranda—try to lay low. For everybody's sake."

"Everybody's sake or yours, James?"

"Both. Send me your information and—and don't call for a while, OK? I mean, telephone before you leave on the *Cameronia,* but . . . just lay low in the meantime. All right?"

"Fine, James. Just grand. You can even give the Bureau a message for me: next time, I won't aim for his fucking legs."

She slammed the phone down with a clang and sat against the black leather, heart thumping in her chest.

*

The Four Roses bottle was almost full.

She poured herself a shot and threw half of it back, bourbon stinging down her throat, watching the cars drive by Market Street, watching the trains roar past.

Heartless and promiscuous, fickle and fancy-free, dancing for the highest bidder, flash of gold, flash of gam, pride of the Pacific and pearl of the Bay, the most beautiful city in the world. And San Francisco used the beauty, used it to gather hearts and lives and then cast them aside, worn out and used up until she could gather more, another generation to hold her, to keep her, to save her from herself.

Maybe she couldn't be saved.

Maybe no one could.

The phone rang and Miranda lifted the receiver, half-expecting James again.

"Miranda? Herb here."

Charm poured across the receiver like wine.

"Hello, Herb. What can I do for you?"

"Plenty, but I'm happily married. Listen, Miranda, I know Sanders is flying off to D.C. and not around to squire you anywhere, and seeing that Bea's busy and you and I are both covering the Alexander affair at Gump's, I thought I'd pick you up at seven. Whaddya say?"

"I say yes, as long as you're not looking for an exclusive."

Fake gasp on the telephone. "I? No, this is strictly for fun. Of course, if you do come through with the details, I'd like an exclusive at some point. When you're ready."

"I already owe you big for helping with Louise. I promise you, Herb—if I can get a handle on this thing, you'll get it first—the whole story—which you won't be able to print, I know that much."

"You'd be surprised at what this bright boy can do with three dots. All right, beautiful, the office or your apartment?"

"My apartment. 640 Mason Street, number 405. I'll see you then."

She rang off, checked the clock. Locked the manila envelope with her name on it in a desk drawer.

Whatever Allen found out about Linkletter would have to wait.

Three o'clock—time to meet Emily.

*

Alexander Publishing was humming with voices, the clatter of typewriter keys and the electricity of a deadline.

No reporters camped outside, no bored cops.

Louise's desk sat forlorn and alone, a pariah of inactivity. Miranda ran a finger along the top of the typewriter, still coated with fingerprint powder.

Bunny flew out of Alexander's former office and took three steps toward the side rooms before she realized Miranda was standing in the waiting area. She stopped abruptly and twisted her head back.

"What the hell happened to you? You look like crap. Jesus—is it three o'clock already? Emily's in here." Bunny nodded toward the door dividing the office suite and shoved it open. "C'mon in."

Hank Ward and Emily Kingston were arguing, Hank looking a little less rumpled and a little more sober. Emily's hat—a good five years old and top-heavy with a bunch of dilapidated flowers above the brim—trembled with indignation.

"—the subjunctive mood, Mr. Ward, not the indicative, and I thank you not to erode what little standards of grammar are left in American English—"

Bunny put two fingers in her mouth and whistled shrilly. Hank jumped, glancing from Bunny to Miranda, lingering on Miranda's bruises, then made a motion with his eyes and head to suggest Emily was crazy and walked back to his desk. Emily blinked a few moments and smiled, teeth large and slightly yellowed.

"Miss Berrigan—so sorry—Mr. Ward and I were discussing that most interesting case, the second conditional, and how it relates to the future less vivid in Latin . . ."

"Yes, yes, Emily, glad to see you two getting your manuscripts ready. It's past three, and Miss Corbie here wants to talk to you."

Emily's pale blue eyes intently poured over Miranda's face. "Oh yes, Miss Corbie. Do you mind if I take notes? I must say, you look—well, you look like you got the 'dry gulch'—was it a Mickey Finn? A sap, perhaps? I'm developing a list of American idioms related to criminality, and I'd be so pleased if you could help—"

"Over here, Miranda." Bunny opened the door to the larger meeting room across the foyer. She lowered her voice and spoke close to Miranda's ear. "Just yell if you need help."

Miranda grinned. Emily entered and sat primly on the edge of a chair, holding a notepad and a pencil as though she were about to take dictation. Bunny rolled her eyes and shut the door.

The copy editor looked Miranda up and down. "You should ice that cheek before the swelling gets worse. Was it a 'button man'? A 'chopper squad'? Or maybe just a 'bad gee' on 'giggle juice'? How thrilling the gumshoe life must be, Miss Corbie, I'd love—"

"I'm here to ask you some questions, Miss Kingston, not to discuss my injury, however unfortunate it is. I'm afraid your criminal philology will have to wait."

Emily nodded. "I understand. You're 'behind the eight ball,' shall we say, and don't wish to 'bump gums.' I must say, you speak English extraordinarily well for a woman of your—your pursuits."

"That may be because I earned a degree in it."

Emily blinked. "What—what did you want to speak to me about, Miss Corbie?"

Miranda pulled out a chair and sat down, shaking out a Chesterfield. "Do you mind?"

Emily looked horrified but fascinated, and shook her head no.

"Just this—Alexander Publishing, like all publishers, was besieged by people who wanted to publish a book but couldn't write a parking ticket. I'm thinking of people like Geoffrey Hutchinson, Esquire. One of them may have killed Mr. Alexander—or Louise."

The older woman wrinkled her brow. "I thought Louise committed suicide. A mortal sin, yes, but—"

"What makes you think so?"

"The papers, Miss Corbie. The *News* all but said it was suicide because she was involved in Mr. Alexander's death."

"Maybe, maybe not. So what about Hutchinson or anyone else who was on the 'crackpot' list?"

Emily tilted her head for a moment, then shook it decisively. "I should think not. Many people are delusional about themselves—some think they're handsome when they're not, some think they're talented or lucky when they aren't. I don't think anyone I've met here could qualify as homicidally delusional . . . though Hutchinson would come the closest. His temper is certainly explosive."

Miranda leaned forward. "Over what?"

"He became quite irate when I explained that he'd borrowed—perhaps 'stolen' would be more apt—the plot of *The Petrified Forest*. Mr. Alexander had to intercede and threw the man out of the office. I was so—so shell-shocked, as it were, I had to immediately go home and lie down for the rest of the day." The copy editor put her hand on her chest and took a deep breath, reliving the memory. "To be honest, Miss Corbie, I find his particular post-nominal to be highly suspect."

Miranda grinned. "In other words, he's a fakeloo artist."

Emily scribbled on her pad. "Is that f-a-k-e-l-i-e-u?"

"Two o's, not derived from the French." Miranda reached across the table to rub the cigarette out in an ashtray. "One more question, Miss Kingston. What kind of writer is Mr. Smith? I mean, what is your opinion of his talents?"

Emily paused. "I would call Mr. Smith a gifted storyteller. Perhaps too gifted for the exposés Mr. Alexander sought."

"Did you read any of his Alcatraz book?"

"I? Heavens, no. They kept it under lock and key. Mr. Alexander was the only one to edit that and he would probably have given it to Hank to copy edit when the time came. I've read Mr. Smith's other work, though, one about unfair labor conditions in Salinas—heavily influenced, of course, by Mr. Steinbeck—and his fiction. Not his latest fiction, mind, Niles was even more secretive about that than the Alcatraz book. He read the first draft very quickly and had high hopes for it—a thriller but possibly award-worthy, from what he said. I understand Smith was finishing his final rewrite when Niles was killed."

Miranda nodded. "How does Smith compare to other authors—Roger Roscoe, for instance?"

"Oh, dear Roger. Such a charming man. He's a far better stylist than Smith, on the surface at least, but he does leave one a bit empty, if you know what I mean."

"No substance?"

The copy editor frowned. "No heart. Roger is so busy impressing us all with his turns of phrase that he forgets about the mechanics—his plots are notoriously weak—and our feelings, the emotions involved when we read. Not in person, of course, Roger is, as I said, a dear. As for Mr. Smith . . . well, the least said about his personality, the better. I would say he will become a bestseller before poor Roger does, though one never knows. That muscular, Hemingway prose is quite popular."

Miranda stood up. "Thanks, Miss Kingston. You've been a great help."

The older woman smiled graciously. "My pleasure, Miss Corbie." She flicked up her eyes, ever-hopeful, pencil poised over the paper. "Would you mind leaving me with one or two particularly vivid expressions for my list?"

Miranda paused, hand on the doorknob. "Well, I guess you could tell that Ward hombre to go climb his thumb next time he throws an ing-bing and confuses his protasis with an apodosis."

She smiled at Emily's open-mouthed look of astonishment and closed the door behind her.

*

Music drifted into John's Grill from the bar across the street, new tune by Glenn Miller. Miranda pushed the plate aside and studied Allen's report again.

Precious little on Frank Linkletter. Arrested for assault in Hayward five years ago, charges dropped. Since then, a bull at San Quentin, then Alcatraz, now captain of the guards and Miller's right-hand man.

Icy blue eyes on her face, memorizing detail . . . too bad it wasn't Linkletter she'd shot.

And now here she was, back on familiar ground. Forget what she'd done about the Musketeers, forget about her success working for James; forget about any protection.

She was on a list somewhere, stamped, tagged, and labeled—and Hoover was the kind who never shredded a list. No telling how far the Red brand would go, if they'd try to track her, spy on her. Depended on how much influence Miller had and how far Hoover was willing to run.

Miranda sipped the bourbon, noting the diners around her, an eye on the entrance.

And then there was James, the man who helped start her on a new life, who made her legitimate and not just a sideshow carnival act, escort turned gumshoe, only clients on the gray side of legality.

"Let it go," he said. As though she were in some sort of petty dispute at the beauty parlor. "Just lie low."

She shoved the report on Linkletter back into the envelope, signaled for the check.

A man was murdered. A young woman almost was. And men—criminals, yes, some of them deserving the worst the law could hand out—were being raped on Alcatraz.

Which amendment was it? The Eighth? "Cruel and unusual punishment" . . . ancient tortures like the iron maiden and the oubliette, not here in the new Republic, not here in America, where all men were created equal . . .

As long as they were white, rich, and Protestant.

Miranda drained the glass and set it down with a clink as the waiter smiled perfunctorily and handed her the bill.

She looked around the dark room packed with insurance men from the Flood Building and newshawks from the De Young, City Hall supervisors and an occasional tourist wandering off Market Street for a taste of real San Francisco.

Murmur of City gossip swirled around her, deals soured and deals made, every clink of an ice cube another sawbuck in someone else's pocket . . .

Miranda closed her eyes. Her face hurt, she was smoking too much, and she almost made a wrong turn with Gonzales. Rick . . . Rick was lost, lost before he could truly be found.

Everything at once, all in one goddamn week. Maybe she was leaving the country just in time.

She stood up, tucking the manila folder under her arm, and pulled out her wallet.

She'd send what she had on Miller and Linkletter to James and hope he'd come through. Maybe they'd talk to Smith, slap him with a subpoena. Maybe they could force Miller's hand and put his captain behind another set of bars. Maybe she could fight the cruel and unusual punishment on Alcatraz, Miller and Linkletter, one sitting, the other standing, hands on bully sticks, smirking, fog swirling and thick off the Bay . . .

Miranda threw a dollar and two bits on the table.

Fuck "lying low."

Thirty-Three

*

Herb Caen carefully placed a gin and tonic at the foot of the enormous gold Buddha, clapped his hands together and made a low, theatrical bow.

"How I love the Gumps. The family motto should be 'making China safe for the rich American since 1861.'"

Miranda laughed and then touched her cheek. "Ouch. You'll make my face swell up again."

The reporter gave her an impish grin. "Your face is always swell, beautiful. Sanders is a chump for missing this. You know he left for D.C. early? Requested the transfer be immediate. I don't know what's cookin' with you two kids, but you'd better get it off the stove."

Miranda looked down at the highball in her hand and shook it until the ice rattled. "Rick and I are friends, Herb. Just friends. We go back a long way."

He cocked his head at her, curls dropping on his forehead despite a copious amount of Wildroot hair oil. "To the cradle? C'mon, Miranda, don't kid a kidder. You two are crazy about each another. Any fool—even this one—can see it." His eye caught a glimpse of a socialite at the other end of the room. "Oops—gotta amscray. There's a Phelan I oughta be feelin'. Be back to check on you later."

Miranda nodded, watching the dapper young man charm his way through the crowd. She smoothed the front of her dress—an aquamarine number, almost glacial, with two straps in a faux-Greek style, plunging neckline and a lot of pleats. She hoped it would divert attention from the bruises on her cheek and eye—couldn't hide them fully, not even with thick makeup.

She sipped the bourbon and set her glass down next to Caen's in front of the Buddha.

The main floor was packed with Blue Book types, silver mine heirs and Junior League misses, ladies' club auxilliaries and a smattering of literary intellectuals from Berkeley and beyond.

Probably half the socialites didn't know who the hell Niles Alexander was, but they appreciated good hootch and a chance to mingle with famous and not-so-famous writers in Gump's private playground.

Thousand-dollar statues from ancient temples perched on the second floor like five-and-dime mannequins, looking down with distaste on the crowd below. Silk tapestries and water-colored scrolls lined walls above Ming vases, while cases of jewelry stood sedately in a dark corner, shining with pearls and gleaming with stones, jade trinkets ornate with age, treasures bargained for in decaying palaces and ancient, crumbling shrines.

Quick, Marge, this one's on sale from $700—how much of your monthly allowance do you have left? I feel like going Oriental for the opera this year . . .

Sandalwood incense added to intoxication levels and exotic music played softly on a well-tuned Victrola. Not quite like the Chinese violin Miranda normally heard in Chinatown, plaintively crooning "Red River Valley" . . .

Gump never missed a trick. He mingled with the crowd, bestowing charm and well-worn anecdotes of adventures overseas to the favored attendees, while well-trained staff made sure all questions of price and payment were immediately answered.

Toward the front of the room, near the podium and a table laden with flowers, Roger Roscoe was showing off a magic trick—something to do with cards and disappearing coins, from what Miranda could see—to a gaggle of young women.

Sylvia—the adored, soon-to-be-wed Sylvia—sat next to him, looking up with a new glow of life, grief and position otherwise lending her an air of exquisitely feminine dignity.

Her son was nowhere to be seen and neither was Howard Carter Smith.

A tap on her bare shoulder made Miranda spin quickly enough to force the man to step backward. He was tall, thin, with burning blue eyes and curly dark hair and an intense, wolfish smile.

"Miss Corbie, isn't it? Bunny Berrigan told me you wanted to talk to me. I'm Charlie Segal—Howard's agent."

Miranda smiled and held out her hand. "Nice to meet you, Mr. Segal. Have you seen your client?"

"You mean at the party?" The agent shook his head. "Howard's perpetually late. What is it—eight o'clock or so? I never expect him until an hour in at any party. I'm sure he'll arrive soon."

A waiter in a red silk cummerbund whirled close to them with a tray of champagne glasses. Segal picked one up and handed it to Miranda.

"I supposed this is for a toast. Poor Niles. He would have enjoyed this so much."

The agent sipped at the champagne, looking up at Miranda, eyes shrewd.

"Now then, Miss Corbie, what did you want to ask me?"

Miranda glanced around and motioned for the agent to join her behind the Buddha. It sat alone toward the rear of the main floor, isolated from the more popular sales tables and counters, amidst an eclectic arrangement of sacred statues, temple bells and other objects for the serious collector.

She lowered her voice. "Did you read any part of Smith's book on Alcatraz?"

"Afraid not. Howard's like any writer in some respects—they all have their quirks and superstitions. He never lets me read anything unless he deems it finished. Oh, I know it sounds strange—he was working with a publisher—who was also a damn fine editor, believe me—but he wouldn't let his own agent read the book. That's because Howard associates me with the—how do I put it— 'filthy lucre' side of the business. He sought out Niles as a fellow artiste. Plus, there was nothing for me to do—the contract had already been signed, so I wasn't really involved."

Miranda frowned. "That doesn't exactly dovetail with what I've observed, Mr. Segal. Your client seems very interested in money—and very aware of the value of the manuscript."

The agent took another sip of the champagne. "Oh, he's aware, all right. He was born aware, you might say. But when he's writing—like he's supposed to be doing now on his new thriller—he separates the work from the business aspect. Once he's done with a book, he's done—and then he can haggle with the best of them. Sometimes I think he ought to be his own agent . . ."

"So as far as the Alcatraz book goes, he treated you like a member of the public, then?"

Segal laughed. "Well, hopefully not as badly as Howard treats most members of the public. But essentially that's true. I'm just the guy that makes sure he gets paid."

She smiled. "Which is how you get paid, if I'm not mistaken."

The agent shrugged. "It's a living. And not always all that profitable—ten percent of nothing is still nothing. But I've got high hopes for this novel Howard's finishing up—I was actually relieved whoever it was took the Alcatraz book. I mean, I'm sure Niles would've promoted it and it would've sold some big numbers in the first month or so, but these exposé-type stories . . . they don't have legs. Your royalty numbers are good for the short term, then it's yesterday's news. Tough to build a career that way. The novel on the other hand— Howard's got passion for it, a real emotional investment. Plus, he's been talking to Steinbeck—he's here tonight, by the way, he and Howard'll probably go out after the party—and I think some of that genius may've rubbed off. Hope so, anyway."

The agent downed the rest of his glass. Miranda said: "Is that why you flew out? To make sure he finished the novel?"

"Partly. I was vacationing in Tuscon, so I thought I'd better check on Howard before going back to New York. Plus, I've been worried about him, what with Niles' murder. Alcatraz gangsters? I mean, sounds like something from Niles' pulp list. It's no secret I wanted Howard to get out of his contract and let me find him a real publisher in New York. Somebody like Knopf, who likes to take chances and loves the tough guys. Now, with Niles gone . . . maybe he'll listen to me."

The agent looked at the crowd assembled by the table. "I think they're about to make a toast. Mind if I find Bunny? I hope I answered your questions."

Miranda nodded. "Of course, Mr. Segal. And thank you."

He smiled. "Call me Charlie. Anytime, Miss Corbie."

The thin man pushed his way past a fat matron eyeing a silk dress and merged into the roar of the party.

Charlie Segal—another man who stood to profit from Alexander's death. Hell, maybe the publishing world was breathing a collective sigh of relief . . .

Richard Gump was at the podium, attempting to quiet the crowd. Roger was rubbing Sylvia's arm as they huddled close, while Bunny stood behind Gump, red hair shining under the lights.

"Ladies and Gentlemen, please . . . may I have your attention . . ."

Gump was a skilled raconteur, known for his wit and savoir faire. Unfortunately, those talents didn't carry over into public speaking. He seemed to lack wind, voice straining to reach the third or fourth row of partygoers. Miranda could catch only every few words.

". . . literary giant . . . humble man . . . beloved . . ."

"Conscience might make cowards of us but death turns us into heroes." The voice was soft, amused. "Niles must be chuckling from below. Maybe Richard is planning to run for something."

Miranda turned toward her right. A tall, dark-haired man with surprisingly vulnerable eyes, set closely together in a rough-skinned face. He wore a thick mustache and was dressed in a simple white shirt, blue tie and jacket. He was smoking a brown cigarette and holding a flask of brandy. He smiled at her.

"I—your last book should be required reading, Mr. Steinbeck."

He arched his eyebrows, high forehead creasing. "Thanks. The Pulitzer helped. Henry Fonda helped even more." He tilted the flask. "You're the woman private eye, aren't you?"

"My name's Miranda Corbie."

He nodded. "That's the one. Howard was impressed by you. Said you were a true woman of the people . . . whatever the hell that means when Howard says it. Have you seen him?"

"No. When did you speak with him last?"

Steinbeck squinted at the crowd. "This morning. He said he'd meet me here at seven sharp—wanted to show up for Niles' sake, then hit Chinatown and Telegraph as soon as the toast was over. Which, it appears, is now."

Gump was raising a champagne glass. After a brief flourish, he threw it back and everyone else followed suit.

Collective sigh, soft exhale, and the party started up again, salute made, mourning over.

Miranda turned to the author. "You sure he said seven, Mr. Steinbeck?"

"Call me John. Sure I'm sure. I was surprised—Howard's always late. I think I even bet him five bucks he'd never make it on time."

"Thanks. Nice to meet you, Mr. Steinbeck."

"John. You, too."

The author melted into the recesses of the store, looking for a back exit, while Miranda hurried across the floor to Herb Caen.

He turned around at the tug on his arm.

"What is it, beauti— oh, Miranda, sorry I never got back to you—"

She lowered her voice, spoke rapidly. "I'm worried. Smith should've been here by now. Look, Herb—call Inspector Fisher. Tell him to send someone to Smith's apartment, pronto. Can you do that?"

The curly-haired reporter blinked his eyes. "Sure, if you really think—"

She'd already pushed her way to the crowds and out the main Gump's door.

*

She hailed a Luxor cab on Post Street and promised him an extra buck if he could push the hack to the top of Nob Hill in less than ten minutes.

The five-year-old Ford managed to reach 1201 California in seven minutes flat.

She tipped the cabbie and hurried to the door, wishing for the tenth time she wasn't in an evening gown.

The ornate apartment house looked curiously empty. No flatfoot with careful eyes and dirty fedora waiting in the shadows. Had Fisher taken the watch off Smith? Or had the cop followed Smith to wherever he'd gone?

Miranda climbed the stairs and hit 602 three times. No answer. She bit her lip and hit it again.

A stocky man with red hair threw open a second-floor window, face softening when Miranda looked up, shielding her eyes.

"I'm the superintendant, miss. Just getting the apartment ready now . . . I'll buzz you in."

Miranda nodded. A few seconds later she was back inside the lobby, sleek front desk empty, sounds of heavy feet climbing down from above.

She started up the stairs but he was already on his way down.

He was about thirty-five, sweat under his armpits, with the air of a good time in the backseat and Sunday dinner with his mother.

"Hold on, miss, we can take the elevator. I'll go ahead and show you the apartment, since these are hard to come by and we expect a lotta interest—but the ad did say tomorrow morning, not tonight—"

She cut him short. "I'm not here to rent—I'm trying to reach a resident, Mr. Howard Carter Smith in number 602. He didn't answer."

The freckled face fell into tighter, disappointed lines. He gave her an up and down and lingered on her cheek.

"What Mr. Smith does is his business, but . . . what happened to you, lady? Somebody hit you when you was doing something you ought'nt'a been doing?"

"Speaking of business, why don't you mind yours and get going? Unless, of course, you want me to report what you said to Mr. Smith . . ."

His bravado caved like a toothless mouth. "Forget I said anything, lady, please. You should take the elevator the rest of the way up." He yanked his thumb in a direction behind him and hastened around the corner toward an unmarked door.

Miranda made her way to the self-service elevator and pushed six.

Goddamn it, hurry up, hurry up . . .

The door slowly opened and she shoved herself through, half-running down the hallway toward the stairs . . . 608, 606, 604 . . . 602.

She knocked. No answer.

Knocked again, held her ear to the door.

Nothing.

Miranda remembered the last time she saw him and shoved the door with both hands.

The heavy door slowly swung open a few inches.

"Smith? Smith? Howard, you here?"

Miranda walked quickly into the living room. Strong odor of tobacco and booze, probably seeped into the paint.

At least the place was tidier, carpet cleaned, no leftover glasses. No sign of Smith . . .

She moved to the kitchen. Bright yellow and modern, with new appliances and a breakfast nook, cereal bowl and spoon still on the table. She opened the refrigerator door. Milk bottle half-full, some leftover Chinese food.

Miranda's stomach hurt. Goddamn it . . .

Bathroom next, signs of a shower, probably earlier that day. Used razor left above the sink. She felt the soft cotton towel . . . dry.

She pushed open the door to the bedroom. Blue wallpaper, with a heavy antique chest of drawers and man's vanity, Corrubias and a Picasso on the walls. Bed wasn't made, definitely slept in, closet door open. A hair tonic promoting a cure for baldness stood front and center on the vanity, along with a bottle of Bay Rum and a flask of Pour un Homme.

One more room.

She entered the study through the adjoining bedroom door, dark brown wood and heavily masculine, with a photo of Steinbeck and Smith sitting on the messy walnut desk.

But no Howard Carter Smith . . .

Miranda took a few deep breaths, trying not to panic. Her eyes fell on the typewriter, a late-model Royal.

Paper fragment—apparently torn from a sheet ripped out in authorial pique— still hugged the platen. She flipped the paper release and pried it out.

Left-hand corner, uneven tear, paper heavier and more expensive than what Alexander used in his office.

It read:

license
hesitation can
She gave me a look and I
Dusty, decayed, dead, like all
"I would—if only I knew how. She

Miranda frowned. No fucking help. She grabbed a pile of bills and paperwork on the desk and thumbed through it quickly.

Bekins Storage invoice, royalty statement from Charlie Segal, Incorporated, bills from Mausner Custom Tailoring and Magnin's. She picked up the Bekins Storage invoice and looked at it again.

What the hell was Smith storing? He wasn't a collector, didn't place much value on what he had—didn't even realize how lucky he was to have it . . . so what the hell did he keep at Bekins?

She folded the yellow invoice and stuck it in her purse along with the torn paper.

Looked around the apartment once more before shutting the door.

Goddamn it.

*

It was 8:45 by the time she got to Bekins on Geary, a tall brick building that loomed on Laurel Hill, brooding over the empty graves and abandoned cemeteries, rates and number and an advertisement for privately locked rooms painted in large white letters against the brick.

Miranda held on to her hat and approached the office. A thin man in a blue uniform, stubble dotted on sallow cheeks, ambled to the doorway.

"What's wrong, lady? Forgot your key?" He looked her up and down. "Ain't you dressed a little too fancy for storin' something? It's dusty in there."

She gave him a dazzling smile. "I'm just here to meet a—a friend." Lowered her voice to a conspiratorial whisper. "My family doesn't want me to see him . . . he works in a garage down the street. But Howard and I are planning on—oh, I shouldn't tell you. It's a secret."

The thin man nodded knowingly, and spat a wad of tobacco with a sharp zing into a spittoon behind him. "One o' them society elopements, I expect. Make sure he treats you right, though, miss, that's all I can tell you. Name's Frank. Whaddya need?"

"He—he asked me to meet him here. His name's Howard—Howard Carter Smith. I'm not sure which room . . ."

"Just a minute, I'll check." The thin man retreated into the small, well-lit office and thumbed through a ledger. "Howard C. Smith, was it? Rents room number 167, one of our small specials. Says here he came by at 4:15 today. I weren't on duty, so I didn't see him. Say . . . your fella must be on the forgetful side, miss—he never did sign out. You sure he said to come by tonight?"

Miranda grabbed a map from the counter. "Frank, do as I tell you, please, and don't ask questions. Give me the key to number 167. Call the police and ask for Inspector Fisher. Tell him to get someone up here right away—tell him Miranda said so."

Frank blinked twice and spat another wad of tobacco. Plucked one of the many keys hanging on hooks and handed it to her.

"I 'spect you ain't exactly what you seem, miss. I'll make the call. Bekins don't want no trouble. Number 167 is middle aisle, first right and then two lefts."

Miranda started to run, pushing through the large main doors into a cavernous warehouse with small rooms, alcoves, and shelving filling every possible square foot. She found a large middle aisle, passing a fat man in a cheap tan business suit who stared at her while locking his cubicle.

One left . . . two left. The rooms here were medium size, enough for maybe a few boxes and a couple of pieces of furniture, wooden doors hollow and cheap. Someone was talking or arguing in #152.

She burrowed deeper, counting the doors, running, out of breath, must and mildew thick and heavy, and in this section a charred odor, like burnt wood . . .

Number 167.

She pounded on the door with her fist, catching her breath. Light was filtering beneath the flimsy door.

"Howard? Howard, you all right?"

The sound of her voice fell flat and powerless against the hallway with a hundred doors.

Grasped the key, slick with sweat from her palms. Fit the lock on the second try and pushed the door open.

The scent of carbon stung Miranda's nose and she blinked. The electric light switch was still on, dim but bright enough.

Dark, antique furniture loomed over the sides of the room and a few shallow boxes stood on shelves. An old typewriter, broken and worn, sat forlornly on an ancient desk.

The concrete floor was lined with a faded Persian carpet and stretched across it, fingers almost touching a pile of charred paper, was a man's body.

Howard Carter Smith.

Thirty-Four

*

M iranda swallowed the bile rising in her throat.

Smith's skull was fractured on the right side. Brain and blood and fluid lay in a small puddle, restoring the color-faded carpet to a crimson red. A small end of rusted-out pipe, about two inches in diameter, was next to him, hair and skull fragments clinging to the jagged end.

At least he was facedown, probably hit from behind . . .

She knelt, careful not to get the hem of her dress near what was left of his head. Swallowed again and looked at the charred paper.

Most of it was black tissue or gray ash, but a few fragments of brown-edged white were still discernible. She could clearly make out "island" and "priso" on one near the top.

Goddamn it. The Alcatraz manuscript.

On Smith's left side was another piece of paper, not brown. In dark, penciled capital letters it read "DEATH TO STOOLIES."

Miranda stood up, stomach clenched.

Too many goddamn clues, too many goddamn gangsters, too many goddamn murders. Sure, they'd saved Louise but Smith was under her watch, too, and for all of his pomposity and nascent social conscious and pseudo-intellectual posing, he was a human being and a talented one, a writer who could have, would have, made a difference.

And now he was dead.

Another one lost, another one killed, maybe not in the line of duty, not in cannon fire behind gray stone walls or under a hot summer sun in Aragon, but still a victim of war, while Hoover chased red shadows behind bedroom doors, and prison guards ran island kingdoms, dictators, potentates, fascists fucking all.

She inhaled sharply, turned away.

No time for mourning, no time.

Miranda looked around the room more carefully. Still had a few minutes before the boys in blue showed up and threw her out of the crime scene.

The furniture in the room was expensive, old and reserved, probably inherited or given to Smith, who'd rejected it for the sleek modernism of his apartment. Most of it was dusty, as was the old typewriter—surely a sentimental relic. But the boxes . . .

The ones on the highest shelves were unmoved, black, low boxes with labels like "Salinas" and "MSS 2" and "1936." Cleaner and newer boxes lined the lower shelves, neatly stacked and lidded except for three, which sat askew, lids pried off: "Crime," "New," and "MSS 4."

Miranda's eyes widened. This was Smith's vault, the place he kept his papers, first drafts, manuscripts, notes. Probably figured on donating them to a library when he was dead, last bid at immortality, take his place among the literary giants he so desperately wanted to join.

Poor bastard never guessed it would be this soon.

Quickly, she pulled a footstool from the desk—probably left there for the purpose—and climbed on it for a better angle.

She stared into the open boxes.

Nothing left.

Footsteps outside. She stepped down from the stool and the door flew open, two uniforms with drawn guns and a plainclothes detective.

Gonzales.

He was as awkward as she was, not following up with any specific questions, assuming Fisher would handle the rest.

She watched him move. Even through the blood and smoke, she caught the scent of French cigarettes and leather.

She wondered if she'd been right. Wondered if she'd ever been right.

Then the moment fled, the weakness of needing comfort, of needing an act against the end, last call for life, last chance to make life, last call, last call . . .

Miranda sighed and shuddered and sat on a crate a few doors down the warehouse aisle, smoking a Chesterfield.

Frank answered Gonzales' questions, still chewing his tobacco. Fisher was at Smith's apartment, which was getting the once-over now that they knew he was dead.

A hand fell on her shoulder and she looked up.

His voice was gentle. "I see no reason to keep you here, Miranda. Inspector Fisher will want to see the crime scene for himself and will then return to the station. You could wait for him there, if you are not too exhausted."

She pinched the end of the stick, flicked her eyes up.

"I'm all right. Thanks, Gonzales . . . I'll go."

The hand squeezed her shoulder. "You must be more careful." He nodded his head toward her cheek. "We are . . . we are friends, you and I. You can always call me."

Green eyes searched brown and she gave him a small half-smile.

"That wouldn't be playing fair, Mark. But I appreciate it—I really do."

She stood up, adjusted her hat, and started walking down the corridor, every door shut behind her.

*

It was nearly midnight before Fisher could see her.

"Fitzgerald's one of my best shadows. Had to do it, Miranda, the Mission District arson case turned into homicide last week, and I figured Smith wouldn't pull anything, not after you talked to him—"

"He didn't. He wasn't trying to ditch anybody. He was either meeting someone at Bekins or somebody followed him."

Fisher looked up, eyes shot through with red. "Yeah, we got that much from the scene. Smith was killed between four-thirty and five-thirty, the ME says. Hit with the pipe—and goddamn it, kids can pick up pieces like that all over the city, wherever there's construction—plus junkyards, basements, you name it. Nothing there. But from the angle we know his back was turned, so it was either somebody he knew or somebody who surprised him."

"You got a man back on Louise around the clock?"

The inspector sighed. "Yeah, but it won't last. I'm telling you, Miranda, confidentially"—he lowered his voice—"they want this over and done with. The note clinched it—Dullea wants to put it out there that it's a criminal gang and now that Smith is dead and the Alcatraz book is destroyed it's over—meat for the

Gangbusters, not SFPD. Got a lotta uppity-ups worried because Alexander got murdered and now Smith, think it's a crime wave against the rich—"

"Making Louise an afterthought. I guess secretaries don't count."

"Miranda—"

"Yeah, I know, I know, Inspector. If it's all the same to you, tomorrow I'm gonna move Louise to Dante's. I've worked with them before."

He grunted. "Go ahead. I'm still holding Blankenship, by the way."

"You won't for long if he gets a lawyer who can read. George is lucky he was in police custody tonight—he can't be a suspect for Smith's murder, and if he's not a suspect for Smith's murder, it lets him off for Alexander's . . . along with a tight alibi."

Fisher leaned back in his chair until it squeaked in sympathetic agony. "Don't you think I know it? We put a trace on Smith's calls from the last couple days, see if someone lured him to Geary. We're talking to neighbors and I got a couple of men rounding up people at the party—even Steinbeck is staying in town—anyone who knows Smith. But Dullea's friends with Gump and knows Smith's father and Dullea wants this to be some crony or cronies of two men already in prison—"

"That would make it all neat and tidy for Dullea and the DA, wouldn't it? Smith's killed because he wrote about two bank robbers, not because he uncovered rape and torture in a federal prison." Miranda shook her head. "Somewhere out there is a sick bastard who murdered two men and thinks he murdered Louise, and the city's best homicide cop is hamstrung because Dullea plays golf at the fucking Olympic Club."

His voice was quiet. "I'll keep at it, Miranda."

"I know you will. But the trail's gonna go cold and I don't have a lot of time. Neither does Louise."

She stood up slowly, shoulder hurting again, legs wobbly. Leaned over his desk.

"Ask yourself three things. Why destroy the Alcatraz manuscript now and not when it was first stolen? Why kill Smith at Bekins? And why the note—'Death to Stoolies'? That's out of a George Raft picture, not how button men work . . . and we both know it."

The cop's head lowered until his chin nearly hit his chest. "I'll do what I can, Miranda."

She stared down at the almost-broken man in front of her.

"So will I, Inspector. So will I."

*

She stayed up until after two, listening to the radio, listening to the world fall apart.

At least they'd saved Louise . . .

She tried to fill her mind with the one thought, wedging it in.

No storage room left, lady, too many dead bodies, too many crushed-in skulls, too many dead girls on street corners, too many babies killed in a carnival road show.

Too many, too many, too many . . .

She turned the knob on the radio, Kaltenborn and Murrow and Elmer Davis, Wynken, Blynken, and Nod, intoning stoic disapproval or admiration of British pluck, war from a distance and let's keep it that way, America, forget the refugees, forget the Nazis, forget the war.

Europe was cleaning house and there wasn't room there anymore, no room for yellow stars or pink stars, just jackboots and spider flags, black shirts and the Blitzkrieg, no gentleness, no empathy, no art. No room here, either, unless you could make movies or make bombs, keep us distracted or keep us safe, otherwise sail back home on the *St. Louis* and into the arms of the Gestapo.

There's a quota on Jews, remember?

She turned the knob, around and around, worldwide band, organ music here, band remote there, and everywhere refugees, bombs, war.

A car barreled down Mason from the top of the Hill, back from a night at the Top of the Mark, while ferries rocked gently, docked at the Ferry Building and ready for Treasure Island, ready for doughnuts and Maxwell House Coffee and nude girls on donkeys and transparent cars, because this was America, Martha, land of the free and home of the brave and everything else was just news, only news, like a murdered publisher or a dead Red author, something to marvel at, something to read, something to pass the fucking time.

Miranda downed another shot of bourbon and tried to sleep for three hours.

*

Thelma was at Louise's bedside by the time Miranda got to Children's Hospital.

Another cop, not so bored, waited outside.

It took the better part of four hours to get the secretary transferred to Dante's Sanitarium. She'd be safer there, under Renata Dante's care, a woman and not an institution. Children's was a fine hospital but doctors and nurses and orderlies could make mistakes, look the other way, and Louise had already been there too long.

Had to move around, keep one step in front of the killer . . .

The secretary was better, more like herself, but still vague and childlike. Remembered more about the milkman, remembered he was wearing a kind of uniform she didn't recognize, remembered he didn't take any money.

Thelma said in low tones that she'd pay Miranda back. She looked better, too, not as frayed around the edges. She was staying at the Potter Hotel, Pandora Blake's old rooming house.

Miranda smiled sadly, wondered if it still smelled like cabbage.

She didn't mention Smith, but bought the papers at the hospital newsstand on her way out the door.

Chronicle headline, page two: CRETZER GANG STRIKES AGAIN: AUTHOR MURDERED. *San Francisco News,* page one: CRIME WRITER MURDERED BY GANG. *Call-Bulletin,* page two: WRITER KILLED AT BEKINS STORAGE: CRETZER-KYLE GANG SUSPECTED.

She lit a cigarette and rolled down the taxi window.

*

She wasn't hungry but ate lunch anyway, cheeseburger and fries washed down with Coca-Cola. Needed energy to walk, to talk, and most of all, to think.

Tascone's was busy for a Monday afternoon, full of telephone operators and newshawks from the De Young and *Examiner* buildings. Gladys wasn't working and Miranda's stomach unknotted, no explanations of the still-visible bruise necessary, no worried friend to lie to.

She punched the elevator button for six.

The large double doors of Alexander Publishing were shut, doorknobs dull. She knocked loudly.

"Bunny? It's Miranda."

After three more loud bangs one of the doors opened a crack. Miranda recognized the bloodshot eye of Hank Ward.

"I need to speak to Bunny."

He grunted and opened it wide enough for her to squeeze past. "Bunny's in a bad way, Miss Corbie. We all are. Don't know whether there's going to be an Alexander Publishing, frankly. She called Emily and I in this morning to tell us about Smith."

Miranda nodded. "Where is she?"

"In the big office. Go on in—all she can do is yell, and I'd honestly feel better if she would."

Miranda softly opened the door to the large office. Bunny was sitting at Niles' desk, staring at a manuscript, body hunched over and tense. She looked up.

"C'mon in, Miranda."

Miranda sat in one of the black leather chairs and lit a Chesterfield. Said: "I'm sorry, Bunny. More than I can say."

The redhead leaned back, hands shaking and eyes too wide.

"Sure looks like somebody's out to destroy Alexander Publishing, doesn't it? First Niles, then Louise, and now Smith—on the very night we hold the memorial for Niles."

"The papers are pushing the Cretzer gang angle."

Bunny waved her hand in the air. "Bullshit. You know it and I know it. That may be how it winds up going down—and God knows, if you print something often enough, people will believe it, I mean, Jesus Christ, I'm public relations and marketing, I know that better than anyone—but that doesn't make it true." She bent forward across the desk, eyes glowing. "I'll tell you one thing, though, Miranda—it won't work. We're not going away."

Miranda raised her eyebrows. "You've got enough material—good material?"

"It doesn't have to be good, just saleable. And thanks to Roger Roscoe, we've got saleable right here." She patted the manuscript on her desk. "Saleable AND good. Surprising, really, it's different from his other stuff, but he did say he was trying something new. Came in with it not half an hour ago, said he wouldn't think of going anywhere else with it and he was in for the long haul. Of course it helps that he and Sylvia got married, you know, despite the horrible news about Smith. Found a JP in San Mateo and tied the knot."

Miranda exhaled a stream of smoke. "So they actually did it. I wonder—have you heard from Jerry? I didn't see him last night . . ."

Bunny shook her head. "Not a word. Roger didn't mention him. But of course, with this horrible murder—another horrible murder—we're just reeling. I thought I'd have to close up shop. That's why I called in Hank and Emily this morning. Goddamn it . . . poor, poor Howard."

"Did he leave any other manuscripts you could publish posthumously? Or was that in his contract?"

"Charlie Segal's going over all that. Phoned this morning and said he's working with the coppers—going through everything Howard left, trying to find something we can publish. I know Howard was finishing up a novel Niles was very high on—almost as much as the Alcatraz book—so maybe." She glanced at the clock on her desk. "Holy Shit—two-thirty. I gotta talk to Emily and Hank, get them busy on this."

Miranda crushed out the stick in the ashtray and stood up. "Keep me posted, Bunny."

"Will do. Jesus—Niles had a few enemies, but this—" She shook her head. "But as long as we've got one good book to publish, we're in." The redhead stood, moving out from behind the desk with her usual alacrity. "See you in the funny papers, Miranda."

✳

The phone was ringing when Miranda unlocked the door.

Name in the paper, "notorious" female private investigator, and dirty jobs poured in from the social register and gambling joints, with a few insurance companies thrown in for good measure . . .

She picked up the heavy headset.

"Miranda? Fisher. Got your message about Louise."

Miranda fell into the black leather desk chair and swiveled to face the window.

"Good. You know where to find her. Thelma's at the Potter Hotel, by the way."

"Yeah, one of our men tracked her there. Listen, Miranda, I've got maybe one more day on this before Dullea and the DA shut it down. O'Meara rang up the Bureau—"

"That sycophantic bastard. Let me guess—they're all in favor of turning the investigation over to Hoover, doffing their hats and saying 'after you,' passing up jurisdiction on a local murder case to suck at the federal tit. That about sum it up?"

Fisher's voice was heavy. "My hands are tied. The papers haven't helped much, either—jumped all over that goddamn note. I don't even know who the hell leaked it."

"Doesn't matter, not now. The Bureau will bury any and all connections to Linkletter or Miller. They'll blame the murders on some redhot already on their 'wanted' list and keep sniffing under bedroom doors for Communists. Hell, Smith was a Red, so they'll do what they can to placate Daddy Warbucks, but the sooner this case is yesterday's news, the better."

Sirens started to wail in the background. After a few seconds she could hear them through the window.

Fisher spoke quietly. 'We've still got today, maybe tomorrow. I'm sending you a copy of the inventory from Smith's apartment and the storage room. Take a look at it. And I've had to let Blankenship go, but told him if he skips town I'll lock him up and throw away the key."

"He give out with anything?"

"Only what you already know. Got a mouthpiece and clammed up quick."

"Figures. You interview Jerry Alexander yet?"

The inspector made a noise. "We can't find him! I was about to ask you if you knew where the hell—"

"I don't. He wasn't at the party last night, either. Contact a Dr. Arthur H. White . . . he's a syphilis specialist and Jerry's supposed to be getting treatments. You won't find him in the usual dives—I warned him off the Settlement and Chinatown with the help of Sally Stanford. Try South City or maybe San Mateo, any well-established house that would cater to the bastard's tastes."

Fisher's voice held a note of incredulity. "Syphilis? Sally Stanford? Jesus, Miranda—"

"I'm sorry I didn't get a chance to tell you sooner. And listen—Roger Roscoe and Sylvia Alexander got married this morning. If you're planning on interviewing them, better make it quick. And Louise's memory is returning— slowly. That dim image of a milkman in an odd uniform isn't going away."

More loud wailing in the background, and a kind of clatter, like something or someone falling over a chair.

"Gotta go—I'll talk to you later, Miranda. Oh, one more thing—someone called Smith yesterday morning from a pay phone at Schwabacher-Frey on Market—not too far from you. The other calls were Charlie Segal and Smith's father."

"Just who the hell *is* Smith's father?"

"Jefferson Hamilton Smith."

Miranda frowned, recognizing the name from social columns and the business pages, a factory owner and Coolidge-era industrialist known for hiring scabs and smashing unions, with holdings in Oakland and San Francisco.

"Thanks, Inspector, that explains a lot. Be seeing you."

She hit the switchhook rapidly and dialed the operator.

"Long distance, person-to-person please."

A woman's voice answered, monotone, emotionless.

"I've got a message for Mr. James MacLeod. Tell him 'Gangbusters taking over. If BOP doesn't step in it, the newspapers will.' Got that? Good."

She set the phone back in the cradle again.

Big money men owned the papers, but maybe, if word got out about what was happening, if it spread . . .

She shook her head.

Maybe.

Thirty-Five

*

Miranda closed the compact mirror, frowning at the blue and purple under her makeup.

Hell, count herself lucky. Lucky little girl blue . . .

A soft knock made her jump, and she opened the right side desk drawer, fingers touching the .22.

Allen poked his head through the door.

"Hey, Miri. I'm about to head out for the day—thought it might be time for that trip to the Rusty Nail." His smile dropped and he stared, squinting. "What the hell happened to you, kid? Some jackass wallop you or something?"

She waved him in. "C'mon in. G-man broke into my apartment while I was sleeping. Threw a flashlight at me after I shot him in the leg."

Allen's eyes opened wide, fine lines around the corners deep. He started to laugh.

"Miranda, what the hell am I gonna do with you? You're more grizzled than half the men on the Pinkerton payroll. What happened? Why was a federal cop in your apartment?"

She brought out the bottle of Four Roses and a couple of Castagnola glasses, and they drank bourbon and smoked while Miranda talked. Shadows stretched along the walls by the time she finished. His eyes lingered on her face.

"Miranda . . . you're a hell of an investigator. A hell of a shamus. But maybe—maybe you should get out of this game. It's damn tough without resources behind you. I don't particularly like Pinkerton, don't even agree with most of what they do. But when push comes to shove, it's like havin' an army at your back. It's why my missus can sleep at nights."

Miranda traced a circle on her desk with a fingernail. "I don't need to worry about someone else's sleep. I don't know, Allen. I just can't see myself doing anything else. I'm not the kind of girl that gets brought home to a four-room cottage and cooks dinner for the mother-in-law every weekend." She looked up and smiled at his worried face. "But thanks for listening. And caring. And who the hell knows—maybe the world will end and we won't have to worry about it."

They clinked glasses and downed another shot.

*

Miranda pushed the Big Chief tablet aside and closed her eyes.

Too many notes, too many clues, too many coincidences.

If she could just get a handle on the case . . .

Motive. Motive, motive, motive. It all came down to motive, and the only real one she'd dug up—the one that connected Smith, Louise, and a stolen manuscript—was what Linkletter and Miller were hiding.

Rape, corruption, torture on Alcatraz, all stamped and approved by the associate warden.

Sure, maybe covering that up was enough to kill for, though it looked as though Miller, at least, had friends in high places that were a better bet than cyanide or a blunt instrument.

Goddamn it. How it happened—how everything unfolded—none of that made sense with Linkletter or Miller behind it.

She sighed for the tenth time and stubbed out the Chesterfield.

Alexander. His death was unplanned—in the way that it happened, the struggle, the spilled drink. But there had been a plan—that's where the cyanide came in.

Why kill him if the manuscript was the goal? Simply because he'd read it?

And what about Louise? She was set up for a fall—those attempts on her life were blinds, maybe even practice. She could either take the blame for Alexander's death—which would explain the cyanide planted in her desk, the second suicide note, and the letters typed on her own machine, suggesting she'd faked the earlier attempts as a cover for her own guilt—or maybe look like the intended target, if the improvisation of Alexander's murder hadn't been necessary.

But why go through all the trouble of framing her if she was a murder target? Insurance?

The killer wanted it both ways and all ways, Louise as a dupe or Louise as a victim or Louise as a scheming killer . . .

And then there was Smith. She could understand the murderer wanting to examine Smith's storage room—make sure there were no other copies of the Alcatraz manuscript—but why burn it and leave it by his body? The whole scene reeked of contrivance, of unnecessary drama, page 113 of a locked-room mystery with a gimmick at the end.

Maybe Bunny was right . . . maybe someone was trying to destroy Alexander Publishing, piece by fucking piece . . .

Miranda was rubbing her temples, trying to think, when the phone rang.

"Miranda Corbie, private investi—"

"Miss Corbie? Charlie Segal here."

She sat upright, opened her eyes. "Yes, Mr. Segal, how can I help you? I'm terribly sorry about Mr. Smith—"

His voice was heavy. "We all are, Miss Corbie. Howard was destined to be a literary heavyweight. And now . . . well, that promise is unfulfilled. I just hope they find this gang or whoever they are. I hope they find them and kill them." He took a breath. "I think you understand how I feel. Death's too good for some people. They've destroyed more than a man—more, even, than his exposé on Alcatraz, uncovering crimes we'll never know about. The fact is, I can't find Howard's new novel anywhere . . . I've searched his apartment with the police, I've checked and notated the list from Bekins . . . nothing. I know you spoke with him the day before—before he was killed. Did he say anything—anything at all—about the novel and where it might be?"

The words came out slowly.

"No—nothing but the fact that he was nearly finished with it. Are you sure you've looked everywhere?"

The agent sighed. "As sure as I can be, given the fact that I've got to fly back to New York tomorrow and I can't search Bekins for myself. Listen, Miss Corbie—can you continue looking for it? I can't believe the gangsters would destroy it—I mean, why bother? It was a detective story, from what he told me, something in the line of Dashiell Hammett or Raymond Chandler. Howard was very proud of it—considered it a literary triumph, a kind of blend of social drama and thriller. Besides, there was plenty of older material in that storage room, first drafts of published works, and none of it was touched."

"I'll do whatever I can, Mr. Segal."

"Thanks. If you turn anything up—I hope like hell you do, for Howard's sake, or at least his memory—then call me in New York. Bunny Berrigan has my number."

They rang off. Miranda sat holding the phone, staring straight ahead, two fingers on the switchhook.

She hit it twice with force, and dialed the mail room.

"This is Miranda Corbie. Do I have any mail or deliveries? Yes—please bring it up."

She hung up, dug into her purse for change, lit a Chesterfield, and waited, staring out the window on Market Street, watching the DO NOT WALK signs flip into place, watching the neon of the pool halls and bars blink on and off.

The knock was hesitant. She thrust two bits at the blushing kid from the mail room and slammed the door.

Two items: a thick manila envelope from Fisher, hand-delivered by messenger, marked inventory. Underneath it, a standard envelope, handwritten and addressed.

To Miranda Corbie . . . from Rick Sanders.

*

She stared at the typewritten list from Fisher, holding it in her hands and reading it for the second time.

Glanced at the unopened letter on the desk.

Miranda stood, shoulder sore, body aching from the rough and tumble of the last few days. She walked to the window and looked out at the San Francisco evening, purple light of twilight and coming blue-black sky.

A White Front roared by, advertising the last days of the 1940 Golden Gate International Exposition, gone forever and a dream remembered after September 29th, only six days to go . . .

She shut the window.

Best not to dream, an old lady told her once when she'd run away again. The old woman was toothless and smoked a pipe and hunkered in a corner of an alley off Pacific. She patted the girl in the thin dress, patted her on the head and cheek and told her not to dream and Miranda stared at her and ran away.

She passed a shaking hand over her cheekbone, glancing again at the letter on her desk. Her jaw clenched, and she scooped up the list and the letter.

Maybe she just needed a change of scenery.

*

She grabbed a sandwich at White Star Tuna and chased it with a Threlkeld scone, not as fresh as a morning batch but still delicious, especially with a cup of Maxwell House.

The Gayway was thronged, Greenwich Village and Madame Zorina's Nudist Colony doing brisk business. The line to get inside Sally's circled the fence, and the Headless Girl and even "Have You Seen Stella?" were attracting crowds, desperate to cram in a final look at the future, past, and present before it became someone else's discarded and forgotten dream.

A couple of the barkers smiled when they saw her and she ran into Edna, one of Sally's girls. Carnival life revolved like a carousel, up and down like the notes on a calliope, and new people she'd never met were selling tickets to the Astro-Mentalist and Roll-O-Plane and Ripley's Odditorium.

She sat in a red leather booth nursing the coffee, watching the neon lights run up the doughnut tower.

Charlie Segal was right.

No manuscript—no fresh manuscript—from Smith.

Nothing about a new novel, detective or otherwise.

Miranda glanced up at the window again, red light reflected on her face. She set aside the inventory list and opened Rick's letter.

> *Dear Miranda,*
>
> *Hope you're OK. I'm on the way to Washington. Asked for an early transfer. I'll be there for the duration—until the fighting starts, anyway— so it's my new home and I want time to get to know it.*
>
> *Speaking of knowing something, I thought I'd let you know that Annabelle and I—well, it didn't work out quite the way I wanted it to. Her parents had some objections. Some legitimate, some not. Most importantly, I had objections, too. They're down on the Commander-in-Chief and had plenty to say about other things. I just can't see myself eating Thanksgiving Dinner with in-laws who frankly ought to be shipped to Berlin. I was never involved in politics quite as much as you and John, but I'd like to do my fighting on the front, not at home.*
>
> *I don't understand people like that. I guess I never will. And I guess that spending so much time with you . . . well, a little of you rubbed off.*

Annabelle's a nice kid except when she gets around her folks and starts talking about Jews. And that was enough of that.

Anyway, please write and let me know when you leave San Francisco and when you get to Britain. You know me too well to believe I won't worry. And I hope you know I'll always be there if you need me.

Take care of yourself, Miranda. I'll be seeing you.

Rick.

She rubbed her cheek absent-mindedly, eyes lingering on the words.

I'll be seeing you, in all the old familiar places . . .

Except nothing was familiar, nothing. She was leaving for a war-torn country, bombed and on its knees, and Rick was in Washington, D.C., ready to fight a battle with his typewriter, waiting for the mortars and machine guns to start.

Even how she felt wasn't familiar, the years she spent pushing him away, irritated at having to hurt him, over and over. Now—now all she could think of is being close to him, wondering if he could accept her—if she could accept him—if they could love each other like . . .

Like she and Johnny.

She lit a cigarette and gathered up the papers and Rick's letter, walked out of Maxwell's and onto the Gayway, step right up, little lady, and meet the man of your dreams . . .

Too late for that, Miranda. Too late.

Johnny was dead. Spain was dying. The world was on its way out.

She started walking toward the amusement section, the Fun House calling her, with trick mirrors and laughing clowns and topsy-turvy slides.

Just the ticket to examine her life.

Miranda inhaled the Chesterfield before stamping it out and bought a ticket from the bald barker, a man with a thick Russian accent she'd never seen before. Her shoes skidded on the sawdust and she entered to the tune of a tinny organ and a laugh like Laffing Sal's, wandering through the surreal landscape with twelve-year-old boys and couples on first dates.

She stood in front of the fat mirror, not really seeing herself. All she could see was Rick and Johnny, Johnny and Rick.

Did she really love Rick? Or did she miss Johnny so much that she willed herself to love him as soon as he was in uniform, as soon as he was doing something Johnny would have done, dressed how Johnny would have dressed . . .

Miranda closed her eyes and let memories wash over her, not memories of Johnny but of Rick, the meeting at Lotta's Fountain, his eyes when he saw her again, and how they fell and then steadied when he knew she was working for Dianne . . . his bent brown hat and the way he always talked her into dinner at John's Grill, the way he helped her catch the clown on the Ferris Wheel, how he waited with her in the dark in the Incubator Baby exhibit, how he dressed up as Robin Hood and rescued her from Fritz Wiedemann.

How he saved her life in the Napa woods, when she thought she'd have to end it herself.

Her eyes opened and she stared at the three-hundred-pound Miranda.

Memories of New York, of Spain, of Johnny burned with a fire that would never go out, never leave her, always there, just below the surface, a laugh, a dance of sunlight, a note of music, the smell of oakmoss and red, red wine . . .

But she loved Rick, too. And she loved him for himself.

For now, that would be enough.

She opened her purse to put the letter inside it and a small piece of paper fluttered to the ground.

She picked it up.

It was the fragment from Smith's room:

license
hesitation can
She gave me a look and I
Dusty, decayed, dead, like all
"I would—if only I knew how. She

Miranda looked at it, surrounded by distorted nightmare doppelgängers, fat Mirandas, tall Mirandas, Mirandas with heads too big and legs too long, Mirandas cracked and Mirandas whole.

And she remembered . . .

Remembered magic and illusion and the tricks of makeup.

Remembered timing and alibis and improvisation and planning.

Remembered character and plot and motive and how she'd lost track of time reading *The Maltese Falcon* and *The Thin Man* and *The Big Sleep*.

She nodded to herself, the bright bulbs reflecting garishly in a hundred mirrors, a thousand mirrors, Miranda backwards, not forwards, upside down and not right side up.

It would be difficult to prove, at least with the time limit they were working under.

The mirror Mirandas nodded back soberly, all in unison.

The mirrors would help.

Thirty-Six

*

S he slept well that night.

No dreams, good or bad. No intruders, either.

She called Fisher and Herb Caen as soon as the sun rose, Fisher grumpy and Caen not awake. Neither one held out much enthusiasm, but both were willing to play.

Miranda splurged for breakfast at the St. Francis, hungry for eggs and sausage for the first time in days. Left the surprised waitress, an older woman in her fifties, a dollar tip.

She spent the morning on the phone, dialing every druggist in San Francisco. Phoned scientific supply companies—only two in the city—and made notes, nodding, in the Big Chief tablet.

She called Goldstein's Costumes and asked for Peg. The girl had just started her senior year but any beginnings of cool professionalism melted away when Miranda identified herself. She squealed, the seventeen-year-old who'd helped Miranda catch a Nazi spy . . .

Miranda laughed and spoke with her, asked her about boyfriends and classes and any plans she had. Peg, as always, was happy to help.

Lunch was from Tascone's, ordered up to the office, while she fended off phone calls for more jobs and a few panicked messages from Fisher and Caen. Allen wasn't in; she left an urgent message with the bored secretary.

Renata Dante called to report that Louise was much better today, about seventy-five percent herself. Miranda phoned Meyer and gave him the good news. The attorney sounded better, too, almost caught up with his rest.

After half a cheeseburger, onion rings, and a large cherry Coke, she walked the two flights upstairs, working tired muscles, stretching her legs. Alexander Publishing was quiet, gloom not quite receded. Hank and Emily were arguing in the outer room, and Miranda waited until they could hear before she dropped the story.

Relief erupted like Vesuvius. Miranda smiled, and left them in a whirlwind of activity.

She finished her notes and preparations in the late afternoon, then headed down to see Gladys.

"Sugar—it's been days! I—Miri . . . what happened to your eye?"

The blonde's large blue eyes welled with concern. Miranda smiled.

"I'll give you the whole story over lunch. We're overdue. How about—how about day after tomorrow? I've got a lot to tell you."

"Sure, honey. That will be—let's see—Thursday. I get off at twelve, OK?"

Miranda gave her a big hug. God, she'd miss Gladys.

Never truly realized how comforting it was to have someone always there, always happy to see her, always watching over her.

She purchased all the afternoon editions and checked them back in her office.

Chronicle, page two: Female Detective Finds Lost Manuscript.

News, page one: Woman PI Discovers Last Book of Murdered Writer.

Call-Bulletin, page two: Girl Gumshoe Locates Howard Smith's Final Book.

Examiner, page one: Woman PI Finds Missing Manuscript of Murdered Man.

Miranda took a deep breath. All the articles stated the necessary facts.

. . . *the lost manuscript, thought to be an early draft of the author's latest work, has not yet been examined by the police. Miss Corbie suggests that it could be combed for clues to Smith's recent murder. She will be presenting it to Inspector David Fisher tomorrow morning and is "keeping it under lock and key" in her Wells Fargo safe. Miss Corbie further suggested that it is safer with her than with Alexander Publishing, where Smith was under contract and whose owner, Niles Alexander, was also recently and mysteriously killed.*

She nodded.

The trap was set.

*

Light filtered in from the window, from the pool hall up on Kearny and the Top Hat Club and the bar half a block down. Red lights, too, from cars, the few that drove down Market Street at three in the morning.

The sky was black and she could almost hear the water breaking surf along the Bay.

She stretched her legs under the desk, trying not to make a sound . . .

There.

Outside.

Could be a footstep.

Miranda slid her hand toward the .22 until she could feel the cold metal. Hell, everything felt cold on the floor behind the desk, even with the wool blanket she brought from home. At least she'd dressed for the occasion, dungarees and a fisherman's cap and man's shirt. Reminded her of trying to pass as a Southern Pacific railroad man in Reno . . .

Again.

Low scuffle, like a . . . yes.

Like a wire in the lock.

The light only illuminated the back of her office. The black desk glinted red from the reflection and the safe and file cabinet could be made out as dim, hulking shapes in the darkness.

Had to rely on sound. She held her breath.

There it was again . . . louder.

A small click and more scuffling. Then the soft, unmistakable hiss of the pneumatic door swinging open and rubber-soled shoes treading softly—hesitantly—into the room.

They stopped once inside, waiting for the door to close again.

Miranda bit her lip. The gun was slippery with the sweat on her palm and she hoped she could hold it steady.

Her left hand held a flashlight.

More scuffles, a skidding sound. Getting closer. A flashlight switched on suddenly, stabbing the darkness and probing it.

Miranda almost gasped, swallowed instead. No view of under the desk, thank God she'd arranged the chairs to block the angle . . .

The light skimmed the top of the desk, hovered for a moment, then swung back to the other side, where the safe was.

The footsteps, louder and more assured now, grew closer.

Sound of a cloth bag hoisted on the ledge, soft grunt. He pulled it open.

She could barely make out thin sticks, like fireworks, held in a hand.

The sonofabitch was planning to blow up her safe.

She shimmied out from under the main part of the desk, toward the window, his preparations loud enough to mask the sound. With an effort of her stomach muscles, she pulled herself upright without a grunt, using the wall as a brace.

He was setting up the dynamite.

Miranda took a breath and raised the gun with her right hand, switching on the flashlight with a flick of her left thumb.

The dark-clothed figure froze with a stick of dynamite in his hand, outlined in white light, pinned against the safe.

Her voice was somber.

"Set the dynamite next to the safe, Roger. The book's not there."

*

He turned slowly, arms not raised, one hand still holding his flashlight, the other, a stick of dynamite.

Thin, dark, narrow face, handsome once, before it became twisted with envy, with jealousy, with misplaced ambition and failed creativity.

He plastered on a smile, hideously forced.

"Miss Corbie—Miranda—I know this must look strange—but believe me, there's method in my madness—"

She took a step forward, .22 pointed squarely at his stomach.

"Spare me the Shakespeare. Quoting the Bard doesn't make you a writer. Neither does murdering Smith and taking credit for his novel. I said to set the goddamn dynamite aside. And drop your flashlight."

Sharp inhale. With a sudden twist, he flung the flashlight at her, but this time—the second time in two days—Miranda was ready.

She ducked sidewise toward the window and squeezed the trigger.

The sound richoted, around and around, cannon fire in Spain, Martini's blood and brains on a bathroom wall, but the .22 was lighter than the Astra, didn't throw her backwards, and she saw Roscoe bend, clutching his stomach, body blinking red and yellow in the reflected neon.

Miranda, breathing hard, raised the flashlight.

"It's over, Roger. Don't move or I'll blow your fucking head off."

The writer slid like jelly, back against the file cabinet, sinking to the floor.

The hand on his stomach was wet and red.

"I'm walking to the light switch and turning it on. Move and I shoot."

He said nothing, breath harsh and rasping, while she backed up toward the office door.

Miranda reached a spot near the light switch, flashlight tucked under her right arm, hand holding the pistol sideways, and groped with her left until she could flick on the overhead light.

She blinked rapidly, letting the flashlight fall with a clank.

Roger jerked against the wall at the sound but made no other movement. Blood was seeping between his fingers.

She walked quickly to the desk, gun still trained on him.

"I'll call the cops and get an ambulance."

He shifted position, thin face stretched in agony as though he couldn't tolerate being seen.

"Operator? Need an ambulance pronto. There's been a shooting and attempted burglary. Fourth floor, Monadnock. Miranda Corbie. Hurry."

She hung up and said: "I'm sorry about the pain. They'll be here soon."

He looked up at her, blue eyes tortured and voice cracked.

"Don't you want to know why?"

Miranda looked down at him, voice softer. "Sure, I do. Why don't you tell me about it."

He was gasping now, writhing like an ant under a magnifying glass.

"I deserved better. I'm . . . I'm a great writer. I'm intelligent, I'm, I'm educated . . . I deserved better. Far better."

Miranda lit two cigarettes and crouched down near Roger, placing one between his lips, pistol still aimed at his chest.

"Better than what? Than how Alexander treated you? Why didn't you change publishers?"

He jerked, inhaling the cigarette gratefully. Sirens started to wail in the distance and he twisted his head toward the window.

"Not much time. You need to understand. I signed a bad contract."

"But your agent—"

"My agent was incompetent." He snapped it out with sudden force, spittle on his lips. Caught his breath and glanced up at her, calmer. "And then it was too late. Don't you see? I was trapped. I wrote beautiful books—literary books, books that could be the equal to Fitzgerald and Steinbeck. But Niles rejected them, held me in chains like the moon, doomed to repeat, tide in, tide out, what he thought the public wanted . . . and what the public mostly wants is drivel, sensationalized and mindless."

"If that were so, Roger, then Steinbeck and Fitzgerald would never have been published."

He met her eyes, ghost of a smile, remnants of charm and charisma clinging like a tattered cape, last vestiges of a gentleman.

"Hemingway, Steinbeck, Lewis, Hilton . . . the lucky few. No, Miss Corbie, I'm no Marxist, but the man had his points. Our opiates are *Fibber McGee and Molly* and *The Saturday Evening Post* and the latest Blondie picture, and books— books written by low men, fit for morons—books that betray the beauty of the tree that was cut down to make them. Those were the kind of books that Niles made me write . . ." He squirmed again, as the siren wail started to fill the room.

"You could have refused."

He shook his head. "You don't understand. Publishers are supposed to give the public what the public needs, not what it wants. They're educated men, men with taste. The truly great publishers support writers that matter, that . . . that make a difference, that should be read. That must be read. But Niles made me write doggerel because doggerel paid and then he let Smith, the imposter Smith, write the books I should have written. I did write them . . . you'll see. You'll see when you find my library."

The sirens were below the Monadnock now, flashing lights revolving around Miranda's office, red and white, red and white.

She looked down at the blood still seeping through Roger's fingers.

"Roger. The ambulance and police will be here in just a couple of minutes. I want you to know . . . you didn't succeed in killing Louise. She's all right."

His eyes opened wide and he sucked on the cigarette, cheeks forming hollows.

"I never—God, I didn't really want to kill her—but that Alcatraz story . . . thank you for telling me. And let Sylvia know—please let her know—that I truly did love her."

He doubled over suddenly. "Oh God—it hurts—"

Instinctively Miranda bent closer and Roger suddenly twisted upright, last surge of strength, grappling with her for the gun.

Surprised, she fell backwards, right hand flung back, and the writer, panting with effort, lunged, holding her wrist with both hands and in a desperate, dying effort pried it loose.

She scrambled to her feet but he waved it at her, smile twisted with pain, still clutching his stomach with his left hand.

His words came out in shuddering gasps, eyes still sharply lit and focused.

"No, no, dear lady. This is my scene. My book, my play. 'I have heard that guilty creatures sitting at a play have, by the very cunning of the scene, been struck so to the soul that presently they have proclaim'd their malefactions; for murder, though it have no tongue, will speak with most miraculous organ.'"

Heavy footsteps in the hall. Roger kept his eyes on her.

"You are the organ of truth, Miranda Corbie, my last reader and my last audience. What would you do, had you the motive and the cue for passion that I have? You would drown the stage with tears. Let it be so . . . I was a writer. I was wronged. There is no play to ease the anguish of a torturing hour."

Heavy banging on the door. "San Francisco Police—Miss Corbie, you there?"

He held her eyes, brown eyes steady. "I have immortal longings in me."

Roger Roscoe held the pistol up to his head and fired.

A uniform broke the door open and rushed to where Miranda was standing, staring down at the dead man.

✳

She sat with Fisher over a bowl of chop suey at Sam Wo. He shook his head.

"You really think that's how it played out?"

Miranda shrugged. She picked at the vegetables, trying not to see the last ten seconds, over and over, movie reel stuck in place . . . Roger Roscoe blowing a hole in his skull with her .22 pistol.

"You'll know for sure when you get something out of Sylvia other than a physician's note from her attorney. I figure she wrote the letters, initially, and Roger used that fact as a springboard for his idea."

"Which was to kill Alexander."

"Which was to kill Alexander and frame Louise for it. He retyped Sylvia's letters on Louise's machine—remember, he lived nearby and probably glommed a key early on and had a duplicate made—and scared her with fake murder attempts so she'd call the cops. He never intended to kill her at that point—just set her up. Remember the chocolates?"

The burly cop crunched on an egg roll. "But she called you instead. That probably worried him—an unknown quantity. It's pretty easy to figure out how cops will react."

She grinned. "Some—not all. He figured if the evidence looked like Louise was lying about the murder attempts, no one would believe her claims of innocence over the eventual murder. So he steals the cyanide from Sylvia—which she bought as part of her previous threats to kill herself. We've got that much from Acme Drug. I suspect that once you've given Jerry Alexander a thorough grilling, he'll admit to having seen the cyanide around the house. Sylvia—at least at first—liked to act as though she was going to off herself at any minute. Once the family got used to it—which didn't take long, considering how self-involved they were—they realized she was crying wolf. That's probably when she started cutting herself, to up the score, taking more drugs, too. And probably when she wrote Louise the letters, focusing on a pretty blonde as the reason for her misery and neglect."

Fisher snorted. "'Misery and neglect'? With all that money? Jesus Christ, with people hopping trains and living in shacks—"

"I know, Inspector, I know. But it was the only reality she knew. And I can't help but think that Roger married her so quickly because in case she realized the cyanide was missing—"

"She wouldn't be able to testify. Makes sense."

The strains of a Chinese violin wafted through the open window, and Miranda turned toward it, light breeze ruffling her hair.

Fisher said: "So Roscoe was after a different manuscript the entire time—Alcatraz had nothing to do with it."

She shook out a Chesterfield. "Mind if I smoke?"

He shook his head. "Go ahead. I'm nearly done."

She clicked the Ronson One-Touch and lit the stick.

"No, that was the clincher. The motive we had wasn't the real motive, and Roger ran with it. He intended to kill Niles, of course, but if he could pass off one of Smith's books as his own to Bunnie or another publisher . . . well, to his sick mind he was the one who should've written it in the first place. Sylvia probably mentioned something Niles said about Smith's book in the safe, and Roger assumed she meant the novel, not the Alcatraz book, which he could never hope to appropriate. He came in and opened the safe—the combination would be easy to pry out of Sylvia, especially with how hopped-up he kept her—and brought the bottle of poisoned gin with him, planning to pour it into Alexander's desk bottle and frame Louise with the cyanide he planted in her desk. Then Alexander walks in early, surprises him, they struggle. Roscoe throws the gin at him to distract him—I know first-hand how 'distracting' thrown objects can be—and clubs him over the head with the sculpture. He probably intended to steal the money, too, to hide the theft of the novel, but got rattled."

Miranda sipped her tea.

"I don't think he expected or wanted to get physical—he preferred murder from a distance—and killing Niles shook him badly. He was insane already but that made it worse."

"So he gets home and realizes he has the wrong book. And then we arrest Louise."

"He probably just saw Howard's name and figured it was the detective novel he wanted so badly, the one he was pretending to work on. Alexander was building it up along with the Alcatraz book—a novel that would make Howard Carter Smith a literary celebrity, which Roger desperately wanted."

The inspector grunted. "And Blankenship leaking the whole Cretzer-Kyle thing . . . I guess that's when Roscoe figured he could throw everyone a curve ball by playing into the Alcatraz motive, plus buy himself time to hunt for Smith's other manuscript."

Miranda nodded.

"Exactly. That's why there were two notes. I figure he first broke into Louise's apartment while she was with you at the Hall. He tampered with the gas, didn't notice the cracked window, and left the first note—the one that made Louise look like she killed Alexander in some kind of love triangle. Then—when the papers came out—he realized the Alcatraz motive was even better cover."

Fisher shoved the plate aside and lit an Old Gold, taking a deep drag.

"Crazy sonofabitch. He took a lot of chances with that nutty milkman getup."

"He was on a high. Like a drug, Inspector, playing for an even bigger hit of what he wanted most: fame, attention, literary recognition. Luckily, I've got a contact at Goldstein's, which clinched him for the milkman."

She exhaled, tapping ash in the chipped glass tray.

"Part of me can't help but feel pity for him, you know. He had charm, maybe even talent once upon a time. Before he shot himself, he said we'd find his magnum opus in his library. My guess is he hasn't been able to write anything for a while. You find any books?"

"Not a one. Notes, ramblings, half-finished, half-baked and all crazy. At least you had the evidence lined up good, if the sonofabitch hadn't shot himself." He shook his head. "But how in the hell was he expecting to get by Louise?"

"She was supposed to be dead, remember? He miscalculated the amount of gas and didn't know about the window. He was damn lucky she was so out of it she couldn't place him right away . . . and of course, he was wearing makeup. I noticed that when he came to see me afterward—it was one of those things that stuck in my mind and made me realize we were looking at everything the wrong way."

Fisher frowned. "He was lucky, all right. Same way with Smith. Calling him from a pay phone—why the hell from Schwabacher-Frey, I wonder?"

"Probably bought a magic trick from them. He performed one at Gump's that night."

"Figures. Magicians and actors—can't be trusted. And I guess we'll add writers to that list. What do you figure he told Smith?"

"I'm not sure. Maybe that he had a lead on who took the Alcatraz manuscript, complete with a phony message to meet up at Bekins. Roger had a key to Alexander's offices, remember. He probably found out about Smith's little storage-cum-manuscript-room and figured the novel might be there. Or he might have just followed Smith to Bekins and snuck in and surprised him. Either way, he had ample time to kill him, burn the Alcatraz manuscript just enough to destroy it, and steal all the drafts of the novel . . . the one Smith brought with him and the one in the box marked 'new.'"

Fisher's brow wrinkled. "Why'd Smith bring the manuscript from his apartment?"

"I'm not sure. Maybe Roger disguised his voice, threatened Smith with a firebomb—the old Sherlock Holmes trick would've appealed to Roscoe. Then Smith dashed out with the most precious thing in his apartment—his new book—and rushed to secure it at Bekins. He had it in his study—that's where I found the fragment."

"Ah yes, the famous fragment. And that one word—'license'—told you everything." He shook his head again. "Hell of a lucky guess, Miranda."

"When you're a PI your license is everything. And I had a little help from a mirror."

He looked at her quizzically and she gave him half a smile. "Look, I've got to get home. I'll type up everything so you have it all nice and neat, but I can get it done sooner if you open my office up again. Speaking of which, don't forget to finish with Sylvia and Jerry and Louise—she'll be out of Dante's very soon. And there's Bunny Berrigan, too—she deserves the full story."

Fisher met her eyes. "The full story . . . the Alcatraz story. Dullea is breathing a sigh of relief, I'm still working in homicide and Hoover—well, who the hell knows what he's up to. Guess it'll never come out. Not now."

Miranda stood, muscles sore and tired. Her eyes glowed green.

"Never say never, Inspector Fisher."

＊

She slept for a couple of hours and spent the rest of the day on the phone, reassuring Meyer she was all right, catching up Allen on the night before, planning dinner with Bente, arranging for the promised exclusive to Herb Caen.

She left four messages for James.

The late-afternoon sun was filtering through the living-room windows when the phone rang.

His voice was tired but better than when they'd last spoke.

"Ducks? Just off the wire with the BOP. Bennett's involved. You can hold off on that interview."

Her voice was careful. "What kind of reassurance do I have, James? Your word for it?"

He sighed, voice sounding far away, as if she were listening to a seashell.

"Look, Miranda, I've done what I can. Bennett said he'd look into it and he's a good man. You've played your trump card, Ducks. Quit while you're ahead."

"You mean quit before Hoover has a chance to smear me even more than he has?"

The State Department man was silent for a few seconds. "You know politics is a dangerous game. Hoover plays for keeps. And if I'm not mistaken, he'll be around for a long, long time."

Miranda's jaw tightened. "I plan to be, too, James. All right. On your word I won't mention Miller or Linkletter. On your word. But if I don't get confirmation that Linkletter was fired—not transferred, but fired—all bets are off."

"Miranda, I can't—"

"Yes, you can. Or Bennett can. And one of you better. We've still got a free press in this country, thank God, and sure, maybe the big papers won't print it, but I'll find someone who will. Word will get out, and there are a few people in government who'd be upset. Maybe more than a few. *Quis custodiet ipsos custodes*, James. And you can tell Hoover I'm watching."

She hung up the phone, afternoon sunlight gleaming red against her hair.

*

The cops unsealed her office at five, tape on the door removed, just a few small pieces left behind to signify that a man killed himself there fourteen hours earlier.

She thought she could still see a blood splatter on the wall by the sink, and she scrubbed at it with a cloth, but it must have been a reflection of the light.

She sat at the desk, re-read Rick's letter.

She'd write, letting him know what happened, send him her travel schedule.

Maybe they'd meet before she sailed . . .

There were messages unanswered, three from Bunny Berrigan. She'd see the redhead tomorrow . . . wondered what she'd do, whether Alexander Publishing was finally over, whether Bunny would salvage the business and try again.

Miranda rose and stood at her window, watching Market Street unfold in the twilight.

White Fronts and late-model cars, tall, soot-stained buildings, ornate and mannerly, rooftop signs advertising Mobile and the Hotel Excelsior; neon blinking everywhere, and everywhere the sound of people and the sea and the foghorns of the Golden Gate.

She breathed it in, window open, soft breeze blowing moist air with the scent of eucalyptus. Breathed it in, drank it in, food, water, all the nourishment that sustained her.

San Francisco.

And she was saying good-bye.

Miranda stared into the colors of dusk.

It was war she was sailing into, a war that would decide the fate of the world, decide whether Shakespeare would be played, whether jazz would be sung, whether books would be read.

A war she had to join.

Waning purples, oranges, and reds gleamed against Lotta's Fountain.

Miranda breathed in again, eyes wide open, trying to hold it, to savor it, to taste it enough so that she could remember it always, the way the City looked, the way the City felt, the way the City was.

She knew it wouldn't be the same.

She'd come back, if she survived, if she found her mother . . . but it wouldn't be the same.

A train roared toward the Ferry Building, sending a man in a brown suit running across the tracks.

A young woman bought a carnation.

Blue neon flashed.

We'll meet again, don't know where, don't know when . . .

Miranda looked at her City.

No matter what changes lay ahead for either of them, San Francisco would be hers . . .

Forever.

Author's Note

*

C*ity of Sharks* is a work of fiction. However, many of the people and events described in the book are historical.

I once had the pleasure of speaking to Herb Caen (and the honor of having a previous family business mentioned in his famous *San Francisco Chronicle* column). He is a life-long inspiration, both as a writer and a transplanted San Franciscan. His City sorely misses him.

Richard Gump became president of his family's company in 1947; he was also a consultant to and inspiration for the detective fiction radio show *The Casebook of Gregory Hood,* created by Anthony Boucher and Denis Green. Hood's character was based on Gump and his life as an importer of artifacts and treasures. The show aired originally on the Mutual network and ran from 1946 to 1950. Today, you can still stroll through Gump's if you're in San Francisco; it is located off of Union Square and is one of the City's treasures.

James Johnston was the first warden of Alcatraz and Edward Joe Miller was his associate warden. Their depictions are fictional, though Miller's background as a correctional officer and other research inspired his characterization. *Hellcatraz* is, indeed, the name of a tell-all book published by Roy Gardner, the "gentlemen bandit," who lived and died as related in *City of Sharks.*

As for the prisoners . . . Ralph Roe and Theodore Cole escaped as described—and, though it is likely they perished, no bodies were ever discovered and reported sightings of the duo persisted through the late '30s and early '40s.

Rufus McCain, Henri (or Henry) Young, and William Martin took part in an escape attempt by Arthur "Doc" Barker and were apprehended. Once they were released into the general population after "isolation," Young eventually killed McCain; his defense attorney claimed that his maltreatment in Alcatraz drove him to insanity. Many modern historians give his narrative little credence.

Joseph "Dutch" Cretzer and Arnold "Shorty" Kyle were apprehended and sentenced as described in the book, though their personal lives are fictionalized in *City of Sharks*. Cretzer was later killed in the 1946 infamous "Battle for Alcatraz" . . . his one last bid to escape.

The veil of secrecy over daily life at Alcatraz created much unease and speculation throughout the "gangster" era—a natural result when an almost absolutely powerful institution seeks to hide all information from the public. *Quis custodiet ipsos custodes?*

I relied on many sources for my research, including contemporary newspaper articles, phone books, and archival material and ephemera. Books that were particularly helpful include *Alcatraz, the Gangster Years* (David A. Ward), *Alcatraz: History and Design of a Landmark* (Donald MacDonald and Ira Nadel), *Eyewitness on Alcatraz* (Jolene Babyak), *Last Train to Alcatraz* (Leon "Whitey" Thompson), and *San Francisco's Playland-at-the-Beach: The Early Years* (James R. Smith).

For more information about Alcatraz and other historical elements in the Miranda Corbie series, please visit my website: http://kellistanley.com.